George William Marshall

Miscellanea Marescalliana

being genealogical notes on the surname of Marshall - Vol. 2

George William Marshall

Miscellanea Marescalliana
being genealogical notes on the surname of Marshall - Vol. 2

ISBN/EAN: 9783337380717

Printed in Europe, USA, Canada, Australia, Japan

Cover: Foto ©Andreas Hilbeck / pixelio.de

More available books at **www.hansebooks.com**

Miscellanea Marescalliana,

BEING

GENEALOGICAL NOTES

ON THE SURNAME OF

MARSHALL.

COLLECTED BY

GEORGE WILLIAM MARSHALL, LL.D

VOL II.

Con VVeLL thIs VVork
yoV then VVILL knoVV
froM VVhere VVe sprIng
anD VVhen VVe go.

PREFACE.

The issue of the second part of this volume brings my notes on the surname of Marshall to a close. The indexes in this and the previous parts will, I hope, to some extent atone for the want of continuity unavoidable in printing a very miscellaneous collection as accumulated. Though by no means exhaustive as to the genealogy of any particular family, I think there are few of the name in England whose pedigree will not be to some extent illustrated by these memoranda. In order to assist the reader, I give here a rough list of the contents of these two volumes; if of no other use, it may save trouble to those who are content with making a superficial enquiry as to their pedigree, and who do not take sufficient interest in it to patiently search out every clue by the aid of the indexes. To those who have been kind enough to take an interest in my researches, I again render my thanks for their assistance.

G. W. M.

CONTENTS.

THE MARSHALLS OF SOUTHWARK.

The earliest ancestor of this family given in the 1620 Visitation of Surrey, is Richard Marshall, of Cockwood, [*i.e.* Coxwold in the North Riding,] in co. York, Gent.[1] His son, Thomas Marshall,[2] was of Stamford, co. Lincoln; he had a son, Richard Marshall, of that town, who married Anne, daughter of Thomas Beckwith,[3] Esq. (and sister of Thomas Beckwith, of Clint, ancestor of the Beckwiths of Alborough, Barts.[4]), by Elizabeth, daughter of ...... Tirrel, of Ockendon, co. Essex, son of Thomas Beckwith, of Clint, co. York, by Matilda, daughter of Henry Pudsey, of Barford, co. Kent.

I have been unable to identify the Stamford Marshalls mentioned in the following extracts with this family, but, I insert them here as they may prove useful for future reference.

From the Register of All Hallowes, Stamford:—

1560. The xxiv of Sept. dynis Whittle servaunte to Richard Marshall was bur.
1561. The xxv of Maye was bapt. Jhon Marshall son of Rychard Marshall. (Buried 12 Feb. 1564-5.)
1564. The 10 of Aug. was bapt. Jone Marshall dau. of Rychard Marshall. Margery, dau. of same, bapt. 20 April, 1565, buried 21 May, 1566. William, son of same, bapt. 17 Oct., 1568. Gregory son of same, bapt. 20 Sept., 1570. Margery, dau. of same, bur. 19 Feb., 1570-1.
1571. July 7, Jhon Coy and Ann Marshall, married.
1571. The xvi of Aprill Rychard Marshall, husbandmũ, was bur.
1657. Mrs. Marshall, an ancient woman, bur. Sept. 1.

From the Register of St. Martin's, Stamford:—

BAPTISMS.

1580.	Alice, the dau. of	Henry Marshall,	23 April, (Bur. 30 June, 1586).
1584.	William the son of	same,	6 Dec. (Bur. 13 Dec.)
1585-6.	Elizabeth, dau of	same,	5 March.
1589.	Lomai (?) dau. of	same,	3 April.
1590.	Roger, son of	same,	21 April.
1595.	Frances, dau. of	same,	6 June.
1596.	John, son of	same,	1 Dec.
1601.	Mary, dau. of	same,	29 March.
1602.	Jone, dau. of	same,	2 May.

MARRIAGES.

1584-5. Edward Willoby and Jane Marshall, 17 January.
1593. Henry Marshall and Margaret More, 6 May.
1600. Henry Marshall and Jane ...., 17 May.
1605. Robert Wylles and Jane Marshall (no date of month).

BURIALS.

1603. Burialls about this tyme sett downe in the tyme of gode visitation [the plague] Henry Marshall, the Labourer. John, the son of Widow Marshall. Jone, her daughter.

[1] See as to earlier Stamford Marshalls, vol. i, p. 202.
[2] Thomas Marshall was plt. re lands in Stamford called Boney-land, Mich. 18 Henry VII. *Feet of Fines, co. Notts. in Pub. Rec. Office.*
[3] Wotton's Baronetage, iii, 680.
[4] Ibid. iii. 677.

Richard Marshall and Anne Beckwith had issue two sons, John, of whom presently, and Henry, eldest son, of the Borough of Southwark, called "late brother," in will of his brother John, 1619, married Margaret, dau. of . . . . Courtney, of London, and had issue:—

Henry Marshall, s.p.

William Marshall, of Southwark, 1623. Mentioned in will of John Marshall, 1619.

Alice, s.p.

Jane, married Henry Vero, of Southwark, and had a son, and a daughter Margaret mentioned in the will of John Marshall, of Southwark, 1627.

John Marshall was of the parish of St. Saviour, in the Borough of Southwark, White-baker, and a Citizen and Tallow-chandler of London. He married Elizabeth, daughter of Richard Heecock, of Clifton, co. Chester. On the 21st December, 1611, he had a grant of Arms from William Camden, *Argent, a chevron cotised Sable between three bucks'-heads caboshed Gules.* CREST. *A greyhound sejant Argent, collared Gules, the ring Or, resting his dexter fore paw on a buck's head caboshed Gules.* In 1623, he entered his pedigree in the Visitation of Surrey. His will is dated 31 May, 1619. He desires to be buried in the parish of St. Saviour, Southwark, in the night time. Mentions wife Elizabeth Marshall. My daughter, Susanna Thicknes. My four children, Thomas Marshall, John Marshall, Richard Marshall, and Elizabeth Marshall. My nephew, William Marshall. My kinswoman Vero, my late brother Henry Marshall's daughter. My two daughters-in-law, my son John's wife, and my son-in-law Maddox his wife. My two grandchildren, John and Thomas Maddox, sons of my late daughter Mary deceased. My grandchild Elizabeth Thicknes. To my cousin Wright, of Grantham, two years' rent of his house which he payeth me. Loving son-in-law William Maddox, and kinsman Charles Yeoman, scrivenor, overseers. Appoints wife sole executrix. There are several bequests to poor, one to Southwark hospital, and one to the poor of the parish of All Hallowes in Stamford. To trustees for poor of Newington Butts, co. Surrey, a rent charge of 20s. *per annum*, out of tenements there. After some alteration the will was re-executed 28 Sept., 1619; and was proved by Elizabeth Marshall, the relict, in P.C.C., 10 August, 1625. (83 Clark). They had issue, besides John, George, Edward, Alexander, William, Richard, who all probably died young; and Sarah, Christiana, Judith, Mary, Anne, Elizabeth, Bridget, and Emma, died *s.p.*, making the number of their children twenty in all :—

1. Thomas Marshall, White-baker, Citizen and Tallow-chandler of London, of the parish of St. Sepulchre extra Newgate. Aged 30 at Visitation of 1623. Will dated 20 April, 1625. Wills to be buried in St. Saviour's, Southwark. Gives to parish of St. Sepulchre £100 for clothing boys. Mentions his father John Marshall. Brothers John Marshall and Richard Marshall. Brother Richard Thickins[1] and his wife. Brother William

[1] *i.e.*, Thickness.

Pickton and his wife. To the first child that my sister Pickton shall bear £20. £100 to parish of St. Saviour, Southwark, for clothing boys. My godson Thomas Maddox and John Maddox his brother. Godson Thomas Thickens. Goddaughter Mary Thickins, and her two sisters Susan and Elizabeth Thickins. Gives his right to fishing in Plymouth in New England to his father. Mentions his "dwelling in the Old Baylie." Loving mother £20 to buy her a ring. Appoints his father sole executor. Brother Maddox and his wife. William Powell and his wife. Administration was granted by P.C.C. 10 August, 1625, to Elizabeth Marshall, relict and executrix of the last will of John Marshall while he lived executor of the will of Thomas Marshall late of the parish of St. Sepulchre extra Newgate, but who died in the parish of St. Saviour Southwark, John Marshall having died before he proved the will (83 Clark).

2. John Marshall, of Southwark. Aged 28 in 1623. Married Elizabeth, daughter and coheir of Richard Taylor, of London, M.D. Ment[d] in will of her mother Elizabeth Taylor, proved 24 Feb., 1635-6. The will of Richard Taylor, Dr. of Physic, was proved in P.C.C., 22 Dec., 1615 (117 Rudd). John Marshall died in March, 1631, and was buried in St. Saviour's Church, the last day of that month. He died without issue (Funeral Certificate, Coll. Arms, I. 23, p. 61[b]). His will is dated 21 August, 1627. Give lands, etc., in trust for Margaret daughter of Henry Vere, under age. Mentions the brother of the said Margaret. Leaves money to maintain poor scholars from Southwark, or Stamford, co. Lincoln, at the Universities. Mentions mother Elizabeth Marshall. Wife Elizabeth Marshall. Money in trust to build a church. My sister Elizabeth Browne. My sister Susan Thicknesse, her eldest daughter Elizabeth Thicknesse, her daughter Mary Thicknesse, and her youngest daughter Suzan Thicknesse. My late Father. To be buried at Sutton, co. Surrey, and then to be removed to the new church he leaves money to build. My brothers Mr. Thicknesse, Mr. Browne, and Mr. Maddox. Proved in P.C.C. 15 April, 1631 (38 St. John). This is a very long will, and further particulars will be found in Manning and Bray's "Surrey," iii. 534—540. See his arms, etc., in Christ Church, Surrey, the church he founded, in Aubrey's "Antiquities of Surrey," v. 156.

3. Richard Marshall, living 1625.

1. Mary (deceased in 1619), married William Maddox, Goldsmith, and had two sons, John and Thomas, who are both mentioned in the will of Charles Yeoman, of London, Scrivenor, 1645-6. Proved in P.C.C. (17 Twisse). William Maddox had married a second wife in or before 1619.

2. Susanna, married Richard Thicknesse, and had issue Elizabeth, Thomas, Mary, and Susan.

3. Elizabeth, living unmarried in 1619. Probably married William Pickton, and secondly, ... Browne.

MARSHALL OF SELABY, CO. DURHAM.

Lord Redesdale, the present owner of the Batsford estates in co. Gloucester, acquired them from the family of ***Freeman***,[1] and assumed that name in addition to his own—***Mitford***. Richard Freeman, of Batsford, Lord Chancellor of Ireland, was twice married; first to Elizabeth, daughter of Sir Anthony Keck, Knt., of an ancient Gloucestershire family, of which it is to be regretted that no good genealogy exists in any printed work (but collections for one will be found in the *Genealogist*, vol. iii., p. 173); and secondly, to Anne, sole daughter and heir of Richard Marshall, of Selaby, and of Gray's Inn, Esq., of whose family there is a pedigree in Surtees' *History of Durham*, vol. iv., p. 21. This pedigree, which is based upon one entered in Dugdale's Visitation of Durham in 1666, amplified by deeds and parish register extracts, is both incomplete and inaccurate. The following notes correct some of the errors contained herein.

It begins with Gilbert Marshall of Newcastle-on-Tyne, who married Agnes daughter and coheir of Cuthbert Brakenbury, (*see* Plantagenet Harrison's *History of Yorkshire*, i, 268) and had two sons, Richard, of Denton (*see* Inq. in App. to 44th Report of D.K. Pub. Records, 473), and Thomas Marshall, of Pearce Bridge End, who had two sons, Gilbert of Houghall, aged 45 at Dugdale's Visitation, and Richard. Gilbert married Elizabeth, daughter of Sir John Bourchier (called by Surtees Sir *Thomas*): *see* Dugdale's *Visitation of Yorkshire*, published by the Surtees Society. p. 140. He is said by Surtees to have been "living at Selaby, 1683," but no authority is given for the statement, which is evidently incorrect. Administration of his goods was granted by the Prerogative Court of Canterbury, 5 March, 1680, in which he is described as of Houghall, co. Durham, but deceased in Gray's Inn, co. Middx., to Gilbert Marshall, Esq., his son, Elizabeth Radcliffe *alias* Marshall, relict of said deceased, and Alexander Radcliffe, her husband, having renounced. So far, therefore, from his having been alive in 1683, his wife had married a second husband before the 5 March, 1680! Administration was also granted by the Prerogative Court of York (Prerogative Act Book, York, for 1679-1705), 8 July, 1684, to Gilbert Marshall, his son, in which he is again described as "of Houghall, co. Durham, but who died at Gray's Inn, co. Middx." This leaves no doubt that the two administrations relate to the same person.

Richard was twice married. His first wife is said by Surtees to have been "Jane, daughter of Thomas Neile, of co. Herts., bur. 20 Feb., 1663, at St. Oswald's." At the time, however, when she married Richard Marshall, she was, I believe, the widow of ..... Cannon, as there is in the Vicar General's Office a licence, dated 25 Feb., 1662-3, for Richard Marshall, of Gray's Inn, Esq., bachelor, aged about 34, and Jane Cannon, of St. Giles', Cripplegate, widow, about 30, to marry at St. Giles', Cripplegate, or St. James', Clerkenwell. The date of burial is no doubt intended for 1663-4. Adminis-

[1] As to the Freemans, *see* Rudder's *Gloucestershire*, p. 265; add. et corr., p. viii.

tration of the goods of Jane Marshall *alias* Cannon, of the parish of St. Oswald, Durham, was granted to her husband, Richard Marshall, 5 March, 1680. I feel no doubt as to the identity of this person with the Jane of the marriage licence, but am entirely unable to explain the reason why so long a time was allowed to elapse before letters of administration were taken out. Richard Marshall married for his second wife Elizabeth Robinson. Marriage licence in Vicar General's Office, dated 24 April, 1666. He of Gray's Inn, Esq., widower, aged about 38; she of All Hallowes, Honey-lane, widow, aged about 36,—to marry at St. Mary Magdalene, Old Fish-street. The marriage took place at that church the same day. By his first wife Richard Marshall apparently had no issue. By Elizabeth Robinson, his second, he was father of Anne, who became the wife of Richard Freeman. Here it is that Mr. Surtees makes his worst and most inexcusable blunder. Anne, wife of Richard Freeman, in Surtees' pedigree of the family, is made to be the daughter of his nephew, also named *Richard* (who was the third son of his elder brother Gilbert), by Mary, daughter of the Rev. Edmund Fotherby. That this descent is entirely erroneous the subsequent history of the descendants of Gilbert will show. Richard Marshall's will is dated 10 February, 1695-6, and was proved in P.C.C. (Leeds 141), by the said Anne, 23 June, 1713, He is described as of Gray's Inn, co. Middlesex, Esq. Devises lands in Selaby, Gainford, etc., in Co. Pal. Durham, and Harpeden, in the parish of Welhampsteed, co. Hertford, and in Luton, co. Bedford, to daughter Anna Marshall. Mentions "her mother, my dear wife," and her jointure in the Hertfordshire estates. Appoints said daughter sole executrix. When she died in 1726, administration was granted 17 May, 1727, to Richard Freeman, Esq., son of Anne Freeman *alias* Marshall, widow, deceased, while she lived daughter and executrix of Richard Marshall. Richard Freeman,[1] the husband of Anne, was married to her in 1702. Marriage licence, Faculty Office of Archbishop of Canterbury, 1702, August 12, Richard Freeman, of Battisford, co. Gloucester, widower, and Anne Marshall, spinster, aged 24, daughter of Richard Marshall, Esq., of St. Sepulchre's, Middlesex, to marry at St. Benet's Paul's wharf, or .... Surtees says that she died 11 January, 1726, *aged thirty-one*. Another evident mistake! She must have been more, as, if thirty-one was her age at death, she must have been married when only seven! The licence proves her to have been then twenty-four, and consequently her age at death would be 48. Richard Freeman had issue by her, Ann, died 1728, aged 23, and Richard who administered to his grandfather Richard Marshall, and died *s.p.* in 1741.

Gilbert Marshall had issue, 1, *Gilbert*, 2, John, 3, *Richard*, five other sons, and eight daughters, who all apparently died *sans* issue, except *Margaret* the third. Gilbert Marshall, the eldest son, was born in Milk-street, London, and baptised at St. Mary Magdalene, Milk-street (or Knight Rider-street, as now called), 27 January, 1653-4. Surtees states that he was buried 29 December, 1675, but

[1] His first wife was Elizabeth dau. of Sir Anthony Keck, Knt. *See* Rudder's *Gloucestershire*, Add. and Corr., p. viii. As to her grandson, see p. 265.

omits to state *where*, and thus prevents enquiry as to who, if such a person existed, the Gilbert Marshall was who was buried at that date. We have seen that in 1680 and 1684 he was administrator to his father. On July 16, 1672, he had a licence (Vicar General's Office) as Gilbert Marshall, gent., junr., of Gray's Inn, bachelor, aged about 19, to marry, with consent of his father, Gilbert Marshall, Esq., Mrs. Jane Cannon, of St. Andrew's, Holborn, spinster, aged about 22, parents dead, at St. Mary Savoy, St. James' Clerkenwell, or St. Clement Danes. She was probably the daughter of Jane Cannon, the first wife of his uncle Richard; at least a comparison of the dates mentioned, and the fact that her parents were dead point to this conclusion. The date given by Surtees as that of the burial of Gilbert, viz., 29 December, 1675, may have been the date of *her* burial. He married secondly, Elizabeth ......, and died without issue by either wife. Will as of St. James's, Westminster, Esq., dated 10 April, 1719. Mentions, wife Elizabeth Marshall, grand-nephew Marshall Richardson, my sister Margaret Snowden, my brother Richard Marshall, Esq., and his wife. Houses and lands in Sackville-street and Calverdine-row, near Tunbridge, co. Kent, and in the Minster-yard of York. My other grand nephew Benjamin Marshall, brother of the said Marshall Richardson. Appoints wife executrix, and after her decease Marshall Richardson. She proved in P.C.C., 14 Sept. 1721 (Buckingham, 165). The original will is sealed with "a chevron between three crescents." He was buried in the chancel at Hampton, where there was a monument to him on the floor. (Lysons' *Middlesex Parishes*, p. 78.) The will of "Elizabeth Marshall, of the parish of St. James's, Westminster, widow and relict of Gilbert Marshall, Esq., deceased," is dated 30 November, 1727. Desires to be buried at Hampton, co. Middx., in same grave with late husband. Whereas upon the marriage of my grand-nephew Marshall Richardson *alias* Gilbert Marshall with Anne Blew, daughter of James Blew, gent., his now wife, etc. Mentions sale of late husband's house in Minster-yard at York. My husband's grand-nephew Benjamin Richardson. My late husband did some time before his death dispose of his house at Tunbridge, co. Kent. My loving brother and sister Richard Marshall, Esq., and his wife. To Col. James Campbell £20 for mourning. To my nephew Gilbert Richardson and his wife £20 for mourning. To my grand-nephew Marshall Richardson *alias* Gilbert Marshall's now wife, all my Japan China, etc. To my kinswoman Jane Thrift, wife of Gabriel Thrift, £10 for mourning. Kinswoman Mary Carty, wife of Timothy Carty, £10 for mourning. My cousin Mrs. Catherine Blakiston.[1] To my kinswoman Judith Thomas *alias* Ager one shilling. Marshall Richardson *alias* Gilbert Marshall, and Benjamin Richardson, executors. Proved by Marshall Richardson, and power reserved to Benjamin Richardson, 16th December 1727, in P.C.C. (Farrant 302.)

Richard, third son of Gilbert Marshall, of Selaby, and brother to the above named Gilbert, was born 14 August, 1659, and was of Selaby

[1] The only mention I find of this name in connection with Marshall is the marriage at Gilling, co. York, of Marmaduke Blakestone and Elizabeth Marshall, 15 January, 1705-6.

and Gray's Inn. He appears to have bought church lands during the Commonwealth from Sir John Wollaston and others appointed by Parliament Commissioners for the sale of them. *See* Deeds enrolled on the Close Rolls, viz.—1651, Part 59, No. 2; 1649, Part 4, No. 33, and Part 14, No. 17; 1650, Part 23, No. 26, etc.; 1652, Part 30, No. 23, and Part 34, No. 2. He married Mary, daughter of Edmund Fotherby, Vicar of Gainford, 1 March, 1691. She was born in 1665. His will, in which he is described as of the New Lodge in Hampton Court Park, in the county of Middlesex, Esq., is dated 28 March, 1725. No mention is made of any child. He appoints his wife Mary sole executrix; and she proved 2 April, 1728, in P.C.C. (Brook 118.) She survived till 1750, at which time she must have been 85, and was, I have no doubt, the "Mary Marshall of the parish of St. George's, Hanover-square, co. Middlesex," administration of whose effects was granted by the P.C.C., 15 March, 1750, to John Fotherby, nephew by the brother, and one of the next of kin.

Margaret, sister of Gilbert and Richard, and daughter of Gilbert Marshall, of Selaby, was born 3 July 1658. Married 1st, 6 Jan., 1679, Richard Richardson; and 2ndly, Tobias Snowdon. On the 4th December, 1728 (the year after the death of Elizabeth, wife of her brother Gilbert,) she (and her then husband Tobias Snowden), as *sister and heir of Gilbert Marshall, Esq.*, released all her equity of redemption in lands at Alwent, a hamlet to the east of Selaby. (Surtees, vol. iv, p. 22). By her first husband, Richard Richardson, she must have been mother of the father of Marshall and Benjamin Richardson, the *grand*-nephews of Gilbert Marshall, who as, through their mother, his presumptive heirs, were called *alias* Marshall.

Marshall Richardson *alias* Gilbert Marshall, married at Chelsea, 14 April, 1726, Anne, daughter of James Blew, and had issue:—Gilbert Marshall, bapt. at Chelsea 5, and buried there 15 Dec., 1726; Mary, bapt. there 21 Dec., 1727; Elizabeth, bapt. there 8 March, 1729-30, and buried 10 May following; and Henrietta, bapt. there 6 June, 1733.

The name "Gilbert" is somewhat uncommon, and with the following exceptions I have not met with it in other families of Marshall.

I. Gilbert Marshall, will dated 2 May, 1708, appoints sister Mary executrix and universal legatee; she proved in P.C.C., 4 June, 1712. (117 Barnes).

II. Gilbert Marshall, of the parish of St. Paul, Shadwell, co. Middx., marriner, will dated 15 August, 1723. Mentions Thomas Beck and Katherine, his wife. Proved in P.C.C. by Thomas Beck, 2 April, 1726. (76 Plymouth).

The notes of Durham wills *(post)* will throw further light on this pedigree. Mr. C. M. Carlton, of Durham, informs me that in a MS. in the Chapter Library at Durham, Gilbert Marshall is mentioned as being seized in fee of a tenement in Giles-gate, Durham; he had a son Thomas, who had issue John Marshall, only son and heir, died 6 March, *1736* (?). Will proved at York by John Thomas, his executor. Gilbert Marshall had also a daughter Ann, who married

William Thomas, and had issue by him :—John Thomas, gent., above mentioned, only son and heir, and devisee of the said Thomas Marshall. From the same source it appears that Edward Marshall, of Darlington, married Margaret Rippon, of Eggleston, 25 Oct., 1581.

THE MARSHALLS' OF EXETER.

During the seventeenth century a respectable family of this name flourished in the city of Exeter, two of whom, John and James, father and son, were Mayors, the former in 1615, and the latter in 1658.[1] The only notice of it in any printed work is a brief pedigree, which appears to have been compiled between 1627 and 1635, in Westcote's *Devonshire Families*, edited by Geo. Oliver and Pitman Jones, p. 502. It is probable that this family was connected with the Marshalls of Teigngrace, under which place Westcote says (p. 439), "Here also is a tribe of the Marshalls." At p. 502 he gives their arms as, *Or, a milrind Sable*, with this entry, "John Marshall, one of the four coroners of Devon, married Agnes daughter of Walter Ossingold of East Ogwell, and had issue Thomas, John, and Katherine." The arms, however, recorded to them in the *Visitation of Devon*, 1572 (Coll. of Arms, MS. G 19, fo. 22^b), are, *Or, a milrind Sable, on a chief Gules three antelopes' heads Or.* Westcote attributes this coat to the Marshalls of Exeter.

The first of the name mentioned by Westcote is William Marshall, who had issue Robert Marshall, who married Joan, daughter and heir of ...... Owsley of Chillington, co. Somerset. His will, dated 7 August 1576, was proved by her 9 October following in the P.C.C. (Carew 29). He is described as of Ashewill, in the parish of Ilminster, and desires to be buried in the churchyard of Ilminster. Gives to son Edward Marshall "his Rynes and bark and half my Tanne vates with a mill to grind Bark." From this bequest it seems that he was by trade a tanner. Mentions sons, John, Nicholas, William, John "the younger," and Thomas, all under age; and appoints wife Joan sole executrix and residuary legatee. He appears to have had two other children besides those mentioned in his will, Roger and Anne, who may possibly have been twins, born posthumous. I take them, therefore, according to the presumable order of their births :—

1. Edward Marshall, mentioned in the will of his sister Anne, 1616, as then deceased; had a son *Nicholas*.
2. John Marshall. I suppose this person to be "John Marshall of Chellington, co. Somerset, Tanner," whose will, dated 14 July, 1590, was proved by his relict in P.C.C., 31 July following. (Drury 54). He mentions therein his son Robert Marshall, and youngest son John Marshall both under age. Appoints wife Elizabeth sole executrix, and Nicholas Osborne and Robert Marshall supervisors.
3. Nicholas Marshall, of Ilminster, co. Somerset, shoemaker. Will dated 10 November, 1625. To be buried in the churchyard of

[1] Izacke's *Antiquities of the City of Exeter*, Lond. 1731, 8vo., 3rd ed., pp. 146, 165.

Ilminster. Lands at Coxbridge to son John Marshall.[1] Wife Christian, sole executrix. Son William Marshall. Daughter Agnes Marshall. Daughter Jone, wife of John Ashton. Brothers-in-law Richard Chicke, Robert Webb, and John Chicke, overseers. Son Nicholas Marshall under age. Proved by relict in P.C.C. 18 Feby. 1625-6. (Hele 21). He had also a son Thomas Marshall, who proved the will of his aunt Anne Marshall, 1616.

4. William Marshall, of Dinnington, in the diocese of Bath and Wells, co. Somerset. Will dated 1 Decr. 1623. Gives money to poor of Ilminster. Mentions, brother Nicholas Marshall,—four children of son-in-law John Braggs,—Elizabeth, Susanna, James, John, and Richard, children of my brother John Marshall of Exeter, all under age,—my brother Roger's children, that is his son John, daughter Jane, and daughter Mary, all under age,—Edward the son of my brother Thomas, and Joane and Judith (under age) his daughters,—Anne, Elizabeth, Margaret, Joane, and Phillip, the daughters of my cozen John Marshall, all under age,—Mary Geare myne apprentice,—John Reinolds my man,—Stenchlie Bennet,—Julian Stucchie my god-daughter,—to my brother Thomas my chattell lease of Chipplecome and Longhills in the parish of Winsham, co. Somerset,—Nicholas son of said Thomas,—gives legacy to said brother Thomas on condition that he makes over his land in West and Middle Chinnock to his (the said Thomas's) son Robert "on his retorne home,"—John son of my brother Thomas,—William Marshall my brother Thomas his son to be executor,—he proved the will in P.C.C. 5 March, 1623. (Byrde 28). Administration was granted 4 April, 1624 to Thomas Marshall, brother of the testator, because William Marshall, the executor, was dead.

5. John Marshall, called the younger in his father's will, Mayor of Exeter in 1615, of whom presently.

6. Thomas Marshall, of Chillington, tanner, devisee of Chippelcombe and Longhills, in the will of his brother William. Will dated 22 August, 1641. Gives house at Chillington to his daughter Agnes Stuckie for life, with remainder to her son Thomas Stuckie,—her other children John, Judith, and Nicholas are all mentioned as under age,—my daughter Joane Weeks, her

[1] I take this John to be the John mentioned in the will of William Marshall, 1623, as his *cousin* (cousin at this date usually means *nephew*), who had five daughters, Anne, Elizabeth, Margaret, Joane, and Phillip, all under age. There were four other Johns, as will be seen from the pedigree, who stood in the relation of nephew to this testator, all of whom, so far as can be ascertained, died without issue, or had no issue in the year 1623. His father Nicholas is described in his will as of Ilminster, it is probable that the son also resided at that place. These considerations, coupled with the name of his youngest daughter, vizt. *Phillip*, lead me to the conclusion that he is identical with "John Marshall of Ilminster, co. Somerset, yeoman. "Will nuncupative, dated 13 April, 1635. He gave all he had to Elizabeth his wife, in the hearing of Katherine Goodland, the wife of Christopher Goodland, and of his (testator's) daughter Phillip Marshall. Administration to relict 26 May 1635." This will is registered in P.C.C. (Sadler 45).

four children Anne, Marshall, Rebecca, and William, all under age,—to my wife Judith Marshall my now dwelling house, etc., in Chillington.—whereas I am to pay unto my son Edward Marshall £100 given to him by his uncle William Marshall deceased, and also £100 which was given him by his brother William Marshall deceased, etc.—appoints cozens Richard Knight, Thomas Marshall, and Robert Marshall, executors. The will was proved by all three in P.C.C. 30 September, 1641. (Evelyn 113.) This testator probably reached an advanced age, as several of his children predeceased him. It will be noticed that, like his father, he had two sons named *John*. His issue was :—

i. William Marshall, of Chillington, will nuncupative and undated,—William Stuckey son of William Stuckey,—to all my brothers and sisters £100 apiece,—money to poor of Dinnington and Ilminster,—my father Thomas Marshall executor. He proved the will in P.C.C. 10 April 1624. (Byrde 36.)

ii. John Marshall, of Exeter, made his will nuncupative, 24 May, 1622, in which he is described as *the younger*. The term younger is no doubt used to distinguish him from his uncle John Marshall (Mayor and Alderman) of Exeter, and not from his brother John, who was citizen and fishmonger of London. He bequeathed to each of the children of his uncle John Marshall, Alderman of Exeter, £50; to Grace Challis, £10; to the poor of Chillington, £10; and a like sum to the poor of St. Mary Arches; to his cousin John Marshall, £100; to Mary Wall, £10; residue to his brother Robert Marshall, and appoints him executor. Administration to John Marshall the uncle, 5 July 1623, because Robert Marshall the executor renounced. Administration 3 March, 1628, to Alice Marshall, widow and executrix of John Marshall, senr., deceased, while he lived, administrator of the goods of John Marshall the younger. Administration 17 June, 1631, to James Marshall of the city of Exeter, merchant, because the said Alice was dead. (Swan 72.) This James was eldest son of the alderman.

iii. Nicholas Marshall, "of Chillington, co. Somerset, tanner, one of the sons of Thomas Marshall of Chillington aforesaid." Will dated 14 January, 1627. Gives to his brother John Marshall, citizen and fishmonger, of London, a messuage called Puphills and other lands at West Chinnock, Middle Chinnock, and Puphill, co. Somerset, and lease of Longhill and Chippelcombe, in the parish of Winsham, and appoints him executor. He proved in P.C.C. 27 Octr. 1628. (Barrington 92.)

iv. Robert Marshall.

v. Edward Marshall.

vi. John Marshall of St. Mary le Bowe, citizen and fishmonger, of London. Will dated 1 October, 1630. Appoints wife Anne Marshall sole executrix. Mentions the four children of my sister Anne Stuckey of Chillington, co. Somerset, all under age,—Jeromie Leeche, parson of St. Mary le Bowe, where I now dwell,—my servant Susan Langworthe,—my father in law John Lynne and Mr. William Spurstowe overseers,—wife "now going with child."—Proved in P.C.C. by relict 12 October, 1630. (Scroope 88.)

John Lynne was of Exeter, and entered his pedigree in the Visitation of Devon, 1620. See *Harleian Society*, vol. vi, p. 176; and *Genealogist*, vol. i, p. 348.

i. Joane married .... Weeks, and had issue.

ii. Judeth, living in 1623.

iii. Agnes, married William (?) Stuckey of Chillington, and had issue. She is called *Anne* in the will of her brother John above.

7. Roger Marshall of Aishwell, in the parish of Ilminster, clothier. Will nuncupative, dated 10 April, 1635. Mentions daughters Marie and Joane,—Joane to be executrix. Witnesses, Thomas Marshall and William Marshall. Proved in P.C.C. by said Joane Marshall 10 June, 1635. (Sadler 69.)

Besides the above daughters he had a son John Marshall, who is mentioned in the will of William Marshall, 1623, as then under age. He probably died in his father's lifetime.

1. Ann. Her will, as of the parish of Ilminster, co. Somerset, spinster, is dated 12 December, 1616, and was proved in P.C.C. 14 February, 1616-17 by the executor therein named. (Weldon 11.) She wills to be buried in the churchyard of Ilminster. Mentions brother Roger Marshall and his three children,—Nicholas Marshall, my godson, the son of my brother Edward Marshall, deceased,—Edward Marshall, the son of my brother Thomas Marshall of Chillington,—Jone Ayshton, the daughter of my brother Nicholas Marshall,—my kinsman Thomas Marshall, son of my brother Nicholas Marshall, sole executor and residuary legatee. Christian Marshall is one of the witnesses.

John Marshall, the Alderman, and Mayor of Exeter, probably settled in that city early in life. He married at St. Mary at Arches, 30 August, 1595, Alice, daughter of Richard Beavis[1] (or Bevis) of Exeter. I have the following notes of his will, and that of his wife :—

"John Marshall, Esq., one of the Aldermen of the citty of Exeter. Dated 8 August, 1624. To be buried in St. Mary Arches church. Property to be divided into three equal parts according to the custom of the city of Exeter. First portion to wife, one other portion amongst my two daughters and three sons, vizt., James Marshall, John Marshall, Richard Marshall, Elizabeth Marshall, and Susan Marshall. The other third in the following legacies. To son James

[1] Arms.—Azure three helmets Argent attired *(sic)* Or.—*Alphabetical Register, etc.*, by Rd. Isacke, p. 22.

Marshall so much as shall with the legacy given him by his cousin John Marshall deceased make up his portion to £300. The like sum to sons John and Richard. The same to make daughter Elizabeth's portion up to £400, and the same to make daughter Susan's up to £350. All these children under age. To my daughter Alice Harris my second best 'guilte bowle.' To my daughter Jane third best gilt bowl. Thomas Milford, Ebott Groot, Agnes Groote, and Mary Wall. Lands in parish of Northtowne called Eastercombe, Westercombe, and Luckerdon. Brother in law Peter Bevis, Esq're. Estate 'of and in the sheafe and Rectory' of Bampton, co. Devon. Proved by Alice Marshall the relict and executrix in P.C.C. 17 September, 1624." (Byrde 74.)

"Alice Marshall of the city of Exeter, widow. Dated 30 December, 1630. To my son and heir apparent James Marshall the manor of Daccombe, in the parish of St. Mary Church, co. Devon. My brother Richard Bevis. My daughter Elizabeth Trowbridge. My daughter Alice Harris. My daughter Jane Golde [*i.e.* Gould]. My daughter Susanna Marshall, under age. Legacies bequeathed to said Susanna by her cousin John Marshall, and her brother John Marshall. Son Richard Marshall, under age, and legacy left to him by his cousin John Marshall, and mentions death of the said Richard's brother John Marshall. My five grandchildren, Bartholomew Harris, James Golde, John Golde, John Trowbridge, and Elizabeth Trowbridge. To my dear mother M^tis^ Jane Martyn one silver bowl with my coat of arms graved or pounced thereon. My brother Peter Beavis. My sister in law M^ris^ Susanna Beavis.[1] My four nephews, Richard, William, Peter, and Henry Beavis, sons of my brother Peter Beavis. Son James Marshall sole executor. He proved in P.C.C. 24 February, 1630-1." (St. John 23.) Alice Marshall died 7 Jan., 1630. M.I.

John and Alice Marshall had the following children :—

1. John, bapt. 17 June, 1599 ; buried 20 March, 1600.
2. James, bapt. 22 January, 1608 ; of whom presently.
3. John, of the City of Exeter, bapt. 19 July, 1610 ; buried 16 December, 1630. Administration granted by the Archdeaconry Court of Exeter to Alice Marshall his mother and James Marshall, merchant, 18 Dec., 1630. Bond is entered by which Alice Marshall, widow, James Marshall, merchant, Peter Bevis, Esq., and Dudley Copplestone of the City of Exeter, merchant, are bound to Thomas Barrett, clerk, and Wm. Kiste, in £1000.
4. Richard, bap. 15 March, 1612.
5. Richard, bap. 3 Nov. 1613 ; buried 9 June, 1635.

1. Jane, bapt. 29 June, 1598 ; buried 30 May, 1600.
2. Alice, bapt. 29 June, 1600 ; married, 29 June, 1621, George Harris, who was born at Barnstaple, and had issue.
3. Grace, bapt. 6 May, 1602 ; buried 11 January, 1620.
4. Elizabeth, bapt. 24 March, 1602-3 ; married, 26 March, 1627, Thomas Trowbridge of Taunton, and had issue.
5. Jane, bapt. 18 March, 1603-4 ; married, 26 September, 1624,

[1] See *Harl. Soc*, vol. vi, p. 181.

James Gould[1] of Exeter. (See *Prince's Worthies of Devon*, new edition, London, 1810, 4to, p. 436; and *Visitation of Devon, Harl. Soc.*, vol. vi, p. 132.)

6. Susanna, married, 30 June 1635, Richard Laut.
7. Anne, bap. 26 March, 1607; buried 14 Nov'r, 1607.

James Marshall, second, but eldest surviving son, was Mayor of Exeter in 1658. Married, 29 May, 1632, Susanna, daughter of ...... Taylour. He was buried 26 January, 1664. The register describes him as some-time Mayor. His monumental inscription is still extant, "Here lyeth the Body of [Jame]s Marshall, Marchent, Mayor of this City, who departed this life ye 20 (?) Jan., 1664." Administration of his effects was granted by the Prerogative Court of Canterbury, 11 February, 1664-5, to Susanna his relict. They had issue:—

1. John Marshall, bapt. 16 April, 1635.
2. James Marshall, bapt. 26 Nov., 1637. Administration granted by P.C.C., in which he is described as "James Marshall senior of the City of Exeter, but at Guinney in parts beyond sea deceased," to John Marshall his brother, 10 May, 1677, James Marshall his son having renounced. Administration *de bonis non* to James Marshall the sonl 6 Oct., 1694.
3. Richard, bapt. 12 April, 1640.
4. Samuel, bapt. 9 July, 1648.[2]
5. Joseph, bapt. 31 March, 1650.
1. Elizabeth, bapt. 29 May, 1642; buried 13 October following.
2. Sarah, buried 20 July, 1656.

The persons mentioned in the following extracts from the register of burials at St. Mary Arches were no doubt connected, but I am unable to say how. "1678. April 8. Mrs. Sarah Marshall." "1697. Dec. 5. Mrs. Ann Marshall."

The earliest entry of the name, and the only one which has not been already mentioned, in the register of St. Mary Arches, is the marriage of "Thomas Marshall and Eleanor Trubodye," which took place 16 January, 1544. The only other Eleanor Marshall I have met with belonging to Exeter made her will 4 October, 1607, as of Crediton, in the co. of Devon, widow. She mentions her daughters Agnes Coleman, Grace Woode, and Mary Dennys and her children Thomas Dennys and Ellinor. Thomas Dennys my son in law. Appoints John Tuckfield of Crediton, gent., and Nicholas Ware of the same parish, yeoman, executors. Both proved the will 7 May, 1608, in P.C.C. (Windebank 44).

[1] There was at a later date another match between a Marshall and one of the Exeter Goulds. Sarah, born in 1697, daughter of George Gould of Exeter, by Elizabeth his wife, married .... Marshall of Exeter. George Gould was of the city of Exeter, mercer; will dated 22 Octr. 1694, and codicil 16 June, 1702. Proved in P.C.C. 7 August, 1702 (Herne 131). In the codicil there is a bequest of 40s. to "the nurse of my daughter Sarah deceased," but no other mention of her is made.

[2] Perhaps identical with "Samuel Marshall of Fremington, co. Devon, clerk.' Will nuncupative, dated 14 July, 1681. "His whole study of bookes and all whatsoever he had he gave to Mrs. Susanna Marshall his deare mother." Witnesses, Mrs. Mary Berry, Mrs. Sedwill Kimpland, Mrs. Penelope Kimpland. Admon. to Susanna Marshall his mother 25 July 1681, in Principal Registry of Exeter. Inventory £173 5s.

MARSHALL OF URSWICK, HADHAM, BLEWBURY, BOSBURY, ETC.

This family appears to have been resident at Urswick in the time of Henry VIII., if not earlier, and members of it, or at all events persons of the same surname, have resided in that parish in comparatively recent times. A pedigree in a MS. of Vincent's in the College of Arms (No. 122, fo. 132), traces a descent from the Marshalls of Pickering, co. York, but varies so much from the authentic accounts of that family, besides assigning entirely different arms, that it appears if not fictitious, at all events doubtful. The arms of the Pickering Marshalls, were, *Barry of six Argent and Sable, a canton Ermine*, quartering, Bruse, Hawyke, and Browne. This, so-called, branch of that house never appears to have pretended to this coat, which affords *prima facie* evidence that it was not part or parcel of it. I shall not therefore give the earlier part of Vincent's pedigree, but commence with William Marshall of Carlton, co. Nottingham, who he asserts to have been the father of Thomas Marshall of *Steventon, co. Lincoln.* There is a copy of Vincent's pedigree in Harleian MS., 6147, signed "Will'm Marshall." The coat assigned by Vincent is, *Gules, on a fess Argent between three mascles Or as many lions' heads erased Azure.* The portions of the following pedigree derived from the Visitation of Berkshire, 1623, will be found in Add. MS. (British Museum) 4961, fo. 58; the arms there given are, *Or, two bars gemelles Sable, in chief a chess rook between two mullets of the second.* Harleian MS. 1441 states that this coat was granted by Bysshe, 14 Decr., 1647, to John Marshall of London Vintner, one of the Common Councilmen. See also Harl. MS. 1532, fo. 111; and Add. MS. 14283, fo. 66.

Nicholas Marshall was inducted Vicar of Urswick, 2 Feby. 1620. He was still Vicar in 1650 when the Church Survey was taken. The jurors then returned, "That ye Viccar Officiating ye Cure of ye Church is Mr. Nicholas Marshall, both Viccar of ye Church and Maister of a ffree School, but that he is scandelous in life & negligent in both his callings.[1] Numerous extracts from the Registers of Urswick will be found in "Local Gleanings, relating to Lancashire and Cheshire," edited by J. P. Earwaker, Vol. ii, pp. 239, 249. The only notes I have from wills are the following.

Will of William Marshall now living in Nagg's Head Court between Gracechurch Street and St. Clement's Lane in the parish of St. Clement's Eastchip, dated 2 March, 1676. To be buried in Deptford churchyard where I buried my mother, my father having been buried there before, and where if it might have stood with her liking I would have buried my deceased wife. Makes "my vertuous trusty diligent and careful servant Anne Marshall daughter of Thomas Marshall of Stainton in the parish of Urswick, co. Lancaster," sole executrix and universal legatee. She proved in P.C.C. 17 Decr., 1683. (Drax 142.)

[1] Record Society's Publications, vol. i, p. 138.

Administration of the goods of Thomas Marshall of Urswick was granted 8 February, 1711. (Richmond Wills, Furness Deanery).

John Marshall of Stainton in the parish of Vrswicke, yeoman, made his will 20 March, 1646. Gives to grandchild Thomas Marshall my tenement of Skaitbreake within Osmotherly, also all my part of the tythe of Stainton and Adgarley. Household goods to said grandson reserving to my son William Marshall the use during his life. Jennett Marshall my grandchild. The three sons of my son Thomas Marshall 15s. equally amongst them. My grandchild Marg. Fox. Anne, Isabell, and Frances Marshall, daughters of my son William Marshall. Sons William Marshall and John Marshall executors. John Richardson and William Ashburner supervisors. No date of probate appears. (Richmond Wills, Furness Deanery).

It will be seen that this family was connected with Stoke-Lacy, co. Hereford. The will of John Marshall, the elder, of that place, yeoman, dated 3 October, 1649, was proved in P.C.C. by Jane Marshall, his widow and relict, 11 February 1649-50. He mentions his daughters, Elenor, Susanna, Anne, Isabell, and Jane. Grandchild Elizabeth Pitt. Appoints wife residuary legatee and executrix. Witnesses, James Rawlins, John Marshall, and Martha Marshall. (Pembroke 25.)

PEDIGREE OF MARSHALL.

William Marshall of Carleton in co. Nottingham. (Said to have died s.p. Harl. MS. 1484, fo. 17). ═ Katherine, dau. of Thomas Leeke.

Children:

- John Marshall, married Elizabeth daughter of Ralph Bingham. ↓
- Thomas Marshall of Steventon in co. Linc. (? Stainton in parish of Urswick, co. Lanc.). *See* Vincent MS. in Coll. Arms, No. 122, fo. 132. ═ Margaret, dau'r of Thomas Hartley of Adgarley in co. Lanc.
- Robert Marshall.
- Joane.

Son of Thomas and Margaret:

William Marshall of Urswick in co. Lanc. ═ Isabell, da, of Robert Penyngton of Lanreghod *(Langroyd)* in co. Lanc.

Children:

- William Marshall of Much Hadham, co. Hertford, Kenwick in the parish of Tilney, co. Norfolk, and Lambeth, co. Surrey. Will[1] dated 1 July 1579, proved in P.C.C. 20 January following (Arundell, 2). *See* Morant's 'Essex,' 2nd edition, vol. ii. p. 172, ═ Alice, dau'r of John King of co. Suffolk. Mentioned in her husband's will 1579. Mar. 2ndly Sir Richard Gibson of London.
- Christopher Marshall, citizen of London. Mentioned in will of his brother William Marshall 1579. ═ Eleanor dau'r of Samuel Gillman. Mentioned in will of William Marhsall 1579. Buried at New Windsor. (M.I. Ashmole's Berks, iii, 91).
- Thomas Marshall of Littlebury, co. Essex *(? of Salesbury, Lanc., see* Harl. MS. 1504, fo. 48). Mentioned in will of his brother William Marshall 1579. ═ His wife, mentioned in will of Will'm Marshall, 1579.
- Margaret, mentioned in will of her brother William Marshall 1579. Mar. John Toenson of Olverston in co. Lanc.
- Agnes, mentioned in will of her brother William Marshall 1579. Mar. Leonard Gardiner.

Children of Thomas Marshall of Littlebury:

- A
- Thomas Marshall of Much Hadham. Mentioned in will of his uncle William Marshall 1579. Will[2] dated 11 and adm'on 23 Feb. 1596 in P.C.C. (Cobham 14).
- Mary, m. at Blewbury 21 Oct. 1558 to Hierome Quartermaine. Mentioned in will of her uncle William Marshall 1579, and in will of her brother Thomas Marshall 1596. Mar. 2ndly John Bradford, clerk,
- Elizabeth, mentioned in will of her uncle William Marshall 1579, and in will of her brother Thomas Marshall 1596.

A

Christopher Marshall of Blewbury, co. Berks. Proved will of his uncle William Marshall 1579-80. Adm'on in P.C.C. 21 Nov. 1593, and again 23 Feb. 1601-2 to Thomas Blunte of Blewbury, Anne Marshall *alias* Blunte, who administered in 1593 being deceased. = Anne, dau. of ... Slade. Administratrix to her husband 1593. Then described as Anne Blount *alias* Marshall.

John Marshall of Much Hadham and Blewbury. Mentioned in will of his uncle William Marshall 1579. Adm'or to his brother Thomas Marshall 1596. Adm'on in P.C.C. 26 June, 1629, to his sister Mary Bradford, wife of John Bradford, clerk. = ...

Edmond Marshall of Bosbury, co. Hereford. Bur. at Blewbury March 21, 1615. Will[4] undated, proved in P.C.C. 14 June 1616. (Cope 60). Mentioned as deceased in will of brother William Marshall 1631. = Dorothy, dau. of Thomas Goddard of ..., co. Wilts. Proved her husband's will 1616 Married 2ndly at Bosbury, Dec. 19, 1620, to Philip Winston of Stoke Lacy, co Hereford.[6]

William Marshall of Blewbury, bapt. there 20 Dec. 1590. Mentioned in will of his brother Edmond Marshall. "Entered as heir male by reason of the state of entail of his uncle William," in Visitation of Berks, 1623. Then living in Old Windsor, co. Berks. (College of Arms MS., C 18, 139[b]). Buried at Blewbury 26 July 1632. Will[3] dated 8 June, 1631, 2nd codicil dated 3 July, 1632, proved in P.C.C. 14 May 1633. (Russell 39). Inq. p.m. dated 22 Feb., 8 Car. I, 1633. (Cole's 'Escheats,' vol. iii, p. 152). = Margery, dau. of Richard Windlow of Chinnor, co. Oxford, mentioned in her husband's will 1631.

Henry Marshall, mentioned in will of William Marshall 1631. = Merialle, buried at Bosbury, 1 April, 1611.

Edmund,[5] born 11 and bapt. 24 March, 1611 at Bosbury. Buried there 14 Jan. 1612.

Children of Edmond Marshall and Dorothy:

William Marshall, bapt. at Blewbury 22 Oct. 1609. Died before 1615.

Thomas Marshall, bapt. at Bosbury 12 and buried there 25 Sept. 1615.

Dorothy, married at Bosbury to (Sir) Thomas Blackwall 7 Dec. 1625.[7] Mentioned in will of her uncle William Marshall 1631. *See* 'Reliquary,' vol. vii, p. 20; 'Genealogist,' vol. vii, p. 144.

Anne, married at Stoke Lacy 3 Oct. 1628 to William Bridges' (Bosbury Par. Reg.). Both mentioned in will of her uncle William Marshall 1631. *See* 'Landed Gentry,' 2nd edn., p. 1524.

Elizabeth, mentioned in will of her uncle William Marshall 1631.

—

Catherine, mentioned in will of her uncle William Marshall 1631. Mar. 26 May, 1634, to William Cartwright of Ossington, who was aged 54, 26 Aug. 1662, when he entered his pedigree in Visitation of Notts. *College of Arms*, MS. C. 34, fo. 25[b].

Children of William Marshall and Margery:

William Marshall, buried at Blewbury 27 Dec. 1620.

Margery, mentioned in her father's will 1631. Called dau. and heir, aged 12, 16 Jan. 1632, in her father's Inq. p.m.

D

[1] Will of "Willyam Mershall of Lambithe, co. Surrey, Esquire.' To nephew Christopher Mershall the eldest son of Thomas Mershall my brother all that my mannor of Kynwick, co. Norfolk, and also my manor of Howchins, co. Essex, and all my other lands in Norfolk and Essex to him and his heirs males, remainder to John Mershall second son of said Thomas Mershall, remainder over to Thomas Mershall third son of said Thomas Mershall, remainder over to right heirs of testator. Houses at Cheshunt to said Christopher Mershall. Copyholds at Mochehadh^{m} to said Christopher for term of two years, then to Christopher Mershall my brother for six years, remainder to John Mershall and Thomas Mershall. To nephew Christopher Mershall the parsonage of Blewberry, co. Berks, for term of five years to pay £10 a year to Edmond S^{r}geant, then for term of ten years more to pay £20 a year to my sisters Margaret and Agnes to either of them, the residue of the profits of the said parsonage to be imployed by said Christopher in erecting a free school either in Little Urswicke, co. Lancaster, or in Mochehadham afs^{d}, the stipend of the schoolmaster to be £15 per annum; and also three schollarships in the University of Cambridge, in Pembroke Hall, Clare Hall, and Jesus College, to each of them five marks yearly for ever. The maintenance of the said school and schollarshipps to be taken out of the moiety of the manor of Brantingthorp, co. Leicester which I lately purchased in the said Christopher's name to the use aforesaid. The said schollarships to be for Lancashire, Cumberland, Hertfordshire, and Essex. Lease of Castlecamps co. Cambridge to nephew Christopher to pay to said brother Christopher £20 a year during the lease. Mentions "the patent of the office" of brother Christopher, which it appears had been pledged to testator as security for a debt. My brother Kinge. George Mershall my servant. Thomas Pygott, Anne Finche, Henry Strong, Thomas Lanye, Wm Newmarche, and Edmund Hungate. Mr. Webbe. Frequent mention is made of the then Archbishop of Canterbury, and legacies given to all his household. To John Mershall, saddler of London, and his wife 40^{s} each. Margaret Kinge my wife's sister. To my sister Christopher Mershalls wife £20 toward bringing up of my brother Thomas Mershall's daughter. Lease of Manor of Scrowby, co. Nott^{m}, to John Scott of Lambith, Esqr, and Anthony Nichols, Gent. Witnesses—John Bullock, John Scott, Willm Webb, Thomas Ballarde, Peter Morten, and Willm Woodhall.

[2] Will as of Much Haddam, co. Hertford, Gent., lying sicke at Watlington, co. Oxford. Nuncupative. "One Rose Hoptro the same day did come to visite him who lyinge vppon his bed in his accustomed apparell she saide vnto him theise wordes or like in effect, viz. Mr Marshall remember yourselfe and make your Will, etc." He then mentioned his sister Elizabeth Marshall and gave her £200. To sister Mary Quartermaine £200,—" and with that gave a great gaspe and dep'ted this life," being present Rose Hoptro, Thomas Quartermaine, Margery Benson, and Jerome Quartermaine.

[3] In his will he desires to be buried in the parish church of Blewbery; and devises to loving friends James Hallywell of Blewberry, Gent., and to my cosen Fraunces Slade of Wantinge, co. Berks, clerk, his manor of Kenwicke in parish of Tilney in Marshland, co. Norfolk,

and also manor called Howchins *alias* Fowchinges in parish of Feeringe, co. Essex, to hold said manor of Kenwicke for 15 years, and manor of Howchins for 30 years, first to pay off mortgage on them, and then to raise 200 marks for a portion for my daughter Margery Marshall. Bequeaths to Henry Marshall, Gent., my cousin german, annuity of £30 after decease of Dorothy Winston my sister-in-law, or after decease of Margery my now wife, which shall first happen. To the four daughters of Dorothy Winston, my neices Dorothy, Anne, Elizabeth, and Catherine, £20 apiece. To my aunt Staunton's children 40s. apiece. To my aunt Bradford's children 40s apiece. My aunt Elianor Marshall. Aunt Bradford's son Thomas Bradford. As touching the fee simple of the manors hereinbefore devised for term of years to my executors, and which were by William Marshall, Esq., my great uncle deceased, by his last will given to Christopher Marshall, Esq., my father deceased and his heirs with divers other remainders over in tail,—recites that testator was heir male of his great uncle and that he has no issue male, and has suffered a recovery to bar entail,—devise to right heirs males of his great uncle William Marshall, but if they interfere with executors in the execution of the trusts before recited,—then I devise the said manor to the right heirs of my brother Edmond Marshall, Esq., deceased, for ever. To Margery my wife household goods at Old Windsor but not elsewhere. My uncle Gregory Slade and kinsman William Bridges overseers. Published 26 March, 1632. Codicil, dated 27 March, 1632, whereas there is a legacy of £10 in my late testament to my well-beloved aunt Mary Bradford, of Aston, co. Berks, and she being since deceased, test[r] gives said legacy to his servant Henry Hulles. Codicil, dated 3 July, 1632; mentions kinswoman Mrs. Anne Bridges wife of William Bridges, Gent., and afterwards calls him his 'cousin.' Test[r] mentions his trunk at William Bridges' house. Proved by sentence of Court by James Hallywell one of the executors, 14 May, 1633.

[4] In his will he devises his lands in Blubery and Bosbery to wife Dorothie to educate children till age of 18, and then portions to be raised for them at discretion of my brother M[r] Francys Goddard, Esq[r], my brother William Marshall, gent., and Giles Winston, gent., and Mr. Hughe Keate my beloved friend.

[5] 1611. "Die Martis mane inter horas quintam et sextam undecimo die dicti mensis natus est primogenitus Henrici Marshalle generosi et Merialle uxoris ejus, qui primogenitus baptizatus est vicesimo quarto die et nominatus Edmundus."—*Parish Regr. of Bosbury.*

[6] He was churchwarden of Bosbury, 1630. Giles Winston was churchwarden there in 1610.

[7] Catherine dau. of Tho[s] Blackwall, gent., of Old Court, and Dorothy his wife, was bap[t] at Stoke Lacy, 7 Jan[y], 1627, and bur[d] at Bosbury Oct., 1628—*Bosbury Register.* John son of Thomas Blackwall, gent., and Dorothy his wife was bapt. at Bosbury 23 May, 1630, and buried *same day (?)*

[8] 26 Sept[r] 1630. "Dorothea filia Gulielmi Bridges, gener., et Annae uxoris ejus baptizabatur."—*Bosbury Register.*

PEDIGREE OF MARSHALL OF WOODWALTON, CO. HUNTINGDON, AND FINCHINGFIELD, CO. ESSEX, ETC.*

... Marshall of Eltisley, co. Cambridge. = ...

William Marshall of Eltisley, collector of the subsidy, temp. Hen. VIII, elder brother to John. *See* Inq. p.m., vol. i, p. 327.

John Marshall of Wintringham, near St. Neots.† = Alice, dau. of ... Percy of Barford, near St. Neots.

John Marshall of Woodwalton, co. Huntingdon. = Johanna, dau. of ... Ayre of Higney.

William Marshall of Woodwalton, living at the time of the Visitation of Huntingdonshire, 1613. Will of 30 Jan. 1627, pro. at Huntingdon 1 April 1628. *See* 'Genealogist,' vol. v, p. 93. = Johanna Martendale of Gretton, co. Northampton.

Matthew Marshall of Eltisley aforesaid, and of Sawtrey, co. Huntingdon. = Johanna, dau. of Philip Hatley of Caxton, co. Cambridge. (*Gayton*, in Visitation of London).

Sarah, mar. Robert Hawes of Bedford, both mentioned in her father's will 1627. She is mentioned in will of her brother John Marshall 1649.

Joane, mar. William Hodilowe, both mentioned in her father's will 1627.

Gilbert Marshall, Merchant of London. Mentioned in wills of his father 1627, and of his brother John Marshall, 1649. = ...

William Marshall.

Michael Marshall. Mentioned in his father's will, 1627. = ...

Robert Marshall. Mentioned in wills of his father, 1627, and of his brother John Marshall, 1649. Was of London, grocer, in 1664, when he entered his pedigree in the Visitation of London. Coll. Arms, MS. D 19, fo. 5. Called "kinsman Mr Robert Marshall" in will of John Marshall 1668. Will dated 20 March, 1671, pro. in P.C.C. 21 Aug. 1676. (Bence 103).‡ = Mary, dau. of Roger Dutton of London. Mentioned in will of John Marshall 1649.

William Marshall. Mentioned in will of his grandfather 1627, then under age.

Gilbert Marshall. Mentioned in will of his grandfather 1627, then under age.

Sarah. = John Widdowson.

A

B

A — B

John Marshall, son and heir. Mentioned in his father's will 1627. Will of 21 April, 1649, proved in P.C.C. 9 April, 1652 (Bowyer 77). To be buried in church or chancel of Woodwalton. Mentions "the three dau'rs of my eldest son Thomas Marshall deceased," all under age. ╤ Verney, dau. of William Godard of Carlton, co. Bedford, Esq.

Thomas Marshall of Woodwalton. Proved his father's will 1628. Will of 24 Sept. 1628, pro. in P.C.C. 22 Jan. following (Ridley 2). To be buried in church or chancel of Woodwalton. Mentions "my mother Dalton." ╤ Elizabeth. Proved her husband's will 1628-9.

George Marshall. Mentioned in his father's will 1628, then under age, and in the will of William Marshall 1627.

Anne, and Sarah. Both mentioned in their father's will 1628, then under 18. Anne is also mentioned in will of William Marshall 1627.

Philipp Marshall of Eltisley, son and heir. Mentioned as deceased in will of his brother John Marshall, 1668. ╤ Mary, dau. of John Brett of Little Gransden, co. Cambridge. Mentioned in will of John Marshall, 1668.

Matthew Marshall. Called "late brother" in will of John Marshall, 1668. ╤ ...

John Marshall of Clifford's Inn, London, 1634, when he entered his pedigree in the Visitation of London. Attorney-at-law. Buried in the Temple Church, 23 Dec. 1668. Will as of the Inner Temple, dated 15 Dec. 1668, proved in P.C.C. 14 Jan. 1668-9§ (Coke 8). = Martha, da. of Obedia Smith of London. Bur. in the Temple Church 8 Feb. 1665-6.

Edward Marshall. Called "late brother" in will of John Marshall, 1668. ╤ Mary, mentioned in will of John Marshall, 1668.

Matthew Marshall, 1613. Mentioned in will of John Marshall, 1668. ╤

Samuel Marshall. Mentioned in will of John Marshall, 1668; and in will of Philip Marshall. 1704.

Philip Marshall of Eltisley, devisee of lease of Parsonage of Lees Downe (Leysdowne), in the Isle of Sheppey, in will of John Marshall, 1668.

Joane, wife of Richard Gynn. Mentioned in will of John Marshall, 1668.

Anthony Marshall. Mentioned in will of John Marshall, 1668; and, as also his children, in will of his brother Philip Marshall, 1704.

Philip Marshall. Mentioned in will of John Marshall, 1668. Will as of the Parish of St. Leonard, Shoreditch, dated 7 Aug., proved in P.C.C. by testator's cousin, Moses Burton, 6 October 1704 (Ash 205.)

Mary, wife of Moses Burton. Mentioned in will of John Marshall, 1668.

Rebecca, wife of Richard Rogers, devisee of messuages near Temple Bar, called "the Green Quishion," and "Jacob's well," in will of John Marshall, 1668.

Mary. a dau.

Devisees of "tenement now in tenure of Walter Trevilian, at Hemingby, near Horncastle, co. Linc." in will of John Marshall, 1668.

D — C

D ... C

Miles Marshall. Mentioned as deceased in will of his brother John Marshall, 1668. = ... Mentioned in will of John Marshall, 1668.

- Daniel Marshall, devisee of messuages in Shorelane, co. Middx., in will of John Marshall, 1668.
- Martha, mentioned in will of John Marshall, 1668.

Joseph Marshall, 1613.

- Frances. 1613.

Elizabeth, wife of James Desborough, 1613.

Joane, wife of ... Isaac. Mentioned as deceased in will of her brother John Marshall, 1668. =

- Elizabeth, and others, 1668.

Mary, wife of ... Naull, called "late sister" in will of John Marshall, 1668. =

- Two dau'rs, 1668.

Margaret, wife of John Long. Mentioned as deceased in will of her brother John Marshall, 1668. =

- Mary, 1668.

---

1. Thomas Marshall[1] of Woodwalton and Cambridge. Will nuncupative dated 1 Jan. 1645-6, proved in P.C.C. 5 May 1646 (Twisse 67 and 74). ¶ = Elizabeth, dau. of Roger Rant of Swaffham, co. Cambridge, Esq. Married at Swaffham Prior 31 Dec. 1638. Proved her husband's will 1646. Mentioned in will of John Marshall, 1649. Mar. 2ndly Rev. Owen Stockton. Carthew's 'Launditch,' vol. iii, p. 461.

- E

2. William Marshall[1] of Caxton, co. Cambridge. Proved his father's will, 1652. Will of 26 Sept. 1667, proved in P.C.C. 25 May 1669 (Coke 58). All to wife Mary and dau'r Anne Marshall, to be equally divided between them. Friends Mr. Peter Webster, and Mr. Hodilow, overseers. Witnesses, John Torrant, and John Godfrey. = Mary. Proved her husband's will 1669.

- Anne Marshall, 1667.

3. John Marshall[1] of Wood Walton. Mentioned in his father's will 1649. ? if buried at St. Andrew, Holborn, 27 March 1657 as "John Marshall, gent. from Mr Osborne's Fetter Lane." = Elizabeth. Will of 4 Jan. 1675, proved in Commissary Court of the Bishop of London, 1 May, 1676.**

4. Joseph Marshall,[1] devisee of lands at Kingston Burnes, and Caldecot, co. Cambridge, in his father's will, 1649.

Joane,[1] eldest dau'r aged 6 in 1613. Married Benjamin Dodd, clerk. Both mentioned, as also their four children under age in will of her father, 1649.

Edith,[1] second and youngest dau'r. Married ... Jackman. Both mentioned in will of her father, 1649.

[1] Mentioned in the will of their grandfather William Marshall, 1627.

Dorothy, dau. and coheir of John Meade, Esq. of Swaffham Prior, co. Cambridge. Marriage Licence (Vicar Gen. Off.) dated 12 Dec. 1668, then a spinster aged about 21 *(sic)*, with father's consent, to marry at Swaffham Prior or Quy, co. Cambridge. Died 26 April 1685, æt. 45. Buried at Finchingfield. M.I. (Her sister Joane married Roger Rant of Swaffham, co. Cambridge. Morant's 'Essex,' second edition, vol. ii, p. 366).

= Sir John Marshall, Knt., of Woodwalton and Much Hadham, co. Herts. of Raveley, co. Huntingdon, and of Finchingfield, co Essex; and at the time of his first marriage of the Middle Temple, Esq. bachelor, aged about 24 *(sic)* (Mar. Lic.) Had the manor of Sculpins, in Finchingfield, by his first wife. Called "kinsman John Marshall barrister of the Middle Temple," in will of John Marshall, 1668. Entered his pedigree at Visitation of Hertfordshire, 1669. Coll. Arms, M.S. D 24, fo. 70b. Proved the will of Elizabeth Marshall. 1676. Knighted 1681. Le Neve's Knights (*Harl. Soc.*), p. 356. Will dated 5 Aug. 1716, proved in P.C.C. 28 Jan. 1723-4 (Bolton 13). Mentions "my godson, John Rant, son of Thomas Rant, Rector of Sturmeere. My cousin Elianor Marshall widow and her son John my godson." Died 21 Jan. 1723-4, aged 82. Buried at Finchingfield M.I.††

= Lucy. dau. and coh. of Sir John Wiseman of Bradokes in Wimbish, co. Essex. Marriage Licence (Fac. Off.) dated 17 Dec. 1689, then a spinster aged about 28 *(sic)*. Died 11 June 1699, aged 46. Buried at Finchingfield. M.I.

Eleanor. Mentioned in her father's will 1645-6, and in will of Elizabeth Marshall 1675. Married Edmund Tooke of Dartford, co. Kent, Esq.

Elizabeth. Mentioned in her father's will, 1645-6; in will of Elizabeth Marshall, 1675; and in will of Sir John Marshall, 1716. Second wife of Sir Francis Theobald, kt. ('Le Neve,' p. 222).

Thomas Theobald and his wife, both mentioned in will of Sir John Marshall, 1716.

Mary, mentioned in will of Elizabeth Marshall, 1675.

Dorothy, only daughter in 1669.

Elizabeth, married Sir Maynard Jenour, Bart. Living 14 Dec. 1696.

"My four grandchildren, Sir John Jenoure, Bart. and his two brothers Maynard and Joseph Jenoure, and his sister Elizabeth wife of the Honble Captn James Bellenden, £20 apiece." (Will of Sir John Marshall, 1716).

William Marshall, Esq. Bapt. at St. Andrew's, Holborn, 21 Jan. 1691-2. Mentioned in his father's will, 1716.

= Elizabeth, second da. of Sir William Blackett, Bart. and coheir of her brother Sir William Blackett, Bart. (Hodgson's 'Northumberland,' vol. i, part ii, p. 259; 'Memoirs of Sir Walter Blackett, Bart,' Newcastle, 1819, 12mo., p. 49).

John Marshall. Proved his father's will, 1716. Thus mentioned therein, "All my estate in Finchingfield to my son John Marshall as by a conveyance dated 6 July 1703, may appear." Died 28 Nov. 1760, aged 66. Buried at Finchingfield. M.I.

William Marshall, Esq. = ... dau. of Samuel Gatward of Cambridge, Barrister-at-Law.

Anne. Married at Chelsea 28 May 1767, to Peter Standley (or Stanley) of Little Paxton, co. Huntingdon, Esq., widower. Died *s.p.*

Lucy. Married at Chelsea 30 May 1767, to Nicholas Wescombe of Flamstead, co. Hertford, Esq. Died *s.p.*

* For the Herald's entry of this pedigree in 1613, see Visitation of Huntingdonshire, Camden Soc. Vol. xliii. p. 34; and Coll Arms, MS. C 3, fo. 15.

† Inq. p.m taken at Gamlingay, 22 May, 9 Eliz. (1567), on John Marshall, yeoman, died 12 Oct 1566. John, his son and heir, then aged 40. Land in Eltesley and Papworth Everard. (Cole's Inq., iii., 265.)

‡ Will as "Robert Marshall of the Charterhouse, Citizen and Bowyer of London." Bequeaths to cousin Anne Mathewes £5; to cousin Sarah Field, widow, £5, to Mary Bell, wife of John Bell, shoemaker, £5; residue, and that which is "in my chamber at the Charter house where I now live" to son-in-law John Widdowson, and makes him sole executor. He proved 1676.

§ The following persons not named in the pedigree are mentioned in the will of this testator. Richard Smith my late wife's brother's son, legatee of all testator's Divinity and Philosophy books. The children of Samuel Burdett by Anne his late wife, my late wife's kinswoman. The children of Elizabeth now wife of John Bentley late wife of Peter Frisby. The children of John Smith by his late wife Mary, my late wife's kinswoman. Thomas Marshall, Taylor, of St. Giles in the Fields, 'who calls himself my brother.' My cousins Samuel Gabry, John Gabry, Mark Gabry, and Mary wife of Mr. John Nedham. My cousin Mr. William Cosyn Minister of God's word. Kinsman Richard Cosyn. Susan Smith, widow of his (testator's) late wife's brother. Moses Burton and John Gabry to be executors.

‖ Mention is made by this testator of his cousins Thomas Cullen and Thomas Johnson; and "my first cousin Elizabeth Morley, who has been very careful of me in my sickness."

¶ Memorandum That Thomas Marshall being sicke in body but in perfect sence bequeathed to his sonne John Tenn shillings. Vnto Elienor and Elizabeth his two Daughters two hundred pounds Provided that if his wife now left behind be with child, the Child borne shall have an equall share with the two daughters in the two hundred pounds. Likewise he did ordaine his wife sole Executrix of this his will. Jan. 1, 1645. Witnes John Eyre, John Marshall. Testator is described in the Probate Act as "late of the Town of Cambridge."

** Elizabeth Marshall of the parish of St. Sepulchres without Newgate, London, widow, relict of John Marshall, late of Woodwalton, in the co. of Huntingdon, gent. deceased. Dated 4 Jan. 1675. To be buried in the parish of St. Andrew Holborne. Forty shillings to Dr. William Bell to preach funeral sermon. There is due to me from S[r] Robert Vyner £90; Mr. Isaac Mennell deceased £100; and from Mrs. Lindsey £100. Gives out of these sums £40 to my sister Jane Hicks the wife of Adam Hicks, and to her son and dau'r Edward and Jane Hicks £20 apiece. Forty shillings each to poor of parishes of St. Andrew Holborne, St. Sepulchres, and St. Dunstan in the West. To Mr. Thomas Bostock, girdler, £5, and to his wife Mrs. Joane Bostock, 40s. To friends Ann Ryley, and Lucretia Weaver of the parish of St. Sepulchres 20s. apiece Anthony Osborne, Girdler. Margaret Pendrith, widow. The Lady Elizabeth Thibalde, Ellenor Marshall, and Mary Marshall. Residue to loving friend John Marshall of Finchingfield, co. Essex, Esq. and appoints him sole executor. He proved the will 1 May, 1676.

†† See 'East Anglian,' iii., 6.

The following are notes of wills of persons probably related to this family.

Mary Marshall, "of the parish of St. Bartholomew the Less within the Citty of London widdow," will dated 5 May, 1714, proved by her son, Henry Marshall, in P.C.C. 22 Dec. following (Aston 244). She mentions, My dau'r Elizabeth Butler. My dau'r Jane Marshall. Mary Cartwright, Elizabeth Cartwright, William Cartwright, and Thomas Butler, the four children of my said dau'r Elizabeth Butler. My sisters Thomasin Martin and Hannah Pelling. My son William Butler, and brother John Martin. My sister Elizabeth How. My sisters Elizabeth Marsh and Catherine Rilythe (*sic*). My brother Martin's children. Elizabeth Day. Alice Ryly my niece. Household goods to be divided between my son Henry Marshall, Elizabeth Butler, and Jane Marshall. Elizabeth Cooper. Ann Pelling. Abigall Harris. Sarah Perkins. Son Henry Marshall ex'or and residuary legatee. Codicil dated 13 June, 1714, mentions my relation Mr. William Cox. Second Codicil dated 28 Nov. 1714.

Thomas Marshall, the eldest son of this testatrix, was of Lincoln's Inn, co. Middx., Gent. Will dated 28 Jan. 1713, proved by his brother Henry Marshall in P.C.C. 17 Feb. 1713 (Aston 32). Gives to dear and honoured mother £1000. Mentions his sister Elizabeth Butler, brother Henry Marshall, and sister Jane Marshall. To Mary Cartwright, Elizabeth Cartwright, William Cartwright, and Thomas Butler, the four children of my sister Elizabeth Butler, £300 apiece. My aunts Elizabeth How, Thomasin Martin, and Hannah Pelling. My clerk Samuel Hamett and his mother Susanna Hamett. Friends Mr. Thomas Woodford, and William Mowbray. My gold watch to Mr. John Warner, goldsmith.

Jane Marshall, above mentioned, was of the parish of St. Peter the Poor, London, spinster. Will of 27 Dec. 1753, proved by her brother Henry Marshall in P.C.C. 13 June 1757 (Herring 197.) To brother Henry Marshall £1500, and appoints him ex'or. My niece Elizabeth Cartwright. George Garrard. Mrs. Thomzin Hurnard. Mrs. Elizabeth Martyn. Mr. Chamberlayne. Mrs. Jane Martyn. Mr. Thomas Martyn. Mr. Thomas Martyn, the son of Mr. John Martyn late of Maryland Point. Mr. John March. Mr Richard March. Mr. Robert Riley. Mr. George Riley. Mrs. Mary Riley. Mr. . . Riley's son. Mrs. Sarah Baxter. Mr. Charles Corker. Mrs. Bean. Sarah Alexander. Rings of 20s. each to Mrs. Eliz^{a} Martyn, sen., Dr. Martyn and his wife, Mrs. Ann Dewell, Mrs. Gratiania Dewell, Mrs. Mary Brown, Mrs. Mary Simson (Sunson?) Mrs. Ireland, Mr. Francis Cooper, Mrs. Masket, Mrs. Helmsley, and Mr. Tho. Roe.

Henry Marshall, who proved these wills, made his will, in which he is described as Citizen and Painter-stainer of London, 24 June, 1757. To niece Elizabeth Cartwright £3000. To Mrs. Thomasin Hurnard £300. To Mrs. Mary Chamberlain £200. To Mr. Thomas Martin £20. To Mrs. Jane Martin £500. To Mr. Thomas Martin, now or late of Jamaica, £100. To Mr. George Garrard £100. Francis Cooper. Mr. Richard March. George Riley, sen. George Riley, jun. Mrs. Mary Riley. Mrs. Mary Bailey. Mr. Thomas Roe. Mrs.

Mary Brown. Mr. Charles Gisbey. Mrs. Sarah Baxter. To worthy friend Mr. Timothy Helmsley £100. Niece Elizabeth Cartwright, Timothy Helmsley, and Charles Corker, ex'ors. Codicil dated 25 Aug. 1757. Witnesses Marshall Rant, Thomas Rant. Proved by two last named ex'ors 3 Feb. 1758.

WILLS OF BEDFORDSHIRE MARSHALLS IN P.C.C.

The oldest will of a Bedfordshire Marshall I have met with is that of William Marchall "dwelling wt'in the place of the blacke freres of Dunstaple in the Countie of Bedfford, gentilman," dated 8 July 1531. He bequeaths to the mother church of Lincoln 4d., and to parish church of Todington 20s. Mentions, his late wife Alice, his father John, and mother Joan. His daughters Dorathe and Margaret. Mary, Jane, and Alice, daughters of his son Richard Marchall. Devises farms at Chalton, &c., to son William Marchall. Mentions, daughter Elizabeth Brockas, her late husband John Brockas, Esq., and their children Mary Brockas and Robert Brockas. Gives residue to wife Mary, and appoints her, and son William Marchall executors. My good lady of Wilshere to be overseer. Proved by relict 6 February, 1531 (13 Thower, vol. i.) A pedigree of Brockas will be found in Berry's *Hampshire Genealogies*, p. 91. "My good lady of Wilshere" was Elizabeth daughter of Thomas Howard, Duke of Norfolk, and wife of Sir Thomas Boleyne, K.G., Earl of Wiltshire.

William Marshall devisee of the farms at Chalton may be identical with "William Marshall of Hitchen, co. Hertford, yeoman," at which place a numerous family of the name appear to have resided. His will is dated 15 May, 1573, and was proved by Annys his relict and sole executrix, 3 June following. (Peter 20.) He mentions his daughter Johan, under age. Devises tenement in Chalton in parish of Ipolits, to Edward Laurence the son of William Laurence late of Gosemor my brother deceased. Also mentions, the children of John Draper late of Chalton which he had by my sister; the four children of William Laurence late of Gosemer deceased, viz., William Laurence, Annys Laurence, Margaret Laurence, and John Laurence; Johan Braye and Kirchin Braye the daughters of Thomas Brayo which he had by Johan his wife my sister.

William Marshall, the elder, of Hippolets, co. Hertford, yeoman, apparently a member of this family, made his will 23 December, 1624. He names, son and heir William Marshall, executor; 2nd son Robert Marshall; 3rd son Christopher Marshall; 4th son John Marshall; 5th son James Marshall; daughter Grace Marshall; Alice my wife. To Mr. Marshall minister of the parish of Hippoletts 10s. Codicil dated 26 December, 1624. Proved by within named executor, 24 February, 1624. (Clark 20.)

James Marshall fifth son of this testator was a citizen and Merchant Taylor of London. In his will dated 19 August, 1625, and proved by Jane Marshall his relict and executrix 10 November, 1626, (Hele 126) he mentions his late father William Marshall of Ippoletts in co. Hertford, yeoman; brother William Marshall of Ippoletts aforesaid;

son William Marshall; two daughters Rebecca and Sara Marshall; brothers John Marshall, and Christopher Marshall.

Robert Marshall, perhaps the brother of this testator, had a daughter Elizabeth, wife, first of Ralph Radcliffe of Hitchin, and secondly of Thomas Norton. Her arms were: Gules on a fess Argent between three mascles Or as many lions' heads erased Azure. See Cussan's *Herts.*, Parts vii and viii, p. 66; Le Neve's *Knights*, p. 214; Berry's *Kent Genealogies*, p. 130; *Herald and Genealogist*, iii, 277; and *Genealogist*, v, 125.

Edward Marshall of Hitchin, another of this family made his will 19 May, 35 Elizabeth. He mentions his sons Thomas Marshall, and John Marshall, both under age; his wife Alice; daughter Alice, wife of William Abbot my son-in-law, their children William, Thomas, Abraham, Marye Abbott, and Joane Abbott, who are legatees of 40s. each; daughter Elizabeth Marshall; daughter Joane; and appoints son Edward Marshall sole executor. He proved 29 May, 1593. (Nevell 41.)

My next note of a Bedfordshire Marshall is the will of "William Marshall parson of Marston, co. Bedford," dated 16 February, 1558. To be buried in the chancel of the Assumption of our blessed Lady Marston nigh unto my mother's grave. To my niece Beatrix Frevell a cup of silver double gilt. Haselden Bury my nephew, and James Hutton his father-in-law. Devises his house at Royston, co. Cambridge, to his sister Jane Haselden. Nieces Elizabeth and Beatryce (Haselden?). Cosen Edward Chambers. Samuel Peto and Elizabeth his wife. William Peto. Maude Marshall, widow. Francis Marshall and Dorothy his sister. Robert Frevell, gentleman, is one of the witnesses. Proved 9 March, 1559 (Mellershe 20).

William Marshall of Royston, the first of whom I have found any notice as connected with that place, made his will 8 February, 1506. He desires to be buried in the church of SS. John Baptist and Thomas Martyr of Royston before the altar of the Blessed Mary of Piety. Devises to wife Elizabeth tenement called "Marshall at the well" in the town of Royston till son William is of age, remainder to daughter Johanna. Mentions Agnes my wife's sister. Appoints Christopher Grene, Robert Marshall my brother, and Robert Hall of Royston executors. Witnesses:—Thomas Taverner my confessor, John Sutton of Mylrede, and James Rogerson of Royston. Proved at Lambeth by Robert Marshall, 26 November, 1507 (Adeane 29.)

I find no further mention of Bedfordshire Marshalls till a much later date than this. Mr. Robert Marshall appears to have been minister of St. Peter de Merton, Bedford, from 1647-1660, during which period several of his children were baptised there, viz.:—William, 24 December, 1648; Margaret, 7 April, 1650 (buried 18 May following); John, 22 April, 1651; An, 30 April, 1654; Robert, 25 March, 1656; Elizabeth, 9 November, 1657; and a child of his still-born was buried 20 April, 1660.

James Marshall of Harpenden, in co. Hertford, yeoman, in his will dated 30 December, 1719, devises his lands at Luton, co. Bedford, and lands at Harpenden to wife Anna for life, she to pay my brother Phillip Marshall £16 a year for his life; the said annuity to be paid after decease of said Phillip Marshall to my cousin Phillip Marshall son of my brother Phillip Marshall for his life. Lands before mentioned to cousin Phillip Marshall after decease of my wife, remainder to his children if he have any. Devises lands to churchwardens and overseers of Wheathampstead and Harpenden to put out poor men's children apprentices. Wife Anna sole executrix. Mr. Thomas Marson, junr., of Luton, grocer, and Hugh Smith of St. Albans, Malster, to assist executrix. Proved by Relict, 10 July, 1722. (Marlborough 142.)

William Marshall of Hitchin, Herts, and Mary Harvy of St. Giles Cripplegate, were married at St. Mary Aldermanbury, 18 November, 1714.

The Marshalls of Ippolits appear to have remained at that place till a later period than that previously mentioned. Nicholas Marshall of the parish of St. Pulcker's, London, in his will, undated, desires to be buried in Ippollits churchyard at south side of Chancel. Mentions his wife Saray. Appoints John Doe trustee. Mentions also, my daughter Ann now wife to John Stevens; my son Josiah Marshall, and his children; granddaughter Mary Marshall daughter to my son Mathew; my grandchildren, sons and daughters of Danill Gootteridge, who is mentioned as deceased as also his wife; William Marshall my grandson son of my son Christopher (dead but his wife living); grandson William Marshall son of William Marshall executor. December 9, 1737, appeared William Marshall, senior, of the parish of St. Mary Whitechapell in the co. of Middlesex, gentleman, and Ann Steventon wife of Thomas Steventon of the parish of St. Sepulchre, London. and swore that the will was in handwriting of testator who died 2 December. December 10, 1737, appeared John Wilmer of the parish of St. Andrew, Undershaft, merchant, and deposed that he knew Nicholas Marshall late of the parish of St. Sepulchre, but in the Fleet prison, London, deceased, and swore to the interlineations in the will. This will was proved by William Marshall the younger, the sole executor, 12 December, 1737. (Wake 280.)

NOTES ON LANCASHIRE MARSHALLS.

A considerable family of the name was resident at, and in the neighbourhood of Cartmel during the seventeenth and eighteenth centuries. The following inscriptions are from monuments in Cartmel Church :—

Here lyes ye Body of Mr. John Marshall late of Aynsom, who died the 5th day of October, 1729, in the 75th year of his age.

Here lyes ye Body of Mr. Henry Marshall late of Aynsom, who died the 9th day of Ianvary, 1736, in the 42^d^ yeare of his age.

Katharine Marshall, buried the 22 Day of Ivne, 1714.

Here lyes yᵉ body of Mr. Edward Marshall son of Mr. John Marshall of Aynsom, who died the 22ⁿ day of December, 1728, in the 38th year of his age.

Here lyes yᵉ Body of Margaret Marshall relict of Mr. John Marshall of Aynsome, who died the 23rd day of February, 1735, in the 75th year of her age.

The following inscription is on a brass chandelier in the church :—

The gift of Margaret the relict of Mr. John Marshall, late of Aynsome, to the Parish Church of Cartmel. Anno Domini 1734.

This is accompanied by the following extraordinary coat of arms, on a lozenge :—Quarterly, 1. Per pale Or and Vert, a lion rampant Gules. 2 and 3. Argent, two bars Gules, a canton Ermine. 4. Or (?) three chevrons (Gules or Sable?) ; a label of five points over all. Impaling: Ermine, a chevron Sable. The first quarter is the coat of the Marshals, Earls of Pembroke, a coat the right to use which ceased except as a quartering to the descendants of their coheirs on the extinction of that earldom. The second and third quarters are evidently intended for the coat of the Yorkshire Marshalls. The fourth the coat of De Clare, quartered by the children of William Marshall, Earl of Pembroke, in right of his marriage with Isabel de Clare, daughter and heir of Richard, Earl of Pembroke, the celebrated Strongbow. Anyone conversant with ancient heraldic bearings will see at once that whoever bore this coat must have been one of the most impertinent of pretenders, indeed it is, with one exception, the only instance I have met with of its usurpation. That instance is the pretence to bear it of one William Marshall of Newton Kyme, co. York, a militia colonel, whose daughter and heir married Randal Gossip, who assumed the name of Hatfield. William Marshall was descended of a respectable family of yeomen, long resident at Tadcaster, and certainly not entitled to this coat, nor so far as can be ascertained to any coat at all.

I have taken some trouble to find out who the Aynsom Marshalls really were, and some of the "Richmond Wills" now at Somerset House, lead me to believe that they were a yeoman family, pretty numerous in that district, with no pretence to coat armour, till the benefactress of the parish chandelier adopted by its gift an easy and not very expensive method of asserting their nobility, and thus perpetuated a fraudulent coat of arms for the *benefit* of her posterity.

The Deaneries, the wills from which were proved in the Consistory Court at Richmond, situate in the county of Lancaster, are Furness, Amounderness, and Lonsdale.

Furness Deanery.

1. George M'shell of Ludderburne. Dated 18 Jan'y, 1575. To be buried in churchyard of Cartmell. Robert Herryson, my sonne in law, to have fermhold according to the covenant that I made him

when he married my daughter that he should have my holle fermhold. To Anne, my daughter, when she comes to marriage £6 13s. 4d., and the same the year following. £6 13s. 4d. to my daughter Esabell, when at what time she comes into the countrye. Richard Allayne, my son in law 13s. 4d. if he come into the countrye. Robert Gurnell. Catheren, my daughter. God children John Herryson and Robert Herryson. Genat M'shell. Robert Gurnell, Anne my daughter, and Robert Herryson, executors. Thomas Swenson, Robert Swenson, and Bryan Gurnell, supervisors. Inventory dated 25 Jan'y, 1575. Robert Marshall was one of those who made it.

II. Richarde Marshell of Ludderburne in Cartmelfell of the parish of Cartmell. Dated 22 April, 1619. To be buried in Cartmell Church. Brother Myles marshall, executor and universal legatee. Will'm Marshall, Edwarde Swainson, and John Harrison supervisors. Proved by Myles Marshall, 3 July, 1619.

III. John Marshall of Akes in Cartmelfell, w^tin the pishe of Cartmell, Husbandman. Dated 6 Feb'y, 1625. To be buried in my Parish Church of Cartmell. My whole messuage and tenement to Edward Marshall my son, and to his heirs for ever. Agnes my wife. Anthonye Marschell my brother, and his son Richard. I give to Winster Chappell 10s. Son Edward Marshall executor and residuary legatee. Edward Swaynson and John Swaynson supervisors. Proved 30 Oct., 1634.

IV. Myles Marshall of Addifeild in Cartmelfell, shereman. Dated 2 Jan'y, 1634. To be buried in Cartmell Churchyard. To Agnes my daughter, £6 13s. 4d. To Elizabeth my daughter, £6 13s. 4d. Mabell my wife, executrix, and residuary legatee. Edward Marshall, my brother, and Rowland Harrison, tanner, supervisors. Proved 22 May, 1635.

V. Edward Marshall of Aynesom in Cartmell. Dated 27 April, 1670. Messuage and tenement at Ayensome to son John Marshall in fee. Messuage at Fellege to grandson Edward Marshall, son of the said John. My grandson John Marshall, his brother Henry Marshall, his brother James, his sister Mary, Edward Marshall their eldest brother. My cosen Anthony Marshall and his son, his daughter Isabell. My cosen Ann Searll of London. My cosen Myles Marshall, and his brother James. My cosen Isabell Strickland. Myles Strickland late of Corkerhowe, and his brothers and sisters. Kathren the wife of Thomas Askew. My cozen Nicholas Strickland and his son John. Thomas Muckelt of the Moore, Edward Turner, and my grandson Edward Marshall, executors. Residue to Edward, John, Henry, and James, sons of John Marshall, or to which of them are most needful. Bond[1] and obligation dated 9 Nov., 1671. Inventory dated 11 July, 1671, amounts, after deducting funeral expenses £9 10s. 0d. and apparel given, to £284 8s. 0d.

VI. William Marshall of Ludderburne in Cartmelfell, in co. Lancaster, yeoman. Dated 31 May, 1692. James Marshall my son. Ellin Pull my daughter. "Agnes, Elizabeth, and Isabell Harrison my grandchildren of Michal Harrisons." Isabel my daughter, and her three daughters. Bridgett my daughter. Agnas and Ellin my

[1] Date of Bond is date of Probate.

two daughters. William Harrison my grandchild. Margaret Strickland living at Olhousbecke. Edward Marshall my natural son[2], and Michael Harrison my son in law, executors. Bond dated 28 Jan., 1692. Inventory dated 1 Dec., 1692. Total, £172 0s. 2d. The funeral expenses were £3 11s. 0d.

VII. William Marshall of Northscale. Dated 28 Jan'y, 1697. Wife Mary executrix and universal legatee. John Marshall of Dalton, Nicholas Marshall my brother, and Thomas Banks supervisors. Inventory dated 3 Feb., 1697. Bond dated 5 Mar., 1697, by which Mary Marshall of Walney, in co. Lancaster, widow, Thomas Marshall of the city of London, gentleman, and Thomas Bunnes, are bound, &c.

VIII. Thomas Marshall of the Hole within the parish of Dalton, co. Lancaster, yeoman. Dated 18 April, 1700. Nicholas Marshall my father. Elizabeth my wife executrix. [Testator had no children.] Inventory dated 27 May, 1700. Bond dated 1 Oct., 1700.

IX. John Marshall of Dalton in Furneis. Dated 15 Dec^r, 1701. To be buried in Dalton churchyard neere ye side of ye church If I die in Furneis. House at Dalton which I purchased of Mr. Woods to wife Jennet Marshall for life, and then to my grandson Henry Marshall in fee. John and Edward Marshall my grandsons the sons of James Marshall deceased. Grandson Edward Marshall and his three sisters Jennet, Mary, and Ellen. My grandson John Fletcher. Forgives son John Marshall £40, which I paid towards the purchase of Smithy Croft and Cow Close. To son John and his wife, and to my son John Fletcher, and to my daughter in law Katherine Marshall each a piece of broad gold. My nephews John Berry, Thomas Berry, and William Berry. Thomas Askew. Ellen Preston and her three daughters. William Rawlingson 20s. towards putting him to a trade. To poor of low end of Broughton township £10 to be added to £10 left by my father[3] in his will. Wife and son John Marshall executors. Thomas Michelson and Thomas Barrow of ye Hill, supervisors.

This will is endorsed "12 Oct. 1704. Then this will found good by the Jury and Allowed by me Wm Simpson seneseal' ib'm."

Inventory dated 20 June, 1705, £501 15s. 0d. Bond from John Marshall and Jenet Marshall, widow, and Wm Fletcher of Broughton in Cartmell, dated 24 Oct., 1705.

X. Mary Marshall[4] of Newbarns, in the parish of Dalton in Furnes, co. Lancaster, Widow. Dated 19 March, 1708. To each and every of my grandchildren 5s. a-piece. To grandchild Nicholas Nunns £5. Grandchild Thomas Nunns. Grandchild Jane Nunns executrix and residuary legatee. Witnesses, Tho. Bankes, Tho. Bunnes, John Wood. Bond dated 7 July, 1709.

Amounderness Deanery.

I. The will of Alice Marshall of Bare, begins thus:—"Item. I give to my daughter Margret all my clothes but for one vnder Coate."

[2] "Natural" means no doubt "natural and lawful."

[3] Edward Marshall of Aynesom, will dated 27 April, 1670. See above.

[4] Widow of William Marshall of Northscale. See above.

Mentions daughters Elizabeth and 'Ann. Son William. Grandson Brien. "Cateren and Ellin my tooe doughters shalle Be my Executers." Witnesses, Robert Fairer, Thomas Lodge. Inventory of goods of Ales Marshell of Bare dated 31 Decr., 1670, made by Edmond Marshell, John Barker, and Thomas Lodge. Bond, Catherine Marshall and Ellen Marshall bound, 31 Dec., 1670.

II. Thomas Marshall of the Lodge within Warton, co. Lancaster, husbandman. Dated 17 Jan., 1680. To be buried in church or churchyard of Kirkham. John Marshall son of William Marshall of Pillinge, husbandman, lawful heir of all my estate. Tenement lying at the Poole houses. Alice my now wife. To William Singleton £10. To Joney Taylor my natural sister £5. To Margret Rydeinge her daughter 50s. Jenet Anyon the wife of Robert Anyon 10s., and both her children. James Smalley and Grace his now wife 20s. each. Everyone of the children of George Cowborne 6s. 8d. apiece. Thomas Balle. John Shawes. All the children of William Singleton 10s. apiece. To William Marshall my brother 20s. Robert Halle and Thomas Bonney of the Bank, husbandman, executors. Adm'on 7 Feb., 1680, to John Marshall next of kin because the executors renounced. Their renunciation is dated 5 Feb'y, 1680.

III. The will of Alice Marshall of the Lodge within Warton, in the co. of Lancaster, widow, (evidently widow of the last testator), is dated 23 Jan'y, 1680. To be buried in the parish church or churchyard of Kirkham. Christopher Coleborne, Margaret, Alice, and Elline Coleborne his sisters, the son and daughters of George Coleborne of Warton, miller. Robert Dobson and Jenet his sister, son and daughter of William Dobson of the Bank within Warton. William Smalley my brother in law. James Smalley my natural son. Calls Richard Dobson and George Coleborn "my sons in law." My daughter Elizabeth's children. James Smalley and William Smalley executors. John Marshall. Inventory dated 7 Feb'y, 1680. John Marshall of Pillinge, husbandman, was one of those who took it. Proved by James and Willm Smalley, 7 Feb'y, 1680. Bond dated 7 Feb'y, 1680.

Lonsdale Deanery.

I. Edmund Marshall. Dated 23 May, 1558. To be buried in the parish church of St. Wylfryde of Mellyng. Farmhold half to wife and half to William my son, and after wife's decease whole to said William. Son Thomas. To Igeett Marshelle my son's son one lamb, &c. Wife executrix.

II. Alyse Marshall of Wray. Dated 1 Sept., 13 Elizabeth. To be buried in parish churchyard of Mellyng near unto my husband. To my daughter Margarethe one quye, and to every one of her children a lamb. To every child that my son Robert hath one lamb. Son Robert executor and residuary legatee. Witnesses, Wyll'm Marssalle, and Roberte Walker.

III. Robert Marshall of Wray. Dated 20 ……, 15 Elizabeth. Agnes my wife. My son Thomas. Thomas (?) to be good to his brother. "Agnes my wyf, …… my son, and Allye and Jane my dog[hters] I make my executors." Witnesses … Walker, Wm. Marshall. Inventory dated 6 November, 15 Elizabeth.

IV. Agnes Marshall of Wray, widow. Dated 20 May, 1585. Thomas Marshall my son. Margret my daughter. John Marshall my son. To Cristofer Gronger one yowe. Joane my daughter. Thomas my son and Elizabethe my daughter residuary legatees and executors. Proved 9 June, 1588.

Besides the wills above noted there remain in the Richmond Registry the following :—

In Furness Deanery. Administration of Frances Marshall, of Pennington, dated 22 Jan'y, 1668. Will of Katherine Marshall, of Holker in the parish of Cartmell, dated 8 Jan'y, 1714. Administration of Janet Marshall, of Aynsom, in the parish of Cartmell, dated 4 Feb'y, 1714. Will of Edward Marshall of Gillhead in Cartmell-fell dated 25 Feb'y, 1715.

The will of John Marshall of Stainton in the parish of Urswick, 1646, and administration of Thomas Marshall, of Urswick, 1711, will be found together with some genealogical notes on the Urswick Marshalls at page 15 of this volume.

In Amounderness Deanery :—

John Marshall, of Bare. In. & Bond. 29 Jan., 1663.
John M., of Pilling. Inv. & Bond. 27 April, 1675.
William M., of Pilling. In. & Bond. 27 Jan. 1682.
James M., of Bare. Will. 7 May, 1692.
Henry M., of Lancaster. In. & Bond. 7 Mar., 1693.
John M., of Pilling. Inv. 30 June, 1694.
Robert M., of Wray. In. & Bond. 13 Nov., 1697.
Margaret M., of Pilling. Bond. 7 Oct., 1703.
Edward M., of Bare. Will. 22 March, 1706.
Henry M., of Lancaster. Will. 14 March, 1711.
Mary M., of Lancaster, Ad. & Bond. 14 Mar., 1714.
Robert M., of Lancaster. Will. 3 Oct., 1717.

In Lonsdale Deanery :—

Thomas Marshall, of Wraye in par. of Melling. Will. 21 Aug 1623.
Thomas M., of Wraye. Inv. 5 March, 1634.
William M., of Hornby. Inv. 1 Feby., 1648.
John M., of Wray. Will. 28 Nov., 1650.
William M., of Roberindale. Inv. 31 May, 1665.
Margery M., of Horneby. Inv. 10 April, 1667.
John M., of Wray. Adm'on. 13 April, 1667.
Robert M., of Wray. Will. 30 Jan., 1668.
Jenet M., of Wray. Will. 2 Nov., 1670.
William M., of Wray. Will. 17 Sept., 1673.
Jenet M., of Wray. Will. 28 Jan., 1674.
John M., of Wray. Will. 10 July, 1676.
Mary M., of Wray. Inv. 3 June, 1682.
Thomas M., of Graystongill in par. Bentham. Will. 1 Sept., 1687.
Thomas M., of Caton. Inv. 20 Feb., 1689.
Thomas M., of Wray. Will. 12 Oct., 1699.
John M., of Mewith. Will. 19 Nov., 1707.

William M., of Wray.[1] Inv. 31 March, 1709.
Elizabeth M., of Wray. Will. 19 Sept., 1717.
Esther M., of Wray. Adm'on. Bond. 24 Dec., 1719.

The following will of a Lancashire Marshall is registered in the Prerogative Court of Canterbury, 110 Abbott :—William Marshall of the parish of St. Buttolphs without Aldgate in the city of London, perriwig maker. Dated 15 Feb., 1728. Friend John Johnson of Worleys Court in the parish of St. Buttolphs Aldgate, gunsmith, £10. Benjamin Johnson £10. Loving uncle Thomas Beckett of Lancaster £10. My father in law Philipp Johnson of Ellen in Lancashire, yeoman, my interest in house called 'Eagle and Child' at Lancaster. Loving uncle John Marshall of Lancaster, shop-keeper. Said John Johnson sole executor and residuary legatee. He proved 11 April, 1729.

Those wills hereafter given in abstract are omitted from the following calendars :—

In the Three Eastern Deaneries, viz., Richmond, Catherick, and Boroughbridge.

Adam, of Langton, died 1579.
Agnes, of Asenbie, died 1571.
Alice of Asenbie.
Christopher and Franciss', of Huton Conyers, 1584.
Christopher, of Huton Conyers p' porco'e Jane filie sue 1593.
Cuthbert, of Thwayte p'ish of Romald' 1586, and letters of Adm'on to *same* (?) 1588.
Elizabeth, p'sh Rypon, (of Aldfield) 1574.*
Henrye, et Hird, Eliz. in ca ma^{li} oblig. 1598.
Isabella, of Newstead, ob. 1608, Adm'on.*
Maior or Mauger, clerk, 1608.
Margaret, of Raynton, 1577, Adm'on.*
Richard, of Asenbie, 1591.
Robert, of Langton, 1595.
William, of Aldbroughe, ob. 1541.
William, of Mylbie, 1541.
William, of Mowton[2], 1542.
William, of Maulton (? Mowton), 1548.

Only those marked * exist, the others are entries in the Calendar, the documents being lost.

George et Eliz'th eius ux., of Sweetingsike, the inventory dated 1 July, 1619. Inv. & Adm'on, 1623.
Thomas of Azenby, par. Topcliffe. Adm'on 18 Nov. 1630.
Dorothy, of Hornby. Inv. and Bond, 11 Aug. 1684.
Brian, of Kirkhammerton. Inv. and Bond, 20 June, 1694.
John, of Long Moores, par. Easby. Inv. and Bond, 21 Dec. 1695.

[1] See pedigree of Marshall of Wray in Coll. Arms, H. MS., vol. 17, fo. 83. The heir married Leeming who took the name of Marshall by Royal Licence 23 Dec. 1802.

[2] ? Morton on Swale. cf. vol. i. p. 25, *note*.

John, of Richmond. Adm'on, 1701.
Richard, of Marton cum Grafton. Adm'on, 1705.
Henry, of Hudswell. Adm'on, 1709.
Christopher, of West Appleton. Adm'on, 1711.
William, of Caldbergh. Adm'on, 1714.
John, of Green Hamerton. Will, 1717.
Oswald, of Melmerby. (?), 1717.
Robert, of Melmerby. Will, 1728.

All the above exist.

1363792

Deanery of Kendal.

John *alias* Walles. Inv. 28 June, 1632.
Anthony, of Windermer. Will. 8 Feb. 1633.
Richard, of Windermer. Inv. 18 April, 1634.
Brian, of Bare. Inv. 30 Oct. 1650.
Anthony, of Undermilnebeck. Will. 3 March, 1676.
Anthony, Highate in Kendall. Inv. 28 May, 1684.
Robert, of Kirkby Kendall. Will. 28 Sept., 1689.
Edward, of Undermilbeck. Will. 9 June, 1694.
James, of Holme. Will. 12 July, 1694.

Deanery of Coupland.

Dorothy, of Branthwait. Will. 21 Jan., 1622.
Thomas, of Hallthwait, par. Millam. Will. 10 Octr., 1626.
James, of Thwaites. Inv. 24 Jan'y., 1634.
James, of Millam. Adm'on & Bond. 24 Jan., 1638.
John, of Edge, par. Deane. Will. 1 June, 1661.
Elizabeth, of Branthwait Edge. Will. 13 March, 1661.
John, of Branthwaite. Inv. and Bond, 1664.
William, of par. of St. Bees. Will. 8 Feb., 1664.
Richard, of Tarnchow. Will. 25 Jan., 1668.
Anthony, of Gilgarron. Inv. Bonds. Acct. 4 Nov., 1671, 1673.
William, of Gosforth. Will. 12 Aug., 1675.
Abigal, of Broughton. Inv. and Bond. 12 Sept., 1682.
William, of Branthwaite. Will. 4 Sept. 1683.
Anthony, of St. Bees. Will. 16 Feb., 1685.
Isabella, of Dean. Inv. and Bond. 12 Dec. 1687.
John, of Gosforth. Will. 15 Sept. 1693.
Samuel, of Gosforth. Will. 15 Sept. 1693.
Richard, of Graysothen. Will. 4 June, 1694.
Janet, of Deanscales. Inv. and Bond. 7 June, 1697.
John, of St. Bees. Adm'on and Bond, 30 March, 1698.
Thomas, of St. Bees. Inv. and Bond, 5 Oct., 1700.
Joseph, of Branthwaite Edge, par. Dean. Will. 15 Sept., 1701.
Mabell, widow, of Workington. Adm'on and Bond. 28 Sept., 1702.
Edward, of Gosforth. Will. 24 Feb. 1702.
John, of Branthwaite Edge, in Deane. Inv. and Bond. 4 Oct. 1706.
William, of do. do. Will. 19 May, 1710.

Nicholas, of Bootle. Will. 15 May, 1714.
Bridgett, of St. Bees. Adm'on. Inv. and Bond. 16 Oct. 1714.
Sarah, of Gosforth. Will. 25 Jan., 1715.
William, of Whitehaven. Will. 12 May, 1718.
Mary, of St. Bees. Adm'on. 25 Jan., 1720.

Wills from Eastern Deaneries.

Thomas M'sall cap'l's de C'ndall. Dated 20 January, 1475 (?), Corp' ad sepelliendū in choro ecc'lie omn' sanctor' Ap'd Merstone. It. p'mortuario meo optimā meā Togam. It. do et lego vxori Th......... vj^s. viij^d.—vxori Thome Blyght vj^s......—filie vxor' Thome Hudson vj^s. viij^d.—Thome......filie eiusd' Thome viij^d.—Maryon Scott...—... Bedfforth Cap'no xv^s. Joh'ni Haknay vj^s. viij^d....Bell vj^s. viij^d.—Roberts Allanson' vj^s. viij^d. Appoints Robert Allanson exōr.. ...[Bed] forth cap'us and Joh'ne Haknay supervisors. Witnesses, Thomas Sclater, William Staynfforth, and others.

John Marshall. Dated 10 March, 1550. To be buried in the churchyard of Topclyff. Agnes my wife to have occupation of six acres of land I now occupy for her life, then to William my son. One rood of rye to dau'r Margaret, same to dau'r Mald, same to son John. To Will'm and Rychard my sons one gray mear (?) equally between them. Wife and Agnes and dau'rs Mald and Margaret ex'xs, and residuary legatees. Witnesses, William Kettlewell, John Atkynson.

William Marshall. Dated 7 Oct., 1557. To be buried in the church earth of Topcliff. To George my son one fely of 5 (?) years old. To Margaret, Elizabeth, and Dorythe, my dau'rs two ewes apiece. John Marshall my brother. Mald my sister. Thomas Thompson my uncle. My wife and all my children to occupy my farmold during her widowhood, and after her widowhood son George to have it. Margaret my wife, George my son, and Margaret, Elizabeth, and Dorothy, my dau'rs, exo'rs. John Sherp and Richerd Yeats supervisors. Witnesses, Richard Ray and William Allenson.

Wyll'm Marshall, of Aldfield, in the countie of York. Dated 7 July, 1566. To be buried in the churchyard of St. Peter and Wylfryde at Rypon. Farmhold to wife for life and then to son John Marshall, and he not to sell it except to some of his brothers. Whoever has farmhold to find my son Marmaduke, meat, drink, and clothing all the time of his prenticeship. My sister Agnes. My wife and Jone my youngest dau'r residuary legatees. Wife and son John exōrs. Witnesses, Marmaduke Abbot, Wyll'm Dauson, John Bowland, Thomas Langseroth, and John Braythwayt.

William Marshell, of Assonby, w'in the p'yshe of Topcliffe. Dated 27 January, 1570. Lease of my Fermold to wife Agnes. Children Rychard Marshell, Steven, Thomas, and Agnes. Son John Marshell. Wife and all children, except John, exo'rs.

Adam Marshall, of the parish of Langton, dated 6 Nov., 1572. To be buried in the parish church earth of Langton. Farmolde to wife, and three children, George, Thomas, and Raufe, and appoints said three children ex'ors. To my brother Thomas my beste blewe Coote. My brother Robert Jackson. John Cocke. My brother son Robarte Marshall his fower children. Richarde Marshall. My dau'r Dorithe. Raufe Sadler and Richarde Inglishe supervisors. Robert Thornton a witness. Proved 21 January, 1572, by Elizabeth the relict, the three children being minors.

Richard Marshall, of Borobrig. Dated 28 Feb., 1573. To be buried in the churchyard of Aldburgh. To Thomas Marshall and William Marshall my two sonnes ij stedes, etc. To Agnes my daughter one brasse pott. Emmott my wife, and above mentioned three children, ex'ors. Witnesses, Thomas Sowerby, clerk, Will'm Browne, and Franc' Smythson. Proved 18 March, 1573, by Emmott Marshall and Thomas Marshall.

Tuition of children of Christopher and Frances Marshall, late of Huton Conyers, dated 8 M......1584. Adm'on and Tuition of George, Christopher, Janet, and Dorothy, to Thomas Cooke, of Huton Conyers. [In very bad condition, see next entry in index.]

John Marshall of Kirkby Fletham, dated 4 March, 1590. To be buried in parish church-yard of Kirkby Fletham. To James Marshall my eldest son lease of Farmhold in Kirkby Fletham, he to suffer my dau'r Ann Marshall to enjoy half an acre of land and one little Chamber in my messuage house, &c. Mentions a white stirk given to his dau'r by her aunt Jane Surham. Richard my son. Issabell my dau'r. Appoints all four children ex'ors. Inventory is dated 11 May, 1590.

George Marshall, of Asenbie, in the Countie of Yorke husbandman. Dated 9 April, 1597. To be buried in churchyard of Topcliffe. Jenet Marshall my wife. George Marshall my son. Fermhold to wife for life, then to son George. To Thomas Marshall my son the yoñgest bay stagg, etc. Roger Marshall my son. My two dau'rs Elizabeth and Jenet Marshall. To Thomas Owrom a ewe and lamb. I give to M^{r}. Vicar 12^{d}. Son Thomas to be brought up in learning at the school. William Clarke, Arthure Dadley, Richard Husthwait and Raif Browne my welwillers supervisors. Wife and children all exo'rs. Witnesses, Raife Kay, Richard Huswait and Raif Browne, etc. Inventory taken 16 April, 1597. Amount £109 10 9.

Thomas Marshall of Disfoorth in the co. of York, smyth. Nuncupative. Dated 21 Sept^{r}., 1603. Dau'r Elizabeth Marshall. Wife Jenet Marshall. Gives them his smithy between them, and to use of Elizabeth if wife marries again. There is an erased bequest which mentions "Katherine and Marie Marshall" his brother's children. To William Marshall my brother's best coat, etc. To Thomas Ray workday Jackett. "He did make Jenet Marshall his wife the bringer up of his two children during their minority." Wife and dau'r Elizabeth ex'ors and residuary legatees. Witnesses, John Barughe, Will'm Marshall, and Raiphe Kay. Proved by relict 15 Nov^{r}, 1603.

Guy Marshall of Grenehandton. Dated 8 April, 1607. To be buried in my parish church earth at Whixley. Grace my wife. Mathew my son. Bryan my son. Will'm my son. Gilbart my son. Elizabeth my dau'r. Anne my dau'r. To Will'm my son "one why stirk" in con'son of a calf given him by my brother William. Mr. Savaile. Wife sole ex'x and residuary legatee. Witnesses, Walter

Ellis, clerk, Thomas Rawlinson, Thomas Mershall, and Richard Mershall. Proved 30 June, 1607, by Grace Mershall the relict.

Mychaell Marshall of Dytherstone grainge in the county of Yorke yeoman. Dated 19 Dec., 1614. To be buried in churchyard of Melsonby at the discretion of Katherine my wife. Son John Marshall and daur's Margarett and Elizabethe. John Messenger of Newisham, Anthony Richardson, Wm Guthord, and John Raynoldson my bretheren in law, to put forward children's portions for them. Bro. in law Anthony Richardson of Ravenswathe sole ex'or. He proved 5 April, 1615.

John Marshall of Goldisburgh in co. York, grassman. Dated 12 July, 1623. To be buried in parish churchyard of Goldisburgh. Sister Isserbell Holmes and her children. My brother's son Robert Marshall. To Edward Conyers my lether dublett and my leather breeches and my graye hatt. William Winder the elder and his wife and dau'r. William Winder the younger. Jenett Bickerdicke. Elizabeth Walker and Jane Walker her dau'r. Richard Dodgoone. Wife ex'x. Proved by Mary Marshall the relict 11 Nov^r, 1623.

Will'm Marshall, of Aldburge, in co. York, Blacksmith. Dated ...Feb., 1624. To buried in churchyard of Aldburghe. William Raynolde the son of Ninian Raynolde. John Waddington. Katheren Raynolde my dau'r. Thomas and Jayne Raynolde children of Ninian Raynolde. Dorothy and Ann Scroton dau'rs of John Scroton. John Scroton my son in law sole ex'or. Witnesses, William Aldburgh and Humfrey Ward. Proved by John Scroton 11 March, 1624.

George Marshall, of Asenby in co. York, yeoman. Dated 13 April, 1639. To be buried in parish churchyard of Topcliffe. To my sister Jennit Allandson 5s., and to every one of her children 5s. "I giue unto John Barughe, of Disforth [my] brother-in-law, euerye one of his Children ffive shillings." Thomas Foxe of Asken and Dorithie his sister. Roger Marshall my brother and his wife. John Barughe, of Disforth, my brother-in-law, and his wife Marie. To Maister George Kay vicar of Topcliffe 10s. John Barughe my father-in-law. To Richard Slinger my servant which is gone into the King's service £5 if he come home lame, and if he come home safe 10s. and my gray horseman coat. Jane Precious my servant. Robert Peacocke my servant. To Marye my dau'r all my lands and goods. Roger Marshall my brother and John Barughe my brother-in-law to have education and bringing up of her till she be of lawful age. App'ts her sole ex'x. She proved 17 May, 1639.

George Marshall, of Hutton Coniers, in co. York, yeoman. Dated 19 June, 1637. To be buried in the churchyard of Ripon. Whereas I intend to take to wife Mary Browne, of Hutton Coniers afs'd, widowe—gives all to his children by her, if any—if none, then £12 equally among my sister Dorothy Thompson, widow, and her three children. Appoints said Mary Browne residuary legatee, and her, and her son Anthony Fawber ex'x and ex'or. Inventory dated 27 July, 1644.

Marmaduke Marshall, of Richmond, in the co. of York, Blacksmith. Dated 9 May, 1645. To be buried in the churchyard at Richmond. To son Expofer Marshall the burgage house and garth in Franchgate, etc. To Isabell my doughter one Burgage house in Bergate, etc. To my other dau'r Susanna Marshall the reversion of a lease at Ravensworth now in the possession of Leonard Marshall my father. Son Expofer ex'or. My brother Thomas Fogg and my brother Allan Barker guardians to my said three children. Witnesses, John Barker, James Amyes, and Robert Holmes. Inventory 9 Sept., 1645, at the foot of it is this mem. :—"It. it is vpon record in the reg'r of [Rich]mond that Mary Marshall wife of the dec' had an Administration of the porcõns of Crfõer Halmegill her brother dec' in minority amountinge vnto Tenn pounds for which there is security entred by Hen. Hardy, of Brompton juxta North Allertonn. And in Regard Ann Almegill grandmother to ye Administratrix is to have ye consideracõn of the money for her life by the dr't direccõns, therefore this minute or note is thus described." (The note following is illegible.)

John Marshall, of Hudswell, in the Co. of York, yeoman. Dated 13 Nov., 1645. To be buried in the Chappell of Hudswell in that seat where I did vsually sitt. Isabell my wife. To my two sons George Marshall and Peter Marshall all my land at Gilmonby equally between them. To my other two sons John Marshall and William Marshall reversion of a lease I have of the grounds belonging to the hospitall of Kirkby Hill to be divided between them when 14 years of age. To my dau'r Jane £60 and £40 besides which was given her for a legacy by her grandfather Raine deceased. To William Raw and Anne his wife 5s. in full satisfaction of her filiall or childes por'con. My Grandchild Grace Raw. My three grandchildren Christopher Raw, John Raw, and William Raw. To Marmaduke Binks, and Isabell his wife 5s. in full satisfaction of her filial childes part or por'con. Elizabeth Binks my grandchild. My son-in-law Marmaduke Binks, Wife Isabell, and son George, ex'ors. My wellbeloved in Christ Robert Loftus, son-in-law William Rawe, and Marmaduke Binks to be supervisors. The will is sealed with: *Arms*, Two bends. Inventory is undated, and there is no date of probate to be found.

Elizabeth Marshall, of Greenham'ton, co. York, widdowe. Dated 9 April, 1666, William Marshall, Ann Marshall, Brian Marshall and John Marshall the two youngest children of Brian Marshall, Mathew Marshal, Isabell Plewman. My daughter Margaret, Mary Johnson, Elizabeth Dawson, Brian Dawson, Thomas Johnson. Son Brian Marshall, ex'or. He proved 20 Nov., 1666. Inventory £7 4s.

To all christian people, &c., I Anne Marshall, of Rowcliffe, co. York, widdow, know ye that I Anne Marshall in consideration of £110 which I owe unto John Marshall my only son and heir, of the same town and county, Batchelor, have etc., granted to said J. M. and John Rosse, of Minskepp, co. Yorke, yeoman, my beloved friend, all goods, etc. Dated 9 Sep., 1678. Witnesses, Rich. Gilbertson, John Buckle. Sealed with Arms, On a chevron 3 roses, a bordure engrailed; Crest, A bird. Proved by John Marshall and John Ross, 3 Dec., 1678. This document is endorsed "Anne Marshall bill of sale to Jo. Marshall and Jo. Rosse."

Guy Marshall, of Greenham'ton. Dated 9 Sept., 1678. Gives House and Garth in Greenhammerton to his two sons, Brian and Mathew Marshall, in fee. Wife Jane Marshall, and dau'r Dorothy

Marshall, residuary legatees and ex'ors. Witnesses, Thomas Johnson, and Bryan Marshall. Proved by relict, 3 Dec., 1678.

Richard Marshall, of Scorton, in the Chapelry of Bolton-upon-Swale, in the vicarage Catherick, co. York, husbandman. Dated 9 Feb., 1699. To my sister Elianor Scurray 10^s. To my sister Phillis Jakes 10^s. To my nephew Francis Jakes 1^s. To Elizabeth Rhodes my neice 2^s 6^d. To Elizabeth Floore, of Catterick, 2^s 6^d. Well-beloved friend Christopher Ramshay, of Tunstall, yeoman, sole ex'or. He proved (name spelt Ram*shaw*) 24 Feb., 1699.

Peter Marshall[1], of Richmond, co. York, grocer. Dated 4 May, 1693. To son John Marshall, son William Marshall, and dau'r Anne Marshall, 10^s each. Lands at Katskins in the Constablery of Hudswell, and in the Westfield in the parish of Richmond, to wife in fee. Gives her all his personal estate and makes her sole ex'x. Witnesses, H. Allen, William Kay, Fran' Blackburne,[2] Ann Forth. Proved 24 April, 1700, by Faith Marshall the widow and relict. Inventory 49*l*.

Faith Marshall, of Richmond, co. York, widow. Dated 20 Aug., 1708. To my dau'r Ann Harland all my Closes at Catskins in the Constablery of Hudswell, for life, remainder to her children. Land in Westfield of Richmond to son William Marshall "to enter upon at the time of his returne into England," if he do not return, then to dau'r Ann Harland in fee. To Ann Forth 3*l*. To my granddaughter Dorithy Harland 20*l* which is now owing me by my nephew Mr. William Kay. Dau'r Ann Harland residuary legatee and executrix. Witnesses, Jane Kay, Fran. Blackburne, Alice Blackburne. Seal of Arms, A fess nebuly between three mullets, a mullet for difference. (Blackburne.) Proved by the ex'x Anne wife of Edward Harland, 20 March, 1709.

Wills from Kendal Deanery.

George Marshall of Kendall. Dated 15 March, 1565. To be buried in parish churchyard of Kendall. Richard my son to have my house if he come into the contre paying to Annes my daught'r 6^l 13^s 4^d. To Christofer my son, "a syd of quite lether, and of my shope gere as mitche as Annes my daught'r will give hime." Two children of son Christopher. A child of Elsabethe my dau'r. Elizabeth (?) Marshall my dau'r ex'x. Thomas Fox and Richard Atkinson supervisors. Inventory dated 27 March, 1567, 13^l 15^s 4^d.

Thomas Marshall, of Staveley, in the parish of Kendall. Dated 1 April, 1588. To be buried in Stavele churchyard in the above side. Elizabeth Marshall now my wife to have houses in Staveley on condition that Augnes Marshall my sister have a bedroom in house where wife dwells. John Ayraye sonne of Henrie Ayray. Wife ex'x. Robert Hareson and Richard Tubman supervisors. Witnesses, Myles Hareson, George Ayraye. Proved 4 June, 1588, in the Church of Bethom. Inventory dated 7 May, 1588.

[1] Peter Marshall, Mayor of Richmond in 1682 resigned his alderman's gown in 1693. Boyne's Tokens, p. 516.

[2] *See* Clarkson's "History of Richmond," pedigree of Blackburne, p. 257.

CALENDAR OF DURHAM WILLS, &c.

This Calendar as well as the Notes of Wills, proved in the Consistory Court, appended thereto, was made by Mr. C. M. Carlton of Durham.

1550.	Nicholas Marshall.[1]	
1562.	George [2]	„
1565.	John [3]	„
1566.	John [4]	„
1567.	Cuthbert [5]	„
1568.	Thomas [6]	„
1572.	John [7]	„
1575.	John [8]	„
1580.	Thomas [9]	„
1581.	Richard [10]	„

[1] Will dated 23 March, 1550. To Anne Wylde my sister one ring. To sister Anne Harbottle one other ring. Residue to brother Richard Harbottle. Witness, George Marshall.

[2] Will dated 6 April, 1562. Described as of the parish of Lanchester, to be buried in the parish church there. My wife [not mentioned by name] to ha. the third part of all my goods. Residue to children, Thomas, William, Elizabeth, Anne, Jennet, Allison, and Christabell.

[3] John Marshall of Norton. Dated 14 May, 1565. Mentions sons, William, Roger, and Anthony. Daughter Margery. Residue to wife Margaret and sons Roger and Anthony.

[4] John Marshall of East Raynton in the parish of Houghton le Spring. Dated 11 July, 1566. Mentions Roger Maugham my kinsman and servant. Anthony Maugham William Marshall. To Mr William Maugham of Newbottle one black filly. To Jane Gleson and Elizabeth Marshall a ewe each. To Richard Marshall 10s. Residue to Wife Margaret.

[5] Cuthbert Marshall of Cockerton in the parish of Darlington. Dated 2 Jan., 1567. To be buried in churchyard there. To Jennet my daughter £20. To John Marshall my son farming stock. To son William Marshall a kye and all the iron gear. Cuthbert Marshall my godson. The heir looms left by my father's will to remain at the house of my son William, and makes him residuary legatee.—(Vol. 3, p. 50).

[6] Thomas Marshall of Barmpton in the parish of Haughton, yeoman. Dated 22 Feb., 1568. To be buried in Haughton church. To daughter Margaret Marshall £20. Mr. Swynburn and Roger Maddison to be supervisors of her till she is 21. Residue to wife Margaret. Proved 31 July, 1573.

[7] John Marshall of the parish of Chester. Dated 21 Feb., 1572. To be buried there. Frances Marshall my daughter. Lease of land to wife Agnes. Proved 1573.

[8] John Marshall of Cockerton. Dated 3 Nov., 1575. To be buried in Darlington church. To William, John, and Jenet Marshall, certain farm stock. To my son Edward Marshall an iron bound wayn. Wife Jenet and son Edward executors.

[9] Thomas Marshall, clerk, Vicar of Haltwhistle, co. Northumberland. Undated. To good master and mistress Nicholas Ridley and his wife some sheep. Anthony and William Marshall my brother's sons. My brother John Marshall's children. To my sister Margaret Marshall her daughter a gown. Anthony, William, and Richard Marshall my brother John's children. My brother John, and John Marshall of Hexham. Gilbert Liddell and my sister his wife and their two youngest children. My sister Anne, and Thomas her son. To William Prockter for the furthering of his apprentice William Marshall in all his affairs 5s. Residue to said William Marshall and appoints him executor. Anthony Marshall his brother to be good unto him. Proved 17 March, 1580.

[10] Richard Marshall of the city of Durham, public notary. Dated 11 Feb., 1581. To Thomas Watson, D.D., Bishop of Lincoln an old ryal of gold. To my sister Johan Williamson of London 20s. To Richard Marshall of Selaun my godchild 12d. To Elizabeth Blythe and Richard Jaye 3s. 4d. each. My house in King's Gate, Durham, to my wife Jane for life, and after her decease to my son Thomas

1582.	James [1]	Marshall.	
1579.	Robert [2]	,,	Harbottle.
1579.	William [3]	,,	Ouston.
1583.	George	,,	Lanchester parish.
1583.	Margery [4]	,,	
1591-2.	Janet [5]	,,	
1604.	Henry	,,	Billeraw.
1609.	Richard [6]	,,	Denton.
1609.	John [7]	,,	Cockerton.
1613.	Richard	,,	Seaham.
1615.	Thomas [8]	,,	Durham.

Marshall and his heirs, remainder to son John, remainder over to daughter Margaret, remainder over to daughter Jane, remainder over to daughter Susan, remainder over to daughter Elizabeth, and then to next of kin. All my leases &c. and lands in diocese of Durham to wife Jane, Thomas and John my sons, Margaret, Jane, Susan, Isabel, and Elizabeth, my daughters. To my cousin Margret Marshall, widow, of East Renton, late wife to my cousin John Marshall, 12d. Cousin Mr. Richard Marshall, parson of Stainton, clerk, supervisor. Proved 4 April, 1581. (Vol. 5, p. 143.)

[1] James Marshall of the parish of Shotley. Dated 3 June, 1582. To my sons Nicholas, and John, and Margery my wife all the title I have to the tenement or farmhold that I and my father are possessed of. My wife to have the custody of Nicholas and John my sons till they are 21. In case of their deaths their interest in the farm to go to my wife. If my wife die before my sons Nicholas and John come to the age of discretion then I will that Oswald Ward otherwise Blumer my father in law and Cuthbert his brother shall have the custody of my two sons. To George Marshall my brother my best jacket and breeches. Proved 16 July, 1582.

[2] Robert Marshall of Harbottle in the co. of Northumberland, yeoman. Dated 13 May, 1579. To be buried at Harbottle. Mary Marshall my sister. Mabel Marshall my sister. Residue to Margaret my wife. Proved 19 May, 1579.

[3] William Marshall of Ouston in the parish of Whitfield. To Jennet my daughter a cow. To my sons Nicholas, George, John, Thomas, and Christofer Marshall, my cattle, Proved 8 April, 1580.

[4] Margery Marshall late wife of William Marshall of Bedlington in the County of Durham. Dated 23 Dec., 1583. Household goods to son John and daughter Elizabeth. To son John a copyhold tenement in Bedlington. Proved 1583.

[5] Janet Marshall, widow of John Marshall of Darlington. Dated 4 March 34 Elizabeth, [1591-2]. To Anthony, Thomas, William, Laurence, Jane, Agnes, Elizabeth, and Jennet, sons and daughters of my sister Dorothy Glover, 20s. each. To Margaret, Agnes, Elizabeth, and Robert Johnson, children of my brother John Johnson 20s. each. To John, Jane, and Joan Neasonn, children of my sister Catherine 10s. each. To Margaret Wilkinson my Aunt 20s. To Richard son of Peter Glover 2s. 6d. My Sister Dorothy Glover to have £20 of my daughter Elizabeth's portion to be paid on her attaining 21. Thomas Laton of Cleasby to keep my daughter Agnes and to have other £30 to the £60 he already has. Peter Glover my brother to take George my son and his portion. George, Agnes, and Elizabeth Marshall my children, residuary legatees. Brother John Johnson to take daughter Elizabeth and her portion. Proved 1592.

[6] Inventory only. Richard Marshall of Denton deceased, dated 19 Oct., 1608. "Item. One signet with arms, and one other ring with a blood sapphire £5. *See* an *Inq.* in App. to 44th Report of D. K. Pub. Rec. p. 473.

[7] John Marshall of Cockerton in the parish of Darlington. Dated 22 April, 1609. Brother Francis Marshall. Sister Isable. Sister Margaret Marshall. Brother Richard Marshall. Residue to wife Katherine and daughter Dorothy.

[8] Thomas Marshall of the city of Durham. Dated 28 June, 1615. To be buried in the church of St. Giles in Durham. To wife Jane £20. To daughters Mary, Jane, and Margaret £20. To daughter Mary two Kye. To brother George a grey mare. To Cousin John Lewis 2s. for a token, and to his two sons John and Christopher 5s. each. To aunt Jennet Marshall 5s. To aunt Dorothy Wright 5s.

1617.	William Marshall.		Morpeth.
1618.	Lionel	„	Seaton Burn.
1621.	Nicholas	„	Brancepeth.
1622.	George	„	Darlington.[1]
1623.	Isabella	„	widow, Newcastle.
1623.	George	„	weaver, Newcastle.
1625.	George	„	Brancepeth.
1629.	William[2]	„	Haydon Bridge.
1633.	John[3]	„	Seaham.
1633.	John	„	Bramley Burn. *Inventory.*[4]
1634.	Thomas	„	Hawthorn.[5]
1636.	John[6]	„	Haydon Bridge.
1636.	William	„	
1638.	Elizabeth[7]	„	Haydon Bridge.
1642.	William	„	Hartlepool. *Inventory.*
1643.	John	„	Corbridge.
1660.	Elizabeth and Samuel.		*Tuition.*
1662.	Ingram	„	
1670.	William	„	*Adm'on.*
1671.	Henry	„	
1675.	John	„	*Adm'on.*
1676.	John	„	*Adm'on.*
1679.	Isabella	„	
1681.	Gilbert	„	*Adm'on.*
1681.	Bartram	„	*Adm'on.*
1682.	John	„	*Adm'on.*
1684.	Richard	„	*Adm'on.*
1686.	Elizabeth	„	*Tuition.*
1686.	George	„	*Adm'on.*
1686.	John	„	*Adm'on.*
1687.	Peter	„	*Tuition.*

To sister Elizabeth Blenkinshipe 8s. To Thomas son of George Marshall 5s. for a token. Proved 1615.

[1] *See* an *Inq.* in App. to 44th Rept. of D. K. Pub. Rec. p. 473. Another on George of Scott's Hill, p. 474.

[2] William Marshall of Haydon Bridge. Dated 17 April, 1628. To Elizabeth my now wife a house in Haydon Bridge for life and then to my daughter Jane Marshall. To daughter Dorothy Marshall a stone house, etc., on the north side of the water. My sister Jane Eshton. To daughter Jane a close on the hill granted to me by my Lord Annandale. Proved 1629. In the inventory annexed George Marshall appears as a creditor.

[3] John Marshell of Seaham, co. Durham, yeoman. Dated 13 Nov., 1633. My father Richard Marshall of Seaham. Wife Christable, and daughter Alice. Proved 1633.

[4] *See* an *Inq.* in App. to 44th Report of D. K. Pub. Rec. p. 475.

[5] *See* an *Inq. ibid.*

[6] John Marshall of Haydon Briggs, yeoman. Dated 8 May, 1636. To be buriey in the Chancel or Quire of Haydon Briggs church. To Elizabeth Marshall my sister reversion of lease of house in Haydon Briggs for her life, and after her decease to go to John Marshall servant to the Rt. Hon. Willm Howard of Howard Castle. Proved 1636.

[7] Elizabeth Marshall of Haydon Bridge, spinster. Dated 20 May, 1628. Lease of my lands to Anne wife of Richard Stokoe and her first husband's children for life, and after her decease to John Marshall of Haward. To George Marshall a branded cow. Anne Stokoe residuary legatee.

1687.	William	Marshall.	*Adm'on.*
1688.	Robert	"	
1690.	John	"	*Adm'on.*
1690.	James	"	*Adm'on.*
1694.	Sampson	"	*Adm'on.*
1694.	Samuel	"	*Adm'on.*
1695.	John	"	*Adm'on.*
1696.	Jane [1]	"	
1699.	Elizabeth	"	*Adm'on.*
1702.	Francis	"	*Adm'on.*
1705.	John	"	
1707.	John	"	
1708.	John	"	*Tuition of infants.*
1712.	James	"	
1712.	George	"	
1713.	Elizabeth	"	
1715.	Thomas	"	*Tuition.*
1715.	Thomas	"	Billingham.
1716.	Isabell	"	*Adm'on.*
1722.	William	"	
1722.	Thomas	"	Parish of Haltwhistle.

CALENDAR OF WILLS AND ADMINISTRATIONS AT LICHFIELD.

Consistory Court, 1656—1725.

The date in the second column is that of Probate or Administration.

William	Marshall of	Heanor.	25 July, 1661.
Edmund	"	Youlgreave.	3 Jan., 1662-3.
John	"	Staveley.	27 Oct., 1663. [2]
William	"	Tatenhill.	28 April, 1664. [3]
William	"	Yoxall.	20 May, 1664. [4]

[1] Jane Marshall of Hurworth upon Tees, spinster. Dated 1695-6, (no day or month). Her aunt Jane Jenison of said place universal legatee. Proved 1696.

[2] John Marshall of Woodthorpe in the parish of Staveley, co. Derby, husbandman. Dated 7 December, 1662. To be buried in the churchyard at Staveley. £30 to son Thomas Marshall if he be obedient to his mother and his uncle John Wollton, if not obedient then to son John Marshall. Appoints wife Mary Marshall and son John Marshall executors. Both proved 27 October, 1663.

[3] William Marshall of Tatenhill, co. Stafford, yeoman. Dated 30 January, 1663. Devises tenement in Dunstall to wife Dorothy for life, remainder to daughter Dorothy "for full term of my lease." Son in law Roger Midleham and Mabell his wife, and Mary their daughter. To my daughter Ann £30. Appoints wife executrix. Richard Green of Little Worley and Walter Hollier of Whichnor overseers. Proved by Dorothy Marshall his relict 28 April, 1664. One Richard Marshall signed the Inventory which amounts to £72 10s. 0d.

[4] William Marshall of Yoxall, co. Stafford, yeoman. Dated 12 October, 1659. To be buried in church or churchyard of Yoxall. Devises lands after decease of wife to John and Henry the children of Walter Holliar; and all copyhold land in the manors of Agarsley and Yoxall to William and Elizabeth Marshall the children of my brother Richard Marshall of Longdon. Appoints wife Katheren residuary legatee and executrix. Richard Marshall a witness. Proved by Katheren Marshall

Francis Marshall	of	Castleton.	2 May, 1667.
Richard	,,	Wolfhamcote.	9 Dec., 1668.
Thurston	,,	Barlborough.	22 Oct., 1668. *Adm'on.*
Richard	,,	Yoxall.	1 Oct., 1669. *Adm'on.*
Elizabeth	,,	Nuneaton.	22 Feb., 1671-2.
Catherine	,,	Stanton.	22 Oct., 1672.
Thomas	,,	Castleton.	30 April, 1673. *Inventory.*
William	,,	Whitwell.	3 Sept., 1673.[1]
John	,,	Newcastle.	10 Jan., 1673-4. *Adm'on.*
John	,,	Staveley.	30 Sept., 1674.[2]
John	,,	Alton.	6 Sept., 1675. *Inventory.*
Ann	,,	Atherston.	12 July, 1678. *Adm'on.*
Richard	,,	Tansley.	23 March, 1679-80.
Francis	,,	Derby.	13 July, 1681. *Adm'on.*
John	,,	Brinklow.	15 July, 1681. *Adm'on.*
Edward	,,	Derby.	22 Sept., 1681.
Thomas	,,	Scarcliffe.	23 March, 1681-2.[3]
Thomas	,,	Derby.	24 April, 1683.
Humphrey	,,	Youlgreave.	26 March, 1684. *Adm'on.*
William	,,	Hampstal Ridware.	27 Nov., 1685.[4]
Thomas	,,	Killamarsh.	22 Sept., 1686.[5]

the relict 20 May, 1664. The Inventory annexed is dated 4 November, 1659. It is therefore evident that some time elapsed between the death of the testator and the proving of the will.

[1] William Marshall of Whitwell in the co. of Derby, yeoman.* Dated 23 April, 1673. House and lands in Whitwell parish to his two daughters Elizabeth and Anne after the decease of his wife Mary. Twenty shillings each to his five brothers and sisters, viz. George, John, Thomas, Elizabeth, and Barbary. "To John Ramsdale and William sons of John Ramsdale of Ratcliffe and to Ann and Elizabeth daughters of James Walker of Walesby to each of them two shillings and sixpence apeece." Wife Mary Marshall sole executrix. Robert Major and Tho. Marshall both of Whitwell parish to be tutors and guardians to two children Elizabeth and Ann in case my executrix die or marry again. Witnesses, Roger Cotes, Tho. Marshall, Robert Major, Ann Rostby. Proved by Mary Marshall the relict, 3 Sept., 1673, and tuition of the two children granted to her at the same time. Inventory £221 19s. 3d.

[2] John Marshall of Stanley Woodthorp, co. Derby. Dated 1 June, 1674. My now wife Elizabeth Marshall. Eldest son Edward Marshall. Lands at Stavley, and in Bolsover parish called the Coppy. Mentions wife Elizabeth as the mother of son Edward. Second son John Marshall. Daughter Elizabeth Marshall. Daughter Margaret Marshall, under age. Brother Thomas Marshall, and brethren in law John Smith, Robert Smith, and Peter Smith, supervisors. Wife and son Edward executors. Both proved 30 Sept., 1674. Inventory £323 11s. 5d.

[3] Adm'on to Alice Marshall his widow 23 March, 1682 (*sic*). Her affidavit that he died without having made a will 22 March, 1681. Inventory of goods of Thomas Marshall of Scarcliffe, co. Derby, lately deceased, dated 3 Jan., 1681, amounts to £170 1 2. Edward Marshall is one of the prisers.

[4] William Marshall of Hamstall Ridware, co. Stafford, Blacksmith. Dated 23 Oct., 1685. Wife Elizabeth Marshall sole executrix. Testator mentions his children, but not by name. Brother John Oldacres overseer. Proved 27 Nov., 1685. Inventory (which is signed by Hugh Marshall) amounts to £15.

[5] Thomas Marshall of Killamarsh, co. Derby. Dated 6 Sept., 1686. Devises land at Killamarsh to son John, under age. Mentions daughter Ann, under age. To Margrit Watson £5. To Thomas Spencer of the Hobline in the parish of Whitwell and John Shotleworth of Chorche Anston £2 10s. 0d. apiece, and appoints them executors. German Pole of the Parke Halle in the parish of Barlborough

* *See* his mother's will, vol. i, 127.

Thomas	Marshall of	Hilton.	23 Mar., 1686-7. *Adm'on.*
Richard	,,	Churchover.	6 August, 1688.
Richard	,,	Trysull.	18 May, 1688.
John	,,	Newton Solney.	9 Jan., 1690-1. *Adm'on.*
William	,,	Tamworth.	13 Nov., 1691. *Adm'on.*
Sarah	,,	Wolfhamcote.	25 Feb., 1691-2. *Adm'on.*
Hester	,,	Bradley.	10 Jan., 1692-3.
John	,,	Checkley.	16 June, 1694. *Adm'on.*
Richard	,,	Lullington.	20 Aug., 1694. *Adm'on.*
Isabel	,,	Atherstone.	20 Nov., 1695.
Humphry	,,	Doveridge.	17 April, 1696. *Adm'on.*
Edward	,,	Derby.	19 Jan., 1696-7. *Adm'on.*
William	,,	Alton.	18 Oct., 1697. *Adm'on.*
Ellen	,,	Church Broughton.	19 Oct., 1699. *Adm'on.*
John	,,	Moreton.	12 April, 1699. *Adm'on.*
John	,,	Hathersage.	2 Oct., 1700.
John	,,	Crich.	24 April, 1702.
Ralph	,,	Youlgrave.	30 Sept., 1702.
Ann	,,	Derby.	16 April, 1703.
Richard	,,	Shawbridge.	14 Oct., 1703.
Josiah	,,	Tamworth.	1 Mar., 1703-4. *Adm'on.*
Dorothy	,,	Stanton.	5 Oct., 1705.
Joshua	,,	Atherstone.	24 July, 1707.
Edward	,,	Staveley.	12 April, 1710.[1]
Hannah	,,	Derby.	6 Nov., 1710.
James	,,	Ashborne.	17 Nov., 1710. *Adm'on.*
John	,,	Staveley.	27 March, 1711. *Adm'on.*
Peter	,,	Rocester.	14 April, 1712.
Edward	,,	Heath.	20 Aug., 1712. *Adm'on.*[2]
Samuel	,,	Crich.	5 April, 1715.
William	,,	Barlborough.	7 Oct., 1715.[3]

Gent., supervisor.* Proved 22 September, 1686. Inventory dated 15 Sept., 1686, amounts to £85 17s. 8d. Tuition of John and Ann children of testator granted 22 Sept., 1686, to Thomas Spenser of Holme in the parish of Whitwell, yeoman, and John Shottlewell of Church Anson, co. York, and John Poole of Killamarsh, yeoman.

[1] Edward Marshall of Staveley Woodthorpe in the parish of Staveley, co. Derby, husbandman. Dated 31 Oct., 1709. To daughter Judeth Marshall £50, and the possession of Farm and Coppe-land. To daughter Barbara Marshall £50. To daughter Elizabeth Marshall £50. To daughter Sarah Marshall £50. Residue to son John Marshall of Staveley Woodthorpe and appoints him sole executor. Witnesses, John Marshall, senor [senior], Thomas Turnor, John Steemson [? Tryson]. Proved by said executor 12 April, 1710. Inventory dated 6 January, 1709, £290 6s. 10d.

[2] Adm'on to George Marshall of Heath, taylor, his son, 20 Aug., 1712. William Clay of Heath, blacksmith, and Christopher Lowe of Lichfield, plummer, parties to the bond.

[3] William Marshall the elder of Barlborough in the co. of Derby, yeoman, being aged and infirme. Dated 15 June, 1715. Tenant right of Farm to wife Elizabeth for life, remainder to son William Marshall. Daughter Elizabeth Milner. Daughter Anne Short. Daughter Mary Marshall. Sons George Marshall and John Marshall. Wife Elizabeth sole executrix. Proved 7 Oct., 1715, by William Marshall eldest son of the deceased, (*i.e.* adm'on with will annexed.) Inventory £99 3s. 4d.

* German Pole ob. 1686-7, *vide* Glover's 'Derbyshire,' ii, 79.

Elizabeth	Marshall of	Barlborough.	4 April, 1716.[1]	
Elizabeth	,,	Chellaston.	29 March, 1720.	
Joseph	,,	Chellaston.	20 Sept., 1720.	
Richard	,,	Monk's Kirby.	28 Sept., 1721.	*Adm'on.*
George	,,	Whitwell.	4 Oct., 1721.	
Thomas[2]	,,	Heynor.	6 Oct., 1721.	*Adm'on.*
William	,,	Hilton.	6 April, 1722.	
Francis	,,	Marston.	19 Oct., 1722.	
Mary	,,	Dore.	3 Oct., 1723.	
Ann	,,	Rocester.	21 Oct., 1724.	
Robert	,, *alias*	Marsh of Staveley.	30 Sept., 1724.[3]	

The Deans Peculiar.

Elizabeth	,,	Lichfield.	26 Aug., 1699.	
George	,,	Lichfield.	15 Dec., 1719.	
John	,,	Adbaston.	--Nov., 1603.	*Adm'on.*
Mary	,,	Lichfield.	2 June, 1820.	*Adm'on.*
Thomas	,,	Lichfield.	23 Aug., 1681.	
William	,,	Lichfield.	10 Dec., 1701.	

Prebendal Court of Alrewas.

Godfrey	,,	Alrewas.	31 Oct., 1684.	
John	,,	Mavesyn Ridware.	20 Oct., 1681.	*Adm'on.*
Richard	,,	King's Bromley.	18 June, 1685.	
Richard	,,	King's Bromley.	24 Nov., 1727.	*Adm'on.*
Thomas	,,	Edingale.	30 May, 1701.	

Prebendal Court of Colwich.

William	,,	Great Haywood.	8 July, 1723.
Thomas	,,	Haywood.	4 Feb., 1733.

Prebendal Court of Longdon.[4]

Richard	,,	Longdon.	22 Aug., 1718,
Richard	,,	Longdon.	22 Sept., 1721.

[1] Elizabeth Marshall of Barlborough, in co. Derby, widdow. Dated 20 Feb., 1715-16. Executor to discharge all the debts of late husband William Marshall and legacies yet unpaid. My two grand children Anne Milner and George Short. My four children, William Marshall, George Marshall, John Marshall, and Mary Marshall. Son William Marshall executor. He proved 4 April, 1716. Inventory £134 19s. 1d.

[2] Of Heynor, co. Derby, labourer. Adm'on to Mary his widow. Goods appraised at £8 13s. 6d.

[3] Robert Marshall of Middle Handley in the parish of Staveley, co. Derby, husbandman. Dated 18 July, 1724. Son Thomas Marshall. Grandson Paul Marshall and his brother Robert Marshall. Richard Marshall my grandson another of the brothers of the said Paul and Robert Marshall. Grand-daughter Anne Marshall daughter of the said Thomas Marshall. Grand-daughter Mary Marshall. Grand-daughter Elizabeth Marshall sister to the said Anne. Son Richard Marshall sole executor and residuary legatee. He proved as Richard *Marsh*, 30 Sept. 1724. The testator is called *Marsh* in the Inventory which amounts to £119 17s. 8d.

[4] There are more wills of Marshalls in this court at subsequent dates.

Dean and Chapters' Peculiar.[1]

Anne	Marshall	of Abney.	8 May, 1640.	
Anthony	"	Bradwell.	29 July, 1641.	
Clement	"	Hope.	16 Nov., 1635.	
Edward	"	Hope.	20 April, 1647.	*Adm'on.*
Edward	"	Smaldale.	... ... 1672.	
Clement	"	Abney.	19 Mar., 1689.	*Adm'on.*

MISCELLANEOUS NOTES OF WILLS AND ADM'ONS.

(Continued from Vol. i, p. 318.)

Will of Richard Farnefolde, Citizen and Merchant Tailor. Dated 5 and proved in P.C.C. 16 July, 1574. Mentions brother in law John Marshall, Draper. (31 Martyn.)

Will of Margaret Cotton of Milford Lane in the parish of St. Clement's Danes, widow. Dated 22 May, 1622. Names godson Thomas Marshall eldest son of Thomas Marshall, deceased, and the four other children of the said Thomas Marshall, viz. John, Elizabeth, Mary, and Lucy. Proved in P.C.C. (9 Swanne.) *cf.* Vol. i, p. 97.

Will of Robert Bassock, Serjeant of the Vestrie to the Queen. Dated 12 Aug. and proved (in P.C.C.) 30 Oct., 1575. Mentions, brother Clement Bassock alderman of the city of Canterbury; sister Katherine Marshall wife of Simon Marshall of Cranbrook, and gives her "a ring of gold with a turkies which I daily wear." To be buried in the church or churchyard of St. Mary at Hill nigh Billingsgate. (36 Pickering.) *See* adm'on of Simon Marshall, Vol. i, *app.* 1.

Will of Elizabeth Ibotson of Woodhouse in chapelry of Bradfield, co. York, widow. Dated 10 July, 1595. Residue to be divided into four parts, one fourth to Henry Ibotson my son, three fourths to Henry and John Ibotson and Ann Ibotson *alias* Marshall my children. Proved in Exchequer Court at York 4 Oct., 1598. *See* Vol. i, p. 236.

Will of William Dale of parish of St Martin's, Seamer, co. York. Dated 27 Sept., 1528. To Elizabeth Marshall my sister two ewes. Proved in Exchequer Court at York, 12 Dec., 1528.

Will of John Daile of Sheriff Hutton, co. York. Dated 6 June, 1521. To Francis Marshall for celebration of a mass xxd. To Matilda Marshall my servant xxd.

1668. April 20. Judith Pollard *alias* Marshall of Potter Heigham, co. Norfolk. Adm'on to Bridget Goodin *alias* Marshall and Catherine Larkeman *alias* Marshall her sisters. (*Norwich Probate Court.*)

The will of Thomas Marshall of Burrowe Peter, 1621, was proved in the Consistory Court at Norwich. "Hud." 26.

Gilbert Marshall of Sibton. Will proved at Ipswich, 1481—1498, 23; also, John Marshall of Nacton, 1518, 260.

The following is a list of Marshall wills at Ipswich, 1660—1735:—

1661. Leonard Marshall, Beccles. Lockier 32.
1670. Edward Marshall, Gorleston.

[1] There are many more wills at subsequent dates.

1679. Thomas Marshall, Buttly. Edgar, file 67.
1684. Robert Marshall, St. Margaret's Ilketshall. Book 444, file 143.
1693. Margaret Marshall, Woodbridge. Book 480, file 146.
1708. Samuel Marshall, Framlingham. Book 168, file 64.
1714. John Marshall, Beccles. Book 142, file 53.

These notes are from the Books from the Archdeacon's Registry, now in Probate Court at Ipswich :—

1610. July 4. Adm'on of goods of Robert Marshall of Stonham Comitis to his daughter Rebecca Harte.
1610. Oct. Scrutetur Test^{m} Thome Marshall de Beccles.
1612. Nov. 14. Reference to the proving of the will of Robert Marshall of Pakefield.
1632. Dec. 10. Marriage Licence. Thomas Cheanie and Mary Marshall, single, of Aldeburghe.

Will of Anne Worth of St. Olave, Southwark, 1665. Proved in P.C.C. (129 Hyde). Mentions "my brother Stephen Marshall now living in Oxford."

Will of John Leigerd of South Kelsey, co. Lincoln, Husbandman. Dated 22 Apr., 1655. Mentions wife Elizabeth Leigerd and her three children William, Mary, and Anne Marshall. Adm'on (in P.C.C.) with will annexed to the cousin and curator[1] lawfully assigned to Jane, Ann, Mary, Margaret, and Helline Leigerd children of the testator, 6 July, 1655. (312 Aylett.)

Will of Henry Parker, Cittizen and Paynter Stayner of London. Dated 12 March, 1669. Wife Margaret Parker executrix. My daughter Margaret Marshall. Eldest son Henry Parker of the Inner Temple, London, Esq. To "my sonne Marshall the husband of my said daughter Margaret my whole Studie of Bookes." Proved by relict in P.C.C. 29 April, 1670. (50 Penn.) *See* Vol. i, *app.* p. 24.

Will of Thomas Langham[2] of Clapham in the county of Surrey. Dated 1 Feb., 1694. Houses in Petticote Lane to niece Elizabeth Lane. To niece Sarah Nicholas £300. To niece Alice Pickus £300. To niece Elizabeth Wilcocks £200. To niece Mary Harvey annuity of £10. To Mr. Peter Smith £100. To Mr. Marshall Smith £100. To Mr. Stephen Nye £50. To Mrs. Elizabeth Benson £50. Mr. Stephen Boughton. To Jane Harvy daughter of my niece Jane Harvy my house and land at Finchingfield, co. Essex, called Little Winsey. To Mary Harvy daughter of said Jane house at Finchingfield called Waseys. To Peter Harvy son of said Jane £500. To niece Elizabeth Juxon my late wife's Jewell as also her velvett gown and petticoat, etc. To ... Wilson dau'r to my late niece......Bush annuity of £10 for her separate use without intermedling of her husband. Nephew Thomas Juxon. Friend Thomas Barnesley. To Dame Rebecca Atkins £20 for mourning. £400 to Mercers Company for a weekly bread

[1] He is not mentioned by name, but I suppose him to have been John Leigerd called in the will 'loving kinsman' and one of the supervisors therein named.

[2] See will of his wife's father, Stephen Marshall, Vol. i, p. 120. In Painter's Work Book, $\frac{II}{1}$ fo. 123, in College of Arms, there is a note of Arms painted for funeral of Thomas Langham, Esq., *Argent, a fess Gules, a label Azure*, impaling the coat belonging to the Marshalls of Woodwalton, Finchingfield, etc.

charity for Clapham. Nephew Thomas Juxon and niece Jane Harvey,[1] executors. Both proved in P.C.C. 30 May, 1695. (75 Irby.)

Will of Thomas Martin of Doncaster in the co. of York, gentleman. Dated 17 January, 1688. To be buried near father and mother in Doncaster church. Settles lands upon the children of his sisters Mrs. Alice Cowley and Mrs. Penelope Rutter. Mentions cousin Mrs. Mary Greenwood, and Alice Box apparently her daughter by a former husband. Aunt Clavalo of London. "To my cozen John Marshall of Grantham one hundred pounds." Proved in the Exchequer Court at York by William Walker, gent., and John Burton, gent., the ex'ors named in the will 24 May, 1690.

Will of Francis Astlin of Halloughton al's Hawton next Southwell, co. Nottingham, yeoman. Dated 9 Feb., 1651. Devises land in the Eastfield and Westfield "which my father Marshall hath for his life" to son and heir Francis Astlin. Mentions wife Elizabeth, and daughters Mary and Elizabeth both under age. Makes father-in-law Troth Marshall and brother Richard Astlin executors. Both proved in P.C.C. 4 August, 1653. (87 Brent.)

Thomas Meller by his will dated 18 June, 1636, and proved in P.C.C. 8 July following (86 Pile), bequeaths to Margaret Marshall, widow, relict of Thomas Marshall, taylor, deceased, inhabiting near Charing Cross, £50.

Will of Thomas Stone of Taunton, co. Somerset, gent., 1675. Mentions cosen Thomas Marshall son of my brother Nicholas Marshall; brother Thomas Marshall and his sons Thomas and Nicholas. Proved in P.C.C. (79 Dycer.)

Will of Elizabeth Baker, widow. Dated 7 January, 1616. Bequest to poor of Eltham, Kent. Mentions Bridget Marshall daughter of my late son Arthur Marshall. Dau'r Anne Saunderson, widow. Sister Dorothy Saywell, widow, late wife of John Saywell, citizen and grocer of London. John Philipson and Margaret his wife my grandchild. Cousin Peter Phesant, Esq. Proved in P.C.C. 13 Sept., 1620. (79 Soame.)

Will of Anne Hesketh[2] of the parish of St Margaret Westminster, widow. Dated 2 Nov., 1650. To be buried in the parish church of St Margaret Westminster as near as may conveniently be to my well beloved husband George Marshall. Mentions her son George Marshall, and his daughter Elizabeth Marshall. Her youngest son Thomas Marshall, whom she makes executor, and his daughter Anne Marshall. He proved in P.C.C. 8 July, 1651.

Will of Benjamin Marshall of Allesley in the co. of Warwick, clerk. Dated 21 Feby, 1748. "I appoint that Sexty's mortgage for £700 be assigned to proper Trustees to be chosen by my wife Phœbe Marshall and my son George Marshall on trust for making good my engagement to my said son relating thereto." Mentions son-in-law Thomas Hardman. MSS. Sermons, etc., to son George. My brother Mr. Richard Marshall of London[3] and his son Francis Marshall, £5

[1] She proved as "widow."
[2] Entered as *Jane* in Calendar. See her marriage Vol. i., p. 56, *cf.* pp. 17—20.
[3] *See* will of Richard Marshall, Vol. i. p. 170.

apiece for mourning. Appoints wife residuary legatee and executrix. She proved, in Consistory Court at Lichfield, 7 April, 1719.

Will of Edward Rennick,[1] dated 6 August, 1639. Was a parishioner of St Catherin Creechurch. To my uncle Robert Marshall of Dartford in the parish of Warsop, co. Notts, £40. To my cosen William Marshall £20. To my cosen Thomas Marshall £20. To every one of the children of my uncle William Marshall of Warmsworth £5. Proved in P.C.C. 17 Nov., 1645. (135 Rivers.)

Will of John Marshall of Screveton in the co. of Nottingham, yeoman. Dated 20 January, 1719-20. To brother Edward Marshall £5. To Elizabeth Morr...... my wifes sister £5. To my nephew Edw...... £1. To my nephew William Marshall £1. To my nephew Joseph Harker £1. Godson William Howett. Wife Mary Marshall sole executrix. Proved in Exchequer Court at York. (Vol. 75, p. 15.) *See* Vol. i. p. 300.

Will of Hannah Marshall of the town of Kingston upon Hull, widow. Dated 7 Nov., 1694. Appoints friends Mr. John Lyth of Kingston upon Hull, Master and Marriner, and Mr. David Crossby of Gunins (?) in the co. of Lincoln, Master and Marriner, executors. To my brother Edward Ruckle in Pensilvania 10s. My sister Sarah his wife. To John Odling of Glandford Brigg 5s. To my sister Elizabeth the wife of John Markham of Burringham 5s. My cousin Robert Ruckle. My son David Wake residuary legatee if he returns to Hull, but if he dies abroad then amongst the other legatees, etc. Sister Elizabeth Markham's three children she had by her late husband Joshua Stutting.

Codicil dated 10 Nov., 1694. Gives to each of the following persons a pair of gloves:—

John Whitehead of Thistorton near Lincoln, and his wife. Mr. Joseph Storr of Hilston in Holderness; his daughter Katherine. Mr. John Lyth, and his wife. Mr. David Crosby, and his wife. Mr. Thomas Harrison, and his wife. Dr. Longmire of Wistead, and his wife. John Raines of Carlton in Holderness, and his wife; his wife's daughter called Hannah Marshall. Joseph Smith of Easington, and his daughter Hannah Smith. Isaac Storr of Owstwick, and his wife. Thomas Pinder of Halsome in Holderness, and his wife. Thomas Wilson of Hull, and his wife. John Odling of Glanford Brigg, and his wife. Edward Ruckle of Pensilvania and his wife. John Markham of Burringham, and his wife. Robert Ruckle. Benjamin Graves. Hannah Williamson. William Williamson of Rawby near Brigg, and his wife. John Sharp of Brigg, and his wife. Also the following bequests, to the poor of Hull meeting £2; to the poor of Owstwicke meeting £2; to the poor belonging to the meeting in the East end of Holderness £2; to Rose Mary [rosemary] for Posies,[2] 10s.

Bond dated 8 Oct., 1695, and Inventory which amounts to

[1] *See* "Doncaster Charities," by Charles Jackson, p. 127.

[2] For her funeral, as it comes in with other amounts for her coffin, and £2 for Sack to be drunk then. This note is taken from the original will, there being no transcript.

£121 5s. 0d., are annexed. Testatrix is described in the Inventory as "sometime of Kingston upon Hull, and late a sojourner at Carleton in Holdernesse." *See* note of Probate, Vol. i. p. 279.

Will of Francis Marshall of Newark upon Trent, Felmonger and Glover. Dated 12 Sept., 1750. My grandchildren Francis Marshall, Mary Marshall, Elizabeth Marshall, William Marshall, and Ann Marshall, sons and daughters of my son John Marshall, all under age. Sons John Marshall, and William Marshall, executors. Mentions his house in Castlegate Street, Newark. Proved 6 January, 1753, in Exchequer Court at York. (Vol. 97, fo. 205.)

Will of Elizabeth Marshall of Wadworth in the co. of York, widow. Dated 9 June 1722. Mentions, daughter Elizabeth Radley; Mary Tyas of Consborough; my son John Marshall; my son Tho. wife; my daughter Anne Beedle; my daughter Mary Wigfield. Appoints son Thomas Marshall sole executor. Bond is dated 5 July, 1722. Proved in peculiar court of Wadworth. The original will is in the Probate Court at York.

Will of William Marshall of Tuxford in the co. of Nottingham, yeoman. Dated 3 Feb. 1686. My sister Ann Nicholson and her two children, "all now living at Cunsborrow." [Conisborough, co. York.] Residue to wife Elizabeth, and Elizabeth Marshall my only daughter, and makes them executrixes.

Inventory dated 15 Feb., 1686. Bond dated 25 Feb., 1686. Proved 2 May, 1687. Original will is among the Vacancy Wills in Probate Court at York.

1648. May 10. Probate of the will of Robert Marshall, Gent., of Selby, to Michael Marshall, clerk, his son, and power reserved to Mary Marshall the relict. Estate over £300. (This will cannot be found.) *Prerogative Act Book, York. See* Vol. i, p. 310.

Will of Anthony Marshall of Stoxley, co. York, yeoman. Dated 30 July, 1708. To be buried in churchyard of Stoxley. To brother Thomas Marshall, 15s. To brother Robert Marshall of Ellerburne 10s. Brother Francis Marshall and his wife Jane, and his daughter Elizabeth. Godson Anthony Marshall. Sister Mary Brotton. Richard Snowdon my son to enjoy house and harth at West End of Stoxley which I lately purchased of Marmaduke Palmer after decease of my wife. Appoints wife executrix. Proved in Exchequer Court at York. (Vol. 65, fo. 319.)

Will of Francis Marshall of Leckenfeild. Dated 24 July, 1630. William my son. Jane Marshall her two children. Ann my wife, and William my son, executors. They proved in Exchequer Court at York, 3 June, 1630. (Vol. 41, fo. 64.)

Will of Peter Marshall of Leaserige. Dated 1627. To be buried in churchyard of Egton. Appoints wife and son William executors. William to pay his brother Thomas Marshall 10s, and to Jane Marshall, and Elizabeth Marshall, 5s. each, (apparently his sisters.) Mentions, Richard Smallwood, Thomas Smallwood, Thomas Dawson, and Roger Munckman. Registered at York, Vol. 41, fo. 52.

Will of Anne Seoley of Wentworth in the parish of Wath, co. York, widdow. Dated 25 Dec., 1671. Mentions Robert and John sons of John Charleton. To Margrett, Richard, Elizabeth, and Katherine children of Richard Marshall, to each of them 20s. Proved at York 19 March, 1671-2. (Vol. 52, fo. 251.)

Will of William Marshall of Newall cu' Clifton in the parish of Otley, co. York. Dated 6 June, 1705. To Miles Oddy of Yeadon in the parish of Guiseley, yeoman, £15. To Robert Murgatroyde of Mythom in Stansfeild, Linnen Weaver, £20. To Mr. Hodgson, Mr. Ingerson, Gentleman, of the parish of Kendall, trustees about the estate of Mr. Thomas Murgatroyd late vicar of Kendall, and to Robert Murgatroyd of Mythom, £20 in trust for children of Thomas Murgatroyd when Alice his daughter shall attain the age of 18. To Nathan Collyer of Ashill 20s. To Mary Tomson of Bradford 20s. To Thomas Snawden of Ottley 20s. To Grace Marshall of Ashhill 5s. To Rebecca Pullon 5s. To Alice Beane of Bealdon 5s. To Mary Marshall of Yeadon 5s. To Margaret wife of Jeremiah Collyer of Ashhill 10s. To Sarah Younge of Ashhill 10s. To Anthony Whitehead of Farneley 2s. To my brother Josiah Marshall of Rawden 2s. To Josiah Marshall, junr., 1s To Jeremiah son of Hugh Marshall of Rawden 5s. To Sarah wife of Isaack Dawson of Yeadon, Cordewayner, one open bedstead, etc. To Anne wife of William Mitchell of Bouling one close bedstead. Hugh Marshall of Rawden aforesaid, yeoman, to pay to said Anne Mitchell his sister £5. Appoints Jeremiah Collyer residuary legatee and executor. (Vol. 65, fo. 288.) *See* Vol. i, 269.

Will of Richard Marshall of Dunnington, co. York, yeoman. Dated 10 Feb., 1630, To be buried in churchyard of Dunnington. To mother Alice Marshall dwelling house in Stockton. My nephew John Marshall. Brother James Marshall. Richard Marshall my nephew son of Rowland Marshall. Anne Smetton my sister. John Marshall my brother. Rowland Marshall my brother. Anne Smeeton the daughter of Thomas Smeeton. Ann Marshall the daughter of Rowland Marshall. To poor of Dunnington 20s. To poor of Stockton 20s. Thomas Burne. Appoints wife and brother James Marshall executors. Both proved in Prerogative Court at York, 17 Feb., 1630. Vol. 41, fo. 297.)

Will [original] of John Marshall thelder of Donigton [Dunnington] in the co. of York, yeoman. Dated between Martinmas and Christmas 1643. He made his will at this date "which was plundered or taken away in these troublesome tymes." The said will was acknowledged and subscribed by testator in the presence of George Smeeton and Thomas Burne, and said Thomas Burne being literate doth testify that after disposing of his soule and body he did devise give and bequeath as followeth :—To his wife Mary Marshall eight Kyne, etc. Second son James Marshall. Appointed said wife, and James Marshall, and Richard Marshall, his sons, executors. Proved at York by James Marshall, 26 Oct., 1644.

(*Original Will.*) Will of John Marshill. Dated 28 Oct., 1639. Bodie to be buried in the Church Earde in Bilbroughe. Daughter Elizabeth. To Robart Cawood of Stillingflet tuition of two youngest daughters Ellen and Easter. John Cawood of Stillingflet. Said three daughters executors, all under age. Ad'mon to Thomas Cawood of Stillingfleete to use of said executors, in Exchequer Court at York, 21 Dec., 1639.

Will of William Marshall of Tickhill. Dated 5 May, 1579. To wife Elizabeth an acre of arable land in Wadworthe field, and an acre of arable land in Tickhill field nigh unto Allhalowes Church, in fee. My children Thomas, Robert, Henry, and Janett vj^{s}. viij^{d} apiece. Wife executrix. John Marshall is one of the witnesses. Proved at York 5 Feb., 1582, by Elizabeth the relict. (Vol. 22, fo. 250.)

Will of John Marshall of Tickhill, Dated 6 Oct., 1589. To be buried in churchyard of Tickhill. Daughters Elline, Jennett, and Jane. Elline my wife executor. To my bretheren and sisters children, to wit, Henrie Marshall 3^{s}, Joh'o Farneworth 16^{d}, and to Nicholas Farneworthe 16^{d}. Wife to be Gou'nor of daughters during their noncage. Proved by relict, at York, 28 January, 1589. (Vol. 24, fo. 194.)

Will of William Marshall of Rossington, co. York, yeoman. Dated 20 June, 164... To Roger Nicholson of Edlington, co. York, yeoman, and to Jennet his wife £60 in the hands of John Peirpoint of Wadworth, co. York, Esq. for their lives on condition that they seal a general release of four acres of land in Long East field in the parish of Tickhill to the said John Pierpoint and his heirs, and after the decease of the said Roger and Jennet Nicholson their executors shall pay the said £60 within one year after their decease in the south porch of the parish church of Stainton to Margaret, Mary, and Sarah, daughters of John Saunderson of Stainton and Winefride his wife. Testator also bequeaths to said Margaret, Mary, and Sarah, £20 apiece. To John Saunderson aforesaid and Winefride his wife one kowe now in their possession and 40^{s} apiece. To John Oglethorpe of Wadworth, co. York, husbandman, and Anne his wife £4 which I lent them. To Christopher Woadeson, Henry Woadson, Thomas Oglethorpe, Margaret Oglethorpe, and Susan Oglethorpe, children of the said Anne Oglethorpe my sister goods mentioned in a bill of sale made betwixt said William Marshall and said John Oglethorpe dated 23 August, 1637, to be equally divided among them. To Dorothy Gressam of Rossington, widow, £10 she oweth me. Her son John Gressam, and her daughters Anne Gressam, and Jane Gressam. Thomas Gressam servant to said Dorothy Gressam. To Thomas Marshall of Tickhill myne Vncle one hat and suite of apparell and 5^{s}. My brother Roger Nicholson to be sole executor. He proved in Exchequer Court at York, 16 April, 1647. *(Original Will.)*

Will of John Marshall of Selbye, plumer. Dated 11 Dec., 1580. To be buried in churchyard of St. Augustine in Headon. To Roger Awmonde my cote. Agnes Marshall my wife. William Marshall my son. Jane Marshall my daughter. Wife Agnes and son William executors. Proved in Exchequer Court at York by relict and power reserved to son William, 13 July, 1581. (Vol. 22, fo. 79.)

Adm'on of Thomas Marshall of Glusburne in parish of Kildwick to Margaret Marshall his relict, in Exchequer Court at York, 5 April, 1715. (Craven Act Book.)

Will of Ralph Marshall of Scalby, husbandman. Dated 10 August, 1647. Son George Marshall. Son Thomas Marshall. To said son Thomas's wife a goose and a gander, and to his daughter Isabell a ewe which was her grandmothers. Daughter Jayne Hinderwell. Sowerby *(sic)* my daughter. To every one of my grandchildren one lamb. Thomas Hinderwell my grandchild. Jonathan Sowerby my grandchild. Son George sole executor and residuary legatee. (*Original will*) Proved at York.

Will of Roger Marshall, clarke. Dated 21 May, 1562. To be buried in chancel at Kelham. To Mr. Person of Kellam all my bookes of Sancte Augustyne workes and my best gowne. To M^ris Roche 20^s. Mr. Maxe. To Sr James my thirde gowne with narrowe sleves and foure bookes of Sancte John gresostomes [Chrysostom] workes. Mr. John Marshall. To Mr. Henrie Marshalles wiffe one oulde Ryall. "To Mr. ꝑson of Kelham and to Mrs. Roche all my beddinge heare in his house in recompence for theire greate paynes taken wth me." Residue to Thom's Hill, Thom's Marshall, John Marshall, and Roger Marshall, whome I make my full executors, saving my sister to have all my lynnen. Witnesses, John Taverham, Robert Maxe, gentleman, Will'm Soden. Proved at York by Thomas Hill and power reserved to other executors, 11 July, 1581. (Vol. 22, fo. 79.)

(*Original will.*) Will of Richard Marshall of Streete in the parish of Wath, co. York, Gardiner. Dated 29 April, 1692. To be buried in the Chappell or Chappell yard of Wentworth. To Amorous Hoyland my son in law 1s. To Margaret Hoyland my daughter 1s. To Margaret Marshall my daughter in law 1s. To Anthony Smeaton my son in law 2s 6d. To Elizabeth Smeaton, my daughter 2s. 6d. To William Marshall my son £5 to be paid at decease of Katherine my loving wife. To Mary my daughter £5. To Christian my daughter £5. Wife Catherine executrix. She proved, in Exchequer Court at York, 23 May, 1693.

(*Original will.*) Will of Robert Marshall of Hatfield, co. York, yeoman. Dated 26 Nov., 1690. To my two brethren Joseph and John, to each of them 2s. 6d. Same to two sisters Rosamund and Margarett. Wife Elizabeth executrix and residuary legatee. She proved in Exchequer Court at York, 9 August, 1693.

(*Original will.*) Robert Marshall of Nether Bradfield in the Chapelry of Bradfield, yeoman. Dated 8 June, 1723. Wife Mary Marshall. Son Thomas Marshall. Anne Chapman my daughter. Martha Chapman my daughter. Francis Marshall my son. To Elizabeth Marshall, Hellen Marshall, Catherine Marshall, and Mary Marshall, my daughters, 40s. apiece. Thomas Marshall my brother. Son Thomas sole executor. He proved, in Exchequer Court at York, 29 April, 1724.

Will of William Stanley of Leicester, mercer. Mentions brother in law Richard Marshall of Mount Sorrell and his children Mary, William, and Thomas Marshall. (74 Huddleston.)

Will of Robert Webb of Ilminster. Daughter Mary wife of Thomas Marshall; Nicholas the son of Thomas Marshall. (91 Harvey.) *See* vol. ii, p. 9.

William Marshall overseer of will of George Bedford of Sarum. (10 Huddleston.)

Will of Agnes Atkinson of St. Olave's, Southwark, dated 17 March, 1605, proved 15 April, 1606. Brother in law Thomas Marshall of Southborough, Kent, and his son Thomas Marshall. My mother

Powell. Late uncle Robert Atkinson. Brother John Whaley. (26 Stafford.)

Will of John Pyne of Curry Mallet, Esqr, dated 1 June, 1607, proved 6 Feb., 1609. Daughters Anne Harvey, Mary Knapton, Frances Marshall, and Elizabeth Langford. (19 Wingfield.)

Will of Mary Simcox, of Budleigh, co. Somerset, dated 12 May, 1608. Daughter Johane Marshall; Mr. George Marshall her husband (54 Windebancke.)

Will of Ellen Launce of Ashe, widow, dated 24 April, 1610 Daughter Ellen Marshall. (56 Wingfield.)

Will of Edmond Sheringham of East Dereham, co. Norfolk, yeoman. To Pleasaunce the wife of William Marshall,[1] Rector of Woodnorton £5. Proved 3 Nov., 1612. (100 Fenner.)

Will of William Markham. Dated 15 May, 1608. To be buried at Sidbrooke amonge my ancestors. My brothers George and Charles. To Mr. Marshall owing for my boord £30. My three brothers-in-law Mr. Molinax, Mr. Swichcottes, and Mr. Eire. Aunt Hornesey. Aunt Markham of Newbe Abbey. My three cosens the children to my uncle Richard Markham, Anne Markham, Theadothia, and Thomas. Mr. Raphe Marshall of Shelltonn executor. To my cosen Fraunces Marshall my black nagge. To my cozen Raphe Marshall my satin doublett and taffetie breeches. To my cozen Mawde Marshall, £40. Proved by said Ralph Marshall 21 June, 1608. (54 Windebancke.)

Will of Robert Bence of Harwich, Merchant. Dated 26 May, 1611. Mentions sister Marshall. (51 Wood.)

The following notes of Probates and Adm'ons from the Act Books at York, are in continuation of those given in Vol. i, pp. 305–309 :—

City of York Act Book.

1702. Jany 2. Probate of will of John Marshall of York to Elizabeth Marshall his relict.

1729. March 20. Probate of will of Thomas Marshall of York to Jane Marshall his relict.

Dickering Act Book.

1667. May 31. Probate of will of John Marshall [2] of Staxton to Sara his relict.

1668. Oct. 22. Probate of will of Sara Marshall [2] of Staxton to Thomas Marshall her son.

1697. Sept. 13. Adm'on of Richard Marshall of Osgarby to Richard Marshall of Osgarby aforesaid husbandman (*agricola.*)

1711. Dec. 24. Probate of will of William Marshall [2] of Staxton in parish of Willerby to John Smith.

[1] Vicar of Scarning, 1583, and Rector of Woodnorton, 1600. Blomefield's "Norfolk," vol. x, p. 45; viii, p. 317. *See* "38th Report of Deputy Keeper of the Public Records," app. p. 683.

[2] *See* Vol. i, p. 276.

1712-13. Feb. 4. Adm'on of Thomas Marshall of Bridlington to Mary Marshall his relict.

1716. May 24. Probate of the will of Anne Marshall of Scarborough to Thomasine Sellar, widow, her daughter [1].

1724-5. Feb. 11. Tuition of William, Mary, and Thomasine Marshall, children of William Marshall of Bridlington, and same day probate of his will, both granted to John Bilton.[2]

Ainstie Act Book.

1725. Oct. 26. Adm'on of William Marshall of Leeds to Martha Marshall his relict.

1728. May 23. Probate of the will of John Marshall of Cliffe in Rawden, parish of Guiseley, to Joseph Marshall his son.[3]

1728. July 5. Probate of the will of Samuel Marshall of Horsforth to John Hird.[4]

1728. Aug. 10. Adm'on of Mercy Marshall of Rawden to John Marshall her son.

1729. Aug. 7. Probate of the will of Samuel Marshall of Wyke in the parish of Bardsey to Mary Marshall his relict; and same day care of Mary Marshall daughter of the said Samuel Marshall to Mary Marshall her mother.[5]

1729. Nov. 4. Probate of the will of Samuel Marshall of Horsforth to Timothy Marshall.[6]

1730. May 7. Probate of the will of Abraham Marshall of Burley Woodhead to Jeremiah Whalley and Isaac Grimshaw.

1730. May 7. Probate of the will of Mercy Marshall of Burley to Jeremiah Marshall.[7]

1730. July 21. Probate of the will of Martha Marshall of Moor Monkton to Major Freer.[8]

1731. Aug. 4. Care of Elizabeth Marshall, aged 16, daughter of Henry Marshall late of Eltoft to Peter Heartfield, according to her voluntary election.[9]

Buckrose Act Book.

1685. April 16. Probate of the will of Henry Marshall of Settrington to Mary, wife of John Cole, his daughter, and power reserved to the other executors.

1693-4. Jan. 11. Adm'on of John Marshall of Thixendale to Alice Marshall his relict.

1728. April 20. Probate of the will of William Marshall of Thixendale in the Parish of Wharram Percy to Christopher Marshall.[10]

Cleveland Act Book.

1712. June 17. Probate of the will of Paul Marshall of Oakebridge Holme in the parish of Egton to William Law.

[1] *See* Vol. i, p. 300.
[2] *See* Vol. i, p. 302.
[3] *See* Vol. i, p. 293.
[4] *See* Vol. i, p. 292.
[5] *See* Vol. i, p. 290.
[6] *See* Vol. i, p. 293.
[7] *See* Vol. i, p. 283.
[8] *See* Vol. i, p. 272.
[9] *See* Vol. i, p. 304.
[10] *See* Vol. i, p. 302.

1712. Dec. 17. Probate of the will of Thomas Marshall of Whitby to Jane Marshall his widow.

1714. Dec. 19. Adm'on of Grace Marshall of Marsk to John Marshall her son.

1732. Sept. 6. Probate of the will of Leonard Marshall of Lofthouse to William Marshall and Thomas Marshall.[1]

Bulmer Act Book.

1722. Nov. 2. Adm'on of Thomas Marshall of Cawton in the parish of Gilling to Ellen Marshall his widow.

1724. Nov. 19. Probate of the will of Marmaduke Marshall of Flaxton to Anne Marshall his relict during the minority of John Marshall his son.

1727. Oct. 14. Adm'on of John Marshall of Thormanby to Jane Marshall his widow.

1727. Nov. 4. Adm'on of Richard Marshall of Terrington to Richard Marshall his son.

1729. June 7. Probate of the will of George Marshall of Bransby to Isabella Marshall his widow,[2]

1731. June 12. Adm'on of William Marshall of Bransby to Lidia Marshall his widow.

Harthill cum Hull and Beverley Act Book.

1670. Dec. 22. Adm'on of John Marshall of Scarborough to Francis Thompson his brother and principal creditor.[3]

The following adm'on and will are from the Consistory Court at York, Book "Dawes," (1714—1724.)

Fo. 110. 1719. April 3. Adm'on of Michael Marshall of Selby, gent., to Lucy Marshall his relict.[4]

Fo. 154. Thomas Marshall of the parish of St. Mary's Bishophill jun'r., Linen-weaver. Dated 8 Oct., 1709. Wife Althea Marshall executrix. Mother Elizabeth Marshall. Sister Deborah Marshall. Kinsman William Addinell, and his sister Elizabeth Addinell. Proved by relict 21 May, 1722.

EXTRACTS FROM VARIOUS REGISTERS.

(*Continued from Vol. i, p. 246.*)

1576. Dec. 30. Marcholl (*sic*) son of Mr. John Marshall citizen of London. Buried. *Little Missenden, Bucks.*

1623. July 29. Thomas Marshall and Elizabeth Lunde. Married.

1658. July 17. John Teasdale of the parish of Whixley and Dorothy Marshall of this parish. Married.

} *Little Ouseburn, co. York.*

[1] *See* Vol. i, p. 304.
[2] *See* Vol. i, p. 302.
[3] *See* Vol. i, p. 315.
[4] *See* Vol. i, pp. 310, 327.

1744. Aug. 1. Sara Marshall. Buried.
1784. June 27. Richard Marshall and Elizabeth Walker, married.
1806. Sept. 1. John Marshall and Hannah Rayner, married.
Bilsthorpe co. Notts.

1703. May 16. Thomas son of William[1] and Elizabeth Marshall was baptised. *Abbot's Morton, co. Worcester.*

1654. July 25. Leonard son of Leonard and Rachael Marshall was baptised.
1678. Oct. 8. William Marshall, singleman, and Francis Davye, singlewoman, both of Beccles, were married.
1692. Feb. 13. Elizabeth wife of Timothy Marshall was buried.
Beccles, co. Suffolk.

1676. M[rs] Ann Marshall widdow was burryed September the twenty third.
1690. Jane daughter of Thomas Marshall, bapt. Sept. 20.
Walton in the Vale, co. Nottingham.

1683. Oct. 21. Thomas Marshall and Susanna Graves, both of Cambridge, married. *Milton, near Cambridge.*

1705. John Marshall the son of John Marshall was born Nov. 16; Mary Marshall the mother of this child, buried Nov. 20; John the son, buried 23 Nov.
1707. Benjamin Marshall a child, buried April 4.
1743-4. John Marshall, buried Jan. 23.
1753. Hannah Marshall, buried Sept. 17.
1744-5. Charles Rowell and Eliz. Marshall, married Jan. 3.
Wing co. Rutland.

1614. George Marshall of Cayes College, buried Jan. 20. *St. Michael's, Cambridge.*

1637. John Marshalle, Gent., and Alee Pepys, 17 July. Married. *Cottenham, co. Cambridge.*

1539. Nov. 20. Tho. Marshall and Isbell Horsman. Married. *Maxey, co. Northampton.*

1683. Sept. 6. Gyles Marshall and Alice Maye. Married. *Temple in Bristol.*

1630. Gulielmus Marshall puer quidam mendicans natus in Uttoxeter moriens in Catton sepultus fuit decimo die Maii.
1688. Henricus Marshall et Elizabetha Richards de Croxall matrimonium contraxerunt decimo tertio 13° (*sic*) May.
Croxall, co. Derby.

1608. William Marshall and Grace Vickers, married 4 July.
1616. William son of Robert Marshall, bapt. 1 December.
St. Mary de Castro, Leicester.

1656. Robert Marshall buryed Sep. 10. *West Hallam, co. Derby.*

1697. Richard son of Mr. Edw. Marshall, Exciseman, bapt. 11 April. *Ashburne co. Derby.*

1578. Jan. 28. Roger M'shall and Joan Griffeth. Married. *St. Stephens, Bristol.*

[1] Churchwarden in 1702.

1625. July 31. Rob't son of Rob't Marshall, gen. Buried. *Selby, co. York.*

Mrs. Mary Marshall wife of Mr. Joseph Marshall was buried Jan. 23, 1691.
Joseph Marshall buried Dec. 14, 1719.
Elizabeth Marshall relict of Joseph Marshall buried Jan. 5, (*sic*) 1719.
— *Chellaston, co. Derby. (Transcript at Lichfield).*

1625. Nov. 7. William Marshall and Chartery Dalby. Married. *Edith Weston, co. Rutland.*

1713. George Allen of Thurcaston and Eleanor Marshall of Burton super Oldswere by Licence mary'd March 28. — *Thurcaston, co. Leicester.*

1637. Nov. 7. Matthew Rosse and Alice Marshall. Married. *Wakefield, co. York.*

1578. June ... William Pearcey and Agnes Marshall. Married. *Rotherham, co. York.*

1702. Sept. 10. Robert Marshall and Margaret Baker. Married. *Sprotborough, co. York.*

1652. .... Robert Marshall and Frances Wildes. Married. *Blyth, co. Notts.*

1735-6. Feb. 27. Edward Marshall of Whitby, Buried.
1763. April 14. Court Marshall [1] and Hannah Stamper, married.
— *Scarborough, co. York.*

1702. .... Willoughby Methley and Ann Marshall. Married. *Felkirk, co. York.*

1671. Sept. 22. John Roberts of Barnburgh and Jane Marshall of Terrymore. Married.
1686. May 8. John Marshall and Margaret Hoyland. Married.
1694. May 31. Peter Marshall and Grace Marshall. Married.
— *Pontefract, co. York.*

Extracts from Transcripts of Parish Registers at York.

(*Continued from Vol. i, p. 245.*)

1681. Nov. 24. Thomas Darbyshire and Ann Marshill. Married. *Seaton.*
1681. June 28. Laurence Marshall and Jane Hall. Married. *Sancton.*
1681. Sept. 25. Elizabeth Marshell ye daughter of John Marshell. Bapt. *Birdsall.*
1681. March 29. Johannes Martiall et Maria Dewell. Married. *Lund.*
1681. July 26. Richardus Marshall. Buried. *Nunnington.*
1681. Sept. 15. Thomas Marshall and Susanah Gurden. Married. *St. Mary's Hull.*
1681. Dec. 18. William son of John Marshall. Buried. *Ibid.*

[1] His will was proved at York, June, 1782.

1681. May 11. Wm Marshall[1] and Priscilla Pearson. Married. 1681. July 14. Grace wife of Thomas Marshall. Buried. 1681-2. Jan. 4. Jane d. of John Marshal. Bapt. 1681-2. Feb. 27. Jerom Graves and Eliz. Marshall. Married. 1681-2. March 16. Castina w. of Tho. Marshall. Buried.	*Trinity, Hull.*

1683. Dec. 14. Jane Marshall[2] widow was buried. *Tuxford, co. Notts.*

1683. Dec. 18. Frances Marshall, widow. Buried. *Worksop, co. Notts,*

1683. April 10. Richardus Thomson[3] et Elizabetha Marshall, nupt. *Egmanton, co. Notts.*

1682. June 3. Willm Marshal.[4] Buried. *Langar, co. Notts.*

1673. Nov. 18. Franceas do. of Henry Marshall of Blyth. Buried. *Blyth, co. Notts.*

1673. July 21. Mary the daughter of Richard Marshall and Margaret his wife. Bapt. *East Drayton, co. Notts.*

1673. Aug. 9. Margeret the wife of Richard Marshall. Buried. *East Drayton, co. Notts.*

1673. March 16. Will'm ye son of Tho. Marshall and Añe his wife. Bapt. *Flintham, co. Notts.*

1673. Sept. 11. Robart Marshall and Catharine Dodson. Married. *Wilford, co. Notts.*

1673. Nov. 29. John Marshall and Jane Brett. Married. *East Markham, co. Notts.*

1674-5.[5] Feb. 14. Eliz^th dau. of Tho. and Anne Marshall. Bapt. *Whatton in the Vale, co. Notts.*

1674. April 27. Johannes Ley et Helena Marshall. Married. *Kirkby in Ashfield, co. Notts.*

1682. Dec. 22. Richard Marshall of Alverton. Buried. *Staunton, co. Notts.*

1682. Aug. 7. Thomas Marshall and Mary Shiffin. Married. *Normanton on Trent, co. Notts.*

1682. May 24. Anne ye Daughter of James Marshall and Margret his wife. Bapt. Buried 26 June. *Beeston, co. Notts.*

1683. April 4. Jane the daughter of John Marshall and Jane his wife. Bapt. *Kirton, co. Notts.*

1682. July 23. John Owen and Anne Marshall. Married. *Arnold, co. Notts.*

1682. Oct. 5. John Marshall. Buried. *Bulwell, co. Notts.*

1682. Sept. 20. Mary Marshall the daughter of Thomas Marshall, of Gunthorpe. Buried. *Lowdham, co. Notts.*

1674. May 17. Elizabeth Marshall the daughter of John Marshall and of Mary his wife was baptized. *Clifton near Nottingham.*

1674. March 29. John Marshall the son of Thomas Marshall[6] of

[1] See his will Vol. i. p. 279.
[2] See her will Vol. i. p. 118.
[3] Cf. a mar. Lic. Vol. i. p. 142.
[4] See his will Vol. i. p. 297.
[5] The return for this year is in the hand-writing of and signed by Gervas Marshall.
[6] See his will Vol. i. p. 309.

Garthorpe and Mary his wife begotten in fornication and borne in Wedlocke, Bapt. *Lowdham, co. Notts.*

1674-5. Feb. 5. Ann ye wife of Daniel Marshall. Buried. *Cossall, co. Notts.*

1682. July 13. Ann ye daughter of William Marshall. Bapt. *Ratcliffe on Trent, co. Notts.*

1674. April 22. Daniel ye sonn of William Marshall and Elizabeth his wife was baptized.
1674. Dec. 25. Elizabeth ye wife of William Marshall was buried.
1674-5. March 20. Daniel Marshall was buried.
Tythby, co. Notts.

1682. July 30. Mary Marshall ye wife of William Marshall. Buried. *Sutton on Trent, co. Notts.*

1682. Richard Marchshall sone of Richard, baptised apiarill ye 2. *Flawborough, co. Notts.*

1682. Dec. 9. Ralph ye sonne of Rob't Marshall. Bapt.
1682. Oct. 17. John Orrell and Hannah Marshall both of this p'ish. Married.
Mansfield, co. Notts.

1662. June 22. Anthony the sonne of Anthony Marshall, bapt. *Plumptree, co. Notts.*

1663. Sept. 12. Mary Marshall the daughter of Lawrence Marshall and of Ann his wife. Bapt. *Kinolton, co. Notts.*

1665. Aug. 15. Bryan Marshall son of Bryan. Bapt. Buried 25 Aug. following.
1665-6. Jan. 3. William Marshall. Buried.
1671. Nov. 12. Bryan Marshall. Buried.
Scrooby, co. Notts.

1664. Oct. 2. Abraham the son of Abraham Marchell and Mercie his wife. Bapt. *Bawtry, co. Notts.*

1665. Sept. 22. John Marshall and Mary Simson. Married. *Basford, co. Notts.*

1661. April 16. John the sonne of Hughe Cartwright, and Ales the daughter of Will'm Marshall were baptized.
Laxton, co. Notts.

1664. Dec. 21. Andrew Marshall. Buried.
1665-6. Jan. 21. John Marshall son of Lawrence Marshall. Bapt.
Kinolton, co. Notts.

1664. Oct. 18. Thomas Marshall and Anne Coozens. Married. *Normanton on Trent, co. Notts.*

1672. Oct. 15. Will'm Marshall and Eliza: Fox. Married. *Sturton cum Fenton, co. Notts.*

1672-3. Feb. 18. Anne Marshall of Spitlehill in the parish of Clareborough. Buried. *West Retford, co. Notts.*

1664. July 24. Augustus and John the sons of Jaruis Marshall. Bapt.
1664. Sept. 18. Ann the wife of Jaruis Marshall. Buried. *North Collingham, co. Notts.*

1665. Jan. 2. Hellin dau. of William Marshall. Buried.
1665. Jan. 31. Ann dau. of William Marshall. Bapt.
Laxton, co. Notts.

1665. July 4. Katherine wife of John Marshall. Buried. *Basford, co. Notts.*

1664. April 8. Silvester son of Skillen Marshall and Anne his wife. Bapt. 1664-5. March 21. Jane Marshall, vidua. Buried. 1665. June 13. Silvester son of Thomas Marshall and Anne his wife. Bapt.	}	*Sutton on Trent, co. Notts.*

1665-6. Jan. 25. William son of Francis Marshall. Bapt. *Mattersey, co. Notts.*

1661-2. Feb. 28. Robert Marshall of North Marnham. Buried. *Marnham, co. Notts.*

1665. March 29. Elizab. Marshall de Newarke, Gen. and vid. Buried. *Balderton, co. Notts.*

1663. Nov. 6. Thomas Marshall. Buried. 1663. July 2. Robert Marshall and Elizabeth Clayton. Married. 1664. April 7. Mary dau. of Robert Marshall and Elizabeth. Bapt. 1664. April 9. Mary an infant yᵉ daughter off Robert Marshall and Elizabeth his wife. Buried. 1665. May 3. Mary dau. of Robert Marshall and Elizabeth. Bapt. 1672. April 8. Robert the son of Robert Marshall and Elizabeth his wife. Bapt.	}	*Kinton, co. Notts.*

1663-4. Jan. 26. Ann yᵉ daughter of Geo. Marshall was buried. *Treswell, co. Notts.*

1664. Nov. 29. Robert Marshall and Elizabeth Barton both of this parish. Married. *Marnham, co. Notts.*

1663. Oct. 18. Thomas the son of Thomas Marshall. Bapt. 1686. April 1. Anne Marshall, widow. Buried.	}	*Flintham, co. Notts.*

1686. Nov. 16. Thomas Marshall. Buried. *Bawtry, co. Notts.*

1691. July 12. John Marshall and Sarah Kithin. Married. *Clarborough, co. Notts.*

1689. Nov. 14. Francis Morton and Frances Marshall. Married. 1690. Nov. 23. Frances yᵉ wife of Fran. Morton. Buried.	}	*Ollerton, co. Notts.*

1689. May 25. Ann dau. of Henry Marshall. Bapt. Buried, June 30. *Laxton, co. Notts.*

1688. Nov. 22. Robert Marshall of Gresthorp in yᵉ parish of Sutton, Butcher, and Elizabeth Porter of the same. Married. *West Markham, co. Notts.*

1715-16 Jan. 22. Benjamin Buttery and Eliz. Marshal. Married. *Worksop, co. Notts.*

1715. July 13. Thomas son of Robert Marshall. Bapt. *Walesby, co. Notts.*

1689-90. March 8. Marshal yᵉ daughter of Geo. Bower. Bapt. *Worksop, co. Notts.*

1638. Dec. 16. Richard son of Henry Marshall and Elizabeth his wife of Blyth. Bapt. *Blyth, co. Notts.*

1711. Ruth Marshall was Buryed ye 12th of Aprill. *Maltby, co. York.*

1598. June 26. Francis Oglethorpe, gent., and Elizabeth Marshall, widow. Married. *Rothwell, co. York.* *See* Mar. Lic. Vol. i, p. 79.

1539. Oct. 14. Elizabeth daughter of Richard Marciall. Bapt. *Rothwell, co. York.*

EXTRACTS FROM PARISH REGISTERS.

(Continued from Vol. i, p. 245.)

KNARESBOROUGH, CO. YORK.

1568. Joh'es Webster and M'gar' M'shall, married, Nov. 21.
1576. ......(?) Marshall, buried, Mar. 26.
1608. Rob't Marshall of Gyslow and M'gr. Foster (?), married, Nov. 21.
1611. Ralf filius Miles Marshall, bapt, Ap'l 10.
1619. Rob't M'shall and Dorothy Catterson, married, Feb. 6.
1624. Henry M'shall and Mary Woude, married, Nov. 18.
1629. Helena fil. Roger Marshall, bapt. May 27.
1631. Matilda fil. same bapt. May 11.
1633. Joh'es fil same bapt. Jan'y 23.
1635. Elizab. fil. same bapt. Ap'l 19.
1657. .... wife of Thomas Marshall, buried, Dec. 5.
1669. Xpophorus Marshall and Dorothea Yorke, married, Aug. 24.
1674. Brian Marshall and Anna Burton, married, Sept. 2.
1676. Christopher Gibson and Sarah Marshall, married, Nov. 30.
1691. Maria fil. Tho. Marshall, bapt. Nov. 3.
1693. Henric Addinall and Sarah Marshall, married, Sept. 6.
1693. Tho. fil. Tho. Marshall, buried, Jany 27.
1695. Maria fil. Tho. Marshall, buried, Nov. 1.
1698. Martha fil. Tho. Marshall, bapt. Sep. 29.
1700. Joh'es Simpson and Sarah Marshall, married, Feb. 5.

See subsequent entries, vol, i, p. 243.

DONCASTER, CO. YORK. (Vol. i, app. 6.)

Marriages.

1564. Oct. 8. Richard Marshall and Joan Grave.
1570. Oct. 23. William Barton and Elizabeth Marshall.
1571. May 14. Steven Marshall and Dionis Craven.
1575. Oct. 2. Christopher Loryman and Jennet Marshall.
1583. Sept. 2. William Wood and Agnes Marshall.
1588. Sept. 16. Stephen Marshall and Christine Cowburne.
1593. Oct. 16. John Ellyson and Alice Marshall.
1595. March 10. William Donnell and Elizabeth Marshall.
1608. July 17. John Marshall and Joan Sandes.
1680. May 21. Peter Marshall and Elizabeth Scola. [*i.e* Scholey.]
1683. Feb. ... . Marshall and ....
1696. July 12. Gilbert Inkersell and Sara Marshall.

MILTON CLEVEDON, CO. SOMERSET.

1608. Robert Coolles and Briget Marshall, married. Oct. 6.[1]
1616. Richard Marshall, Vicar, buried. May 24.
1616. Ambrose Marshall and Margaret Peine, married. Nov. 3.
1617. Richard son of Ambrose Marshall, bapt. Sept. 21.
1619. Ambrose son of Ambros Marshall, bapt. Sept. 12. (Ambrose Marshall was churchwarden this year.)
1621. Katherin dau. Ambrose Marshall and Mary were bap. Dec. 9. *Twins?*
1622. Katherin Marshall, buried. 22 Jan.
1623. Ambrose Marshall *Junior?* buried. June 11.
[No Register from 1629-1672.]
1675. May 18. Tho's Hodges and Francis Marshall, married.[2]

ST. MARY CASTLEGATE, YORK.

1619-20. Feb. 6. Mary d. of Christopher Marshall, bapt.
1621. July 11. Nicholas Goldsborough of Flixborough parish in Lincolnshire and Elizabeth Marshall servant to Bartil Banester, married.
1625-6. Jan. 10. Roger Johnson and Anne Marshall, married.
1625-6. Feb. 28. Stephen Marshall prisoner at the Castle, buried.
1634. July 21. Jane wife of Robert Marshall, buried.
1635. June 16. Robert son of Robert Marshall, bapt.
1643. July 5. Robert Marshall who died at John Hutchinson's, buried.
1644. June 11. Margaret Marshall, buried.
1682-3. March 12. George son of Arthur Marshall, bapt.
1693. Dec. 31. Thomas Marshall and Susannah Rowntree, married.
1695. July 2. Thomas Marshall and Susannah Smith, married.
1698. April 21. John Marshall, executed, buried.
1797. May 24. Catherine Marshall, Widow, aged 80, buried.

SCARRINGTON, CO. NOTTINGHAM.

1697. April, 16. Sarah d. of Wm Bush, bapt.
1698. Oct. 20. Benjamin s. of Thomas Marshall, bapt.
1700-1. March 7. Winifrith d. of Thomas Marshall, bapt.
1702-3. March 22. Thomas s. of Matthew Hall, bapt.
1703. Nov. 21. Martin s. of Thomas and Winyfrith Marshall, bapt.
1706. Nov. 25. John Caunt of Bridgford and Mary Marshall, married.
1707. Dec. 4. Thomas Marshall, buried.
1708. April 7. Elizabeth wife of Wm Bush, buried.
1728. Augt. 18. Hannah Hall, buried.

BARTON IN FABIS, CO. NOTTINGHAM.

Baptisms.

1583. Feb. 9. Margaret d. of Francis Marshall.
1586. Sept. 11. George s. of same.

[1] 1610. Grace dau. of Robert Colles, Bapt. Apr. 30. 1608. Wm Clarke and Alice Coolles, Married. Feb. 27.

[2] 1676. June 18. Tho's son of Tho's and Francis Hodges. Bapt. Buried, Dec. 11.

1607. Dec. 19. Francis s. of Thomas Marshall.
1610. Nov. 4. Anne d. of same.
1612. Oct. 17. Tabitha d. of same.
1614. Sept. 4. Marshall s. of William Woodward.
1614-5. March 8. Marie d. of Thomas Marshall.
1616. June 24. Thomas s. of same.
1618. May 14. Dorraty d. of Hew Marshall.
1619. June 27. John s. of Thomas Marshall.
1619-20. March 19. Elizabeth d. of Heugh Marshall.
1621. March 17. Elizabeth d. of Thomas Marshall.
1622. Sept. 1. Ales d. of Hew Marshall.
1624. Jan. 23. Ane d. of same.
1624-5. March 13. Dorcas d. of Thomas Marshall.
1628. July 5. John s. of Hew Marshall.
1628-29. Jan. 18. Rowlland s. of Thomas Marshall.
1640. April 6. Joyce d. of Francis Marshall and Mary his wife.
1642. July 10. Theodosia d. of same
1643. April 5. Theodosia d. of same. *Buried.*
1649. April 24. Mary d. of Francis Marshall.
1652. Feb. 6. Thomas s. of same.
1654. ...... Hugh s. of John Marshall.
1655. July 8. Elizabeth d. of Francis Marshall.
1657. June 11. Anne d. of same.
1657-8. Jan. 24. Mary d. of John Marshall.
1661. Feb. 12. John s. of same.
1674. Nov. 17. Anne d. of Thomas Marshall.
1682. Oct. 5. Francis s. of same.
1686. Aug. 22. Elizabeth d. of John Marshall and Ellen his wife.
1686. Jan. 26. William s. of Thomas Marshall and Mary his wife.
1687. Jan. 24. Steven s. of John Marshall the younger and Ellen.
1689. Nov. 5. John s. of John Marshall,
1691. Jan. 19. Ellin d. of John Marshall.
1696. Dec. 6. Alys d. of John Marshall and Ellen.
1698. March 22. Mary d. of John and Ellin Marshall.
1701. March 17. Thomas s. of John Marshall.
1717. Aug. 1. Elioner d. of Stephen Marshall and Anne.
1720. Feb. 12. Jane d. of same.
1726. Sept. 18. John s. of same.
1729. Dec. 11. Stephen s. of same.
1752. Nov. 18. Ann d. of Stephen and Hannah Marshall.
1756. Jan. 25. Jane d. of same.
1759. March 4. John s. of same.
1760. Oct. 26. Hannah d. of same.
1763. May 29. Stephen s. of same.
1764. Nov. 11. Hannah d. of same.
1766. June 8. Thomas s. of same.
1768. May 8. Thomas s. of same.
1770. Sept. 30. William s. of same. "The same infant buried Oct. 2."

Marriages.

1 Eliz. May 11. Robert Hallam and Agnes Marshall.

1602. June 26. Henry Dunne and Anne Martiall.
1611. Nov. 30. William Winfield and Elizebeth Marshall.
1628. April 21. William *Gad* (?) and An Marshall.
1633. ...... William Thorpe and Tabitha Marshall.
1685. Nov. 1. John Marshall bach^lr^ and Ellen Elliot spins^tr^.
1723. Nov. 12. Thomas Hopwell of Widmerpole and Mary Marshall of Barton.
1737. Nov. 28. John Stubs of Stanton on the Wolds and Eleanor Marshall.
1746. April 5. Thomas Cooper and Elizabeth Marshall.

Burials.

1647. July 30. Jane wife of Hugh Marshall.
1653. June 30. Hugh Marshall.
1660. May 30. Thomas Marshall.
1664. March 29. Richard s. of John Marshall.
1665. April 29. Richard s. of John Marshall. (*sic*).
1668. March 15. Francis Marshall.
1673. March 12. Mary [1] wife of Francis Marshall.
1680. March 4. Francis s. of Thomas Marshall.
1683. Jan. 14. Alice wife of John Marshall dyed Sunday 13 Jan.
1687. April 8. Mary wife of Thomas Marshall died 6 Ap.
1700. May 6. John Marshall.
1716. Feb. 7. Elionor wife of John Marshall.
1728. May 8. John Marshall, infant.
1732. Feb. 12. Francis Marshall. (baptized Feb. 11).
1738. Nov. 26. William Marshall.
1747. Oct. 18. John Marshall, Esqr. [2]
1751. Oct. 6. Mrs Ann Marshall Widow of John Marshall, Esq.
1754. June 2. Mrs Ann Sacheverel.[3]
1754. Oct. 2. Mrs Ann Clifton, Widow.[3]
1758. Jan. 1. Ann Wife of Stephen Marshall
1761. April 17. Hannah d. of Stephen and Hannah Marshall.
1765. Dec. 20. Hannah d. of same.

[1] In transcript at York :—1673-4. Mary w^o^ of Francis Marshall. Buried 9 March.

[2] On the south side of the chancel at Barton, on the floor :—

Here lyeth the Body
Of John Marshall, Esq.
Captain in the Royal
Regiment of English
Fuzillers *(sic)* who Departed
this life Octob^r^ 15th, 1747.
Aged 69 Years.

His will as John Marshall, Esq., Captain Lieutenant in the Royal Regiment of English Fuzileers, is dated 5 Oct., 1747. To be interred in the parish church of Barton, co. Nottingham or in the chancel there, at the discretion of wife Ann Marshall, and appoints her executrix. Mentions daughter Elizabeth wife of Mr. Charles Hodges of Nottingham, surgeon. Proved in Exchequer Court at York, 28 Oct., 1747. (Vol. 90, fo. 165).

[3] Two adjoining stones record that, Anne relict of Robert Sacheverell, and dau. of Thomas Marshall of this place, gentleman, died 28 May, 1754, aged 80; and Anne wife of George Clifton, Esq. and dau. of Robert Sacheverell, Esq., by Anne his wife, died 2 Oct. 1754, aged 41. (Fox's History of Morley, p. 57). These still remain, 1884.

1767. April 17. Thomas s. of Stephen and Hannah Marshall
1769. Sept. 20. Stephen Marshall.
1776. July 18. Stephen Marshall.

WINTERINGHAM, CO. YORK.

Baptisms.

1576. Will'm M^r^shall the sonne of Heughe M. was baptised the xxviij^th^ day of July.
1607. Elizabeth Marshall the davght' of Will'm Marshall was baptised the xviij^th^ of June a^o^ p^r^dicto.
1609. Margareete Marshall the davght' of John Marshall was baptised the xviij of August a^o^ p^r^dicto.
1612. Anne Mershell the davghter of John M. was bapt. the xvi^th^ daye of August Anno p^r^dicto.
1618. Elizabeth Marshall the davghter of John of Wint'ingh'm bapt^d^ the xvi^th^ daye of August Anno p'dict.
1637. Laurence ye sonne of Margret Marshall was baptised, 3 Sept.
1644. Thomas the sonne of Marmaduke Marshall bapt. Jan. xiiij.
1648. ffrancis the sonne of Will'm Marshall bapt. March xxix.
1672. Elizabeth the daught. of Willi' Marshall was baptized ffebruary...
1677. George ye sonne of Willi' Marshall bapt. July xxix^th^.
1682. John the sonne of Francis Marshall bap. October viij^th^.
1686. Francis the son of Francis Marshall was baptised January xvj^th^.
1688. An the daughter of Francis Marshill baptized December ix^th^.

Marriages.

1558. Willm Watson & Margaret Marshall were married viij^th^ of Maie.
1566. Heughe M^r^shall & Margaret beuley were married the third of November.
1606. Will'm Marshall & Catherine his Wiffe was married the xxv^th^ day of Maye a^o^ p^r^dicto.
1607. John Mershell and Mary Wav'ller was maryed the xxviii day of Maye a^o^ p^r^dict'.

Ralphe Halliday of ye towne and p'ishe of Ampleforth and An Mershell of Wintringha' were Solemnely Married at o^r^ p'ishe Church in Wintringha' ye 17 day of Nove'ber 1657, by me John Bandinell, Minist.

Will'm Dring Register.

1635. Marmaduke Marshall & Ann Read were marryed ye 22th of November.
1637. Thos Ys^r^wood & Margret Marshall married 17th Novemb.
1664. William Mershell & Barbary Spendely weere married xxv^th^ day of October.
1667. Bartholemew Allen and Elizabeth Marshall weere married Aprill xvj^th^ 1667.

Burials.

1558. Rowland M^r^shall was buried the vi^th^ day of December.
1571. John M^r^shall was buried the xxiiij^th^ day of March.
,, John M^r^shall was buried the vj^th^ of June.
,, Thomas M^r^shall was buried the xxiij day of June.

1575. Kateryne M^{r}shall was buried the second day of March.
1599. Rychard Marschall seivant to Robt. Rychardson was buried the ffirst daye of Marche.
1608. Hugh Mershell was buryed the xxixth of March anno p^{r}dicto.
1618. Ann Marshall the da. of John of Winteringham buried the xxviijth of ffebruarye Anno p^{r}dict.
„ Anne Marshall the da. of Will'm buryed the xxix Aprill Anno predict.
1634. William Marshall of Knapton was buried the iiij day of ffebruarie.
1636. Mary Marshall ye wife of John Marshall was burried the tenth day of Aprill.
„ Elizabeth Marshall the da. of John M. was buried the xxvjth day of June.
1657. Marmaduke Mershell buried the vth day of July.[1]
1663. Elizebeth Marshall Widdow was buried May ye viijth.
1668. Thomas Marshall was buried March viijth.
1679. William Marshall was buried September ijth.
1688. James Mar... was buried Aprill...

WHITBY, CO. YORK, 1600 TO 1795.

Baptisms.

1657.	Nov. 6th.	Wm Marshall, Son of Thos.
1659.	Dec. 5th.	Jno Marshall, Son of Ja^{s}.
1684.	Aug. 16th.	Elezth Marshall, D^{tr} of W^{m}.
1685.	Jan. 17th.	Thos Marshall, Son of W^{m}.
1687.	April 10th.	Wm Marshall, Son of Timothy.
„	Sept. 25th.	Jane Marshall, D^{tr} of W^{m}.
1688.	Aug. 19th.	Math^{w} Marshall, S. of Tim^{thy}.
1690.	Sept. 21st.	Elezth Marshall, D. of Tim^{thy}.
1692.	Aug. 25th.	Mary Marshall, D. of Thos.
„	Oct. 30th.	Henry Marshall, S. of Tim^{thy}.
1693.	Feb. 18th.	Jane Marshall, D. of Robt.
1694.	Mar. 19th.	John Marshall, S. of Thos.
1695.	June 2nd.	Ellis Marshall, D. of Francis, of Saltwick.
„	Nov. 10th.	Thos Marshall, S. of Tim^{thy}.
1696.	Jan. 26th.	Mary Marshall, D. of Robt.
„	Mar. 1st.	Jane Marshall, D. of Thos.
1697.	Nov. 14th.	Jane Marshall, D. of Tim^{thy}.
1698.	Jan. 30th.	Abigal Marshall, D. of Robt.
1699.	Aug. 27th.	Ellen Marshall, D. of Ja^{s}.
1700.	May 19th.	Henry Marshall, S. of Thos.
„	July 28th.	Hester Marshall, D. of Tim^{thy}.
1701.	Oct. 5th.	Thos Marshall, S. of Thos.
„	Mar. 1st.	Math^{w} Marshall, S. of Robt.

[1] Will dated 29 June 1651 (P.C.C. Ruthen 335). To be buried at Wintringham. Debts owed testator by William Marshall of Wharham. John Marshall minister of Skirtenbeck. Wife Ann Marshall. Son Thomas "but young." Daughter Lucy wife of John Duncan of West Heslerton. Admon. to relict 4 Septr 1657.

1703.	Nov. 7th.	Wm Marshall, S. of Thos.
1704.	Jan. 4th.	Mary Marshall, D. of Jas.
1720.	May 17th.	Robt Marshall, S. of Mathw.
1731.	June 6th.	Wm Marshall, S. of Robt.
„	July 4th.	Paul Marshall, S. of Mathw.
1732.	April 2nd.	Ann Marshall, D. of Henry.
„	May 7th.	Rebeccah Marshall, D. of Mathw.
1742.	Dec. 1st.	Mary Marshall, D. of Wm, Fisherman.
1744.	Jan. 6th.	Willm Marshall, S. of Wm, Fisherman.
1751.	Nov. 3rd.	John Marshall, S. of Mathw, Sailor.
1752.	May 10th.	Josph Marshall, S. of Wm, Shoemaker.
1754.	Dec. 30th.	Robt. Marshall, S. of Mathw, Carpenter.
1758.	May 19th.	Mary Marshall, Dtr of Mathw, born 20th Apl last.
„	July 29th.	Mathw Marshall, S. of Mathw, Sailor.
1763.	Aug. 21st.	John Marshall, S. of Robt, Currier.
„	Oct. 23rd.	Jane Marshall, Dtr of the late Mathw.
1765.	Aug. 18th.	Thos Marshall, S. of Thos, Joiner, born 9th July.
1766.	Dec. 25th.	Robt Marshall, S. of Robt. Farmer, born 8th July.
1784.	Feb. 2nd.	Wm Marshall, S. of Robt. Born Jany 28th.
1785.	Dec. 21st.	Peggy Marshall, D. of Jno & Elenor, Labourer.
„	July 10th.	Ann Marshall, D. of Robt & Jane, Boat Br.
1791.	Nov. 10th.	Wm Marshall, S. of Robt & Jane, Carpenter.

Marriages.

1658.	Jan. 9th.	Jas Marshall, to Abigal Gardner.
1685.	June 22nd.	Timthy Marshall, to Elezth Dode.
1689	Nov. 25th.	Robt Marshall, to Margt Whitwell.
1692.	June 12th.	Ann Marshall, Pickering, to Geo. Longstaff.
1698.	Nov. 17th.	Jas Marshall, to Mary Tiplady.
1700.	Oct. 3rd.	Ralph Marshall, to Ann Boles.
1730.	Nov. 2nd.	Robt Marshall, to Hannah Fotherlay.
1735.	Nov. 13th.	Wm Marshall, to Ann Calvert.
1739.	Sept. 23rd.	Wm Marshall, to Elezth Thorp.
„	Nov. 6th.	Wm Marshall, to Dinah Coatham.
1743.	July 10th.	Biggan Marshall, to Jno Harwood.
1756.	Aug. 25th.	Wm Marshall, to Jane Robinson, Widow.
1757.	Jan. 10th.	Ann Marshall, to Henry Allaley, Sailor.
„	Dec. 3rd.	Mathw Marshall, to Alice Sleightholme, Widow.
1762.	May 12th.	Robt Marshall, to Sarah Dobson.
„	Nov. 28th.	Henrtta Marshall, to Jas Lane, Husbandman.
1763.	Mar. 27th.	Ann Marshall, to Benjn Stephenson, Barber.
1764.	Dec. 1st.	Jane Marshall to Wm Croft.
1769.	Aug. 8th.	Sarah Marshall, to Wm Kingston.
1774.	Feb. 19th.	Robt Marshall, Labr. to Sarah Bennison.
„	Dec. 31st.	John Marshall, Sailor, to Susannah Richardson.
1776.	Oct. 24th.	Elizth Marshall, to Benjn Cook.
1779.	Feb. 6th.	Deborah Marshall, to Jno Dinsdale.
„	Feb. 20th.	Mary Marshall, to Roderick Sinclair.
1795.	Nov. 7th.	Jno Marshall, Attorney, to Ann Dale.

Burials.

1660.	Nov. 19th.	Margt Marshall, Wife of Thos.
1676.	Mar. 9th.	Ann Marshall, Widdow.
1681.	Mar. 7th.	Isabel Marshall, Daughter of Jas.
1686.	Aug. 19th.	Mary Marshall.
1687.	Nov. 14th.	Wm Marshall, Son of Timthy.
1696.	May 15th.	Elles Marshall, Daughter of Francis.
,,	Sept. 3rd.	Thos Marshall, Son of Timthy.
,,	Dec. 9th.	Francis Marshall, Son of Francis.
1704.	Aug. 30th.	Wm Marshall, Son of Thos.
,,	Nov. 25th.	Jane Marshall, Dtr of Thos.
1740.	Jan. 7th.	Elezth Marshall. Widow.
1752.	Aug. 13th.	Timthy Marshall, Cobbleman.
1753.	Sept. 2nd.	Margt Marshall, Widow.
1757.	May 3rd.	Henry Marshall, Son of Mathw, Fisherman,
1759.	June 19th.	Mathw Marshall, Senr, Sailor.
,,	Sept. 19th.	John Marshall, Flaxdresser.
1762.	Feb. 23rd.	Susanna Marshall, Widow.
1764.	Feb. 7th.	John Marshall, Son of Robt, Currier.
1767.	Nov. 29th.	Ann Marshall, Widow. Aged 70.
1783.	Sept. 30th.	Robt Marshall, Innkeeper. Aged 49.
1784.	Aug. 12th. Infant.	Wm Marshall, Son of Robt & Jane, Boatbuilder.
1785.	Jan. 11th.	Peggy Marshall, Dtr of John & Honor, Labr.
1786.	Oct. 19th.	Robt Marshall, Son of Robt & Elezth, Sailor. Aged 10 Mths.

Holme on Spalding moor, co. York.

1719.	Oct. 17th.	Mary dtr of Isaac Marshall. Bapt.
,,	Oct. 17th.	Mary wife of Isaac Marshall. Buried.
,,	Decr 21st.	Mary dtr of Isaac Marshall. Buried.
1724.	April 28th.	John son of Isaac Marshall. Bapt.
,,	April 30th.	John son of Isaac Marshall. Buried.
1725.	May 23rd.	Frances dtr of Isaac Marshall. Bapt.
1726-7	Feby 12th.	James son of Isaac Marshall. Bapt.
1745.	Augt 21st.	Thomas Marshall a farmer. Buried.

Harswell, co. York.

1731.	Bapt.	Isaac ye son of Isaac and Frances Marshall, March ye 18th.
1733.	Buried.	John ye son of Isaac & Frances Marshall, July ye 31st.
1734.	Bapt.	Rebecca ye Daughter of Isaac & Frances Marshall, April ye 21th.
1742.	Buried.	Frances the Daughter of Isaac and Frances Marshal, May ye 28th.
1755.	Bapt.	William the son of Isaac Marshall, May 12th.
1756.	Bapt.	James the son of Isaac Marshall, Junr, Augt 22d.

1763. Buried. Isaac Marshall, Farmer, 8 May.[1]
1764. Buried. Frances the widow of Isaac Marshall, Farmer, Jany 9.
,, Bapt. Thomas son of John Marshall, 29 Jan^y.

Marriages.

1762. March 9. Matthew Marshall of this parish and Isabella Ireland of this parish—by licence.
1764. March 15. John Marshal of this parish and Mary Ireland of this parish—by licence.
1798. Octr 29. Ralf Jackson and Isabella Marshall both of the parish of Harswell.

GAMSTON, CO. NOTTS.

1617. James Martiall the sonn of James was baptised the xii^th of October.
1620. Denzill Marshall the sonne of James Marshall was baptised October the xxi^th.
1624. Francis Marshall sonne of James Marshall, baptised ye 29th of June.
1721. Mary ye daughter of Francis Marshall and Mary his wife was baptized Oct. ye 15th.

EGTON, NEAR WHITBY, CO. YORK.

1628. Maria filia Roberti Marshall bap. 27 die Jan.
1629. Elizabeth filia...... Marshall bap. 22 die J ......
1629. ...... fili ...... Radulphi Marshall bap. 6 die Januarii.[2]
1630. Elizabeth filia John Marshall bap. 6 die Septembris.
1634. Thomas filius Radulphi Marshall bap. 14 die Septemb^r.
1636. Lurwis (?) filia Georgii Marshall bap. 20 die Octobris.
1637. Tho. filius John Marshall bap. 8 die Januarij.
1624. Margaret Marshall sepult. 15 die Aprilis.
1627. Petrus Marshall sepult. 5 die Jan.
1629. Anne Marshall sepult. 9 die Augusti.
1630. Robt Marshall sepu. 8 die Jan.
1634. Thomas filius Radulphi Marshall sep. 12 die Feb.
1635. Elizabeth Marshall vid. sepul. 6 die July.
1635. Robert Marshall maritus sepul. 5 die februa.
1636. Willm Marshall senex sepu^l. 3 die July.
1642. Jane Marshall Vidua sepulta est.. ...
1771. Nov. 16. Mary Marshall Widow aged 100 buried.

RAMPTON, CO. NOTTS.

Baptisms.

1566. George, son of William Marshall, Dec. 9.
1595. John, son of Christopher Marshall, Jan. 13.
1596. Elizabeth, dau^r of Christopher Marshall, Nov. 14.

[1] Will dated 24 Feb., 1763, proved in Exchequer Court at York 23 May following (vol. 107, fo. 359), in which he is described as—Isaac Marshall at Harswell, in the East Riding of the Co. of York. Testator mentions his sons, James Marshall, Isaac Marshall, and Mathew Marshall,—Rebeckah Corner the wife of Robert Corner my daughter,—Appoints his wife Frances Marshall and son John Marshall ex'x and ex'or and residuary legatees. Witnesses, John Calverly, and John Wisker.

[2] *See* as to charities at Egton by Ralph and Paul Marshall, Lawton's 'Rerum, p. 481.

1599. Francis and William, sons of Christopher Marshall, Nov. 18.
1602. William, son of Robert Marshall, May 13th.
1603. Hellen, daur. of Christopher Marshall, March 24.
1604. John, son of William Marshall, Sept. 12.
1605. Margaret, daur. of William Marshall, Feb. 9th.
1609. Robert, son of Christopher Marshall, June 6th.
1609. Elizabeth, daur. of William Marshall, Jan. 11th.
1609. Anne, daur. of Robert Marshall, Feb. 6th.
1611. Gertrude, daur. of William Marshall, Dec. 8th.
1612. Robert, son of Robert Marshall, Oct. 20th.
1615. Catherine, daur. of Robert Marshall, Dec. 3rd.
1620. Robert, son of John Marshall, Aug. 9.
1622. Gervas, son of John Marshall, Dec. 10th.
1625. Henry, son of John Marshall, July 22nd.
1630. John, son of John Marshall, April 23rd.
1631. William, son of John Marshall, Nov. 5.
1631. John, son of John Marshall, yeoman, Dec. 25th.
1632. Barbara, daur. of John Marshall, Sept. 23.
1633. Edward, son of John Marshall, by Elizabeth his wife, March ——
1634. William, son of John Marshall, by Frances his wife, July 11th.
1636. Elizabeth, daur. of John and Alice Marshall, Aug. 21th.
1636. Anne, daur. of John and Frances Marshall, Sept. 22nd.
1639. John, son of John and Alice Marshall, March 31st.
1639. William, son of John and Frances Marshall, Sept. 1st.
1642. Mary, daur. of John and Frances Marshall, Aug. 28th.
1656. Robert, son of John the younger and Margaret Marshall, July 3rd.
1657. Mary, daur. of John and Margaret Marshall, Nov. 23rd.
1659. John, son of John and Margaret Marshall, Oct. 3rd.
1663. William, son of William and Jane Marshall, Feb. 8th.
1666. John, son of William and Jane Marshall, June 19th.
1668. George, son of William and Jane Marshall, Aug. 8th.
1673. Gervas, son of William and Elizabeth Marshall, Aug. 7th.
1673. John and William, twins of John and Mary Marshall, Oct. 2nd.
1676. Elizabeth, daur. of William and Elizabeth Marshall, March 4th.
1677. Isabell, daur. of John and Mary Marshall, May 13th.
1690. William, son of Edward and Mary Marshall, Mar. 22nd.
1691. William, son of William and Margaret Marshall, Jan. 1st.
1693. Edward, son of Edward and Mary Marshall, April 22nd.
1695. Thomas, son of Edward and Mary Marshall, Sept. 14th.
1698. Mary, daur. of Edward and Mary Marshall, April 11th.
1700. Elizabeth, daur. of Edward and Mary Marshall, Sept. 3rd.
1703. Mary, daur. of Edward and Mary Marshall, March 31st.
1705. John, son of Edward and Mary Marshall, Aug. 5th.
1709. Elizabeth, daur. of John and Sarah Marshall, Aug. 22nd.
1712. Paul, son of John and Sarah Marshall, May 8th.
1734. George, son of Thomas and Mary Marshall, Aug. 18th.
1735. William, son of John and Grace Marshall, Sept. 11th.
1736. Elizabeth, daur. of Thomas and Mary Marshall, July 14th.
1737. Margaret, daur. of John and Grace Marshall, June 22nd.
1738. Margaret, daur. of John and Grace Marshall, Sept. 11th.
1740. Thomas, son of Thomas and Mary Marshall, Oct. 19th.
1742. Elizabeth, daur. of John and Grace Marshall, March 29th.
1767. Thomas, son of George and Mary Marshall, Aug. 14th.
1777. George, son of George and Mary Marshall, March 29th.

Marriages.

1570. John Marshall and Elizabeth Gully, Feb. 2nd.
1571. Oliver Cottam and Sarah Marshall, Nov. 20th.
1575. Henry Hurdgon and Joan Marshall, Jan. 27th.
1581. Richard Milner and Elizabeth Marshall, Jan. 23rd.
1589. Robert Marshall and Helen Salmon, Sept. 30.
1590. Christopher Marshall and Catherine Justice, Sept. 28.
1603. William Marshall and Sicily Robinson, Nov. 27.
1629. William Dickinson and Margaret Marshall, May 30.

1633. William Peart and Elizabeth Marshall, July 15th.
1639. Robert Walker and Catherine Marshall, July 30.
1645. John Rogers and Gertrude Marshall, June 19.
1649. Edward Gulley and Elizabeth Marshall, May 2nd.
1655. John Marshall and Margaret Ashton.
1688. William Sleeford and Alice Marshall, June 12.
1690. Edward Marshall and Mary Hall, May 1st.
1692. Richard Salmon and Mary Marshall, April 19.
1698. Nicolas Hibberd and Gertrude Marshall, Jan. 27.
1732. John Keyworth and Elizabeth Marshall, July 16.
1766. George Marshall and Mary Butler, Nov. 25.

Burials.

1568. Nicholas, son of William Marshall, Feb. 6th.
1578. Hellen Marshall, Feb. 8.
1587. Originall son of William Marshall, Oct. 13th.
1588. Hellen, wife of William Marshall, June 8th.
1600. Francis, son of *Alexander* Marshall, Oct. 6.
1602. William, son of Robert Marshall, May 19th.
1606. William Marshall, Husbandman, April 13th.[1]
1609. William Marshall, Cottager, June 7th.[1]
1617. Catherine, wife of Christopher Marshall, Sept. 20th.
1626. William, son of Christopher Marshall, Dec. 9th.
1630. William Marshall, Aug. 29th.
1630. Robert, son of Christopher Marshall, Sept. 28th.
1632. Mary, wife of John Marshall, April 2nd.
1632. Christopher Marshall, July 4th.
1635. Robert Marshall, Householder, June 19th.
1635. William, son of John Marshall, Nov. 1st.
1645. William, son of John Marshall, Aug. 12th.
1648. Barbara, daughter of John Marshall, Dec. 5th.
1651. ———, wife of John Marshall, Oct. 11th.
1654. Sicila Marshall, Widow, Sept. 19th.
1657. Mary, daughter of John and Margaret Marshall, Nov. 28th.
1659. John Marshall, buried, May 4th.
1661. John Marshall, June 5th.
1661. John, son of John Marshall, June 10th.
1661. John Marshall, Senr., Feb. 9th.[1]
1662. Jane Marshall, Feb. 26th.
1673. John, son of John and Mary Marshall, Feb. 23rd.
1674. William, son of John and Mary Marshall, Oct. 28th.
1676. William Marshall, Feb. 8th.
1677. Elizabeth Marshall, Widow, March 16th.
1678. Isabell, dau^{r} of John and Mary Marshall, Feb. 2nd.
1688. Mary, wife of John Marshall, March 18th.
1692. William Marshall, son of William and Margaret, Jan. 29th.
1696. John Marshall, Jan. 27th.[1]
1701. Elizabeth, dau^{r} of Edward and Mary Marshall, Sept. 14th.
1703. Margaret, wife of William Marshall, Aug. 16th.
1704. Edward Marshall, March 3rd.
1705. William Marshall, Aug. 28th.[1]
1706. John, son of Edward Marshall, by Mary his wife, Sept. 26th.
1726. Sarah, wife of John Marshall, Jan. 20th.
1727. John Marshall, Senr., Nov.[1]
1730. George Marshall, May 18th.
1737. Margaret, Infant dau^{r} of John and Grace Marshall, June 25.
1738. Elizabeth, dau^{r} of Thomas and Mary Marshall, July 5th.
1760. Mary, wife of Thomas Marshall, March 24th.
1768. Thomas Marshall, Aug. 11th.
1817. George Marshall, June 3rd, aged 85.
1828. Mary Marshall, April 17th, aged 85.
1849. George Marshall, June 29, aged 72.

[1] See Wills of these persons, Vol. I, p. 141.

TUXFORD, CO. NOTTS.

Baptisms.

Ellinor, ye daughter of Thomas and Barbara Marshall, 18 Dec., 1625.
Elizabeth, ye daughter of Abraham and Elizabeth Marshall, 1 Jan., 1628.
George, ye sonn of George and Elizabeth Marshall, 20 August, 1629.
Thomas, the son of George and Elizabeth Marshall, 21 Dec., 1631.
Katherine, the daughter of Thomas and Barbara Marshall, 4 August, 1633.
———, the son of William and Alice Marshall, 13 December, 1634.
Willm. ye sonn of Abraham Marshall, and Elizabeth his wife, 28 Sept. 1634.
Willm. the sonn of Thomas Marshall and Barbara his wife, 22 Nov., 1635.
Elizabeth, the daughter of George Marshall and Elizabeth his wife, 18 December 1636.
Elizabeth, the daughter of Wm. Marshall and Alice his wife, 28 Oct., 1638.
Hester, the daughter of Thomas Marshall and Barbara his wife, 27 March, 1638.
Thomas, the son of George Marshall and Elizabeth his wife, 5 June, 1639.
Ann (Amy ?), the daughter of George Marshall and Elizabeth his wife, 6 March, 1641.
William, the son of William Marshall and Alice his wife, 11 Dec., 1642.
Ann, daughter of William Marshall and Alice his wife, 23 Feb., 1644.
Rosamond, daughter of George Marshall and Elizabeth his wife, 4 March, 1645.
Mary, daughter of James Marshall, 9 July, 1646.
John, son of William Marshall, 30 July, 1646.
Thomas, ye Bastard of Thomas Marshall and Ann Freeman, 28 Nov., 1646.
Harrald, ye son of Thomas Marshall and Jane his wife, 26 Dec., 1651.
Jane Marshall, Jan. 23, 1654 (? Dec. 23, 1653).
Thomas, son of George Marshall, March (?) 22, 1657.
Thomas, son of Thomas Marshall and Jane his wife, 27 Sept., 1657.
Barbara, daughter of Thomas Marshall and Jane his wife, 2 April, 1660.
Jane, daughter of Thomas Marshall and Jane his wife, 2 May, 1663.

Marriages.[2]

John Whitworth and Ann Marshall, 21 May, 1649.
Thomas Sprigge and Elizabeth Marshall, 2 June, 1653.
George Marshall, junr., and Mary Hall, 21 November, 1661.[3]
Thomas Marshall and Mary Brownley, 16 April, 1667.
William Marshall and Elizabeth Sowby, 23 April, 1668.
William Marshall,[4] of Whitwell, and Mary Maior, of Mansfield, 16 June, 1668.
Thomas Fitchet and Mary Marshall, 30 December, 1669.
Thomas Beedam and Jane Marshall, 22 April, 1679.[5]
George Bonnington and Elizabeth Marshall, 25 Nov., 1679.[6]
Robert Maples and Elizabeth Marshall, 6 March, 1688.[6]
John Marshall and Anne Robinson, 28 April, 1706.
Thomas Marshall, of West Drayton, and Elizabeth Cooking, of Tuxford, 11 July, 1730.

Burials, from transcripts of Tuxford Register at York.

1664. Aug. 4. Francis the son of Thomas Marshall.
1665. May 12. Will'm Marshall, Sen.
1671-2. March 8. George Marshall.[7]
1672. Aug. 26. Abraham son of Abraham Marshall.
1672. Nov. 18. George son of George Marshall.
1686. Oct. 29. Abraham Marshall.
1686-7. Feb. 10. William Marshall, Senr.

[2] John Rockley, of Ollerton, and Anne Marshall of Tuxford, were married at Palethorpe, 20 March, 1710.
[3] This marriage is also entered in the transcript of Marnham Register.
[4] Cf. Vol. I., p. 127.
[5] See Mar. Lic., Vol. I., p. 118.
[6] Nov. 22 is date in transcript at York.
[7] Thomas Marshall signs as Churchwarden this year.

The following entries from Tuxford Register are not included in those already given :—

Baptisms.

1627. William, son of Thomas and Barbara Marshall, 13 Nov.
1630. Abraham, son of Abraham and Elizabeth Marshall, 19 Sept.[1]
1631. George, son of Thomas and Barbara Marshall, 15 May.
1641. Thomas, son of William and Alice Marshall, 28 October.
1655. Barbara, daughter of George and Elizabeth Marshall, 29 April.
1659. Jane, daughter of George and Jane Marshall, 19 September.
1662. Anne, daughter of George and Mary Marshall, 11 Sept.
1661. George, son of George and Mary Marshall, 11 (? 21) August.
1665. Anne, daughter of Abraham Marshall, 21 June.[2]
1666. Thomas, son of George and Mary Marshall, 11 August.
1667. Elizabeth, daughter of Abraham Marshall, 21 May.
1667. Elizabeth, daughter of George and Mary Marshall, 1 March.
1667. Elizabeth, daughter of Thomas and Mary Marshall, 24 March.
1669. Elizabeth, daughter of William Marshall, 12 May.
1670. George, son of Thomas Marshall, 12 April.
1670. Abraham, son of Abraham Marshall, 17 June.
1670. George, son of George and Jane Marshall, 8 Sept.
1671. Thomas, son of Thomas and Mary Marshall, 26 June.
1672. Jane, daughter of Abraham Marshall, 15 Oct.
1672. William, son of William and Elizabeth Marshall, 4 March.
1674. Mary, daughter of Thomas and Mary Marshall, 21 May.
1675. Edward, son of Abraham and Anne Marshall, 6 July.
1676. George, son of Thomas and Mary Marshall, 27 April.
1676. Anne, daughter of William and Elizabeth Marshall, 3 Jan.
1680. Thomas, son of Harrold and Mary Marshall, 12 April.
1682. Edward, son of Thomas and Mary Marshall, 18 April.
1682. Mary, daughter of Harrold and Mary Marshall, 6 August.
1684. William, son of Harrold and Mary Marshall, 26 Dec.
1685. Anne, daughter of Thomas and Mary Marshall, 16 Dec.
1686. Elizabeth,[3] daughter of Thomas and Mary Marshall, 13 March.
1687. Harrold, son of Harrold and Mary Marshall, 7 April.
1690. Elizabeth, daughter of George Marshall, 17 January.
1691. George, son of Harrold and Mary Marshall, 28 April.
1706. John, son of John Marshall, 9 February.
1709. Anne, daughter of John Marshall, 27 April.

Marriages.

Harrold Marshall and Mary Wigfall, 18 October, 1679.
Robert Matthews and Elizabeth Marshall, 22 November, 1688.
Edward Marshall and Ann Wimpless, 5 September, 1703.
James Marshall and Anne Ramsdale, 26 October, 1708.[4]
Edward Marshall and Judith Roe, 25 September, 1711.
Francis Taylor and Frances Marshall, 1 December, 1730.
Thomas Marshall and Mary Leverton, of Wellough, 1 June, 1731.

WEST HAM, CO. ESSEX. *(Marriages 1653—1801.)*

1654. Oct. 24. Edward Marshall and Johane Whitland.
1658. Aug. 1, 8, 15. (Banns.) Francis Marshall and Mary Taylor.
1700. April 3. Thomas Barker (?) and Eliz. Marshall.
1711. June 16. Bignall Potter of St. Lawrence Jewry, London, and Rebecca Marshall of St. Giles Cripplegate, London.
1775. May 11. George Easterby, widower, and Sarah Marshall.
1795. Oct. 29. John Marshall and Elizabeth Frisby.
1795. November 2. Hugh Hughes, widower, and Anne Marshall.

[1] 1662. March 29. Elizabeth the wife of Abraham Marshall. Buried. *Transcript of Tuxford Register, at York.*

[2] 1662. Abraham Marshall of Tuxford and Anne Turner of the same towne were married by licence 12 Jan'y. *Transcript of East Retford Register, at York.*

[3] *Esther* in transcript at York.

[4] See Mar. Lic., Vol. I., p. 118.

EAST HAM, CO. ESSEX. (1695—1803.)

Marriage.

1779. June 26. John Marshall and Mary Hawkins. Per Banns.

Baptisms.

1701. July 21. John s. of William and Margaret Marshall.
1704. June 6. William s. of William and Mary Marshall.
1778. June 28. Mary d. of Robert and Mary Marshal.
1781. June 3. Mary d. of John and Mary Marshal.
1783. Dec. 21. Rebecca d. of same born 23 Nov.
1786. March 12. Ann d. of same born 22 Feb.
1788. Feb. 17. Dinah d. of same born 27 Jan'y.
1790. Oct. 31. Susanna d. of same born 8 Oct.

Burials.

1703. March 5. John s. of William Marshall.
1707. Nov. 9. Margaret d. of Will'm and Margaret Marshall.
1707. Feb'y. 15. Sarah Marshall.
1720. June 5. William Marshall.
1726. Dec. 2. Joanna Marshall. } See Vol. I., p. 159.
1727. July 7. Mr. Alexander Marshall. }
1742. April 4. Margaret Marshall, widow.
1756. March 21. Thomas Marshall from Joseph Chandlers.
1769. Oct. 9. Richard Marshall, infant.
1779. July 18. Robert Marshal.
1784. Sept. 19. Rebecca Marshall, infant.
1788. Jan'y. 4. Mary Marshall.
1788. Jan'y. 17. Ann Marsall *(sic)*, infant.

TRUSTHORPE, CO. LINCOLN.

1705. Aug. 28. Robert Marshall, buried.
1721. July 21. John son of Marmaduke Marshall and Elizabeth his wife, baptised.
1724. May 6. William son of Marmaduke and Elizabeth Marshall, buried.
1735. May 20. Elizabeth Marshall from Theddlethorpe, baptised.
1739. June 9. Marmaduke Marshall, buried.

MABLETHORPE, CO. LINCOLN.

1704. May 2. John Marshall, single man, and Mary Smith, single woman. Married.
1707. June 26. Marmaduke Marshall, buried.
1710. Sept. 24. John son of John and Mary Marshall, baptised.
1711. Aug. 12. John son of John Marshall, buried.
1711. Sept. 28. Mary wife of John Marshall, buried.
1715. April 10. John son of John and Susan Marshall, baptised.
1715. June 8. John son of John and Susan Marshall, buried.
1716. Dec. 17. William son of John and Susan Marshall, born.

SOCIETY OF FRIENDS. No. 370. (AT SOMERSET HOUSE.) BALBY, TICKHILL, AND BLYTH.

Leonard Marshall of Cottingworth, co. York, and Ursilea Tomkinson of Everton, co. Nott^m^, married 15th 5th month 1688.

Nicholas Marchall late of Balby, co. York, husbandman, and Elizabeth Sparvold of Bawtry, married 16th 11th month 1728.

John Marshall of Sutton upon Trent and Sarah Bullivant of Blyth, married 27th 1st month called March, 1729.

Phebe Marshall of Scrooby died 5th and buried 8th of 10th month 1717, buried at Friends burying place at Blyth.

Nicholas Marshall of Bawtry died 17th 2nd month 1751, buried in Friends burying place at Blyth 19th.

NOTES FROM SUBSIDY ROLLS (PUBLIC RECORD OFFICE).

Subsidy $\frac{94}{400}$. Hundred of Scarsdale, co. Derby. Car. II. Aº 1663. Hearth Tax.

Barlebrough and Whitwell.	William Marshall.	1 hearth.	
"	John Marshall.	1 "	
Stanisby and Heath.	George Marshall.	2 "	
Staveley.	Widd. Marshall.	1 "	

Subsidy $\frac{94}{371}$. Hundred of Scarsdale, 1672. Hearth Money. 24 Car. II.[1]

Whitwell.	Will. Marshall.	1 hearth.	
Killamarsh.	Mr. Marshall.	3 "	
Stanisby & Heath.	Wm. Earle of Devonshire.	114 "	
"	Hen. Pearpoint, Esq.	48 "	
"	Will'm Clay.	2 "	
"	Edward Marshall.	2 "	
Staveley cu'membris.	Jo. Marshall.	3 "	
"	Wid. Martiall.	1 "	

Subsidy $\frac{160}{331}$. Notts. Car. II. Hearth Tax. Fragment of a Roll.

Orston.	Thomas Marshall, jun.	1 hearth.	
"	Widdow Marshall.	2 "	
Whatton[2]	Mr. Gervas Marshall.	3 "	
Barton in Fabis.	Mrs. Marshall, widow.	4 "	
"	John Marshall.	1 "	
Rampton.	Will'm Marshall.	2 "	

Subsidy $\frac{160}{328}$. 15 Car. II. (1663.) Hundred of Thurgarton and Newark. Co. Notts. Hearth Tax.

Burton cum Bulcock.	Richard Marshall.	1 hearth.	
Gresthorpe cum Normanton.	Tho. Marshall.	1 "	
"	John Marshall.	1 "	not chargeable.
Gunthorpe.	Tho. Marshall.	1 "	
Marnham.	Robert Marshall	1 "	
Ossington.	Willm Cartwright, Esq.	12 "	
"	Cartwright Marshall.	1 "	
Sutton.	WmCartwright, Esq.	7 "	
"	Tho. Marshall.	1 "	
"	Expofer Marshall.	1 "	
Thurgarton.	Gabriel Marshall.	1 "	not chargeable.
Weston.	William Marshall.	1 "	
Newark Town:—			
Apletongate.	William Marshall.	1 "	not chargeable.
Barmbygate.	Widdow Marshall.	1 "	"
Baldertongate.	Thomas Marshall.	1 "	"
Stodmer street.	Mr. Thomas Marshall.	5 "	
Besthorpe.	Huntington Marshall.	1 "	
Coddington.	John Marshall.	1 "	not chargeable.
Harby.	John Marshall.	1 "	"

[1] This is a very well preserved document. At the end of the list of persons charged in Chesterfield parish is this note, "There are 113 p'sons in the p'ish of Chesterfield wch doe receive constant Almes of p'ish & therefore omitted." In most other rolls of Hearth money it is usual to mention certain persons as "not chargeable."

[2] Gervas Marshall was the Vicar there. William and Thomas Flower were also taxed for three hearths each.

North Collingham.	Gervas Marshall.	1 hearth	
"	John Marshall.	1 "	not chargeable.
Thorney.	Richard Marshall.	1 "	

Subsidy $\frac{160}{336}$. Car. II. Hundred of Thurgarton and Leigh, co. Notts. Hearth Tax.

Burton cum Bulcoate.	Richard Marshall.	2 hearths.
Cathorpe.	John Marshall	1 "
Calverton.	[defaced] Marshall.	4 "
Gesthorpe.	Tho. Marshall.	2 "
Gunthorpe.	Widow Marshall.	2 "
Marneham.	Robert Marshall.	1 "
Ossington.	Cartwright Marshall.	2 "
"	William Cartwright.	12 "
"	Hen. Cartwright.	1 "
"	Augustine Cartwright.	2 "
Sutton on Trent.	William Marshall.	1 "
"	Skilling Marshall.	1 "
"	Widow Marshall.	1 "
Southwell.	John Marshall.	3 "
Thurgarton.	Gabrill Marshall.	1 "
Weston.	Wm Marshall.	1 "

CALENDAR OF WILLS AND ADMINISTRATIONS IN P.C.C. 1761-1784.

1761.	Cheslyn.	Francis Marshall.[1]	Leith.	Adm'on, January.
		Frances[2] "	Middlesex.	" February.
		William[3] "	Pts.	" "
		Elizabeth (Marisal.)		Will, 28.
		William[4] "	Pts.	Adm'on, November.
		John "	Pts.	Adm'on with will, 225.
		James "		Will, 293.
		Christopher "		" 322.
		John "		" 401.
		John[5] "	Essex.	" 440.
1762.	St. Eloy.	William "		Adm'on, January.
		William "	London.	Will, 20.

[1] Adm'on of Francis Marshall of Leith, co. Edinburgh, to Christian Marshall his relict, 2 January, 1761.

[2] Adm'on of goods of Frances Marshall, (wife of Edward Marshall,) of Hampton, co. Middx, left unadministered by Francis Marshall since deceased, to Christian Marshall, widow and relict, and administratrix of the goods of Francis Marshall deceased, while he lived the son and only child of deceased, Edward Marshall the husband having died before he administered. *See* Vol. I. App., p. 25.

[3] Adm'on of William Marshall, seaman, belonging to his Majesty's ship the Happy, to Stephen Robinson attorney for James Marshall his father now residing at Newcastle upon Tyne, 6 February, 1761.

[4] Adm'on of William Marshall of his Majesty's Frigate Minerva, bachelor, to John Steward Attorney for Alexander Marshall his father now residing at Newcastle upon Tyne, 21 Nov., 1761.

[5] John Marshall of Finchingfield, co. Essex, Esqr. Dated 18 May, 1756. My two neices Ann Marshall and Lucy Marshall daughters of my nephew William Marshall of Woodwalton in the co. of Huntingdon. Neices Mary Bellenden and Jemima Bellenden, and their brother James Bellenden. Appoints Richard Commyns, Esq., ex'or. To be buried by Father and Mother in Finchingfield church. Adm'on with will annexed to John Yeldham, Esq., the guardian assigned to Ann and Lucy Marshall minors, 13 Dec., 1761. (See *ante* p. 23.)

		Ann Marshall	Worcester.	Adm'on, May.
		William ,,	Pts.	,, ,,
		John ,,	Pts.	,, June.
		William ,,	Kent.	,, September.
		Daniel ,,	Pts.	,, October.
		Christopher ,,	Pts.	,, December.
		Thomas [1] ,,		Will, 390.
		William[2] ,,	Leicester.	,, ,,
		Ann ,,	Kent.	,, 516.
		Robert ,,		,, 517.
		James ,,		,, 519.
1763.	Cæsar.	Edward ,,	Kent.	,, 25.
		Charles ,,	Oxford.	,, 76.
		Hugh ,,	Middlesex.	,, 77.
		Solgard ,,	Norwich.	Adm'on, April.
		George ,,	Southampton.	Will, 143.
		John ,,	Middlesex.	,, 188.
		Thomas ,,	Pts.	,, 192.
		Robert ,,	Pts.	,, 243.
		Sarah ,,	Devon.	Adm'on, October.
		Jervis [3] ,,	Pts.	Will, 296.
		Thomas ,,	Middlesex.	Ad'mon, December.
		Martin [4] ,,	Middlesex.	Will, 440.
		William ,,	Kent.	,, 442.
		Elizabeth Deborah ,,	Middlesex.	,, 478.
		John ,,	Huntingdon.	,, 478.
		John ,,	London.	,, 478.
		Robert ,,	Worcester.	,, 521.
		Thomas ,,	Southampton.	,, 559.
		Thomas ,,	Middlesex.	,, 560.
1764.	Simpson.	William ,,	Middlesex.	,, 58.
		Gunnel ,,	Middlesex.	Will, 60.
		Charles[5] ,,	Middlesex.	Adm'on, March.
		Thomas ,,	London.	Will, 106.
		Benjamin[6] ,,	Middlesex.	Adm'on, June.
		Robert ,,	Kent.	,, July.
		Catherine ,,	Middlesex.	Will, 187 (2nd grant in 1775.)
		Wilson ,,	Pts.	,, 189.
		John ,,	Warwick.	,, 232.
		Margaret ,,	London.	Adm'on, October.

[1] Thomas Marshall, chief mate of the sloop Friendship. Dated 1 May, 1753. Son William Marshall, wife Hannah Marshall and William Trinder Citizen and Joiner of London executors. Codicil dated 28 January, 1755. Richard Wilson, Gunsmith executor in place of William Trinder. Proved by relict 8 Sept., 1762.

[2] William Marshall of the Borough of Leicester, Gent., Lieutenant in the Militia established for the co. of Leicester. Dated 14 July, 1762. Lands at Burrough alias Ardburrough, in said county to wife Rachel Marshall in fee, and makes her sole executrix. She proved 18 Sept., 1762.

[3] Jervis Marshall, marine, belonging to his Majesty's ship America. Dated 26 Jan., 1760. Friend Mary Morris of Portsmouth universal legatee and executrix. She proved 17 June, 1763, as "Mary Graves formerly Morris otherwise Morrison."

[4] Martin Marshall of the parish of St. Giles in the Fields, co. Middx., Baker. Dated 25 June, 1763. To son William Marshall £300. Residue to daughter Winifred Marshall and makes her sole executrix. Proved 6 Sept., 1763, by Winifred Marshall, spinster.

[5] Of Hadley, co. Middlesex, Esq. Adm'on to Ann Marshall his relict. 22 March, 1764.

[6] Of the parish of St. Leonard Shoreditch, a seaman belonging to his Majesty's ship Vanguard. Adm'on to Martha Marshall his relict. 23 June, 1764.

		John	,,	Cornwall.	Adm'on, October.
		James	,,	Pts.	Will, 315.
		Sarah	,,	Worcester.	,, 317.
		Jeremiah	,,	Middlesex.	,, 134.
		Joseph	,,	Middlesex.	,, 136.
		Christopher	,,	Surrey.	,, 136.
1765.	Rushworth.	John	,,	Kent.	,, 25.
		Peter	,,	Pts.	Adm'on, January.
		Elizabeth	,,	Middlesex.	Will, 65.
		Susanna	,,	Devon.	,, 149.
		Amy	,,	Berks.	,, 191.
		Mary	,,	York.	,, 192.
		Mary	,,	Kent.	,, 267.
		John	,,	Middlesex.	,, 302.
		Phœbe	,,	Stafford.	,, 340.
		Nicholas	,,	Worcester	,, 457.
1766.	Tyndall.	John	,,	Hereford.	,, 23.
		Thomas	,,	Derby.	Adm'on, January.
		Ann	,,	Hertford.	Will, 25.
		Edward	,,	Hertford.	,, 149.
		Elizabeth	,,	Kent.	,, 149.
		Elias	,,	Pts.	,, 234.
		Andrew	,,	Pts.	Adm'on, October.
		Richard	,,	Norfolk.	,, December.
		Nicholas	,,	Middlesex.	Will, 313.
1767.	Legard.	William	,,	Devon.	Adm'on, April.
		William [1]	,,	Gloucester.	Will, 104.
		John [2]	,,	Middlesex.	,, 105.
		James	,,	Pts.	Adm'on, June.
		William	,,	Middlesex.	Will, 186.
		Amy	,,	formerly White. Oxford.	Adm'on, July.
		John	,,	Middlesex.	Will, 188.
		William	,,	Hertford.	,, 314.
		William [3]	,,	Middlesex.	,, 348.
		William	,,	London.	,, 380.
		Elizabeth	,,	Middlesex.	,, 382.
		John	,,	London.	,, 454.
1768.	Secker.	Sarah	,,	Middlesex.	Adm'on, April.

[1] William Marshall Captain in his Majesty's Regiment of Foot of Invalides. Dated at Embden 22 Sept., 1761. Dearly beloved wife Charlotte Marshall, daughter of the late Captn Robert Jennings and Cornelia Jennings his wife, universal legatee.

Adm'on with will annexed of William Marshall late of the parish of Westbury, co. Gloucester, Captn in the 81st regiment of Foot to Charlotte Marshall his relict, 17 March, 1767.

[2] John Marshall of the parish of St. Martin in the Fields, Middlesex, Merchant. Dated 28 January, 1767. Wife Mary Marshall, sole executrix. To mother Jane Marshall annuity of £50. Aunt Elizabeth Hardisty of Knaresborough, co. York widow. Aunt Mrs Eleanor Young. Son John William Marshall under 25. Sister-in-law Mrs Francis Hercy. Joseph Harper Reynolds and Lovelace Hercy trustees. Proved by relict 24 March, 1767.

[3] William Marshall of Gray's Inn in the parish of St Andrew Holborn, Esq. Dated 10 May, 1755. My two daughters Ann and Lucy Marshall, both under age. Whereas I have lately sold my estate in Essex unto Mr. Thomas Wolfe of Saffron Walden who is to raise and pay £2,000 secured by my marriage articles—directs all deeds found in his (testator's) possession at his decease to be delivered to said Thomas Wolfe. Makes George Hatch linen and woollen draper of New Windsor, co. Bucks, and Mr Thomas Wolfe, attorney at law, of Saffron Walden, executors. Adm'on with will annexed, the executors having renounced, 23 Sept., 1767, to Ann Standly, formerly Marshall, wife of Peter Standly, Esq., and Lucy Wescomb, formerly Marshall, wife of Nicholas Wescomb, Esq., his daughters. *See ante* p. 23.

		Samuel	„	Esq. Southampton.	Will, 208.
1769.	Bogg.	Margaret	„	Middlesex.	„ 20.
		James	„	Middlesex.	„ 20.
		Jane	„	formerly Cook. London.	Adm'on, December.
1770.	Jenner.	Elizabeth	„	London.	Will, 154.
		Mary	„	Cambridge.	„ 201.
		James	„	Middlesex.	„ 204.
		Jane	„	Sussex.	„ 441.
1771.	Trevor.	Beaumont	„	Middlesex.	„ 69.
		Mary Jane (Marisal)		Middlesex.	Adm'on, January.
		Bathsheba or Barshabe	„	formerly Staples. Middlesex.	„ „ July.
		William	„	Surrey.	Will, 218.
		John	„	London.	„ 264.
		Robert	„	Surrey.	„ 309.
		John[1]	„	Southampton.	„ 347.
1772.	Taverner.	Elizabeth	„	London.	Adm'on, April.
		James Plaxton			Will, 338.
1773.	Stevens.	Leonard	„	York.	„ 119.
		William[2]	„	Lincoln.	„ 171.
		Francis[3]	„	Middlesex.	„ 172.
		Hannah Bella		Middlesex.	„ 214.
		Thomas	„	Bedford.	„ 258.
		Edward	„	Pts.	„ 302.
		John	„	Bucks.	„ 365.
1774.	Bargrave.	Henry	„	Surrey.	„ 22.
		Charles	„	Surrey.	„ 22.
		Thomas	„	Surrey.	„ 56.
		Mary	„	Middlesex.	„ 193.
		Hannah	„	Middlesex.	Adm'on, July.

[1] *See* Vol. i, p. 316.

[2] William Marshall of Theddlethorpe, co. Lincoln, Esqr., dated 28 Dec., 1765. Younger sons, William, John, and Charles-Robert Marshall, and my daughter Anna-Maria Marshall. My aunt Ann Abbott. Wife Grace Marshall, sole executrix. Eldest son Henry Cracroft Marshall. John Allatt of Theddlethorpe, a witness. Proved by relict 3 April, 1773. *See* Vol. i. p. 11.

[3] Francis Marshall of Hampstead in the co. of Middlesex, Esq., dated 6 March, 1772. To Mary Frith, spinster, my wife's sister, now living with me £20. To William Dobson of Twickenham, Esq., £25, and to Rebecca his wife £25. To Elizabeth Scrivenor, spinster, now living with me £30. To Nathaniel Clarkson of Islington, Gent., £30. To Thomas Shirley of the same place, surgeon, £20. To Robert Challand of the Excise office, London, Gent., £20. Recites that late Aunt Mary Arnold of Hampstead, widow, by her will dated 17 Sept., 1767, left him £5,000 in 3 per cents with power of appointment—appoints said sum to wife Rosamond Marshall for life, and then to said Mary Frith, and Ann Marshall and Mary Marshall daughters of the Revd George Marshall* late of Newnham with Badby in the co. of Northampton, clerk, deceased, and to Thomas Hurdman and Benjamin Hurdman sons of Thomas Hurdman of Alrewas in the co. of Stafford, Esq., equally to be divided amongst them. Mentions, James Russell of Fleet S^{t}, Hatter and Hozier. John Bragg Russell of the same Hatter and Hozier. Joanna wife of . . . . Bateman now or late of Bartholemew close, London, Victualler. James Andrews son of Thomas Andrews of East Cheap, London, Printer. Mary Whitehead of Eltham, co. Kent, spinster. Jonathan Watson of Gloucester County, Virginia. Henry Hoare of Fleet S^{t}, London, Banker, son of William Hoare late of St Edmondsbury, Esqr. Money to poor of St Mary Islington, and Datchett, co. Bucks. Wife and William Dobson, executors. Both proved 14 April, 1773.

* Vicar of Badby. Died 22 May, 1753, aged 27. M.I. Bakers 'Northampton,' Vol. i. p. 261.

1775.	Alexander.	Susanna	,,		Warwick.	Adm'on, March.
		George	,,		Northampton.	,, March & April.
		James	,,		Middlesex.	Will, 148.
		Gilbert [1]	,,		Middlesex.	,, 195.
1776.	Bellas.	William	,,		London.	Adm'on, January.
		Bethia	,,		Surrey.	,, February.
		Philip	,,		Pts.	,, March.
		William [2]	,,		York.	Will, 85.
		James	,,		Middlesex.	,, 134.
		John	,,		Pts.	Adm'on, June.
		David	,,		Pts.	Will, 324.
		Elizabeth	,,		Kent.	,, 395.
		Francis	,,	Esq.	Surrey.	,, 432.
		John	,,		Stafford.	,, 511.
1777.	Collier.	Ann	,,		Surrey.	,, 29.
		John	,,		Middlesex.	,, 30.
		James	,,		Berks.	,, 75.
		Peter	,,		Middlesex.	,, 228.
		Eleanor	,,		Middlesex.	,, 228.
		Jane	,,		Middlesex.	,, 276.
		John	,,		Devon.	,, 475.
1778.	Hay.	Catherine [3]	,,		Kent.	,, 123.
		Elizabeth	,,		Surrey.	Adm'on, May.
		Rachell	,,		Middlesex.	Will, 503.
1779.	Warburton.	David	,,		Durham.	Adm'on, April.
		Gregory	,,		Pts.	Will, 164.
		William	,,		Kent.	,, 259.
		William [4]	,,		Southampton.	,, 315.
		Richard	,,		London.	,, 385.
		David	,,		Pts.	,, 388.
		William	,,		Southampton.	,, 385.
		William	,,		Essex.	,, 424.
1780.	Collins.	Jane [5]	,,		Nottingham.	Adm'on, May.
		John	,,		Pts.	,, June.
		Ann [6]	,,		York.	,, July.
		John	,,		Surrey.	Will, 151.
		Bryan	,,		Middlesex.	,, 202.
		Penyston [7]	,,		London.	Adm'on, July.
		Robert	,,		Pts.	Will, 365.
		William	,,		Pts.	Adm'on, December.

[1] Gilbert Marshall of Charlotte St in the parish of St Pancras, co. Middlesex, Esq., Dated 1 Nov., 1774. Son-in-law William Greton of Littlebury, co. Essex, clerk. Son-in-law Walter Serocold of Cherry Hinton, co. Cambridge, clerk, sole executor. He proved 22 May, 1775.

[2] William Marshall of Tadcaster, Esq., Master and Commander in the King's Navy. Dated 6 Sept., 1775. Mother Mrs Elizabeth Marshall of Tadcaster, widow, universal legatee and sole executrix. She proved 16 Feb., 1776. *See* Vol. i. p. 271.

[3] Catherine Marshall of the parish of Charing in the co. of Kent, widow. Dated 10 Decr., 1774. "All my real estate whatsoever I devise unto my dear son Joshua Marshall and his heirs for ever, my son Edmund being already well provided for." Appoints son Joshua executor. He proved 19 March, 1778. *See* Vol. i. app. p. 25.

[4] William Marshall belonging to his Majesty's ship the Centaur. Dated 7 Jan., 1761. Wife Joanna Marshall universal legatee and executrix. She proved 30 July, 1779.

[5] Adm'on of Jane Marshall of parish of St Mary, Nottingham, to Thomas Marshall her husband, 10 May, 1780.

[6] Adm'on of Ann Marshall of Notton, co. York, widow, to Elizabeth Wood, wife of Adam Wood her daughter, 12 July, 1780.

[7] Adm'on of Penystone Marshall of St. Andrew Undershaft, London, to Elizabeth Clarance wife of Peter Clarance his daughter, 14 July, 1780.

1781.	Webster.	Matthew	„		Pts.	Adm'on, January.
		Edith	„		Southampton.	Will, 203.
		Peter	„		London.	„ 399.
		Matthew	„		Middlesex.	„ 487.
1782.	Gostling.	Caroline [1]	„		Somerset.	„ 38.
		Thomas	„		Bucks.	„ 89.
		John	„		Bristol.	Adm'on, April.
		Sarah	„		Kent.	„ April.
		Richard	„		Pts.	„ May.
		Sarah	„		Middlesex.	Will, 189.
		John	„	Esq.	Stafford.	„ 504.
1783.	Cornwallis.	Theodore	„		Southampton.	„ 33.
		George	„		Southampton.	Adm'on, Feb.
		Walter	„		Pts.	Will, February.
		James	„		Worcestershire.	Will, 87.
		Jacob	„		Southampton.	Adm'on, March.
		James	„		Middlesex.	Will, 141.
		Thomas	„		Pts.	Adm'on, April.
		Richard	„		Pts.	„ August.
		John	„		St. Albans.	„ October.
1784.	Rockingham.	Sarah	„		Middlesex.	Will, 35.
		James	„		Pts.	„ 275.
		James	„		Devon.	„ 338.
		Robert	„		Pts.	Adm'on, Sept.
		William [2]	„		Middlesex.	Will, 563.
		William	„		London.	„ 655.

Penelope Elton, formerly Marshall. Southampton. Adm'on, March.

NOTES

FROM THE KNARESBOROUGH COURT ROLLS.

Date of Court.	
1332, Oct. 7.	[Received] Of *William le Mareschall* for a tree thrown down in Harlaw. 3*s.* 4*d.*
1341-2, Feb. 13.	*John Mareschal* amerced for not having John de Erington to answer concerning a trespass.
1342, Oct. 9.	*William Mareschall* plt. (trespass). To next Court.
1342, May 8.	*Alice Mareschal* amerced for cutting green thorn in Folwyth.
1346-7, Jan'y. 3.	*William Mareschal* of Rossist attached for cutting thorns &c. in. Foul[wyth].
1350 [before 22 Dec.]	*John Marcshall* of Wedurby plt. (covenant).
1354-5, Jan'y. 8.	*John Marcshall* of Cayton deft. (trespass).
1349, June 3.	Wm. Fox, younger, plt. *v.* Alice who was wife of Wm. de Bekwyth, *Wm. Mareschall* and others (trespass).
1349, Dec. 9.	*Agnes* daughter of *John Marcschal* took 2 messuages 3 ac. and 3 r. of land in Rossyst, of which her husband died seized, To have &c. Fine 6*d.*
1350-1, March 2.	*John Marcshall* of Wethirby plt. (covenant).
March 16.	*Idem* *non pros.*
	¶ Plaint entered also Jan. 19 and Feb. 9, 1350-1; but membranes disarranged.
1353, June 12.	*John Marcschal* plt. *v.* John Dykmansone who came to town of Knar: 9 June 27th year (1353) and took away

[1] *See* Vol. i. p. 316.
[2] Of St. Mary le bone, Coachmaker. Wife Ann universal legatee.

Isabel dau. of Wm. de Haltoñ, his hired servant, against the King's peace *etc.* Judgment for Mareschal, and John D. amerced.

1355-6, March 9. *William Marcschal* of Ryppelay plt. *v.* Robert Tybsone of Brame, concerning a plea of covenant.

1356, March 30. *Idem* plt. [and at other Courts].

May 11. *Wm. Mareschal* of Ryppelay plt. and Robert T. agree.

1357-8, Feb. 27. *Agnes Marcschal* came and took twelth part of an acre of land in Roscest, To hold to her and her heirs *&c.* Fine 4*d.*

1359, Nov. 23. [ALDBURGH] Order to attach *Richard Mareshall*, *Henry Marshal* [and others] *&c.* to answer for carrying away growing corn taken for money due.

Dec. 13. Defts. appear—say "not guilty." Jury ordered.
¶ By interlineation, jury find them "not guilty."

1360—1361. *William Marcschal* pays for summer agistment had in Haye-park in 35th year.

1363, July 26. [ALDBURGH] *Robert Marsall* plt. and Henry Wryght of Lynton agree in plea of trespass. Said Henry amerced.

1364, Oct. 9. *William Marchall* of Harwode amerced.

1364-5, Jan'y. 22. *Matilda* (or Maud) *Marchale* dft. in debt. (J. Nellesone).

Feb. 12. *John Nelson* plt. *non pros.*

1362. *Roger Marschall* of Quixlay pays summer agistment in Hay-park in 36th year (4*s.*).

1367, Sept. 15. *Roger Mareschall* of Quixley *op. sc.* *v.* Wm. Wilmott, John Frerr', Robt. de Barneby, John Ferour & John Yonge of Thor[n]thwayte in a plea of assise of fresh force. He says that they came on Monday 24 July 41st year (1367) and unjustly disseised him of his freehold, viz. 3 mess. & 24 ac. lands wt appurts in Ferryngesby, Bekwythshagh and Ledhoues *post primam* etc. And the said Wm. & others come & defend *etc.* and pray for Inq. *Roger* likewise. Hereupon Inq. taken by recognitors [named] who say that the said Wm. Wylimot *etc.* unjustly disseised said Roger *etc.* Damages assessed at 20*s.*
Judgment that Roger recover his seisin of said mess. and lands with damages. Defendants amerced.

Oct. 6. *John Marchall* of Ryplay plt. *v.* John Dowe, who owes him 2*s.* 4*d.* for pledge for beasts taken in the Lord's corn at Ryplaye on Monday after Nativity of B.V.M. 41st year (13 Sept. 1367). Deft. acknowledges debt. Plt. satisfied, and Dowe amerced 3-pence.

1366. *Adam Marchall* pays summer agistment of horses in Bilton-park in 40th year.

1369, Oct. 10. The Roll of Suitors of the Court has "Will Wylmot."

1369-70, March 13. Ric. de Merstone and Alice his wife *v.* Richard del Brotte and Agnes his wife in plea of land. They say that Ric. and Agnes deforced them of a messuage, and 3½ acres 1 rood of land in Roset; for one *William Mareschal* who held said lands in fee according to the custom of the forest died, and right descended to *Henry*, son and heir of William, and next to *John* brother of Henry, which John died. After whose death the right descended to *Agnes* his (John's) dau. and heir who died seized thereof without issue. So come said Richard and *Alice* dau. of Wm. *Mareschall* and claim. Said Ric. del Brotte and Agnes come and defend. They say that *Agnes* dau. of *John Marcschall* who last held said lands surrendered the same to the use of Agnes, wife of Ric. del. Brotte, and so they claim. Ric. de M. and Alice say that said *Agnes*, dau. of *John Marcschall*, was not of full age when she surrendered to the use of Agnes wife of Richard del B. And this they are prepared *etc.* A jury ordered.

1370, March 27. Found by Inq. that *Agnes* dau of *John* son of *Wm. Marcschall* was not of full age when she surrendered a mess. 3½ acres 1 rood of land in Rosset to the use of Agnes wife of Richard del Brotte. Therefore Ric. de Merstone and Alice his wife recover, and the others are amerced.

May 29. Ric. del Brotte and Agnes his wife complain of Richard de Merstone and Alice his wife in a plea of land, as to a third part of :—2 mess., 3 acres and 3 roods of land and a waste builded in Rosset, because *John Mareschall* formerly husband of Agnes died seized of said 2 mess. &c., and 3rd part thereof as dower fell to Agnes. As to the waste, said Agnes fined for that in Court at Knar : Ric. de Merstone and Alice say that *John Mareschall* was never seised of said two mess. &c. As to the waste, they say that there is no waste except that contained in 1 mess. which said Ric. and Alice at Court 13 March 44th year (1369-70) recovered and said Agnes never fined for that *etc.* Jury ordered.

1370, June 19. Found by Inq. that *John Mareschall* was never seised of 2 mess., 3 ac. 3 r. land in Bekwyth [before Rosset] ; and, as to waste, Agnes fined for that, and it is not contained in said messuage, but how much waste the Jurors know not. Therefore Ric. del Brotte and Agnes recover seisin in said waste *cum per vicinos extra limitetur.*

July 31. *William Mareschall* who held 1 mess. in Bekwyth *diem suum clausit extremum ;* after whose Death comes *Alice* wife of Ric. de Merstone, dau. & next heir of *Wm.*, and entered *etc.* Relief—4-pence.

1371, Nov. 11. *Robert Mareschall* paid for release of suit of Court up to Michaelmas next (1372).

¶ His name *not* among the suitors in schedule attached to Court 1 Oct. 39 Ed. 3 (1365).

1372, Oct. 13. *Roger Mareschall* pays 6*d.* for release of suit up to Michaelmas next (1373).

¶ In the strip showing "Suitors of said Court," thus :— R Mareschall vj[d]
Will. Wylymot
the pen struck thro' the name of Wm. Wylymot and R. Mareschall written over.

1373, Oct. 5. Schedule of Suitors of Court has (attached) : —
"*Rog'us Mareschall'* mortuus est."

Same date. "heres *Rog'i Mareschall'* ij[d]" amerced for default of Suit.

1375, Oct. 10. "heres *Rog'i Mareschall'*" in Roll of Suitors of Court.

1375, Oct. 10. *Wm. Mareschall* plt'.
"heres Rog'i Mareschall ij[d]" amerced for default of Suit.
John Mareschall presented in township of Scotton for brewing & selling ale *contra assisam.*

Oct. 31. *Wm. Mareschall non pros.* Amerced 2*d.*
"heres Rog'i Mareschall' ij[d]" amerced for default of Suit.

Up to 10 Sept. *Idem.* for same.

1376, Oct. 29. "heres Rog'i Mareschall xij[d]" for release of Suit of Court.

Nov. 12. heres Rog'i Mareschall', [amerced, but sum struck out, because he fined for release of Suit.]

1377, Oct. 13. Heir of *Roger Mareschall* amerced (2*d.*) for default of suit of Court.

1378, Oct. 5. Heir of *Roger Mareschall* amerced *etc.* as before.

1379, April 13. *Matilda* (or Maud) *Mareschall* plt. *v.* Robert Been and Beatrice his wife (trespass.) *non pros* : amerced 2*d.*

1379, Oct. 20. "heres *Rog' Mareschall*" in the Roll of Suitors.

1379-80, March 14. Heir of *Roger Mareschall* amerced for default of suit.

1380—1. *Robert Mareschall* pays 2*s.* 4*d.* } for Summer agistment in
Richard Mareschall pays 16*d.* } Haywra Park.

1380, July 18. King's writ to the Bailiffs of John *&c.*, Duke of Lancaster, of Knaresborough that right should be done to John de Newton and Isabel his wife and William Haliday concerning 3 messuages, 3 bovates and 19 acres of land and six acres of meadow in Feryngesby, Clynt, and Kylinghale, which *John* son of *Roger Marcschall* of Quyxlay (Whixley) deforced *etc.* Dated at Westminster 6 June, 3rd year (1380).

By virtue of which writ the bailiff summoned *John* son of *Roger* to be at next Court, *i.e.* in 3 weeks from this date (18 July), to answer to the said John, Isabel, and William.

1380, Aug. 8.	The plaintiffs appeared.	John summoned	1st time.
Aug. 29.	Ditto.	„	2nd. „
Oct. 10.	Ditto.	„	3rd. „

Oct. 10. *John* son of *Roger Marcschall* paid 12*d.* for release of suit of Court.

Oct. 31. John de Newton and others *v.* *John* son of *Roger Marcschall* who comes in person, and eventually gets judgement in his favour. (Et postea consider' est p'd'ci petent' nihil capiant per breve suū sed in m'ia).

„ „ John Brounstede drew blood from servant of *William Marcschall* for wch he was amerced in 12*d.*

1381, March 27. King's writ (as before) concerning *John* son of *Roger Marcschall* dated at Westminster 26 January 4 Ric. 2 (1380-1). Ric. Brennand, bailiff of the liberty of Knaresbro' ordered to summon "Joh'em fil. *Rog'i Marcschall* de Qwixlay" to be at the next Court, *etc.*

1381, April 17.	*John* s. of *Roger M.*	summoned first time.
May 8.	„	second.
May 29.	„	third.
June 19.	Plea again entered.	
July 10.	„	

July 31. *Marcschall* not coming, Bailiff to seize lands &c. and Demandants to be at next Court.

Sept. 11. The Demandants' case is :—

William son of Wm. Wylymot was seized of the said lands and ten'ts in fee *temp.* Edw. 3, and died without issue ; and the right ascended to Emmota wife of Robert Ingleys, and to Eleanor her sister, as aunts and heirs of said Wm., and sisters of his father. From Emmota the right descended to Isabel, who now demands with John Newton her husband, as daughter and heir of Emmota. From Eleanor the right descended to William Halyday, her son and heir. And they say that the said *John* son of *Roger* entered into the said lands &c. by *Roger Marcschall* of Qwixlay, who disseised the said Wm. (son of Wm.) Wylimot whose heir the said Isabel and Wm. Halyday are.

John son of *Roger M.* says that the descent from the said Emmota is to Isabel alone and not jointly with John Newton her husband.

Court adjourned to 3 weeks after, at which day the tenant comes in person and says that *Roger Marcschall* his father took an assise of fresh force against Wm. son of Wm. Wilimot, John Frere, and others, by which assise it was found that they disseised the said *Roger Marcschall*, and this is of record. The demandants deny the existence of any such record. A day is given to show record in 3 weeks.

Then the tenant says that demandants ought not to have their action because in 41 Edw. 3. *Roger* de Wixlay father of the said *John* (*Marcschall*) whose heir he is arraigned in an assise of fresh force in the Court of Knar : against Wm. Willymot (ancestor of the demandants) of the said tenements by the name of tenements in Ledehous and elsewhere, which places are hamlets and parcels of towns now put in the writ[1]. The said ten'ts were put in view and process

[1] Four original writs are sewn in the Roll under examination ; of which there are two which concern Mareschall, dated 6 June, 3 Ric. 2, and 26 January, 4 Ric. 2.

continued until *Roger* recovered the same. The said *John* prays judgment if action ought to be had against said Recovery by *Roger* his father.

1381, Nov. 13.[1] Judgment postponed.

Dec. 4. John de Newton & others *v.* *John* son of *Roger Marcschall.* The latter made default. Therefore, judgment given that demandants recover seisin of the lands and ten'ts on acc^t of default of the tenant, and that the tenant be amerced 3*s.* 4*d.*

1381-2, Feb. 26. *Joh'* fil' *Rog'i Mareschall* paid 6*d.* for release of suit of Court.

1382, July 2. *Alice,* dau. of *Robert Mareschall* of Quixlay, plt'. *v.* Wm. Turpyn (debt).

1385, July 19. *Adam Marcschall* plt'. (debt).

1385-6, March 7. *John Marcschall* amerced 6*d.* for cutting "husse't 'dni" in Foulwyth.

1386, May 28. *Maud* (Matilda) *Marcschall'* "ponit se in gracia domini" for one dog contrary to the assise.

1386-7, Feb. 6. *Adam Marschall* plt'. (covenant) *v.* Robert Orme. *Non pros.* Amerced therefore.

1386—7. *Adam Marschall* pays pannage for 8 hogs 4*d.* in Knar: and Scriven for 10th year.

1386-7, March 20. *Adam Marschall* deft. (debt); Robt. Orme plt'.

1387. Oct. 16. *Adam Marschall* on jury.

1388, April 1. *John Marschall* to answer for cutting wood in Bilton Park. He and his wife carried away etc. Amerced 6*d.*

1390, Nov. 15. *Adam Marschall* paid 7½*d.* for pannage in Knar: and Screvyn.

1391, Oct. 6. [ALDBURGH.] *Thomas Marschall* of Massam plt. *v.* John Malkynson "in placito plegii." Half a mark to have been paid 7 years ago—not paid—damage 2*s.*

1392, Nov. 6. *Adam Marshall* a juror concerning Mill of Killinghale and other mills.

1392-3, Jan'y 29. *Adam Marschall* plt. (debt) *v.* Richard Warde of Scotton.

1393, April 23. Adam Marshall amerced 1*d.* for a sow rooting up soil in Hay-park.

1392-3. Adam Marshall pays pannage in Knar. and Screvyn.

1391-2. *Adam Marschall* pay pannage in Knar:
Maud (Matilda) *Marschall* ditto.

1391, Oct. 4. *Thomas Marschall* of Massam plt' *v.* John Turpyn (debt).
Idem plt *v.* Wm. Turpyn (debt).

1391-2, Jan'y. *Adam Marshall* surrendered 3 roods of land in Garker, to the use of John son Richard son of Wm. Brennand. John entered.

Feb. 27. *Adam Marshall* 2nd on list of jurors, as to Mill of Knaresbro'.

1392, July 3. *Adam Marshall* plt. *v.* John Doweson.

Oct. 19. [ALDBURGH.] *John Marshall* of Norton plt. in plea of covenant. Settled and def^t amerced.

1393-4, March 18.[1] John de Burton, vicar of Knar: owes *Adam Marshall.*

1394, May 6. *Adam Marshall* recovers 4*s.* against said Vicar.

May 27. *Adam Marshall* amerced 2*d.* "q3 nonh' Joh'em Wayte" *etc.*

1394, Sept. 9. *Adam Marshall* 4*d.* with others of jury for not coming in plea of land. Wm. son of Robert de Nesfelde plt. and Percival de Pensax and Ric. de Brereton def^ts.

Adam Marshall pays pannage in Knar. and Scryveyn.
N.B. The Roll put up in wrong order, and certain Courts of earlier date come in here.

1393, Dec. 30. *Adam Marshall* op. se *v.* John, vicar of Knar. who unjustly detains 4*s.* due for a "materas" sold by said Adam. The money should have been paid a year ago—damage set at 12*d.* Vicar denies *etc.*

[1] *See* under—1393, Dec. 30.

1393-4, Feb. 9.	Vicar of Knar: defends *v.* Ad. Marshall (debt above). ¶ The sum recovered—see last page—6 May, 1394.
1395, April 7.	*Adam Marshall* with others fined—each 2*d.*—because the jurors did not come to Inq. between the Vicar and John del Hill.
May 31.	*Adam Marshall* again (with others) fined for not coming to another Inq.—Forsett & Redeshagh.
1394-5.	*Adam Marshall* pays pannage in Scriven.
1395, October 6.	*Adam Marshall* surrendered a cottage in Knar: To the use of John Walker of Wethirby, who was duly admitted. Fine 18*d.*
1396, August 2.	*Adam Marshall* plt. (trespass) *v.* Adam Hunt.
Sept. 13.	Ad. Hunt distr. to answer to *Ad. Marshall* (debt).
1395-6.	*Adam Marshall* pays pannage in Scriven.
1396-7, Feb. 7.	*Adam Marsc*[h]*all* fined 2*d* (summoned on jury).
1398, June 26.	*Adam Marshall* surrendered 1 acre, 3 roods of demesne land on Boterhill, to the use of Wm. Smith *&c.* Fine 2*s.*
1399, July 9.	*Adam Marshall* presented for cutting "husset'" without licence in Foulwith.
1399, Sept. 10.	*Idem* presented for similar forest trespass.
1400, Nov. 6. [ALDBURGH]	*Robert Marschall* complains of *Geoffrey Marschall* (M'chall) in a plea of debt, and demands 13*s.* detained for six years past, to his damage 40-pence. And the deft. denies *etc.*
Nov. 29.	*Geoffrey Marchall* fails, and *Robert Marchall* (M'chall) gets judgment.
1406, Dec. 8.	*Alice Marshall* obstructed watercourse in divers places, viz. near her house and near her garden in Frogmire. She is therefore amerced.
1406-7, Feb. 10.	*William Marchall v.* John de Burton, vicar of the church of Knaresburgh in plea of debt.
1415, May 8.	*William Marshall* (M'shall) plt. (debt).
Oct. 2.	Robert de Pensax distrained to answer to *William Marshall* of Harwode (plea of trespass). To next court.
1418, Oct. 5.	*William Marshall* of Clint surrendered one mesuage and half an acre of land in Clint to the use of Robert de Wallerthwait of Ripon. Fine 12*d.*
1422, April 1.	Adam Brenand carpenter came into Court and took of the Lord two wastes in Knaresburghe formerly of *Adam Marschall* as next heir of the said Adam, To have and to hold the said wastes to him and his heirs according to the custom of the Manor. And he gives to the Lord for fine 6-pence etc. [By next entry] The same Adam B. on the same day surrendered the said two wastes to the use of John Isacson.
1425, June 30.	*Robert Marchall* plt. *v.* Ric. Kirkby (debt). ALDBURGH.
July 25.	*Robert Marchall* "de B" (Boro'bridge) plt. (debt).
	Richard Marchall of Roundhaw will not pay wages of the Forester.
1427, Nov. 20.	*William Marchall* plt. (debt). [of Wodhall, as appears by next.]
Dec. 10.	*William Marchall* of Wodhall plt. Case settled.
1432, Oct. 22.	Thomas Marchall and Richard Marchall surrendered a messuage with half an acre of land in Kelyngall to use of John Bekwyth [of Kelyngall] *etc.* Fine 6*d.*
1433, Dec. 16.	*William Marchall* of Spofford surr^d by the hands of Geoffrey Smyth, chaplain, *Katherine* wife of the said *William*, Wm. Bogas and John Cragge, 2 acres of demesne lands in Feryngesby to the use of Robert Harton, Minister of the House of St. Robert (near Knar:), & John Blake. Hereupon *etc.* Fine 18*d.*
1436-7, Jan'y 2.	*Richard Marsshall*, servant of Robert Brenand amerced for not prosecuting his plea of trespass *v.* John Stele.

1410, Oct. 12.	*William Marshall* fined 12*d.* for assault on Wm. Webster.
	John Steele fined 12*d.* for assaulting *Wm. Marshall.*
1412, May 23.	*Richard Marchall* on jury in Inq. (right of John Cokill in Tentergate).
Oct. 10.	*William Marchall* laborer drew blood from Tho'm Willam-son, and ran away.
	Also the same *Wm. Marchall* at Erkynden by night lay in wait about the house of Ric. Skalwra to beat said Richard *etc.*
1447, May 3.	*John Marchall* amerced 2*d.* trespass wood (Fulwith).
1452, Aug. 3.	*John Marchall* 6*d.* cutting down oaks (Fulwith).
1453, July 25.	*John Marshall* (in Fulwyth) 6*d.* cutting greenwood.
1460, April 16.	*John Marschll* attached for cutting down wood (in Foulwith).
1461, May 27.	*John Marschall*, 2*d.* for cutting wood (in Harlowe and Fulwith).
Sept. 30.	*John Marchall* of Plompton cut down wood. Fined 6-pence.'
1463, Sept. 7.	*John Marchall* fined 4*d.* for cutting and carrying away wood in Fulwith.
Sept. 30.	*John Marschall* (M'schall) 4*d.* cut greenwood in "Ocden'."
1466, March 29.	[1] *John Marshall* amerced 2*d.* for not coming.
Oct. 1.	*John Marschall* on jury for borough of Boro'bridge.
1466-7, Feb. 7.	*John Marschall* amerced with another juror *re* Robt. Williamson.
1467, April 11.	*Idem* same matter.
July 25.	Jury found verdict *re* Robert Williamson.
1468, Sept. 30.	*John Marschall* took and carried away wood out of the King's forest (under " Fulwith & Harlow ").
" "	*William Marschall* *ditto* ("Ocden' ").
1469, Oct. 2.	*William Marschall*, 2*d.* for cutting down wood. ("Okden' ").
1474, April 25.	*John Marchall* and *Richard M'schall* cut wood and carried away in the Forest.
Oct. 17.	*John Marschall*, 4*d.*; *William Marschall*, 2*d.* cutting wood, (under " Fulwith ").
1475-6, March 6.	*John Marschall*, 8*d.*; *William Marschall*, 8*d.* cutting boughs of oaks, thorns, &c. in Fulwith.
" "	John Marschall, 6*d.*; William Marschall, 4*d.* cutting green-wood in Fulwith and Harlow.
1494, Sept. 10.	*Richard Marshall* (under Swyndon') fined 2*d.*
1508, Oct. 5.	*Thomas Marshall*, juror for the borough of Knaresburgh, and in 1509, 10, 11.
1514, Aug. 9.	*Joan* (Johanna) *Marshall non pros.*—amerced.
Dec. 20.	*William Marshall*, juror for Kn :
1515, Oct. 18.	*Thomas Marshall*, juror Knar : and in 1516, and subsequent years.
	William Marshall late of Connyshethorpe, laborer, assaulted Ric. Thorpe—fined.
1518, Oct. 2.	*William Marshall* juror Kn :
1527, Sept. 20.	*William Marshall*, chosen Constable of Scotton township for year to come.
1532, Oct. 12.	*Wm. Marshall* of Mylby amerced for licence of concord (tres pass at Boro'bridge in the King's Court of ALDBURGH.
1539-40, Jan. 21.	*Wm. Marshall* juror of Boro'bridge in plea of debt.
1540, May 14.	*Idem* ditto " trespass.
1546, Aug. 25.	*William Marshall*, a juror (Knar :)—plea of tres; ass.
1537,[2] April 5.	*Thomas Marshall* and others "asportaver' husset' ib'm [*i.e.* in parco de Haye] sine licenc'. (fined 2*d.*)
1550, Oct. 6.	[3] *Robert Marshall*, juror for Liberty of Aldburgh, in Sheriff's Turn of Aldburgh (Aldeburghte), holden at Boro'bridge 6 Oct. 4 Edw. 6 (1550).
1551, April 4.	[3] *Richard Marshall*, juror for borough of Boro'bridge (Sheriff's Turn).

[1] These entries are on the ALDBURGH Roll.

[2] Date correct, though out of order.

[3] Robert and Richard appear frequently as jurors in subsequent years.

1556, March 28.	*Robert Marshall* of Mylby, deft., plea of debt.
	Robert Marshall of Burghbrygge plt. in like plea. To next Court.
April 25.	*Robt. M.* agreed with plt. *Robert M.* plt. *non pros.*
1558, Dec. 3.	*Robert Marshall* of Mylbye summoned to answer Richard Thornton of Boro'bridge in plea of debt—does not come. Therefore "in exitus."
	¶ At next Court s[d] Robt. came & acknowledged debt (40s.) Judgment for amount and costs. Also fined.
1566, Nov. 9.	Robert Marshall acknowledged debt to Agnes Warde, widow.
1567, April 12.	Robert Marshall of Milbye *non pros. c.* John Clerke of Kirkebye super montem.
1567-8, March 6.	Robert Marshall pays for licence of concord with *Anne* Warde widow.
1586, Dec. 21.	*Thomas Marshall* plt. in plea of debts 20*s.* (Knaresbro')
1587, Oct. 23.	*William Marshall*, juror for Boro'bridge.
1588, Sept. 8.	*Thomas Marshall*, plt. in detinue (Boro'bridge and Aldburgh).
Oct. 4.	*William Marshall*, juror Borobridge, and in subsequent years.
1589-90, Jan'y 17.	*William Marshall* plt. (in trespass).
1602, Sept. 8.	Anthony Smithe surrendered 2 acres of land and meadow with buildings thereon and appurtenances in Hampsethwayte and Rowden within the township of Clint, now in the occupation of *Robert Marshall* to the use of said *Robt. M* : for 8 years from Ladyday next (25 March, 1603) at yearly rent of 13*s.* 4*d.*
1612, Oct. 13.	John Pulleyn of Fuiston surr[d] two closes called Peter Banke and Milne Holme (2 ac. of land and mead.) at Fuiston within the township of Timble (now in the ten[e] or occup[n] of Francis Jeffrey) to use of *Thomas Marshall* of Moorcallerton, his heirs and assigns for ever, according to custom of the forest *etc.*
1613, April 28.	*Wm. Marshall* plt. (with 2 others) in a plea of debt.
1614, May 18.	*Agnes Marshall* amerced for not prosecuting plaint *c.* Wm. Watson (debt).
1617, April 23.	*Thomas Marshall*, who held two closes called 'Peter Banke' and 'Milneholme' (two acres of land and meadow (formerly in the tenure of Francis Jeffrey) at Fuiston in the township of Timble *diem suum clausit extremum* ; after whose death came *William Marshall* as son and next heir of the said *Thomas*, and took said closes *etc.*
"	*William Marshall* gen. and John Bradley surrendered two closes *etc.* [as above] at Fuiston *etc.* now in the occupation of Francis Taskard and Thomas Forest to the use of Robert Michell, his heirs and assigns for ever *etc.*
1623, Sept. 24.	Robert Sayner of Bramham and late of the parish of Hampsthwait surrendered 3 roods of land, meadow and pasture called 'Akers' in the hamlet of Fellescliffe in the township of *Clint* (now in his own tenure) to the use of *Elizabeth Marshall*, her heirs and assigns for ever *etc.*
1624, May 19.	Robert Seyner surrendered half of six roods of land called 'Ackers' in the hamlet of Feliselife within the township of Clint (now in his own tenure or occupation) to the use of *Elizabeth Marshall* her heirs and assigns for ever.
1625, July 9 ALDBURGH.	*William Marshall* lying *in extremis* surrendered one acre of arable land lying in the field of Aldburgh called Sowersykefeilde upon a furlong called Langcells with appur'ts to the use of William Scroton son of John S. his heirs and assigns for ever.
1633, Oct. 17.	*Roger Marshall* elected Constable of "Bilton et Harrogait" in the Great Court holden on Thursday 17 October, 9 Charles I.
1634, Oct. 22.	*Robert Marshall.* Margaret Waid, widow and ex'x of the last *Will of John Waid owes *Robert Marshall* £44 on

a bond not paid by either said John or widow. Therefore he (Robert) recovers debt and damages and costs.

1638-9, Jan'y 23. *John Marshall* plt. in plea of debt *v.* John Umplebie.

1642, May 18. *Elizabeth Marshall* surrendered half of six roods of land called 'Akers' within Fenscliffe [Felscliff] in the township of Clint (now in the occupation of Thomas Lax) to the use of John Kidd, his heirs & assigns for ever.

1648, Oct. 12. "Al' Pene" that *Brian Marshall* put away his Dogg being unlawfull betwixt & ye xxj October Instant sub pena xj^{s} [amount doubtful] "Al' Pene that the said *Brian* shall make a sufficient Moorefenc betwixt his Hall & Bowcher yayt betwixt & the second of february next sub pena xx^{s}.

1649, May 30. John Cheldray *v. Brian Marshall* in a plea of trespass on the case.

1650, 1 May. *Thomas Marshall* of Harrogate co. York 'Taylor' and Anne his wife surr^{d} a mess. and 3 ac. land and mead. thereto belong^{g} with all buildings and appur'ts situate at Harrogate w'in the parish of Killinghall now in ten^{e} or occup^{n} of s^{d} Tho. M. to the use of Wm. Cooke (son & heir of said Anne), his h. & as. for ever.

22 May. John Monnkton of Flasby surr^{d} a mess. and 8 ac. of land meadow or pasture, situate in the hamlet of Harrogate and parish of Killinghall in ten^{e} or occup. of Tho. Marshall to the use of said Tho. Marshall & his ass. for term of 7 years next ensuing yielding therefor to said J.M. £10 yearly at Ladyday & Mic'hmas.

1651-2, March 3. Fine of land—8*d.* Wilferey Harrison surrendered half of a messuage called 'Wrenchill' & 4 acres, "two peniworth & a halfe of Land & meadow" with all buildings thereon in the Hamlet of Timble to the use of *Dorithey Marshall* wife of *John Marshall* & *Anne M:* (dau. of said *John* & *Dorithey*) all of Yeadon co. York, their h. & ass. *etc.*

" " Fine for years—14*d.* *John Marshall* of Yeadon co. York, yeoman, surr^{d} abovesaid half of a mess. (as above) *etc.*, to the use of Wilferey Harrison and his ass. from 25 March next for 5 years paying for the last half year of the said term the sum of *£2 : 6 : 8 etc.*

1652, April 14. Christopher Yeates and Thomas Culburne surr^{d} two closes (one acre of land and meadow) in Timble (now in ten^{e} or occup^{n} of Thomas Culburne) to the use of *Dorithey Marshall*, now wife of *John M.*, her heirs and assigns for ever.

John Marshall surr^{d} the aforesaid two closes to the use of Tho. Culburne and Anne his wife for their lives and life of survivor, paying yearly to said *John M.* his h. or ass. 40*s.* at Mayday and Martinmas.

July 7. John Monkton of Flasby surr^{d} moiety of a messuage and 8 acres of land meadow and pasture in hamlet of Bilton cum Harregate within the township of Killinghall (now in ten^{e} or occup^{n} of *Thom.* [first written *John* and then corrected] *Marshall*) after his (Monkton's) death to the use of Jane Linfoote wife of Mr. Peter L. for her life *etc.* The same John Monkton surr^{d} a mess. and 8 acres (as above) "as it is now In the tenure and occupa'con of *Thomas Marshall*" after his (Monkton's) death to the use of Thomas Ward and James Ward grandsons of said John.

1656, April 30. Peter Linford gent. and Jane his wife, Thomas Ward and James Ward surr^{d} one ancient building and 8 acres of land, mead. and past. in hamlet of Bilton cum Harrogate and township of Killinghall (now in ten^{e} or occup^{n} of *Thomas Marshall* or his assigns) To the use of John Lewis *etc.*

1661, June 5. *John Marshall* surr^{d} half of a mess., a house, a close and an "Intacke" (4 acres land and meadow) with buildings and appur'ts in hamlet of Timble as they are now in occup^{n} of

Will'm Watson to the use of said Wm. Watson & ass. from 25 March last (1661) for term of 21 yrs. next ensuing yielding yearly to said John M. £4 : 4s. at Lady-day & Mich'mas equally, according *etc.*

1661-5, Feb. 22. *John Marshall* of Yeadon surr[d] a close called 'Wrenchil,' containing one acre of land (more or less) with all buildings and appurt's situate in the hamlet of Timble now or lately in the occupation of John Gambling, to the use of the said John Gambling, his ex'ors adm'ors and assigns from Ladyday next (1665) for 21 years, yielding to said *John M.* at the feasts of SS. Philip and James (May 1) and St. Martin-in-winter (11 Nov.) 15 shillings yearly.

1671, Oct. 26. Henry Clint and Mary his wife, Richard Clint and Richard Roome (she Mary sole examined *etc.*) surr[d] one ancient building and three closes, called the 'upper close, nether close and spencie mires' (3 acres of land and meadow) with all buildings and appu'rts situate in the hamlet of Beckwith and Rosset and township of Killinghall (as now in the occupation of said Ric. Roome), to the use of *John Marshall* of Newall his h. & ass. for ever. And hereupon comes *J. M. etc.* and is admitted tenant.

John Marshall of Clifton [*sic*] surr[d] the premises above-named (now in occup[n] of Ric. Roome) to the use of Ric. Roome his exor's ad'mors & assigns from Ladyday next following (25 March, 1672) for the term of 20 years—yielding yearly to said *J. M.* or his assigns £8 10*s.* rent at 1 May & 11 Nov. equally.

1672, May 2. Toby Humphrey esq. surr[d] one ancient building, and 3 closes of land & meadow, called the 'Spencie mires, over close' and 'nether close' (3 acres) situate in hamlet of Beckwith & Rosset and township of Killinghall (now in the occupation of Ric. Roome) to the use of *John Marshall*, his h. & ass. for ever according to the custom of the Forest. Hereupon comes *J. M. etc.*

1675, August 11. Thomas Grayson & Jane his wife (she sole exam[d]) surr[d] one barn and one close called 'Windhill feild' (one acre of land & meadow) with appurts. in hamlet of Birstith and township of Clint (now in occupation of said Tho. Grayson) to the use of *John Marshall* of the City of York grocer, his h. & ass. for ever. Hereupon came said J. M. and took the said premises *etc.* and was admitted tenant thereof.

1677, Sept 5. *Richard Greaves* surr[d] one messuage, half of one messuage, 3 barns & 8 closes of land & meadow called Salmon close and Garth, low croft, and backcroft, long lands, limekill close, far feild & ealand pasture' (containing 5 acres) with all buildings, &c. in the hamlet of Hill within the township of Thurscrosse (now in occup[n] of said Richard) to the use of *John Marshall* of Yeadon, his h. & ass. for ever. Hereupon comes *John M. etc.* admitted tenant.

John Marshall surr[d] the above-named [names all repeated] to be after the death of himself to the use of *Judeth Hanne* and *Susan Marshall* daughters of said *John*, and their h. & assigns for ever, according to the custom *etc.* And hereupon came said *Judeth*, *Hanna* [before Hanne], and *Susan Marshall*, after the death of the said *John* by *Dorothy Marshall* their guardian, and took of the Lady the Queen [Katherine] the premises *etc.*

John Marshall surr[d] one mess. etc. [as before, but the 8 closes mentioned without the names being repeated] to the use of Richard Greaves [then occupier, as by the first entry], for life of himself, yielding to him (*J. M.*) or his assigns yearly £11 at Martinmas during the said term.

¶ All these entries follow, one the other; two on the *recto*, the 3rd on the *verso* (at top).

1678, June 5. *John Marshall* surr[d] one acre of land in Birstith to the use of Thomas Fentyman.

1679, May 15. *John Marshall*, one of two tenants who witness a surrender in Timble.

1681, Oct. 20. John Canler and Anne his wife surr[d] in Bilton cum Harrogate to the use of *John Marshall* of the City of York, who came and was admitted.

¶ I find John Candler in Harrogate at Court 14 June 1682.

1684, April 1. *John Marshall* of City of York surr[d] land in Harrogate now in the occupation of John Candler to the use of Lawrence Danson the younger, who was admitted.

May 7. *John Marshall* of Newall surr[d] messuage and 3 closes[1] of land & meadow in hamlet of Beckwith and Rosset (now in the occupation of Richard Roome) to the use of *Richard Marshall*, his h. & ass. for ever. Hereupon Ric. M. within age by Francis[2] (or Frances) Marshall his guardian, admitted.

1685, Sept. 2. John Marshall came in person and prayed to be admitted to one rood, parcel of the waste within the parish of Pannell. Proclamation made *etc.* *J. M.* to hold &c. yearly rent 1½*d.* Fine 10*s.*

Oct. 22. *John Marshall* of City of York surr[d] one barn and one acre[3] of land & meadow in the hamlet of Birstith and township of Clint (now in the occupation of Thomas Fentyman) to the use of Leonard Askwith his h. & ass. who was admitted tenant.

1686, August 25. Joseph Simpson of Rawden and Anne his wife (she sole exam[d]) surr[d] half a messuage, called 'Wrenchill' and 4 acres 2½ pennyworth of land & meadow in township of Timble (now in the occupation of Wm. Richardson), to the use of *Dorothy Marshall*, her h. & ass. for ever. She was admitted.

1687, Oct. 27. *Dorothy Marshall*, widow, surr[d] half a messuage, 2 barns, 5 acres 2½ pennyworth of land & meadow at Gillbecks within township of Timble to the use of William Richardson his ex'ors and adm'ors from 25 March next (1688) for term of eleven years. Wm. came and was admitted. Fine 18*s.*

1690, Dec. 10. *Richard Marshall* of Clifton surr[d] a messuage and 3 closes (over & nether close & spence mires) at Beckwith shaw within township of Killinghall to the use of Richard Roome his ex'ors and adm'ors from 25 March last (1689) for the term of six years yielding to said *R. M.* £7 10*s.* yearly at the feasts of SS. Philip & James & S. Martin the bishop in winter (*i.e.* 1 May and 11 Nov.). Hereupon Ric. Roome admitted.

1693, May 11. John Hawkin and Ellen his wife (she sole exam[d]) surr[d] one waste builded with appur'ts in Knar: near the river Nid (now in the occupation of said John); to the use of *Sara Marshall*, her heirs & assigns. She admitted tenant.

1694, Oct. 25. *Richard Marshall* lying in peril of death surr[d] one ancient building and 3 closes (upper close, nether close and Spence mires) in hamlet of Beckwith & Rosset and township of Killinghall (now in the occupation of Richard Roome) to the use of *Francis Marshall* and *John Marshall*, their heirs & assigns for ever. Hereupon came *Francis* and *John etc.* and were admitted tenants.

1697, Oct. 21. *Francis Marshall* and *John Marshall* surr[d] one ancient building, 2 barns and 3 closes (3 acres) at Beckwith shaw within the township of Killinghall (now in the occupation of Ric. Roome), to the use of Thomas Stub, his h. & ass. for ever, who is admitted tenant.

[1] Spence mires, over close and nether close.

[2] No sex indicated.

[3] 'Windall feild.'

Nov. 10. *Dorothy Marshall*, widow, surr^d half one messuage, and one close of land & meadow (4 acres) within the township of Timble (now in the occupation of William Richison) to the use of *John Marshall* her son, his h. & ass. for ever. Hereupon *John M.* admitted.

1699, May 4. John Marshall of Yeadon surr^d half a mess. and 5 acres 1½ pennyworth of land and meadow (now in the occupation of Wm. Richardson), to the use of Willam Watson his heirs & assigns for ever. Said Wm. admitted tenant.

1700, Dec. 18. Richard Somergill and Elizabeth Coates, widow, surr^d one waste builded in Tentergate within the township of Scriven to the use of *Sara Marshall*, her h. & ass. for ever. She came & was admitted.

1702, Oct. 22. *Thomas Marshall* elected one of the two constables of Knaresburgh town.

1705, Oct. 24. *Thomas Marshall* one of the Jurors for the borough.

1707, Oct. 29. *John Marshall* of City of York and *John Marshall* his son surr^d a parcel of waste within the parish of Pannell[1] and late in the occupation of Stephen Kitchin or his assigns to the use of Matthew Maunby, his heirs & assigns for ever. Said Matthew admitted tenant.

1715, Nov. 26. John Holdsworth of Kirksmoor with out the Court surrendered by virtue of power and authority given to him by *John Marshall* of Spanish-town in Jamaica by Letters of Attorney dated 2 May 1715 (1 Geo. I) two messuages and 23 acres of land lying & being at Beckwith Shaw within the township of Clint (containing 23 acres more or less) with all buildings and appur'ts (now in the occupation of Matthew Pawson and Wm. Forrest or their assigns) to the use of Mary Spinage, wife of Richard Spinage of Newberry, Berks, and of Elizabeth Marshall of Masham, co. York, their heirs and assigns for ever.

"I *John Marshall* of Spanish Town in the Island of Jamaica in America Gent., nephew & heir at law to Susanna Smith late of London widow deceased, late wife of Joshua Smith late of London merchant have made *etc.* [here naming his two attornies[2]] for me and in my name to surrender *etc.* all and singular such messuages &c. whereunto I shall be admitted Tenant &c. to the use & behoof of my wellbeloved sisters Mary Spenege wife of Ric. S. of Newbury Berks lately called *Mary Marshall Elizabeth Marshall* of Masham, co. York spinster their heirs and assigns for ever. Dated 2 May 1715 and 1 George.

Affidavit sworn 28 June 1715.

Joseph Maxwell late of Jamaica gentleman but now of London, deposes that he is well acquainted with *John Marshall* of Spanish-town gentleman and saw him (John) deliver letter of attorney in due form of law. He (Joseph) thereto set his name as Witness.

¶ John Marshall of Spanish-town in Jamaica, gentleman, says that he is nephew & heir at law to Susanna Smith widow deceased.

Now, I find, as follows :—

1713, Oct. 1. Susanna Smith, widow and relict of Joshua Smith late of the parish of S. Alp[h]age, London, merchant, surrendered 1 Oct. 1713 all the title to 3 messuages and lands (32 acres) in Beckwith & Rossett (lately occupied by said Joshua Smith) to the use of Samuel Smith of Leeds, who is admitted *etc.*

[1] *See* 1685, Sept. 2.

[2] The letters of attorney are made to John Holdsworth of *Kelsmoor*, co. York, Grazier, and to William Beckworth of Masham, co. York, Grocer.

1713, Nov. 11. Joshua Smith of London merchant who held one messuage, 3 ancient buildings and 32 acres at Beckwith and Rossett within the township of Killinghall died; after whose death at this Court (11 Nov. 1713) came Samuel Smith of Leeds brother and heir of Joshua and took premises *etc.*

1714, Oct. 20. Samuel Smith of Leeds and Matthew Drawer surr[d] *etc.* [as above] to such uses as the said Samuel by his last Will or other writing should declare.

1720, Feb. 21. *John Marshall gen.* Richard Spinage *gen.* and Mary his wife, Benjamin Collins *gen.* and Elizabeth his wife (said Mary and Elizabeth sole examined) surr[d] half of two messuages, and half of several closes of land [here named] situate in the hamlet of Beckwith with Rossett within the forest (containing 23 acres), also half of all other customary lands and tenements within the said forest to the use of Richard Spinage *gen.*, his heirs & assigns for ever, *etc.*

1720-1, Feb. 21. *John Marshall gen.*, Richard Spinage *gen.* & Mary, Benj. Collins & Eliz: (as before) surr[d] half of two mess. and half of several closes [named again—all as before] to the use of Benj. Collins *gen.* his h. and ass. for ever. Hereupon at this

March 22. Court (22 March, 172$\frac{0}{1}$) comes to Benjamin Collins &c. and admitted *etc.*

1726, May 5. *Martha Marshall* late wife of *Thomas M.* of Knar: who held half of one waste builded with appur'ts situate in "Le back lane prope Le Town well in Knaresbrough predicta" died; after whose death came *Thomas Marshall*, son and heir of *Martha*, and prayed *&c.* admitted.

August 22. *Thomas Marshall*, Leonard Sibber and Mary his wife of the City of York, and Francis Plumer and Margaret his wife, surr[d] without the Court, viz. 22 Aug. 1726, one waste builded with appur'ts sit[e] in the back Lane near the Town well of Knar: To the use of William Slater, his h. & ass. which Wm. S. is admitted.

¶ Inrolled in Court (Sheriff's Turn) holden 20 Oct. 1726.

1730-1, Jan. 29. Sara Simpson widow without the Court, viz. 29 January 1730-1, surr[d] one waste builded situate near the March bridge in Knaresbrough with the appur'ts (now in her own occupation) to the use of *Thomas Marshall* his h. & ass. for ever. Condition that said Tho. M. his exors &c. pay to Richard Simpson, son of John S. dec'd, the sum of £3 10s. within six months after the death of the said Sarah. Else Ric. Simpson his ex'ors &c. shall enter on the premises etc. until said sum of £3 10s. with all costs shall be paid.

MISCELLANEOUS NOTES OF WILLS AND ADM'ONS.

(Continued from p. 58.)

Richard Aishe, citizen and butcher of London, mentions sister Joane Marshall 1612. P.C.C. (26 Fenner.)

Margaret Snell of Reach in co. Cambridge, widow, mentions cousin Diana Marshall. P.C.C. (35 Fenner.)

William Grey of East Doniland, co. Essex, Esq. gives his virginals to his daughter-in-law Elizabeth Marshall. P.C.C. (74 Fenner.)

Alice Handcock of Capland in parish of Brodway, co. Somerset, widow. Mentions daughter Eleanor wife of Roger Marshall, and their daughter Johan Marshall. P.C.C. (87 Capell.)

Thomas Fisher the elder of Taunton, co. Somerset, merchant. Mentions my wifes daughter Grace Marshall. P.C.C. (105 Capell.)

Thomas Hoale of Battel, Sussex, mentions kinsman Mr John Marshall of London, Fishmonger. P.C.C. (110 Capell.)

Thomas Russell of Willingdon, co. Sussex, mentions his daughters Elizabeth wife of Thomas Marshall, and Mary wife of Thomas Oxenbridge. P.C.C. (2 Lawe.) *See* Vol. i. p. 96.

Thomasine Cattell of Erith, co. Huntingdon. Mentions cousin Thomas Marshall. P.C.C. (73 Lawe.)

Will of Thomas Marshall of Worrall in Bradfield, dated 26 August 1616. mentions his children, John, (under 28), Elizabeth, Mary Ann, and Alice Marshall. Proved at York by Ann his relict, 7 May, 1617. *See* Vol. i. p. 263.

John Tims of London, Gent., in his will dated 29 Dec., 1760, and proved in P.C.C. 26 March, 1763, mentions his cousin Mrs. Sarah Marshall. (158 Cæsar.)

George Dalton of St. Saviour's, Southwark, Citizen and Joiner of London in his will dated 7 Oct., 1626, mentions daughter Elizabeth wife of Thomas Marshall, their daughter Anne Marshall, and their sons Gilbert and George Marshall. Proved in Archdeaconry Court of Surrey, 30 Nov., 1626. (369 Yeast.)

Mary Gray of Colchester, Essex, mentions grandchild Mary Marshall, and cousin Mary Wiseman. 1616. P.C.C. (77 Cope.)

Thomas Wilding, citizen and Dyer of London, mentions sisters Elizabeth Marshall, and Katherine Bigge; also brother Richard Marshall, and brother John Bigge. Proved in P.C.C. 1616. (95 Cope.) *See* Vol. i. p. 77.

Judith Cawdwell of Anstey in co. Leicester, singlewoman. Mentions mother Anne Marshall, and brother Samuel Marshall. P.C.C. (124 Cope.)

John Knighton of Bayford, co. Herts, Esq., son of Sir George Knighton, mentions cousin Anne Marshall wife of......Marshall of Hackney, 1635. P.C.C. (37 Sadler.)

John Ruggle of Glemsford, co. Suffolk, 1594. Mentions sister Elizabeth Firmin, and her four children Edmund Firmin, Anne Tanner, Margaret Marshall, and Katherine Marshall. P.C.C. (16 Scott.)

Will of Thomas Marshall of Wicken Bonhant, co. Essex, husbandman. Dated 7 August, 1637. To daughters Anne Marshall and Dorothie Marshall, £4 apiece. Wife Ursula sole executrix. She proved 13 Sept., 1637. (Consistory Court of London, 296 Allen.)

Francis Barrell heretofore of St. Margaret's Rochester, but now of Upper Grosvenor St. co. Middlesex, Esq. Mentions, nephew the Revd Mr Edmund Marshall, Vicar of Charing, co. Kent; daughter Catherine Barrell; sisters Ann Barrell, and Catherine Marshall; wife Frances Barrell sole executrix. Dated 16 July, 1770. Proved by Frances Barrell the relict, 5 March, 1772, in P.C.C. (81 Taverner.) *See* Vol. i. app. p. 25.

Josiah Frith, minister of God's word, [Rector] of St Alphage, London. Dated 19 Nov., 1637. To Phebe Cartwright of Low Lane, London, £10. To Edward Fuller minister of the word of God all my MSS. Richard Marshall a witness. Proved in Consistory Court of London...January, 1637-8. (354 Allen.)

Gregory Francklyn in his will dated 19 Feb., 1635, mentions cousin M[rs] Martha Marshall. P.C.C. (32 Pile.)

Charles Bigland of Chelmsford, will in P.C.C., proved 1625, mentions his cousin John Marshall, and his wife Sarah Marshall. (7 Clark.)

William Marshall, is called 'son in law' in the will of David Powell of Stretton, co. Gloucester, clerk, proved 1625. P.C.C. (43 Clark.)

Thomas Badily of S[t] Peter ad Vincula, will proved in P.C.C. 1625, mentions his sister Marshall. (146 Clarke.)

Bartholomew Harris of London, Merchant, will proved in P.C.C. 1641, mentions his uncle James Marshall. (45 Evelyn.)

Charles Webster of Richmond, co. Surrey, plaisterer. Will dated 14 August, 1783. Mentions son-in-law James Marshall. P.C.C. (439 Cornwallis.)

This James Marshall was of Newport St. Westminster, Grocer. He is mentioned in the will of Joseph King of Richmond, 1780. (267 Collins.)

Will of Eleanor Brown of Marshgate, in the parish of Richmond, co. Surrey. Dated 24 Oct., 1774. Mentions son James Marshall, Esq., sister Margaret Howard. Alexander French of Rotherhithe, Esq. Nephew John Howard now of the kingdom of Ireland. Son Jackson Brown. Nephew Nicholas Garway. Proved in P.C.C. 22 Oct., 1777 by James Marshall. (409 Collier.)

William Monday of Bilstrop in the county of Nottgā, gen., 18 June, 1648, in parfitt healthe,—unto my daughter Elyzabeth wiffe vnto garves Marshall minister of Whatton all my land at Lenton and at Nottingā to her and her Right hayres, if the said Elyzabeth do dye with[t] heyres before her husband my will is that my son in law Garvis Marshall shall hold all that land for term of his life paying vnto my daughter Juedeth yerely 20[s] and after his decease to come to my daughter Judeth and her heirs, remainder over to Mary Dawson daughter of Thom' Dawson of Morpitt [Morpeth] in the co. of Northumberland, Taner, which daughter he had by my daughter Margarett, remainder to right heirs of testator. To son in law Garves Marshall all my Svaying [surveying] Instruments, etc., and half my printed books, the other half to Samwell Smith my wiffe Soon to be equally divided between them. Land at Blidworth to wife Judith wch Phillop Abbott and William Flint holdeth by lease, for terme of her life and after her decease to my daughter Judith and her right heirs. To my daughter Judeth all my land at Edenstow [Edwinstow] and for lack of her heirs I give the land at Blidworth and Edenstow to my daughter Elizabeth wife of Garves Marshall. To my wiffe To Soons Samvell and John either of them 20[s]. To godson William Leason my Bowe and sheath of arrowes, and to my son Kidson on shilling. To servant Troth Walker 2[s]. Wife Judeth and daughter Judeth executrixes. To my son in law Thom' Dawson who married with my daughter Margaret 12[d].

Witnesses, Gilbert Benet, Rect. eccles. Richard Needham. Henry Preston. Proved at York 5 January 1648-9. ult. 40[li].

John Marshall of Stilton, co. Huntingdon, Inn-holder. Dated 16

Aug., 1763. Wife Ann Marshall, executrix. Nephew John Watson. Larrat Langley. John King. Adm'on with will annexed, the executrix having renounced, 15 Oct., 1763, to Ann Thornhill and Allen Hopkins, creditors, in P.C.C. (478 Cæsar.) *See* p. 80.

John Marshall of Forestreet in the parish of St. Giles without Cripplegate, London, cheesmonger. Dated 30 Aug., 1758, Brother William Marshall of Wandsworth in the co. of Surrey, Gent., sole executor and universal legatee. Mentions grand-daughter Elizabeth Potter. Proved in P.C.C. by said Willm Marshall, 13 Oct., 1763. (478 Cæsar.) *See* p. 80.

FROM DONCASTER ACT BOOK, AT YORK.

1602. July 20. Probate of will of William Marshall of will of Stannington, to Elizabeth his relict, and Elizabeth Greaves, Alice Brigg, and Emott Rose, his daughters. *See* Vol. i. p.

1603. Oct., 6. Adm'on of Robert Marshall of Bradfield to Ann Marshall. 1632, March 29, and 1633, May 14. Tuition of Ellen, Mary, Elizabeth, Margaret, and Emmott, daughters of William Marshall of Bradfield, to Emmott Broomhead, spinster.

1635. April 6. Probate of will of Margaret Taylor of Worrall to John Taylor and Dorothy Perkins, and power reserved to John Crawshaw and Alice Marshall.

1637. May 2. Tuition of Mary daughter of William Marshall of Nether Bradfield to John Smawfett.

PROBATES OF WILLS, AND ADM'ONS FROM THE ACT BOOK FOR THE PECULIAR OF HOWDENSHIRE, 1622--1735.

1624. Dec., 20. Adm'on of William Marshall of Balkeholme to Rosamunde Marshall his relict. Inventory under £20.

1624-5 Feb., 8. Adm'on of Oliver Marshall of Blacktoft to Ambrose Marshall his brother.

1632.* May 16. Adm'on of Rose Marshall, widow, of Bolkholme to Bartholomew Marshall, m'ri ejus. Inventory under £5.

1660-1. Feb., 13. Probate of Jennett Marshall of Cliffe in the parish of Henningborough to Thomas Marshall her son, and one of the executors. Inventory £34 8s. 4d.

1661. April 19. Thomas Marshall of Cliffe in the parish of Henningborough. Adm'on with will annexed to Thomas Marshall his son. Inventory under £40.

1680. March 1. Probate of Anthony Marshall of Howden to Susanna Marshall his widow.

1680. May 25. Probate of James Marshall of Howden to Dorothy Marshall his widow and sole executrix.

1684. Aug., 5. Adm'on with will annexed of Robert Marshall of Ellerker to Thomas Sissons to sole use of Rachel Marshall, widow, and Hanna Marshall daughter of said deceased, the executors named in the will.

* There are no probates or adm'ons from 1643-59.

1689. April 4. Care of person and portion of John Marshall son of John Marshall of Cliffe, according to his voluntary election, to Richard Clarkson.

At end of the year 1691 there is a list of "Wills, Bonds, and Inventories, etc., not entered by Mr. Mawde," among them,

William Marshall of Howden, original will, inventory, and probate bond, 1695.

1697. June 9. Adm'on of Richard Marshall of Gilberdike to Margaret his relict.

1703. June 29. Probate of Thomas Marshall of North Duffield to Sarah Marshall, widow, and sole executrix.

1720. Sept. 1. Adm'on of Elizabeth Marshall of Howden to Anne wife of Thomas Bedford her daughter. Inventory under £5.

1729. April 12. Probate of Mary Marshall of Longcliffe to Nathaniel Andrew and Frances Granger co-executors.

Wills in South Cave Peculiar, 1687-1843.

1706.	Robert Marshall of South Cave.			Will.
1706.	Richard	,,	,,	Inventory.
1713.	Catherine	,,	,,	Will.
no date.	John	,,	,,	Will.

Wills in Alne and Tollerton Peculiar, 1601-1856.

Wills of Matthew Marshall of Tollerton, 1711; and Miles Marshall of Flawith, Merchant Taylor, 1791.

Wills in Knaresborough Peculiar.

1772.	Bundle	R. No. 11.	Capt[n] Marshall.
1772.	,,	R. No. 31.	William Marshall.
1776.	,,	T. No. 24.	Thomas Marshall.

The only earlier document is a Tuition of John Marshall in 1683.

Wills in Masham Peculiar.

1585. John Marshall of Masham Book i. fo. 154.
1585. John ,, of Seirby in parish of Masham. Book i. fo. 166.
1613. Francys ,, of Masham. Book i. fo. 221.
1632. Christopher ,, of Masham, Yeoman. Book i. fo. 381.[1]

Adm'ons of Leonard Marshall of Grewelthorpe (in West Riding), 28 April, 1682; and of Christopher Marshall of Masham, ... July, 1707.

Wills proved in Peculiar Court of Southwell.

John Marshall of Southecarleton, in the p'ishe of Southmuskh'm in the countie of Nott[m]. Dated 13 Nov., 1582. I give vnto my nephewe Rauffe my ring of remembrance. Vnto my brother Rauffe a brace of Angells to make him a ringe of. Vnto my brother Francis, yf he be alive and be able to come into the countrie and to weare it, my best cloke. To my servant William Neave 'Rasfalls abridgement' of the eldest date, the "Justice of Peace" of the eldest date, 'Littleton

[1] Christopher Marshall of Massam, co. York, yeoman. Dated 20th Dec., 1632. To be buried in the parish church of Massam. Son John Marshall. To two daughters Jaine and Susanna £20 apiece when 24. To sister Anne Linge 10s. Wife Elizabeth sole executrix.

and Parkins' of the newest date. To Will'm Ellis of Southmuskh'm my wint[r] boots. My dau'r Ellin'. [Ellinor.] My son Henrie. My nephew Raulfe Marshall, my nephew William Marshall, my brother Raulfe his children, and my brother Meringe children shall have free accesse vnto my written books of lawe, to coppie theme out at their pleasure. These books are bequeathed to Henry Marshall. Wife to be sole executrix. Brother M[r] Henry Marshall and father in law M[r] Ric. Athelston supervisors. Son Henry's portion to be in government of wife till he is twenty-one. Witnesses, Nich'as Irelande,[1] Richarde Irelande, Elino[r] Marshall, William Neave, and Briget Clarke, with Robert Ellyotte. Proved by relict in the peculiar court of Southwell, 28 May, 1583. (Vol. iv. 1567-1592.)

Adm'on granted by peculiar court of Southwell of goods of Robert Marshall of Southmuskham, 24 April, 1604, to John Marshall and Oliver Marshall of Staley Woodthorpe, in co. Derby, husbandmen, his brothers. (Vol. v. p. 484.)

Francis Marshall of North Muskham, gent. To Robert Marshall my nephew, 6[s] 8[d],—[2]Anne Askewe 6[s] 8[d],—[2]Marie Marshall the elder 6[s] 8[d],—[2]Henrie Cawton 6[s] 8[d],—[2]Katherine Cawton 6[s] 8[d], -[2]John Mearinge 6[s] 8[d]. Godsons, Francis Robothom, Francis Strawe, Francis Ashley, Francis Saxton, Francis Deane. Edmunde Platts. Goddaughters, Elizabeth Livesey, and Marie Crookes. Francis Johnson. Elizabeth Garnon. William Livesey and Helnour his wife. Brother Rauf Marshall sole executor and residuary legatee. Dated 27 April, 4 King James. [1606]. Proved by said executor 22 October, 1606, in the peculiar court of Southwell. (Vol. v. p. 583.)

Rauf Marshall of Southmuskham. Dated 4 December, 1610. To be buried in the parish church of South Muskham. Son Robert Marshall. Daughter Anne Askew. Daughter Marie Marshall. Richard Willoughby and Henry Turner overseers. William Willoughby of South Muskham, Knight, executor. He renounced and probate granted to Edward Pim of South Muskham, gent., 7 May, 1611, by peculiar court of Southwell. (Vol. v. p. 798.)

Adm'on of William Marshall of Holme in the parish of Northmuskham to Elizabeth Marshall his relict granted by peculiar court of Southwell 5 April, 1634.

MISCELLANEA.

College of Arms, 3 D 14, 27. Pedigree of Tyler of Boston in New England, relatives of Sir Isaac Heard. Mary Tyler married John Marshall. Lucy Tyler her sister married Samuel Marshall brother to said John, and had issue Samuel, Mary (*sic*), John, and Mary Marshall.

"The Field" newspaper, 18 May, 1878, p. 590. Notice of the town of Marshall, and the old Marshall Mansion, a type of the old Southern planter's home, North Texas.

[1] The will of John Irelande of Batheley in the parish of North Muskham, proved 1604, is registered Vol. v. p. 520.

[2] Evidently all nephews and neices.

College of Arms, K, 9, 209. Hester Meade, daughter of John Meade of Much Hayston, [Easton] co. Essex, who was aged 84 in 1667, married Nathaniel Marshall and had issue by him, Nathaniel, and William.

British Museum. Add. MS. 24,458, p. 294.

Thomas Marshall of Sheffield, was a member of the Revd T. Jollies congregation, and all his children were baptised by Mr. Jollie.

Jeremiah Marshall of Sheffield, Cutler. Bapt. 12 Feb. 1688-9.	= Hannah dau of Luke Winter of Sheffield, Cutler. Bapt. 1 Jany 1698. Mar. 28. Sept. 1719.	Joshua M. Bapt 20 Nov. 1690. ob. inf. — Edward M. Bapt 12 Dec. 1692.	Timothy Marshall of Sheffield, cutler. Bapt. 17 Jany 1694-5 Died 5 March, 1750.	= Helen Pearson. She mar. 2ly 12 Jany 1754-5, to Willm Smith of Sheffield, Cutler, and died 20 Dec. 1777, aged 69.	Sarah. bapt 31 May, 1697. — Mary bapt. 20 Feb. 1698-9. — Joshua M. bapt. 22 April 1700. — Georg M, bapt. 18 June 1702

Samuel Marshall of Sheffield, Ironmonger. Died unm. *circa* 1800. Only son. Was a well known and remarkable character at Sheffield. His will with a multitude of bequests may be seen.	Lydia only dau. died unm.	Hephzibah. Mar. at Sheffield 31 Aug. 1770 to Thomas Vennor of Sheffield, Mercer.

Somerset House. Vicar General's Books. Martin, Pt i, 12. Licence to bury Margarett Marshall, who died excommunicate, in parish church of St Sepulchre, dated 29 August, 1616. Mr. Blinkarne was the parson.

College of Arms. 7 D 14, 96-7. Pedigree of Walter Burrows who married Elizabeth dau. and heir of Francis Marshall of Lambeth. Married at St. George's Southwark 14 Feb. 1743. In Grants xvi. 50 there is a grant of arms to her.

College of Arms. Painter's Work Book, $\frac{11}{1}$, fo. 81 :—

11 Aug. 1683. Argent, a lion rampant gules, a chief Sable. *Impaling* Sable, three bars Argent, a canton ermine. Mr. Russell whose wife's name was Marshall.

This Mr. Russell I suppose to be Ralph Russell, citizen and Cooke of London, whose will dated 4 May 1683, was proved in P.C.C. 21 August following. (97 Drax.) He mentions his wife Susanna; daughter Anne Mudd; and sons, Nathaniel, Robert, and John. *cf.* Vol. i. p. 276.

Painter's Work Book, $\frac{11}{6}$, fo. 20b:—

22 Feb., 1691-2. Sable, a chevron Or between three boars' heads

Argent. (Wormall). *Impaling* Sable, three bars Argent, a canton Ermine (Marshall.)

There is in P.C.C. an adm'on of Israel Wormall of St Stephen Walbrook, London, to Rebecca Wormall his relict, dated 4 May, 1692. *See* Hulbert's "Annals of Almondbury," p. 520.

FROM FUNERAL ENTRIES IN ULSTER'S OFFICE, DUBLIN CASTLE, Vol. i. p. 14.

John Marshall sometime Shirefe of ye cittie of Dublin buryed in St. Patrick's Churche the 14th of July, 1597; he had to wife......... Genninges by whom he had issu:—Edward, and a daughter ma. to Lawrence Ussher, of Dublin, merchante.

EXTRACTS FROM A MS. IN THE "WILLIAM SALT LIBRARY" AT STAFFORD, ENTITLED "STAFFORDSHIRE MARRIAGE REGISTERS, XVIIth CENTURY," 1660-1700.

1660-1.	Midlam,	Roger	Marshall, Mabel	Burton on Trent.
1665.	Marshall,	Humphrey	Scattergood, Ann	Ashow.
1665.	Marshall	Richard	Hodgkys, Ann	Mancetter.
1668.	"	Edward	Hallam, Ann	Derby.
1681.	"	Thomas	Percivall, Alice	Lullington.
1681.	"	William	Short, Mary	Stone.
1684.	"	Henry	Saywell, Mary	Repton.
1684.	"	John	Clerk, Jane	Castleton.
1685.	"	William	Hilliot, Dorothy	Etwall.
1686.	Peirpoint,	Thomas	Marshall, Elizabeth	Marchington.
1687.	Marshall,	Thomas	Ward, Alice	Burton on Trent.
1688.	"	James	Taylor, Mary	Ashbourn.
1688.	"	John	Wordon, Sarah	West-hallam.
1690.	"	William	Wood, Ann	Sutton Coldfield.
1693.	"	Francis	Wolat, Ann	Marston upon Dove.
1693.	"	John	Poyser, Alice	Ellaston, Mathfield.
1693.	"	Joseph	Henshaw, Elizabeth	Chellaston, Osmaston.
1693.	"	William	Cotton, Elizabeth	Trentham.
1694.	"	William	Rolston, Margaret	Alveton.
1698.	"	Peter	Horsly, Ann	Rocester.

Licences for Marriages at St. Mary Magdalen, Old Fish St. from originals in Coll. Arms.

George Marshall of St Peter's Cornhill, bachelor, and Elizabeth Browne of St Clement Danes, spinster, dated 12 Oct., 1691. Married 13th.

John Barnfather of St Stephen's Coleman S^{t}, bachelor, and Elizabeth Marshall of the same, spinster, dated 12 July, 1711. Married 15th.

College of Arms, MS. I.C.B. 90, 738. Arms. Argent, a chevron invected Vert, between three cresents Gules. (A quartering to to the coat of Teasdale.)

George Marshall of Walltown = Mary d. and h. of Thomas Ridley, aged 15, 1615.

John Marshall mar. Jane d. of .... Coalsforth.	Thomas Marshall mar. Catherine d. of .... Scott, and had issue George Marshall, died s.p.	Jane dau. and eventual heir, mar. John Bacon.

Anne Bacon, eldest daughter = Middleton Teasdale.

Historical Register. 1735. June. "George Grantham of Wellingborough, Northamptonshire to Mrs Marshall, a widow, worth £900 per ann. He is her 5th husband, and she his 5th wife." The 'Chronological Diary,' at end of 'Historical Register.'

From a small MS. book in possession of James Coleman, bookseller, 1885:—Thos Marshal Married to Penelope his Wife Oc^{t} 29th An^{o} 1758 By the Revd Mr Richd White in Chequor Church Lincoln.

Anne Daughter of Thos and Pene^{l} Marshal Born Sept^{m} 3^{d} about 3 o'Clock in ye Afternoon An^{o} Dom. 1759.

William son of Thos and Pene^{l} Marshal Born Jan^{u} 24th about 11 o'clock in ye Forenoon An^{o} Dom. 1761. Dy'd in Sumer, 1764.

Thos son of Thos and Pen^{l} Marshal Born Sepr 6th about 3 o'Clock in the Afternoon Ano. 1762.

2^{d} William son of Thos & Pen^{l} Marshal Born May 30th 1768 about 11 o'Clock in the Evening.

I Thomas Marshal Stood Sponser for Mary Daughter of Willm & Eliz. Oliphent, In ye year of our Lord 1759.

Stood Sponser for Anna Daughter of Geo. & Eliz. Bingham, In ye Year of our Lord 1760.

Sponser for Joseph, Son of Joseph & Eliz. Walker, Ano. Dom. 1761. (Thomas Marshall the writer of the above was living in 1771.)

Masons Company. The earliest book in the possession of this Company is lettered "Masonic Accounts, 1620—1706" The following extracts relate to Edward Marshall who was Master Mason of England.[1] (See pedigree Vol. i. app. p. 24.)

fo. 47^b under head "Ingresse money of freemen." "Received of Edward Marshall late Apprentice of John Clerke made free in January 1626, xxiij^s x^d."

fo. 86. In 1631-2 Edward Marshall paid £5 fine for being admitted into the Livery and being discharged of the office of being one of the stewards thereof.

Duchy of Lancaster Court Rolls, No. 1588, Bundle 108. Pub. Rec. Office:—

View of Frankpledge with Court Baron, &c. 3 Oct. 1661. "Anth'us Marshall elect' in offic' co'is imparcatoris ib'm [Plumptre] pro hoc Anno sequen' Jur.'

Inquisitions Post Mortem.

Chancery Inquisition, 1 Elizabeth, 3rd Part, No. 168.

Inquisition taken at Ilmester Sept^r, 1. Eliz. [1559] on the death of Richard Marshall, Esq. who some time (*diu*) before he died was seized of the manor of Goosebraden in the parish of Curry Ryvell containing by estimation 240 acres, and lands in Glaston and Wembdon in co. Somerset, and lands in Walton and East Penn'd. He had granted them to William Porteman, Esq, and John Fry, gent., to use of him the said Richard Marshall and Lore his wife and the heirs of his body in virtue of which the said Wm Porteman and John Fry were seized to said use, and the jurors say that said Richard Marshall was seized in fee of the capital Mansion of Ivythorn, and died so seized, and they say that Richard Marshall died leaving Lora surviving, and that he died [date gone] and that Richard Marshall is his son and heir and is aged 30.

See Gentleman's Magazine, April 1865, p. 486. Collinson's Somerset, iii. 424.

John Marshall died seized of the Manor of Ivythorne. Esc. 11 Edw. IV, No. 20.

John Marshall of Ivythorne, son and heir 11 Edw. IV. [1471-2.] = Joane dau. of John Fitz-James, Lord Chief Baron. His will pro. 12 May, 1542. *See* Foss's Judges.

A

[1] The petition of this Edward Marshall for the confirmation of the grant of the place of Master Mason (May, 1660), and the grant of that place, void by death of Nicholas Stone, dated at Hampton Court, 28 Sept., 1647, will be found in Egerton MS. (Brit. Museum) 2549, fo^s 31, 32.

A

- Elizabeth dau. of Moore of Moore-heyes co. *Devon.* *See* Colby's Visitation of Devon, pp. 161, 162. = Richard Marshall of Ivythorne, Esq. Inq. p.m. dated ... Sept. 1 Eliz. = Lora, dau. of ... Rogers, 2 wife, survived her husband.
- Isabel, wife of Edmund Probal of Weston in Gordano.

Children of Richard Marshall and Lora:

- Thomas Marshall.
- George Marshall.
- Mary, mar. Leonard Horner.
- Elizabeth, mar. John Thomas of Gloucestershire.

Children of Richard Marshall and Elizabeth:

- Richard Marshall of Ivythorne, aged 30 in Sept. 1559. Had a grant of Arms 1573.[1] = Anne, dau. of John Selwood of Chard.
  - George Marshall.
- Barbara, wife of Ralph Whalley of London.

Index of Inquisitions Post Mortem. Court of Wards.
34 Henry VIII. to 10 Charles I.

35 Henry VIII.	William Marshall.	York.	Vol. i,	page	20.
1 Edward VI.	William ,,	Lincoln.	,, iii,	,,	12.
20 Elizabeth.	John ,,	York.	,, xix,	,,	94.
24 Elizabeth.	William ,,	York.	,, xx,	,,	118.
43-44 Elizabeth.	John ,,	Lincoln.	,, xxvi,	,,	204.
1-2 James.	John ,,	York.	,, xxviii,	,,	100.
1-2 James.	Thomas[2] ,,	Sussex.	Bundle vii,	No.	17.
9-10 James.	Richard ,,	Durham.	,, xiv,	,,	13.
10-11 James.	Thomas[3] ,,	York.	,, xvii,	,,	64.
10, 11, 12 James.	John ,,	Leicester.	,, xviii,	,,	59.
14 James.	Richard. ,,	Durham.	,, xx,	,,	40.
12-13 James.	Agnes ,,	Durham.	,, xxii,	,,	233.
v.y. James.	Stephen ,,	Cornwall.	,, xxvii,	,,	100.
v.y. James.	John ,,	Cornwall.	,, xxvii,	,,	127.
18-19 James.	Richard[4] ,,	Lincoln.	,, xxxi,	,,	62.
19-20 James.	Nicholas ,,	Suffolk.	,, xxxv,	,,	15.
2, 3, 4 Charles.	Hugh ,,	Leicester.	,, xlv,	,,	40.

[1] *Argent on a fess betw. three chess-rooks Sable as many mullets Or.*

[2] Inq. taken at Arundel 12 April, 2 James, on Thomas Marshall, yeoman, Messuage in Horsham called the Redd Lyon. He died 12 Feb. 40 Elizabeth. Thomas Marshall is his son and heir and was aged 20 on 19 Nov. last before the taking of this inquisition.

[3] Inq. taken at Wetherbie 18 Sept. 11 James, on Thomas Marshall of Moore Allerton. Messuage &c. in Moore Allerton and in Chapel Allerton. He died 16 August last, on which day William Marshall his son and heir was aged 21 years ten months and six days.

[4] Inq. taken at Sleaford 15 Sept. 15 James [1617] on Richard Marshall of West Laughton, gent., Capital messuage in Aslackby; close in Hawthropp. He died 20 Feb. 3 James [1606], Richard Marshall is his son and heir and was aged 21 and upwards at his father's death.

2, 3, 4 Charles.	William	,,	Huntingdon.	,,	xlv,	,,	62.
8 Charles.	William	,,	Gloucester.	,,	lii,	,,	183.
8 Charles.	John	,,	Surrey.	,,	lii,	,,	246.
9-10 Charles.	Christopher	,,	Lincoln.	,,	liv,	,,	158.
10 Charles.	William	,,	Essex.	,,	lv,	,,	24.
v.y.	Thomas	,,	Lincoln	,,	lxix,[1]	,,	52.

REGISTER OF KNEBWORTH, CO. HERTFORD.

1716. March . . . Edward Marshall and Ann Yeilding, by Licence. (Married.)

REGISTER OF TANNINGTON, CO. SUFFOLK. 1644. Thomas Bennifield and Ann Marshall were married the xith of November.

NOTES FROM THE CLOSE ROLLS.

16 Car. II, Part ix, No. 2. Indenture dated 24 August, 16 Car II. [1664] between Susanna Vaughan of Whitwell, co. York, spinster, one of the three sisters and coheirs of Henry Vaughan late of Whitwell aforesaid Esq. deceased of the one part, and Thomas Marshall of the Ewes in the said County of York, Esq., and Richard Etherington of the city of York, Esq., of the other part, Witnesseth that said Susanna Vaughan in con'son of 5^s sells third part of the manor of Whitwell and her third of lands therein to Thomas Marshall and Richard Etherington to uses and trusts contained in certain indentures tripartite bearing date with these presents between said Susanna Vaughan of the first part, Thomas Marshall and Richard Etherington of the second part, and Herbert Jeffereys of the city of York, Esq., of the third part. Recognizance by Susanna Vaughan, 25 Aug., 1664.

1656, Part 43, No. 1. Indenture dated 22 Feb^y, 1656, between Samuel Clarke of the City of Coventry, gent., son of Richard Clarke late of the same City, gent., deceased of the one part, and Edward Marshall of St. Martin Ludgate, London, Haberdasher, of the other part. Samuel Clarke for £150 sells tenement in Hemingby, co. Lincoln, heretofore in occupation of John Ward, yeoman, and now in that of Edmund Trevellian, and toft or tenement called the house of the Hill close in Hemingby, etc., enjoyed by virtue of the last will and testament of Richard Clarke his father. [rest illegible.]

23 Car. II., Part 10, No. 23. Indenture dated 12 Oct., 1670, between Christopher Alured of Martin in co. Nottingham, gent., of the first part, John Alured of Martin afs^d gent., son and heir of said Christopher of second part, and Fabian Philipps of the parish of St. Andrew-Holborn, Esq., Thomas Moyle of Uffington, co. Lincoln, gent., Thomas Chamberlaine, the younger, of Oddington, co. Gloucester,

[1] Inq. taken at the Bail (*apud Ballinam*) of Lincoln in co. Lincoln, 7 July, 22 James, on Thomas Marshall of Owmby juxta Serby [Searby] yeoman. Messuage and lands in Owmby which he bought of John Wilkinson, and 33 acres in Owmby which he bought of Thomas Greene, gent. He died 10 Oct. 21 James. The messuage bought of Greene was held of Richard Rosseter, Esq. as of his manor of Owmby in free socage at rent of 11 shillings. Thomas Marshall is his son and heir and was aged 24 years 8 months and upwards at his father's death.

gent., and Thomas Marshall of Stirropp, co. Nottingham, Esq., of the third part. Whereas by indenture dated 2 July, 1650, made between Elizabeth, lady Hausby the relict of Sir Ralph Hausby late of Titchill in co. York, Kn't, deceased, Robert Morton, Esq., and William Saunderson, Esq., since deceased, of the one part, and the said Christopher Alured of the other part, the said Elizabeth, Lady Hansby, Robert Morton, and William Saunderson sold to Christopher Alured the manor, etc., hereinafter mentioned for 985 years, and whereas by indenture dated 22 May, 1668, made between the said Christopher Alured of the one pait, and said John Alured of the other part, did demise said manor, etc., to the said John Alured for term of years being residue of the 985 years to come, and whereas a marriage is intended between the said John Alured and Margaret Philipps one of the daughters of the said Fabian Philipps who is to bring with her to said John Alured £1100—settlement of said term to provide portion for said Margaret--settlement of manor of Martin *alias* Morton in co. Nottingham. Fabian Philipps, Thomas Moyle, Thomas Chamberlaine, and Thomas Marshall, being the Trustees. John Alured acknowledged the Indenture 6 March 23 Car. II.

17 Car. II. Part ii, No. 16. Indenture dated 22 May, 1665, between Richard Godfrey and John Godfrey of Wey, co. Kent, gent., of first part, Richard Marshall of London, gent., of second part, and Edward Noell of Clements Inn, gent., of third part, Witnesseth that the two Godfreys in consideration of 10s. paid by Richard Marshall sell him the Manor of Court a Moore otherwise called Court of Moore and 100 acres of marsh land in parishes of Idechurch and New Romney, co. Kent.

26 Car. II. Part iii. No. 18. Indenture dated 15 July, 1674, between Henry Parker of the Inner Temple, London, Esq., son and heir of Henry Parker late of East Barnett in the county of Hertford, gent., deceased and Edward Marshall of the parish of St. Martins in the Fields in the county of Middlesex, gent., and Margaret his wife late the wife of the said Henry Parker deceased of the one part, and the Honble Dame Anne Fanshawe the relict of the Right Honble Sir Richard Fanshawe Knt and Bart, deceased of the other part. Edward Marshall and Margaret his wife in cons'on or £1740, and Henry Parker in cons'on of 5s, sell messuage in East Barnett and closes called Broomefield and Little Coopers to Dame Anne Fanshawe. Henry Parker acknowledged the Indenture, 16 July, 1674.

22 Edward III. Part i. *in dorso.* John Burdeles (Burdeleyes) de Partitione terr. inter sorores et heredes, vizt Elizabeth' nupt' Thomæ Marescall, et Joh'am nupt' Gilberto de la Chamber.

20 Car. II. Part 18. No. 40. Indenture dated 22 June, 1668, between Isaac White of the parish of St. Giles in the Fields in co. Midd'x., Taylor of first part, John Knight of the parish of St. Andrew Holborne, Clothworker, and Thomas Aborne of the parish of St. Clement Danes, Cordweyner of second part, Richard Marshall and Henry Bourne of London, gent., of third part, and John Gopp Citizen and Scrivener of London of fourth part. White sells to Gopp for £400 messuage in Princes Street. *See* Vol. i. app. p. 9.

6 Anne. Part 4, No. 33. Indenture dated 6 Sept., 1707, between

William Hawkins of the parish of St. Andrew Holborn, co. Middlesex, gent., of first part, John Mead of London, Goldsmith, and William Mead, gent., brother of the said John Mead of second part, Elizabeth Marshall and Sarah Marshall of London spinsters of third part and Thomas Frost Citizen and Merchant Taylor of London, and James Reeves Citizen and Shipwright of London, of the fourth part. Whereas David Jones late of the parish of Portsea co. Southampton, Marriner, by his last will dated 23 Aug[t] 1704 did give to his cousins the said Elizabeth and Sarah Marshall £100 apiece, the money to be laid out in land for them, and made his wife Elizabeth Jones executrix, and she proved the will in P.C.C. 3 Oct., 1704, &c. Money invested in a new house called Ailsbury House on site of late priory of St. John of Jerusalem.

2 James II, Part 5, No. 21. Indenture dated 26 April, 1686, between Elizabeth Curtois and Dorothy Curtoys both of Gunnalstone in the county of Nottingham spinsters, daughters and executrixes of the last will and testament of Leonard Curtoys late of Wilford in the county of Nottingham, clerke, of first part, John Strey of Beeston in the county of Nottingham, gent., and Robert Marshall[1] of the town and county of the town of Nottingham, Maltster, of second part, and Samuel Richards of the town and county of the town of Nottingham, gent., of third part—Witnesseth that said Elizabeth and Dorothy for £380 sell to said Samuel Richards messuages late belonging to said Leonard Curtoys. Elizabeth and Dorothy acknowledged the Indenture, 20 May, 1686.

FROM REGISTER OF STUBTON, CO. LINCOLN.

1587. Buried Thomas Marshall y[e] 21 day of May.
1591. Bap. Stephen Marshall y[e] 2 day of June.
1594. Richard Marshall was bap. y[e] 4 of August.
1595. Buried Thomas Marshall y[e] 29th of October.
1626. Richard Marshall and Margaret Northrop married November the 12th.
1627. Thomas Marshall fil. Richardi bap: Decemb: xxvj.

FROM REGISTER OF DAVINGTON, CO KENT.

Marshall, Elizabeth, Bapt. dau. of Henry M. and Mary his wife ... ... } 31 Aug. 1676.
" Elizabeth, Marr. to Henry Martin, seaman, 27 June 1699.
" Frances, Bapt. d. of Henry M. and Mary his w. 2 Apl. 1671.
" Henry, Bur'd. 20 Sept. 1682.
" Mary wid[o]. Mar. William Hawkett, 14 Jan. 1682-3.
" Richard, Mar. Dorothy Dewell, 2 Nov. 1684.
" Willm. Bapt. s. of Henry and Mary, 6 Oct. 1673.
" William, Bur. son of Henry deceased and Mary his wife ... ... } 17 Feb. 1682-3.
Martial, John, Mar. Bennet Phillips, 8 Oct. 1640.

[1] *See* vol. i, p. 302.

From Register of Darrington, co. York.

1574. Aug. 8. John son of Robert Marshall. Bapt.
1578. May 13. Michael son of ,, ,,
1579-80. Mar. 1. Elizabeth dau. of ,, ,,
1582. Nov. 11. Ann dau. of ,, ,, Buried 19 Dec., 1583.
1583. Dec. 22. Jane dau. of ,, ,, Buried 19 Oct., 1589.
1586. April 14. Robert son of ,, ,,
1589. June 8. Victoria dau. of ,, ,,
1587. March 7. Elizabeth wife of Robert Marshall. Buried.
1582. Aug. 24. Lucy dau. of Thomas Marshall. Bapt.
1736. May 13. Thomas Marshall of Kirkthorpe and Martha Perkin of this [Darrington]. Married.
1712. Feb. 10. Edmund Marshall of Pontefract and Elizabeth Steel of this parish. Married.
1748. July 12. Edward Clark of Womersley and Mary Marshall of Darrington. Married.

ADDITIONS AND CORRECTIONS TO VOL. I.

Page 4. See as to the origin of the name of Marshall, 'Notes and Queries' 3 S. viii. 313; L. T. Smith's article on the Marshals and Smiths of York, 'Antiquary,' (published by Eliot Stock,) Vol. xi. 105.

,, 8, line 4. Add after "of Netherthorpe," "and of Everton, co. Notts, see pedigree of Rogers in Hunter's 'Deanery of Doncaster,' Vol. i. 311."

,, 10. See account of the portrait of Sir Henry Marshall, at Goldsmiths' Hall, Malcolm's 'Londinum Redivivum,' Vol. ii. 412.

,, 13. Add as a note to the burial of Peter Lavigne, "See Lavigne *impaling* Marshall, for his funeral, 31 January, 1717, in 'Painters' Work Book' $\frac{H}{8}$ fo. 117^{b}, in College of Arms.

Samuel Bucknall who married Margaret Marshall was 'of Westminster.' She died at Wrexham, co. Denbigh, before 8 June, 1736. He was son of William Bucknall, of Oxhey, near Watford, co. Herts, and died at Oxhey before 1732, and was buried there. See Pedigree of Bucknall in "Miscellaneous Pedigrees, R.B.G. Vol. ii. fo. 139^{b}, in College of Arms."

,, 14, line 22. For "died 3," read "died 5;" and next line for, "aged 46" read "aged 47." And add *see* Vol. ii. 82, *note* 2. Add note to William Marshall who died in 1826, aged 71, *see* 'Gentleman's Magazine,' 1826, i. 477.

,, 22. Add note to William Marshall of Aislaby, *see* app. to 38th Report of Deputy Keeper of Public Records, p. 718.

,, 24. Sir George Marshall married secondly Elizabeth widow of Robert Angell. See "Remembrancia of the city of London," p. 320. Harleian Society, xv. 20.

See as to children of Marmaduke Marshall of Morton-on-Swale, 'Collectanea Topographica et Genealogica,' Vol. vi, 238; College of Arms, MS. H. iii. 168.

,, 27 Add note to Richard Marshall who is called brother in will of Edmund Marshall, "cf. 38 Report D.K Public Records, p. 423."

,, 29. Henry Marshall of Copmanthorpe,— Adm'on of Edward Marshall of Holme in Spaldingmore was granted to his brother William Marshall of Copmanthorpe, 31 March, 1620.

last line. Add note to Will of 'Wm Marshall, May,' *see* Vol. ii. p. 52.

,, 37. At foot. For Thomas M. bapt. 9 Jan^{y}, "1797," read "1697."

,, 42. Under Carburton for "Aprill 22" *read* "Aprill 30th."

" 45. Add to note 2. Robert Marshall was presented to the Rectory of Escrike, co. York, by Sir H. Tompson, Kt, 15 Nov. 1672. Liber Institutionum (Public Record office,) Ser. C. Vol. i. fo. 91.

" 59. Add note to marriage of John Hilles and Anne Marshall—"See Harl. Soc., Visitn of London, vol. i. 385."

" 64. Add note to George Granville Marshall—"See Clutterbuck's Hertford, ii. 347."

" 65, line 11, for "born 1662," *read*, "born 11th of 4th month 1662."

" " 17, add "Sarah Marshall dau. of Thomas and Elizabeth Marshall died and was buried at Skegby 2nd of 2nd month 1671."

" " 4th line from foot, read "Thrifthouse."

" 67. Add note to "Rebecca Stead," "Daughter of William Stead of Sheffield, Mercer, by Rebecca daughter of Nathaniel Baxter, clerk, who descended from the Revels. See Add. MS. 24458, p. 173, for pedigree."

" 70. note 1. Add "William Marshall, M.A. was instituted to the Rectory of Oddingley, 5 Feb., 1605-6.

" 74. After date "1627, July 30," near foot, add after "Mrs Ann Marshall" the word "widow."

" 75, line 22. For "1681" *read* "1687."

" 86. Add to No. IX. "2 Ric. II. 13 May, (1484-5.) Willm Marchall of Coventry, fishmonger, adm'or of John Charyte late of Coventry, mercer. *See* 9th Report of D.K. Pub. Rec. app. ii. p. 90."

" 90. See as to William Marshall, clerk, of Scarning, 38th Report of D.K. Pub. Rec. app. p. 683.

" 94. No. XLVIII. Cf. Consistory Court, at Somerset House, Vol. 6, fo. 66b.

" 95, line 9. Add note to "Barnarde Welles," "He was husband of Barbara. See his M.I. Glover's 'Derbyshire,' ii. 73."

" 117. Add to 3rd line from foot, "Also Richard Marshall of Swinderby, co. Lincoln, whose freehold was at Tuxford."

" 118, line 37. George Marshall of Dunham voted at Notts election in 1722.

" 120. Add note to No. CIX. 1655. Mary the daughter of Mr. John Nye, Rector of this parish, buried 28 Aug. (*Par. Regr. of Cottenham, co. Cambridge.*) *See* Cole's MSS. Vol. 48. fo. 177.

" 134, line 12. Isaac Marshall was born in St Mary Bothaw, 2 Feb. 1637; entered at Merchant Taylors 1647. *See* Merchant Taylors School Register, p. 182.

" 137. See as to Robert and William Marshall, 'Diary of Abraham De la Pryme,' Surtees Society, Vol. 54, p. 158.

" 139. Sarah wife of Joshua Key was buried at St Laurence's, Norwich, in 1679. In the church wardens account book for that year is this entry, "ReceLved for breaking the church for Mrs Key 10s."

" 149. Add to *note* on Benjamin Marshall, "Query his wife's arms in Painter's Work Book $\frac{II}{1}$ fo. 114, in the Coll. Arms, where this coat,—Argent, three bars Sable, a canton Ermine, *impaling*, Gules, a lion rampant Or, a bordure indented of the last. Madam Marshall's funeral, Nov. 21, 1691. Her maiden name Jones of Carmarthen."

" 159. No. CCXXII. In Painters Work Book $\frac{II}{4}$ fo. 3b in College of Arms, under date 31st March, 1699, 'Gules, a lion rampant Argent within an orle of besants' (on a lozenge) is tricked as the coat for the funeral of .. ... Marshall, daughter of Mr Marshall at the Bible in Newgate St. Under the arms is written "Marshall of Oxfordshire."

" 226. No. VIII. This will was also proved at York, and is registered there Vol. 41, fo. 229.

" 230. *Note* 1. for "1687" read 1686.

" 233. Add note to Will of Margaret Marshall of Diseworthe.—"John Marshall of Osgathorpe, co. Leicr, gent., and John Marshall of Dyseworth, co. Leic., gent., and Sarah his wife, parties to a deed entered on Close Roll, 18 Car. ii, part 15, No. 23.

" 236. 7th line from foot. Add note to Ann Ibotson. "Mentioned as child in will of Eliz. Ibotson of Woodhouse in Bradfield, widow, 1595."

" 237. Add note to "William Marshall of Nether Bradfield." "*See* Adm'on of William Marshall of Bradfield to Francis Marshall, 15 March, 1632. *Doncaster Act Book.*"

„ 244. line 15 from foot, for "Jan. 3," read "June 3."
„ 245. Add to note. "*See* Carthew's Launditch, iii. 197."
„ 246. line 13. For "Johnson," *read*, "John son."
„ 256. line 15. For "Welbam," *read* "Kelham."
line 18. *dele* (? North Lofthouse.)
note 5 should read —Proved by Agnes his relict and power reserved to son William, 13 July, 1581.
„ 257. Add note to Thomas Marshall of Raistropp, "Adm'on of Thomas Marshall and Isabella his wife late of Raistroppe in parish of Wharram to Peter, Mary, and Roger, their children, 18 April, 1637."
„ „ Add to note 7, "Adm'on of Thomas Marshall of Hotham to Philice his widow, 5 May, 1625."
„ 260. line 6. Add note to Robert Marshall of Danby, "Thomas Marshall, chaplain, was presented to parish of Danby, 26 Feb. 1483-4. *See* 9th Rept. of D.K. Public Records, App. ii. 36."
„ 261. Add to note 8. "William Marshall, Rector of Todwick died *circa* 1535. Hunter's 'South Yorkshire,' ii. 160."
„ 263. line 1. Note that adm'on of Agnes Marshall of Dimbleton, in parish of Easington, was granted to Mary Smith, 31 Jan., 1625.
„ 266. line 11. *dele* Keckonfield, and *read*, Leconfield; line 17, for "of Skipton," *read*, "of Shipton, labourer."
„ 267. line 12. Add note. "In Marton, 'Katheren Marshall wife of Peter Marshall, rich man.' List of Roman Catholics in the co. of York in 1604. By Edward Peacock, p. 125."
„ „ Add to note 5. "Elizabeth the relict having renounced.
„ 268. Note 6. Samuel Tooley was of Beverley, Mercer. Roger Marshall of Scorborough, clerk, made his will 26 Oct., 1648. Mentions sisters Isabell, and Frances Marshall. Brother George Thompson. Appoints wife Elizabeth executrix and residuary legatee.
Marmaduke Marshall was presented to the Rectory of Scorborough by Henry, Earl of Northumberland, 27 July, 1620. *Liber Institutionum (Pub. Rec. Office.) Ser. A. Vol. i. fo.* 45. *Harthill Deanery.*
„ 270. Add to II. "The will of Edward Marshall, of Tadcaster, gent., was proved at York, in January, 1742.
„ 278. Add after line 2. "Adm'on of Thomas Marshall of Aughton to Elizabeth his widow, 2 Nov., 1625."
Add to footnote. "Jackson's 'Doncaster Charities,' p. 120."
„ 284. Elizabeth daughter of Joseph Oates. In a pedigree of Oates at p. 97, of Whitaker's 'Loidis and Elmete,' he is called *William.*
„ 285. Frances and Elizabeth daughters of John Marshall and Bainbrigge died at Southsea in 1884. *See* 'Times' Newspaper of 2 and 25 June, 1884.
„ 288. Henry Cowper Marshall, died at Derwent Island, Keswick, 14 Oct., 1884, aged 76.
„ 295. No. XXXIII. Anne Marshall was buried at Whatton, 23 Sept., 1676.
„ 296. 11th line from foot. For 1725 *read* 1726.
„ 299. lines 5 and 6. For 293 *read* 294; in following lines for 294 *read* 295; line 12, for 295, *read* 29 ; line 13, for 294, *read* 295; line 14, for 295, *read* 296; line 29, for 296 *read* 297.
„ 302. line 1. Add note to Robert Marshall. "Party to a deed dated 26 April, 1686. *See* Close Roll, 2 Jac. II. Part 5, No. 21."
„ 307. last line. For 'Elem norem' *read* 'electionem.'
„ 308. line 7. Close Roll, 1649. Part 5, No. 12. Indenture dated 9 Oct., 1649, between Robert Clarke of North Dalton, co. York, yeoman, of one part, and George Marshall of Dighton, yeoman, Thomas Meadley of Foggathorpe in said co. yeoman, and Elizabeth Freeman of Manthorpe in said co. spinster of the other part. Said Clarke for £160 sells them a messuage and lands in North Dalton.
„ 308. line 4 from foot. For "William" *read* "Richard." line 7 from foot, add this note, "At the end of the Hull Act Book, 1705, the will of Catherine Marshall of Otteringham, dated 27 Aug., 1677, is said to be in a bundle, marked *reinfecta.*
„ 314. line 24. Add "Mr Richard Marshall overseer."
„ 315. line 16. For "Dated 1515" *read* "Dated 22 Oct., 1513, proved 17 Nov., 1515. (11 Holder.)"

„ 322. John Marshall of Watton was not the first of his name there. Adm'on of Thomas Marshall of Clarkson House in the parish of Watton was granted to Martha his widow, 8 Oct., 1639.
The will of Katherine Marshall of Otteringham, widow, is dated 27 August, 1677. She mentions her sons Matthew and Thomas, and makes her daughter Hellen Clyoate, executrix. She died, and her husband Robert Clyoates did swear to execute the will.

„ 325. last line. For "1s." *read* "1 ;" and to line above add note, "Thomas Marshall of Maltby is mentioned in the preface to Dugdale's Visitation of Yorkshire (*Surtees Soc.*) as one of those summoned, but who did not attend."

„ 326. Inq. on Thomas Marshall 15-16 Henry VIII. For "11 messuages" *read* "40 ;" after Middlethorpe insert. "Bathley, Irleshagh, Westhorpe, and Aykeryng [Eakring]." Add at end "Inq. 16 Hen. VIII, Chancery, No. 74."

APPENDIX.

Page 2. Add to No. 26. "1611. Oct., 23. Adm'on of Matthew Marshall of Aldeburghe to Anne his relict." *Books from Archdeacon's Registry at Ipswich*

„ 6. No. 46. The 'late wife' mentioned in will of Thomas Marshall was Anne Sylyard. *See* Mis. Gen. et Her. 2nd Series, i. 31.
Jennet da. of...... Graves, in the entry of her marriage, in Doncaster Register 8 Oct., 1564, is called 'Joan Grave.'

„ 7. line 8 from foot. For "1641" *read* "1642."

„ „ last line but one. insert date "May 21."

„ 8. line 2. For "Fosterd" read "Foster."

„ 12. No. 71. For "Farnton" read "Farndon." Add, "See as to the lease of the tithes of Farndon to Robert Marshall, 33 Eliz. 38th Report of D.K. Pub. Rec. p. 373."

„ „ No. 82. Add. "See extracts from Register of Seaton. Genealogist, v. 109, etc."

„ 13. No. 87. 'Margeria Marshall de Wysebich,' was widow of Alexander Marshall, and one of the daughters and heirs of Alice Charles daughter and heir of John Davy. Alexander and Margery held a court at Overhall in Buckton 27 Henry VI. Their daughter and heir Elizabeth married David Orrell, whose son Sir Lewis Orrell sold it. Blomefields Norfolk, vii. 300.

„ 16. A further account of Nathaniel Marshall will be found in Malcolm's 'Londinum Redivivum,' iv. 637.

„ „ Two administrations should be added here :—
87a.—George Marshall of Morpeth, co. Northumberland. Adm'on to William Marshall his son, 27 Nov., 1657.
87b.—Ralph Marshall of Pocklington, co. York, bachelor. Adm'on to Margaret Hewett his mother, 18 Dec., 1657.

„ 19. Charlotte Augusta Dring Drake relict of Charles Henry Marshall of the Cedars, Sydenham, married 2ndly, 10 July, 1883, at St Michaels and all Saints, Sydenham, W. Knighton, LL.D, of Mortimer House, Sydenham.

„ 26. No. 130. Add. "Close Roll 12 Car. II, part 14, no. 16. Indenture dated 7 Nov., 1660, between Edward Merriwether Citizen and Haberdasher of London, and Mary Marshall of Lenham, co. Kent, widow. Mary Marshall buys of him for £30 a messuage in Barking, co. Essex, etc."

„ 27. Add note to William Bissell. "Mar. Allegation at Worcester for William Bissell of the city of Worcester, Malster, and Jane Marshall of St Michaels in Bedwardine, co. Worcester, about 18, daughter of Edward Marshall of the same parish, Chirurgeon. Testified by John Marshall brother of the said Jane. Dated 25 Feb., 1660."

„ 29. No. 144. Marriage Allegation Commissory of Surrey. 6 Sept. 1676. John Marshall of St George Botolph Lane, bachr, aged about 24, to marry Anne Lawrence of Crayford, Kent, single woman, aged about 24, at St Saviour Southwark.

„ „ No. 151. Fine Hillary 31 Car. II. Notts. Between Benjamin Marshall and Thomas Palmer, plaintiffs, and John Hanford, gent., and Sara his wife, defendants, of two mess., 50 ac. of land, 12 ac. of meadow, 40 ac. of pasture, etc., in Eastwood, Newton, and Shelford. Consideration £100.

„ 33. No. 189. Transpose the children of Gell and Christopher Marshall. For "monument of St Saviours," *read* "monument at St Saviours."

„ 34. No. 201. "Mr Hezekiah Marshall Chief Clerk of the Check at Deptford." *See* Add. MS. 29587, fo. 82.

„ 43. *Dele* "No. 43. For 'Server' read 'Sewer.'"

„ „ Add to note of will of Richard Marshall of Westlawghton, "Inq. post mortem, (Court of Wards,) on Richard Marshall of West Laughton, gent., taken at Sleaford, 15 Sept., 15 James I. (1617). Was seized of a capital messuage in Aslackby, etc., and close in Hawthropp. Died 20 Feb., 3 James I. (1606). Richard Marshall is his son and heir, and was aged 21 and upwards at his father's death."

Add to Index of Persons :—

Lewes, Robert, 252.
The references to Nicholas and Richard Orell should be 248.
Salton, John, 23 *ped.*

Add to Index of Places :—

Arkesley and Arksey are the same place.
Dele Farnton, and add "ap. 12" to Farndon.
Foggathorpe, 308.
Massem (*i.e.* Massam or Masham), 255.

ADDITIONS AND CORRECTIONS TO VOL. II.

Page 5. Add note to Mary Fotherby. "Her pedigree will be found in Walbran's Antiquities of Gainford, p. 88."

„ 46. Add to note at foot "German Pole was nephew of Ann wife of Thurstan Marshall. *See* Glover's Derbyshire, ii. 324."

„ 47. line 16. For "1820" read "1620."

„ 80. last line. For "Adm'on October," read, "Will 232."

„ 99. line 15. Read "Vol. i, p. 259."

Vol. i, page 145. For "John Lingard Rayner," read "John Lingard executor to Robert Rayner."

INDEX OF CHRISTIAN NAMES OF MARSHALLS.

Note that although a name frequently occurs more than once on the same page only one reference is made.

Names are given under their modern spellings, thus for Bartylmew see Bartholomew, or for Expofer see Christopher.

When a person has more than two names initials only are given.

Wives are here indexed as Marshalls, as well as under their maiden names in the other Index of persons..

INDEX OF PERSONS.

INDEX OF PLACES.

VOLUME II. PART II.

THE MARSHALLS OF PEEBLES.[1]

James Marshall, born in or before 1650, was a Burgess and Merchant of Peebles. He became possessed of three sumes of Cademuir Hill in 1708. He had at least two sons, Robert, born 1673, and John, who appears to have been baptised on 9th September, 1677. Robert Marshall was baptised 24th November, 1673. He is afterwards described in the Parish Registers as a "dweller in Ormiston," which looks as if he had been a farmer. His son James Marshall was baptised 5th October, 1703. In 1731 he was admitted a Burgess and Guildbrother of Peebles, and was for a number of years one of the Bailies of that burgh. When the Highlanders were encamped at Peebles, in 1745, he was Dean of Guild, and went boldly to the Cross of Peebles, where he drank "Confusion to the Pretender." His Will is dated and signed at Peebles, 20th April, 1771, and he died 27th May following, and was buried in St. Andrew's Kirk Yard, Peebles. He married, first a Miss Scott, by whom he had a son, Robert, born 1736; and secondly in 1746, Janet, daughter of William Tait, late tenent in Feathen, Traquair. Their issue was:—

William, born 1747; died young.
James, born 1749; of whom presently.
Margaret, born 1750; died young.
Jean, born 1752; alive 1771.
William, born 1754, Minister of Manor; of whom hereafter.
Alex^r^, born 1758, Banker in London; of whom hereafter.
Margaret, born 1762; died unmarried.
Isobell, born about 1756; married Archibald Robertson.
Janet, died unmarried.

Robert Marshall, the only child of James Marshall by his first marriage, was baptised 22nd February, 1736, and was made a Burgess of Peebles, "free of all Composition or fees" on account of his father in 1754. He was several years Dean of Guild, and died unmarried.

James Marshall, the eldest surviving son of the second marriage was baptised 8th March, 1749, and was a Burgess, Merchant, and many years Bailie of Peebles. Upon the 10th September, 1779, he married Margaret Ballantine, daughter of James Ballantine, of Hollylee. He died 22nd May, 1837, and was buried beside his father in St. Andrew's Kirk Yard. He had issue:—

[1] For this pedigree I am indebted to Captain Robert Seton Marshall.

Isobell, born 1780; married the Revd Thomas Leckie.
Jean, born 1781; died unmarried 1854.
Marion, born 1782; died unmarried 1857.
James, born 1784; died 1850; of whom hereafter.
Janet, born 1786; died 1789.
Robert, born 1788; died 1845; of whom hereafter.
Margaret, born 1790; died unmarried, 1850.
Janet, born 1792; died unmarried 1851.

William Marshall (Minister of Manor) was born in Peebles, 2nd August, 1754, and educated at Peebles Parish School, the Edinburgh High School, and Edinburgh University, where he distinguished himself as a scholar, and in 1788 was presented to the parish of Manor, Peeblesshire, by William, Duke of Queensberry. He was first married at Edinburgh, 30th April, 1790, to Christian, daughter of Mr. William Vair, and by her had one child, who died young. She died 21st September, 1794, aged 21 years, and was buried in Manor Church Yard. He married secondly, at Peebles, 16th November, 1803, Christian Smith (only child of Archibald Smith, Merchant in Peebles, and Elizabeth Govan), by whom he had ten children, viz. :—

Elizabeth, born 1804; married, 1st, Mr. John Anderson, Castlehill; 2nd, Mr. Thomas Thorburn.
James, born 1806; buried at Manor, 1812.
William Forbes, born 1808; died at London, unmarried, 2nd December, 1866.
Janet, born 1809; died unmarried, 1826.
Christian, born 1810; buried at Manor, 1811.
Archibald, born 1812; of whom presently.
Isabella, born 1814; married Mr. John Thorburn, and died 1840.
Agnes, born 1816; died unmarried, and buried at Manor, 1836.
Jane, born 1818; married Mr. John Anderson, and died 1880.
Margaret Christian, born 1824; married Mr. John Hewat, and died 1886.

About 1828 he gave up the ministry, and went to live at St. John's Hill, Edinburgh, where he died, 22nd April, 1830, in the 76th year of his age, and 42nd of his ministry.

Alexander Marshall, born 1758, was made a Burgess of Peebles, 1778, free of all charge, on account of his father and brothers. He was for sometime in Sir William Forbes' Bank, Edinburgh, and afterwards in Hankey's Bank, London. He died before March, 1827.

James Marshall, son of James Marshall and Margaret Ballantine, born 1784, was a Wine Merchant in Edinburgh.

He married Margaret Allen, and died 1st May, 1850, having had issue:—

James, born 1816, a Wine Merchant in Edinburgh, and for many years one of the Bailies, married Jenetta, daughter of Mr. Currie, of Glassmount, and died 1880, leaving issue:—

Elizabeth, born 1851.

James, born 1852; went to Manitoba.

Andrew, born 1854; Banker, Hong Kong.

Allan, born 1856; went to Manitoba.

Janetta, born 1858.

Frank, born 1859; Lieutenant, 25th Regt.

Robert, born 1863; Lieutenant, Duke of Wellington's West Riding Regt.

Isabella, born 1866.

Isabella, born 1817; married William Christie, and died 1881.

Francis, born 1820, a Wine Merchant in partnership with his father; died unmarried 1849.

Robert Marshall, brother of the above, born 1788, was a Commission Agent in Edinburgh, and married the widow of a Newcastle Merchant, named Sewell, and dying in 1845, left issue, James, who went to Australia.

Archibald Marshall, son of Mr. William Marshall and Christian his wife, born 1812, is a Justice of the Peace for the County of the City of Edinburgh, Commissioner of Supply for the County of Peebles, &c., was a Merchant in Edinburgh, but inheriting property through his mother, was enabled to retire from business early in life. He married, first, Margaret Anderson, daughter of Walter Anderson, Cramilt; secondly, Rosina Seton Veitch, only child of John Veitch, H.M. Excise, Somerset House. By his first wife he has issue:—

William, born 1850; died 1870.

Walter, born 1851; Bank of Scotland.

James, born 1853; died 1869.

Elizabeth Govan, born 1854; died 1856.

Oliver, born 1856; went to Manitoba.

By his second wife:—

Rose Seton, born 1861; died 1862.

John Archibald, born 1862; Accountant, Audit Department of the Eastern Bengal Railway, Calcutta.

Robert Seton, born 1864; Captain 3rd Brigade Scottish Division Royal Artillery (Edinburgh Militia).

Edward Govan, born 1866; Bank of Scotland.

Christian Eliza, born 1868.

Charles James, born 1870.

Margaret Seton, born and died 1872.

Jane, born, 1873.

EXTRACTS FROM PARISH REGISTERS.

BLYTH, CO. NOTT$^{M.}$

1572. Dec. 2. William Marshall. Buried.
1578. March 5. Richard Marshall. Bapt.
1581. Sept. 7. Elizabethe Marshall. Bapt.
1588. Sept. 8. Margaret Marshall. Bapt.
1601. June 13. Richard Marshall and Issabell Hawson were maried.
1606. Oct. 19. Rob'te sonn of Richard Marshall of Blythe. Bapt.
1610. Nov. 12. John Martiall and Katherine Dobson. Married.
1615. Oct. 19. Issabell da. of Richard Marshiall of Blyth. Bapt.
1619. Jan. 3. Christofer son of Richard Marshall of Blythe. Bapt.
1623. May 25. Eliz. da. of John Marsiall of Blythe. Bapt.
1632. Feb. 28. Frances dau. of Rob. Sanderson of the Abby. Bapt.[1]
1635. Nov. 25. John Marshall sonne of Henrie Marshall of Blith. Buried.
1638. Dec. 16. Richard sonn of Henry Marshall of Blyth. Bapt.
1640. Sept. 27. Ellen Daug. of Henry Marshall of blith. Bapt.
1645. Sept. 9. Henry Marshall still borne. Buried.
1646. March 25. John son of Henry Marshall of Blyth. Bapt.
1647. Dec. 5. John Chernley and Isabell Marshall. Married.
1652. Nov. 18. Robert Marshall and Frances Wild. Married.
1654. July 25. Elizabeth daughter of Robert Marshall of Blyth borne July 2 and bapt. July 25.

In 1655 Henry Marshall was one of a jury for staking out the ground belonging to the Vicar.

1658. (Commonwealth marriages and publications thereof.) Thomas Marshall of Parkhouse in the pish of Balborough in the Countie of Darby and Mary Smith daughter of Mr Richard Smith of Blyth. Consent published 14, 21, and 28 November.
1659. June 1. Elizabeth wife of Henry Marshall of Blyth. Buried.
1660. July 19. Hennery Marshall and Elizabeth Hill. Married.
1661. Aug. 18. Francis doughter of Henry Marshall of Blyth. Bapt.
1663-4. Feb. 25. Simon son of Henry Marshall of Blyth. Bapt. Buried . . . April, 1667.
1664-5. Jan. 14. Ann wife of Will. Marshall of Oldcots. Buried.
1665-6. March 8. Richard son of Henry Marshall of Blyth. Bapt.
1668-9. March 22. Thomas son of Mr Thomas Marshall of Stirrapp. Bapt. Buried 3 May, 1669. [23 May in Transcript.][2]

[1] Married Thomas Marshall. See Thoroton's *Notts.*, p. 474; Raine's *Blyth*, p. 75.
[2] Transcript of the Register at York.

1669. June 5. Rich. sonn of Henry Marshall of Blyth. Buried. [6 June in Transcript.] [1]
1669-70. Jan. . . . Henry Marshall of Blyth. Buried. [4 Jan. in Transcript.] [1]
1687. May 10. Robert Browne and Elizabeth Marshall. Married.
1701. Nov. 27. Edw[d] Denton and Mary Marshall both of Blyth. Married. [Transcript.] [1]
1713. April 19. W[m] Kitchin of Woodall in P'ish of Harthill and Eliz. Marshal of Torwoth in ys Parish. Married.

Arksey, co. York.

Baptisms.

1586. March 25. Catherine dau. of George Marshall.
1588. Feb. 1. Mary dau. of John Marshall.
1595. April 27. Cecily dau. of Robert Marshall of Shaftholme.
1624. Aug. 24. Alice dau. of Robert Marshall.
1626. April 2. Richard son of Robert Marshall.
1632. Dec. 2. Elizabeth dau. of William Marshall.
1639. Dec. 27. Ann dau. of William Marshall of Bentley.
1676. Dec. 12. Sarah dau. of Joseph Marshall of Bentley.
1679. June 17. Ann dau. of Joseph Marshall of Bentley.
1700. April 14. Ann dau. of Joseph Marshall of Bentley.
1703. Sept. 2. Benjamin son of Joseph Marshall, jun[r], of Bentley.
1706. April 18. Joseph son of Joseph Marshall of Bentley.
1719. June 3. William son of Robert Marshall of Arksey, agricola.
1721. Sept. 19. Susanna dau. of Robert Marshall of Arksey, husbandman.
1723. Jan[y] 7. Susanna dau. of Robert Marshall of Arksey.
1724. Sept. 22. Joseph son of John Marshall of Bentley.
1725. Dec. 20. Sarah dau. of Benj. Marshall of Bentley.
1726. June 28. Mary dau. of John Marshall of Bentley, husbandman.
1726. Sept. 30. Thomas son of Robert Marshall of Arksey, husbandman.
1726. Jan[y] 10. John son of Benjamin Marshall of Bentley, husbandman.
1727. Jan[y] 26. Robert son of Robert Marshall of Arksey, husbandman.
1729. Sept. 14. Thomas son of Benj. Marshall of Bentley.
1731. Nov. 9. Ann dau. of Benj. Marshall of Bentley, husbandman.
1733. March 6. Joseph son of Benj. Marshall of Bentley, husbandman.
1736. Dec. 30. Eliz. dau. of Ben. Marshall of Bentley.
1739. May 17. Joshua son of Ben. Marshall of Bentley, husbandman.

1 Transcript of the Register at York.

1741. Oct. 14. Ben. son of Ben. Marshall, of Bentley, husbandman.
1744. March 29. Mary dau. of Ben. Marshall of Bentley, husbandman.
1746. Aug. 10. Sarah dau. of Benjamin Marshall of Bentley, husbandman.
1757. Sept. 5. Wm son of John Marshall of Bentley, Innkeepeer.
1760. June 9. John son of John Marshall of Bentley, Innkeeper.
1790. Aug. 19. Joseph and Mary, twin children of Joshua Marshall, Farmer, Bentley.
1791. Jany 6. John son of John Marshall, Miller, Bentley.
1794. March 13. Ann dau. of Joshua Marshall, Farmer. Bentley, by Ann his wife.
1794. April 3. Elizabeth dau. of John Marshall, Miller, Bentley. by Margaret his wife.
1795. Jany 5. Jane dau. of John Marshall, Victualler, Bentley, by Jane his wife.
1798. March 22. Elizabeth third daughter of Joshua Marshall, of Bentley, Farmer, by Ann daughter of Thomas Hemsworth, of Barnborough. Shoemaker.

Marriages.

1595. April 23. Allan Cocken and Alice Marshall.
1598. Aug. 13. Robert Potte and Matilda Marshall.
1623. Oct. 28. Robertus Marshall et Joanna Cockine.
1635. Nov. 10. John Green and Ann Marshall.
1655. June 27. William Pigburne of Bentley, shoemaker, and Mary Marshall of the parish of Methley, spinster.
1656. Nov. 27. William Marshall of Bentley, labourer, and Elizabeth Bincliffe of Stockbridge, widow.
1661. Oct. 22. William Otley and Elizabeth Marshall, both of this parish.
1695. Nov. 26. Robert Turner of Burghwallis and Mary Marshall of Bentley.
1705. Nov. 30. Robert Marshall and Ann Crawshaw.
1730. June 25. John Ellison and Elizabeth Marshall, widow, both of this.
1732. April 16. Washington Wroe, Sut. calcear. and Susanna Marshall, vid.[1]
1753. April 26. John Marshall and Martha Rantree.
1756. Nov. 16. John Marshall and Mary Scholay both of this.
1756. Nov. 29. John Booth and Eliz. Marshall both of this p.
1757. Dec. 1. Joseph Hutchinson of Thorn and Elizabeth Marshall of this p.
1766. May 18. Richard Mapplebeck and Mary Marshall both of this p.
1769. Jany 17. Thomas Marshall of Bentley, Farmer, and Ann Huntington, widow, of this, by lic.

1 She was buried at Arksey, 3 Jany. 1752.

1585. Jany 7. Richard Mascall of Almholme.
1595. Feb. 17. Thomas son of Robert Marshall.
1628. Oct. 13. Infans Roberti Marshall.
1655. Dec. 21. Barbara wife of William Marshall of Bentley, labourer.
1659. Jany 17. Ann dau. of William Marshall of Bentley.
1667. Sept. 9. William Marshall of Bentley.
1676. July 8. Elizabetha Marshall, e charitatis ædibus.
1700. April 16. Ann d. of Joseph Marshall of Bentley.
1706. April 12. Ann wife of Robert Marshall of Bentley.
1706. Feb. 4. Joseph son of Joseph Marshall, jun., of Bentley.
1714. Feb. 14. Ann wife of Joseph Marshall, sen., of Bentley.
1722. Nov. 24. Joseph Marshall of Bentley, husbandman.[1]
1722. Feb. 26. Susanna dau. of Robert Marshall of Arksey, husbandman.
1722. Feb. 26. Joseph son of same.
1726. Nov. 28. Thomas son of same.
1727. Nov. 20. Robert Marshall of Arksey, husbandman.
1727. Dec. 18. Sarah wife of Joseph Marshall, of Bentley, husbandman.
1727. Dec. 31. Ann Marshall of Bentley, a virgin.
1727. Jany 28. Susanna dau. of Robert Marshall, of Arksey, husbandman, lately deceased.
1728. March . . . Elizabeth dau. of John Marshall, of Bentley, husbandman.
1729. April 17. John Marshall of Bentley, husbandman.
1729. Dec. 1. Joseph Marshall of Bentley, husbandman.
1730. March 10. Joseph son of John Marshall of Bentley, deceased, husbandman.
1732. March 1. Sarah dau. of John Marshall, of Bentley, husbandman, lately deceased.
1736. Nov. 17. Joseph son of Benj. Marshall of Bentley, Farmer.
1743. April 23. Sarah dau. of Benj. Marshall.
1758. Aug. 8. W^m son of John Marshall of Bentley, Innkeeper.
1774. Jany 7. Mary wife of John Marshall of Bentley, Victualler.
1774. May 20. John Marshall of Bentley, Victualler.
1786. Sept. 6. Eliz^th wife of Benjamin Marshall, Farmer, Bentley, aged 83.
1791. May 10. Benjamin Marshall, Farmer, Bentley, aged 88.
1791. Dec. 26. Martha wife of John Marshall, Farmer, Bentley, aged 69.
1792. Jany 26. Edward Marshall, labourer, Bentley, aged 80.
1799. March 15. John Marshall, junior, of Bentley, Miller, aged 43.

1 Joseph Marshall of Bentley, sen^r. yeoman. Will dated 29 August, 1722. To daughter Ann £100. Joseph son of Richard Doughty. Ann daughter of Robert Turner. Joseph son of Robert Marshall. My daughter Sarah Doughty. To Robert Turner, 1s. Farm to son Joseph, he paying to my son Robert Marshall £10. Proved at York 21 May, 1723. See Vol. i., p. 302. His descendants appear to have been as here set down in tabular form:—

Joseph Marshall of Bentley, in the parish of Arksey, yeoman. Buried 24 Nov., 1722. Will dated 29 Aug., 1722, proved at York, 21 May, 1723. = Ann England of Hutton Pannell. Marriage licence dated 1664. To marry at Felkirk or Royston. Married at Felkirke, 13 Jan^{y}, 1664. Buried 14 Feb., 1714.

- Joseph Marshall of Bentley, yeoman. Ment^{d} in his father's will, 1722. Will dated 28 Nov., 1729, proved at York, 25 Nov., 1730. Bur^{d} 1 Dec., 1729. = Sarah, widow of Joseph Foster, of Bentley. Married at Doncaster, 25 March, 1699. Bur^{d} 18 Dec., 1727. Joseph Foster was buried at Arksey, 2 Jan., 1698. She had issue by him Thomas Foster, ment^{d} in will of Joseph Marshall, 1729.
- Robert Marshall of Arksey. Ment^{d} in his father's will, 1722. Bur^{d} 20 Nov. 1727. = Susanna .... Married 2^{ndly} to Washington Wroe, 16 April 1732. Buried 3 Jan., 1752.
- Sarah. Bapt. 12 Dec., 1676. Ment^{d} in her father's will, 1722. Married Robert Doughty.
- Ann. Bapt. 17 June, 1679. Ment^{d} in her father's will, 1722. Buried 31 Dec., 1727.

Children of Robert Marshall and Susanna:

- William Marshall. Bapt. 3 June, 1719.
- Robert Marshall. Bapt. 26 Jan., 1727.
- Joseph Marshall. Ment^{d} in will of Joseph Marshall, 1722. Bur^{d} 26 Feb., 1722-3.
- Thomas Marshall. Bapt. 30 Sept., 1726. Buried 28 Nov., following.
- Susanna. Bapt. 19 Sept., 1721. Buried 26 Feb., 1722.
- Susanna. Bapt. 7 Jan., 1723. Buried 28 Jan., 1727.

Children of Joseph Marshall and Sarah:

- John Marshall, of Bentley. Ment^{d} as deceased in his father's will, 1729. Bur^{d} 17 April, 1729. Admo'n to Elizabeth his relict, 10 Sept., 1729. = Elizabeth. Ment^{d} as a widow in will of Joseph Marshall, 1729. Married 2^{ndly} to John Ellison, 25 June, 1730.
- Benjamin Marshall of Bentley. Bapt. 2 Sept., 1703. Proved his father's will, 1730. Buried 10 May, 1791. = Elizabeth. Buried 6 Sept., 1786.
- Joseph Marshall. Bapt. 18 April, 1706. Buried 4 Feb., 1706-7.
- Ann. Bapt. 14 and buried 16 April, 1700.

Children of John Marshall and Elizabeth:

- Joseph Marshall. Bapt. 22 Sept., 1724. Ment^{d} in will of Joseph Marshall, 1729. Buried 10 March, 1730.
- Mary. Bapt. 28 June, 1726. Ment^{d} in will of Joseph Marshall, 1729.
- Elizabeth. Buried ... March, 1728.
- Sarah. Buried 1 March, 1732.

Children of Benjamin Marshall and Elizabeth:

- Sarah. Bapt. 20 Dec., 1725. Bur^{d} 23 April, 1743.
- John Marshall. Bapt. 10 Jan^{y}, 1726.
- Thomas Marshall. Bapt. 14 Sept., 1729.
- Joseph Marshall. Bapt. 6 March, 1733. Buried 17 Nov., 1736.
- Joshua Marshall. Bapt. 17 May, 1739.
- Benjamin Marshall. Bapt. 14 Oct., 1741.
- Elizabeth. Bapt. 30 Dec., 1736.
- Sarah. Bapt. 10 Aug., 1746.
- Ann. Bapt. 9 Nov., 1731.
- Mary. Bapt. 29 Mar., 1744.

EXTRACTS FROM VARIOUS REGISTERS.

1731. May 31. Daniel son of Daniel and Jane Marshall Bapt. *Faversham, co. Kent.*

1656. Anne Marshall dau. of Jonathan Marshall, 25 March. Bapt.
1697-8. George Shelford of Hormead Mag: Wid: and Mary Marshal Wid. 26 Jany Married.
1658. Grace Marshall wife of Jonathan Marshall, 9 Sept. Buried.
1658. Jonathan Marshall of Luffenhall, 31 Dec. Buried.
Ardeley, co. Hertford.

1680. Oct. 18. Henry son of Thomas Marshall *alias* Gifford, of Woodmancote, and Jane his wife was bapt.
1681. March 6. Thomas son of Thomas Gifford *alias* Marcher *(sic)* of Woodmancote, and Jane his wife was bapt.
Transcript of Bishop's Cleeve Register at Gloucester.

1637. June 30. Mr Henry Marshall of Gatefulford and Ann Bowes. Married. *Howden, co. York.* See vol. i., p. 19.

1698. Jan. 19. John Marshall, Gent. Buried. *Felkirk, co. York.*

1630. Aug. 8. Roger Marshall and Elizabeth Watts. Married. *Pylle, co. Somerset.*

1691. May 5. Mr George Lench and Mrs Katherine Marshall were married. *Transcript of Grimley Register at Worcester.*

1626. Sept. 26. James Woodes & Marie Marshall were married.
1722. Oct. 18. Mary D^{r} of James & Rachel Marshall Travelers. Bapt.
Brundish, co. Suffolk.

1644. Nov. 11. Thomas Bennifield & Ann Marshall were married. *Tannington, co. Suffolk.*

1572. Oct. 3. Thomas Marshall and Elizabeth Welch. Married.
1573. Feb. 15. The Wife of Thomas Marshall. Buried.
1575. April 29. Thomas Marshall Bapt.
Stifford, co. Essex.

1688. Buried. Mr Francis Marshall Vicar of Hollow, November 23. *Transcript of Hallow Register at Worcester.*[1]

1611. Nov. 5. John Marshall.[2] Buried. *Richmond, co. Surrey.*

1670. Jany 31. Jeffery Brock [of Basford] and Mary Marshall.[3] Married. *Radford, co. Nott^{m}.*

[1] Francis Marshall, clerk, A.B. was instituted to the vicarage of Grimley with Hallow, 13 Dec., 1660, patron the Bishop of Worcester, (Morley). He appears amongst those who disclaimed arms at the Visitation of Worcestershire 1682. He was succeeded in the living by Thomas Pipard, who was instituted on the vacancy caused by his death, 19 Feb., 1688.

[2] See Vol. i., p. 55. *From Index to Court Rolls of Richmond, Gough MSS. Bodleian*, it appears that 9 James I. (1611-12) George Marshall was heir to John Marshall at his death. 5 Car. I. (1629-30) Katherine Marshall was heir of George Marshall at his death.

[3] See *Mar. Lic.* Vol. i., p. 78.

1661. Dec. 17. Mr Wm Marshall. Buried.
1666. June 22. Mr Saml Marshall. Buried.
Basford, co. Nottm.

1562-3. Feb. 1. Jhonnes Marshall and Edetha Grafton. Married.
1593. Aug. 3. Edeth Marshall wife of John Marshall of Hounslow. Buried.
1594. May 13. George Greatrackes and Anne Marshall. Married.
1717. Oct. 10. John Marshall and Mary Hickman both of this parish. Married.
1730. Aug. 9. Ric. Marshall and Hannah Hall both of this parish. Married.
1743. Oct. 5. Robert Stapleton and Mary Marshall. Married.
Heston, co. Middlesex.

1732. Sept. 15. James Marshall and Sarah Shepherd. Married. *Petersham, co. Surrey.*

1699. Jany 25. Joseph Kippax and Sarah Marshall Married. *Harworth, co. Nottm.*

1662. April 15. Williã the son of John Marshall and Anne was (of the Merls) buryed.
1662. April 24. Anne the Daughter of John and Anne Marshall was buryed (of ye Merells).
1689. Nov. 2. Ant. Marshall. Buried. See Vol. i., pp. 297, 321.
Carlton in Lindrick, co. Nottm.

1604. April 9. Mathew Marshall & Brigett Sandars. Married.
1650. April 4. Thomas Marshall of Kew. Buried.
1658. Aug. 18. Kathrine Marshall. Buried.
1680. Aug. 5. William Grant & Eliz. Marshall. Married.
1766. Oct. 19. James Marshall of St Ann's Westminster, and Elizabeth Webster, of Richmond. Lic. Married.
Richmond, co. Surrey.

1623. June 22. Thomas Marshall and Ann Bell of Balcombe in the parish of Howden. Married.
1629. Feb. 4. Henry Marshall of Howden & Duglas Pearcey of Sandholm. Married.
Eastrington, co. York.

1661. Sept. 22. Daniell the sonne of John Marshall. Bapt. *Transcript of Wragby, co. York.*

1661 (1662?). William Marshall . . . die March. ? Buried. *Transcript of Acaster, co. York.*

1661. Aug. 11. Will'm ye sone of Will'm Marshall. Buried. *Transcript of Patrington, co. York.*

1713. April 10. George Short and Anne Marshall. Married. *Cuckney, co. Nottm.*

1615. Feb. 7. Philip Marshall *alias* Milward and Anne Pardoe. Married.
1645. July 15. Justice dau. of Justice and Richard Millerd *al's* Marshal. Bapt.
1668. Sept. 29. Edmund son of Philip and Margaret Marshall. Bapt.
Transcript of Ombersley, co. Worcester.

1634. Oct. 28. Francis Marshall and Jane Wentworth. Married. *Badsworth, co. York.*

1702-3. Feb. 21. Anthony Marshall of Upton. Buried. *Badsworth, co. York.*

1648. Dec. 26. Bernard Marshall and Jennet Pigot. Married. *Frickley, co. York.*

1656. Madglen Marshall wife of John Marshall, buried Aug. 23.
1661. John Marshall, buried 16 Feb.
1681. Othery (?) wife of James Marshall, buried 27 April.
1682. Henry son of James Marshall, buried 16 March..
1687. James son of Thomas Marshall, bapt. 15 Feb.
1691. John Marshall and Elizabeth Baites. Married, 29 Nov.

South Dalton, co. York.

1653. Upon Monday the 13th day of March 1653 John Marshall of Hake [Ake] and Servant to Richard Remington the elder hanged himself and upon the 15th of March he was buried after ye Coroner had viewed him. *Lockington, co. York.*

1549. May 20. Jennet M'shall was bapt.
1699. June 23. Thomas Nornabell and Ann Marshall. Married.
1700. Nov. 28. Thos Marshall and Mary Sherwood. Married.

Holme on the Wolds, co. York.

TICKHILL, CO. YORK.

Baptisms.

1551. March 14. John son of William Marshall.
1553. July 16. Jennett dau. of William Marshall.
1568. Aug. 22. Henry son of William Marshall.
1574. Dec. 16. Hellen dau. of John Marshall.
1579. Feb. 10. Johan dau. of John Marshall.
1583. Feb. 24. Jane dau. of John Marshall.
1594. Feb. 25. Jennett dau. of Thomas Marshall.
1597. May 8. Dorithie dau. of Thomas Marshall.
1599. May 20. Johan dau. of Henry Marshall.
1600. Aug. 8. Francis dau. of Robert Marshall.
1600. Feb. 22. William son of Henry Marshall.
1601. March 7. Henry son of Thomas Marshall.
1602. Feb. 24. Dorytye dau. of Henry Marshall.
1603. July 25. Johan dau. of Robert Marshall.
1603. Sept. 4. Robert base son of Jayne Marshall.
1605. July 14. Margaret dau. of Henry Marshall.
1608. March 30. William son of Robert Marshall.
1610. March 26. Margret dau. of Henrie Marshall.
1612. June 28. Wynifride dau. of Henrie Marshall.
1669. Sept. 14. Anne dau. of William Marshall.

1672. Aug. 4. Elizabeth dau. of William Marshall.
1676. Nov. 7. Dorothy dau. of William Marshall.
1682. Nov. 24. . . . . son of William Marshall.

Marriages.

1548. July 1. William Marshall and Elizabeth Bybb.
1573. Nov. 24. John Marshall and Hellen Birley.
1579. May 19. Richard Marshall and Anne Bower.
1584. June 2. John Vessy and Jane Oglethorpe.
1592. Dec. 4. Robert Marshall and Issabell Stillinge.
1599. Jan. 27. William Powle and Ellen Marshall.
1602. July 11. Thomas Marshall and Dyonis Pashelaye.
1603. Oct. 24. George Fisher and Joan Marshall.
1624. Jan. 20. Roger Nycholsonne and Joane Marshall.
1632. Oct. 28. James Fowler and Dorathy Marshall.
1643. Dec. 8. John Leese and Frances Marshall.
1694. April 10. William Marshall and Jane Norton.
1699. Nov. 28. Jo: Wildsmith and Dorathy Marshall.
1713. July 19. John Marshall and Mary Fanshaw.

Burials.

1546. May 12. Margret Marshall.
1550. March 20. Richard the son of William Marshall.
1552. July 18. John son of William Marshall.
1569. Dec. 1. John Marshall.
1570. Jan. 16. Jennett Marshall.
1570. Jan. 27. Issabell Marshall.
1570. Feb. 6. Margrete Marshall.
1579. May 10. William Marshall. (See p. 54.)
1583. April 23. Jennet dau. of William Marshall.
1586. June 27. Hellen dau. of John Marshall.
1589. Oct. 7. John Marshall. (See p. 54.)
1599. May 12. Dorithie dau. of Thomas Marshall.
1600. March 24. Anne wife of Thomas Marshall.
1604. April 2. Henry son of Thomas Marshall.
1608. Feb. 15. William son of Robert Marshall.
1611. March 28. John son of Henrie Marshall.
1611. Sept. 28.[1] Margarett dau. of Henrie Marshall.
1619. May 20. Anne dau. of Robert Marshall.
1623. March 24. Margaret wife of Henrye Marshall.
1631. July 20. Dorothy dau. of Henry Marshall.
1632. March 18. Henry Marshall.

ST. JOHN'S (LAUGHTON), CO. YORK.

1578. June 7. Elizabeth d. of John Marshall.
1578. Jany 13. Alice d. of John Marshall.
1581. April 24. Thomas s. of John Marshall.

1 See Vol. i., p. 70, where 18 is an error for 28.

1586. April 10. 'Emota' d. of John Marshall.
1588. July 22. Edward s. of John Marshall.
1590. April 21. Robert s. of John Marshall.
1593. March 2. 'Elizeus'[1] s. of Clement Marshall.
1596. July 23. Robert s. of Clement Marshall.
1597. Jany 14. 'Dorithea' d. of Clement Marshall.
1599. Jany 28. Elizabeth d. of Clement Marshall.
1602. Dec. 10. Alice d. of Clement Marshall.

SELBY, CO. YORK.

Baptisms.

1582. Oct. 12. Michael son of William Marshall.
1585. Sept. 14. Richard son of Thomas Marshall.
1587. Oct. 11. Thomas son of Thomas Marshall.
1621. Sept. 13. Peter Marshall the sone of Robert Marshall.
1624. Oct. 10. [Ro] bert Marshall the sone of Rob. Marshall.
1627. March 9. Mary Marshall the daughter of Williā Marshall, Junior.
1629. May 30. Roger Marshall the sone of Robert Marshall, gen.
1643. May 22. Margaret the daughter of Richard Marshall.
1644. Dec. 5. Thomas the sonne of Richard Marshall.
1646. Jany 3. Jane the daughter of Richard Marshall.
1649. Aug. 16. Lawrence the sonne of Richard Marshall.
1650. Sept. 21. Robert the sonne of Mr Michell Marshall.[2]
1651. Sept. 23. Michell the sonne of Mr Michell Marshall.
1652. Sept. 2. Thomas the sonne of Richard Marchell.
1652. March 8. Ann the daughter of Micell Marshall.
1654. Sept. 12. Thomas the son of Michell Marshall.
1656. Jany 22. John the son of Michell Marshell.
1673. April 29. Emanell the sonn of Richard Marchell.
1674. Feb. 10. Ann the daughter of Richard Marshill.
1678. June 20. Sara the daughter of Richard Marshill.
1679. April 8. Henarey the sonn [of] Henarey Marshell.
1679. Feb. 26. Ailize the daughter of Richard Marshell.
1683. June 5. Saray the daughter of Richard Marshell.
1684. June 25. Ann dau. of Thomas Marshall.
1684. Feb. 8. Richard son of Henry Marshall.
1686. June 9. John son of Thomas Marshall.
1694. April 26. Ann dau. of John Marshall.
1695. Aug. 28. John son of John Marshall.
1699. Sept. 27. Emanuel son of Emanuel Marshall, bricklayer.[3]
1701. Nov. 18. Lydia dau. of Emanuel Marshall, bricklayer.[4]

[1] *i.e.*, Elisha.

[2] The following tabular pedigree, p. 16, will assist the reader to place the persons mentioned in these extracts, and in other places in this book, in the proper order of their relationship.

[3] "Emanuel Marshall, Junr, b. 11 March, 1724. Emanuel Marshall, Senr, gent, 17 May, 1740." Monumental Inscription in Morrell's *History of Selby*, p. 234.

[4] "Lydia w. of Robert Anby, and d. of Eml. Marshall, senr. d. 21st December, 1756." Monumental Inscription in Morrell's *History of Selby*, p. 237.

Elizabeth. Buried at Darrington, 7 March, 1587. See p. 110. = Robert Marshall, of Wentbridge, Innholder. Died 1602-3.[1] = Mary, widow of . . . . Boult. See Vol. i., p. 264.

. . . . Marshall =

Victoria. Bapt. at Darrington, 8 June, 1589. Married William Grant, of South Kirby, 1611. See Vol. i., p. 264.

Mary. Ment[d] in will of Robert Marshall, 1602.

John Marshall. Bapt. at Darrington, 8 Aug., 1574.

Michael Marshall. ::: Margaret Fleminge, Mar. at Selby, 10 Aug., 1602. Michael Marshall: Bapt. at Darrington, 13 May, 1578. ? If guardian to his brother Robert Marshall.

Robert Marshall. Bapt. at Darrington, 14 April, 1586. Ment[d] as under age, in his father's will, 1602. Chose Michael Marshall of Selby, to be his guardian. ? Called cousin in will of Edward Marshall of Tadcaster, 1615. See Vol. i., p. 263. = Mary. ? if Mary Bramley. Married 24 Oct., 1609.

Elizabeth, Bapt. at Darrington, 1 Mar., 1579-80. Married Robert Watson.

Anne, and Jane. Died infants. Bapt. and bur. at Darrington.

I believe this Robert to be the same person as Robert Marshall of Selby, gent. Will proved at York by Michael Marshall, clerk, his son, 10 May, 1648. See Vol. i., p. 314, and *ante* p. 52. = Mary. Buried 29 Dec., 1669.

Roger Marshall. Bapt. 30 May, and buried 9 Sept., 1629.

Michael Marshall, D.D., Vicar of Selby. Buried there, 4 Mar., 1657. According to his epitaph he left a will. = Ann Myers of Selby. Married at Trinity, Goodramgate, York, 7 Dec., 1648. Ment[d] as Ann Pickard in will of Alice Oglethorpe, 2 1660. Pro. will of her son Thomas Marshall, 1693. Bur[d] 2 Aug., 1698. = Thomas Pickard, Minister. Ment[d] in will of Alice Oglethorpe, 1661. Dead in 1693.

Peter Marshall. Bapt. 13 Sept., 1621.

Robert Marshall. Bapt. 10 Oct., 1624. Buried 31 July, 1625. See *ante* p. 60.

Robert Marshall. Bapt. 21 Sept., 1650. Bur. 3 May, 1655.

Michael Marshall. Bapt. 23 Sept., 1651. Ment[d] in will of Alice Oglethorpe, 1660.

Thomas Marshall of Selby, Draper. Bapt. 12 Sept., 1654. Will of 23 Apr., 1692, pro. at York, 29 June, 1693. See Vol. i., p. 309. = Elizabeth. ? if dau. of . . . . Purratt, as Tho. M. ment[s] in his will his "mother Margaret Purratt." Bur. 24 June, 1690.

John Marshall. Bapt. 22 Jan., 1656. ? Signed inventory of his brother Thomas, 1693. ? Taxed for 6 hearths at Wistow, *temp.* Car. II.

Ann. Bapt. 8 March 1652-3.

Charles Pickard. Ment[d] in will of Alice Oglethorpe, 1660.

Michael Marshall of Selby. Devisee of land at Wistow in his father's will, 1692. Buried 12 Feb., 1718. Admon to Lucy his widow, 3 April, 1719. See *ante* p. 58. = Lucy, dau. of . . . . Frankland. Mar. at York Minster, 7 July, 1709.

Robert Marshall. Mentioned in his father's will, 1692.

John Marshall. Bapt. 9 June, 1686. Bur[d] 20 Dec., 1689.

Thomas Marshall. Care of his person granted to Ann Pickard, widow, his grandmother, 29 June, 1693.

Ann. Bapt. 25 June, 1684. Ment[d] in her father's will, 1692.

Michael Marshall. Bapt. and buried 25 August, 1710.

Frankland Marshall. Bapt. April, and buried 2 July, 1713.

Robert Marshall. Bapt. 29 May, and buried 9 Sept., 1714.

Elizabeth. Bapt. 14 Feb., 1715.

[1] Robert Marshall of Wentbridge, Innholder. Will dated 9 Oct., 1602, proved at York 27 Jan[y], following. To be buried in the churchyard of Kirk-Smeaton. Mentions an indenture dated 39 Eliz., by Robert Waterhouse of

1709. . . . . dau. of Emanuel Marshall, bricklayer.
1710. Aug. 25. Michael son of Michael Marshall.
1713. April . . Frankland son of Mr Michael Marshall.
1714. May 29. Robert son of Mr Michael Marshall.
1715. Feb. 14. Elizabeth dau. of Mr Michael Marshall.

Marriages.

1595. July 6. William Marshall and Alice Smith.
. . . . Woobanke and Jane Marshall.
1602. Aug. 10. Michael Marshall and Margaret Fleminge.
1606. Dec. 2. William Marshall and Isabell Bolton.
1609. Oct. 24. Robert Marshall and Mary Bramley.
1620. July 9. Richard Parker and Lucye Marshall.
1626. Nov. 28. William Hawley and Mary Marshall.
1630. Sept. 15. William Colbourne and An Marshall.
1632. Sept. 25. William Marshall and Rachell Topham.
1632. Dec. 11. Thomas Knight, Junior, and Margaret Marshall.
1633. Feb. 24. Georg Lawtye of Carleton and Bridgett Marshall.
1635. Nov. 26. Thomas Copley and Ann Marshall.
1687. Feb. 16. James Marshall and Frances Westoby.

Burials.

1625. July 31. Robert Marshall the sone of Robert Marshall, gen.
1628. Feb. 3. Mary Marshall the daughter of William Marshall Junior.
1629. Sept. 9. Roger Marshall the sone of Robert Marshall gentleman. (Buried in the church.)
1629. March 9. Joan Marshall the wife of William Marshall.
1643. May 4. Frances the wife of Robert Marshall senior.
1644. May 28. Alize the daughter of Richard Marshall.

Harthill, gent., demising to him for 19 years at the rent of £11 17s 6d "the house called the Swan in which I now dwell," etc. I will that Mary my wife, and my daughter Elizabeth wife of Robert Watson, enjoy them during the minority of my son Robert. To son Michael £40. To daughter Victoria £20. Son in law Thomas Belte. Mary Marshall my brothers daughter. Robert Marshall the son chose Michael Marshall of Selby to be his guardian.

[2] Alice Oglethorpe of Keilington, co. York. Dated 9 August, 1660. To be buried in chancel of parish church of Keilington nigh to my husband, deceased. To son Thomas Mab £100 or to his child or children in case he die. His daughter Elizabeth Mab. Grandchild William Lewis. To my cousin John Oglethorpe the scholar 40s. Henry, Thomas, Christopher, and William Addams sons of Henry Addams, minister of Rawmarsh. To William and John Everingham sons of Thomas Everingham of Whitley, deceased 16s amongst them. To William Loueday 20s William Shireson. William Sharpaste. Lease of Thornefeild in the lordship of Beale to Edward Pagitt of Beale. Margaret Anby daughter of John Anby of Selby. To Thomas Pickard, Minister, and Anne his wife 40s, and to Michael, Thomas, and John Marshall, and Charles Pickard, sons of Anne Pickard, 20s equally amongst them. Anne Walken of Hadlesay and Thomas Walken her son. Thomas Mab, and William Lewis executors. Thomas Pickard, minister, a witness.—Proved at York 30 December, 1662. (Vol.45, fo. 253.)

1655. May 3. Robart the sonne of Michell Marshall.
1657. Dec. 27. Leonard son of Richard Marshall.
1657. March 4. Michael Marshall Minester of the Gospel.[1]
1658. Oct. 29. Rachel wife of William Marshall.
1667. Oct. 6. Alice Marshill.
1669. Dec. 29. Mrs Marchell. (Buried in the church.)
1679. Sept. 5. Jane the wife of Richard Marshill.
1679. Dec. 22. Richard Marshell. (Buried in the church.)
1689. Dec. 20. John son of Thomas Marshall.
1690. June 24. Elizabeth wife of Mr Thomas Marshall.
1690. Feb. 24. Markerill [? Margaret] dau. of Thomas Marshall.
1692. April 29. Mr Thomas Marshall.[1]
1698. Aug. 2. Mrs Pickard, Woollen draper, buried by her executor Ann Marshall.
1710. Aug. 25. Michael son of Michael Marshall.
1713. July 2. Frankland son of Michael Marshall.
1714. Sept. 9. Robert son of Michael Marshall.
1718. Feb. 12. Mr Michael Marshall.
1719. May 2. Henry Marshall.

CONISBOROUGH, CO. YORK.

1566. June 7. Margret dau. of Tho. Marshall.
1585. Dec. 16. Jane dau. of Will'm Marshall.
1587. March 17. Elizabeth dau. of Will'm Marshall.
1594. June 9. Richard son of Will'm Marshall.
} Baptised.
1648. July 18. Matrimoniū Guliel: Saxton de Harworth clerici et Edithe Marshall celebratū est.[2]
1675. Nov. 21. Thomas Nicholson & Anne Marshall. Married. (See vol. ii., p. 52.)
1688. July . . . Robert Thwaites & Eliz. Saxton, Gent. Married.
1722. May 27. Nicholas Marshal. Buried.

[1] On a ledger stone in South Aisle:—
An epitaph upon ye . . . . . . Michael Marshall, who died . . . . day of . . . .
[Here follow several lines in verse which will be found in Morrell's *History of Selby*, but note that the two which he gives in parentheses are not on the stone.]
Here lieth ye body of Thomas Marshall, Draper, son of Michael Marshall, Doctor of Divinity, late in Selby, who departed ys life ye 27th of April, 1692.
Inf. Hic jacet Michælem *(sic)* Michælis Filius, et Thomæ Marshall, Gen. Nepos, Qui sepultus est 25to die Augusti . . . .

On another stone, near the above:—
Here was buried . . . .
of Mary the wife . . . .
Marshall the 2 of . . . .
1683.

[2] The following entry is in Harworth Register:—
1648. July 18. "Guilielmus Saxton cler' et Editha filia Guil. Marshall, Generosus."

ROTHERHAM, CO. YORK.

Baptisms.

2 Edw. vi. Nov. 19. George s. of Thomas Marshall.
1563. April 4. John Marshall.
1566. Jany 19. Richard Marshall.
1568. July 25. Roger Marshall.
1570. Jany 6. William Marshall.
1570. March 17. William Marshall.
1571. Oct. 7. John Marshall.
1573. Aug. 2. Elizabeth Marshall.
1576. July 1. Margret Marshall.
1581. Sept. 17. Margret Marshall. (illegit.)
1582. Sept. 23. Thomas Marshall.
1586. March 2. Agnes Marshall.
1586. March 4. Henry Marshall.
1586. May 12. George Marshall.
1588. April 21. Ellin Marshall.
1589. July 7. Anne Marshall.
1591. May 12. Betryse Marshall. } gemelli.
1591. May 13.[1] Margaret Marshall. }
1598. Aug. 18. Isabell Marshall.
1601. Sept. 20. Robert Marshall.
1602. March 14. Thomas Marshall.
1602. Nov. 14. Ann Marshall.
1603. Jany 30. Anthonye Marshall.
1607. April 22. William son of Xpofer Marshall, stranger.
1609. April 30. Thomas son of James Marshall.
1643. Oct. 29. Deborah dau. of William Marshall.
1647. April 4. William son of William Marshall.
1649. May 27. William son of William Marshall.
1651. March 14. Jonathan son of William Marshall.
1662. April 13. Mary dau. of Godfrey Marshall.—*Transcript at York.*

Marriages.

1565. Oct. 7. John Marshall and Margaret Hirst.
1566. Sept. 1. John Law and Joan Marshall.
1569. Sept. 29. Robert Marshall and Joan Everingham.
1570. Sep. 3. William Marshall and Margaret Darwyn.
1570. Sept. 4. Robert Marshall and Mary Tincker.
1571. Oct. 2. Richard Marshall and Ellin Whittley.
1578. June 6. William Pearsay and Agnes Marshall.
1583. Nov. 3. James Marshall and Margaret Byncks.
1584. Nov. 15. Richard Marshall and Marjery Jelott.
1587. Jany 30. John Marshall and Elizabeth Cowper.
1595. March 2. Willm̄ Marshall and Issabell Greenwood.
1597. April 10. Xpofer Marshall and Margaret Robinson.
1598. Jany 21. Richard Trewloue and Fraunces Marshall.

[1] In another place "eodem die."

1599. Jany 20. Willm̄ Marshall and Elizabeth Hadfeild.
1608. Oct. 8. Thomas Dodworth and Anne Marshall.
1612. Sept. 8. Henry Marshall and Mary Stringer.
1612. Jany 24. George Marshall and Issabell Swifte.
1618. July 28. Xpofer Marshall and Margret Birkes.
1627. July 11. Xpofer Marshall and Anne Page.
1627. July 29. John Benton and Elizabeth Marshall.
1636. July 25. Robert Roger and Elizabeth Marshall.
1637. July 16. Richard Johnson and Anne Marshall.
1640. Nov. 12. Henry Lilly and Ellen Marshall.
1666. Dec. 3. Rich. Johnson & Eliz. Marshall.—*Transcript at York*.

Burials.

1574. Nov. 9. Frauncys Marshall.
1576. July 21. Rychard Marshall.
1577. Oct. 10. Margert Marshall.
1586. July 10. John Marshall.
1587. Dec. 27. Elizabeth Marshall.
1589. Nov. 25. John Marshall.
1591. June 13. Frauncis Marshall.
1591. June 15. Agnes Marshall.
1640. Jany 1. Mathew Marshall.
1642. Dec. 14. John Marshall.
1646. Oct. 17, Deborah Marshall.
1648. July 20. William Marshall.
1652. April 21. George Marshall.

MASHAM, CO. YORK.

Baptisms.

1604. Masham. Oct. 3. William son of Francis Marshall.
1619. ,, Sept. 10. Susanna dau. of Christopher Marshall.
1639. ,, Feb. 14. Arthur son of John Marshall.
1640. ,, Dec. 17. Elizabeth dau. of same.
1645. ,, Feb. 16. Susanna ,, same.
1674. ,, July 21. John son of Christopher Marshall.
1676. ,, April 25. Mary dau. of same.

Marriages.

1629. Ellingstring. July 7. Thomas Pickersgill and Elizabeth Marshall.
1630. July 1. Francis Marshall and Jane Pickersgill.
1668. Grewelthorpe. May 21. Leonard Marshall and Mary Malthouse, of Aldfield.
1672. Masham. Aug. 14. Christopher Marshall and Bettrice Holdsworth.

Burials.

1603. Masham. Oct. 7. An infant of Francis Marshall.
1606. Fearby. April 22. Anthony Marshall.

1609. Masham. May 7. The wife of Francis Marshall.
1613. Dec. 1. Francis Marshall.
1632. Masham. Dec. 21. Christopher Marshall.
1646. ,, July 22. Elizabeth Marshall, widow.

St. Nicholas, in the City of Gloucester.

Marriages.

1578. May 11. Thom̄s Marchall and Sybbell Pryce.
1618. Jan. 10. John Marshall and Anne Cradocke.
1656. Feb. —. Henry Marshall and Margarett Jones.
1686. Oct. 16. Thomas Marshall and Mary Cibbletts.
1696. Nov. 10. John Window and Elizabeth Marshall.

Kirkby Malzeard, co. York.

1685. Braistywood. Sep. 26. Leonard son of Leonard Marshall of Braistywood. Bapt. Leonard Metcalf, jun., of Studley hall, John Bramley of Golwhay [Galphay] and Margaret Todd of Ripon, sureties.
1688. Galwhay. Ruth wife of Leonard Marshall. Buried. Nov. 18.
1692. Galwhay. William son of Leonard Marshall. Buried. Feb. 1.
1689. Leonard Marshall and Hannah Wikeley both of Galwhay married 13 Jan^{y}, 1689-90.

East Markham, co. Notts.

1621. Nov. 27. Thomas Marshall with Alce Johnson. Married.
1622. June 9. Elizabeth dau. of Thomas Marshall.
1623. March 14. Mary dau. of same.
1625. Jany 28. Thomas son of same.
1627. Dec. 20. Richard son of same.
1630. Jany 20. Edward son of same. Bapt.
1634. Oct. 28. Robert son of same.
1637. March 16. Oliver son of same. and Alce Marshall.
1621. Feb. 26. Mary the dau. of Tho. Marshall. Buried.
1633. Rowland Barker wth Bridgett Marshall. Married 9 May.
1640. Willm Hastings with Sibbell Marshall. Married 13 August.
1642. March 24. Robert son of Thomas and Dorothy Marshall. Bapt.
1673. Nov. 29. John Marshall and Jane Brett. Married.
1673. Dec. 12. Mary dau. of John Marshall. Bapt.

EXTRACTS FROM TRANSCRIPTS OF YORKSHIRE PARISH REGISTERS.

Leeds.

1661. June 18. William Marshall of Kirkgait. Buried.
1661. Aug. 8. An infant of Henry Marshall of Milhill. Buried.
1661. Oct. 24. Hannah daughter of Thomas Marshall of Houlbecke. Buried.
1661. Feb. 8. Thomas sonne of Francis Marshall of Hilhousbankes. Buried.
1662. Nov. 30. Francis Marshall of Hilhousbankes had a child bapt. named Ruth.
1662. March 8. Thomas Marshall of Houbecke had a child baptized named Ann.
1662. April 24. James sonne of Widow Marshall of Kirkgait. Buried.
1662. May 17. Francis Marshall of Hilhousbankes. Buried.
1662. Aug. 27. Mr William Marshall steward of lower house. Buried.
1663. May 6. Mr William Haumshey of Vicar laine and Mary Marshall of Otley parish. Married.
1664. Nov. 13. Thomas Marshall of Houlbecke had a child baptized named Richard.
1665. Nov. 16. John Dovers of March laine and Grace Marshall of Brigait. Married.
1665. Dec. 4. Ruth daughter of Widow Marshall of Almeshouses in Lidgait. Buried.
1666. Jan. 29. X'po. Tomson and Sarah Marshall of Lidgait. Married.
1666. Dec. 27. Ann daughter of Thomas Marshall of Houlbecke. Buried.
1666. Feb. 6. Richard sonne of Thomas Marshall of Houlbecke. Buried.
1667. Jan. 26. Stephen Snell of Headrow and Ann Marshall of New chappell. Married.
1667. April 3. Ann wife of William Marshall of Headrow. Buried.
1667. May 20. Peter Marshall of the Shambles. Buried.
1667. Nov. 15. Henry Marshal of Milhill, Flocker. Buried.
1668. May 14. Beniamin Dyson of Heddingley and Alice Marshall of Shambles. Married.
1668. Jan. 13. Stephen Clarke and Mary Marshall of Milhill. Married.
1669. Aug. 25. William Fletcher of Churchyarde and Isabell Marshall of Kirkgait. Married.
1669. Oct. 12. Thomas Marshall of Houlbeck. Buried.

Terrington.

1661. Sept. 31. Fra'cis the daughter of Thomas Marshall. Bapt.
1662. Jan. 14. Robert Knott and Thomas Marshell was bured.

1664. April 29. Isabell Marshall widow buryed.
1668. Feb. 23. Mathew Marshall and Anne Pennock. Married.
1671. Richard Marshall signs as churchwarden.

Halifax.

1661. April 23. Wid. Sam. Marshall, Hali. Buried.
1661. Jan. 5. Beniamin Martin Marshall, Hali. Bapt.
1661. Jan. 12. Beni'min Martin Marshall, Hali. Buried.
1661. Feb. 5. Tho. Marshall. Hali. plasterer. Buried.
1662. Feb. 29. Maior Marshall and Martha Lawton, Stansfield. Married.
1663. Nov. 12. Joh'es Hoyle and Elizabeth Marshall. Sowerby. Married.
1663. April 12. Vid. Joh. Marshall. Halifax. Buried.
1665. Feb. 27. Joh. Hobson & Judith Marshall. Halifax. Married.
1665. April 16. Tho. Marshall. Halifax. Buried.
1669. April 11. "Jud: Jos: Marchall & Mar: Medley, Halifax." Bapt.
1669. May 11. Joh. Marchall & Gratia Brooke. Shelfe. Married.
1669. Sept. 21. Edw. Marchall & Katherina Wheatley. Halyfax. Married.
1670. July 17. Tho: Ed: Marshell. Halyfax. Bapt.
1670. Aug. 24. Jos: Marshall. Northor'. Buried.
1670. Jan. 15. Marg: Marshall. Halyfax. Buried.

Silkestone.

1661. Dec. 22. Anne the daughter of Martin Marshall of Silkestone was Baptized.
1661-2. Feb. 4. George Marshall of Dodworth was Buried.
1663-4. Jan. 31. John the son of Martin Marshall of Silkston was baptized.
1663. June 18. Richard Marshall of the pishe of Peniston and Mary Crawshaw of Dodworth in the pish of Silkston was maried.
1664. Oct. 1. Sara the daughter of Geruas Marshall of Silkston. Bapt.
1664. Jan. 4. Mary daughter of Geruas Marshall of Silkston. Buried.
1665. Dec. 17. Ann daughter of Geruas & Mary Marshall. Bapt.
1666. Jan. 17. Will. Sonn of Marten Marshall. Bapt.
1667. May 18. Marthin Marshall buryd.

Kippax.

1667. June 2. Anna Marshall sepulta erat.
1663. Jan. 24. Will'm Marshall sonne of Will'm Marshall. Bapt.

1666. July 22. Jacobus Marshall filius Gulielmi Marshall. Bapt.
1666. Nov. 22. Joanna Marshall vidua sepulta.
1668. June 2. Will'm Marshall burrid.
1669. Oct. 24. Eliz. daughter of Wm Marshall. Bapt.
1670. Aug. 26. Cuthbert Marshall buried.

MYTON UPON SWAYLE.

1661. Sept. 25. Anne the daughter of Thomas Marshall, jun^{r}. Bapt.
1661. April 30. Thomas Marshall and Alice Clemmison were marryed.
1661. March 3. Thomas Marshall was buryed.
1664. March 19. Alice the Daughter of Thomas Marshall and Alice his wife. Bapt.
1664. Oct. 14. Anne ye Daughter of Thomas Marshall was buryed.
1669. Nov. 28. Elizabeth the daughter of Thomas Marshall & Alice his wife of ye Parish of Oldbrough was baptiz.
1671. Aug. 30. Alice the wife of Thomas Marshall was buried.

WHITBY.

1661. May 26. Robert Marshall sonn of James Marshall of Whitbey. Bapt.
1661. Jan. 5. Margret Marshall Daughter of Tho. Marshall of Wh. Bapt.
1662. Nov. 29. A child of James Marshalls. Buried.
1663. Dec. 6. Issabell Marshall Daughter of James Marshall. Bapt.
1663. Jan. 31. Timothy Marshall son of Thomas Marshall. Bapt.
1663. Feb. 7. Francis Marshall son of Francis Marshall. Bapt.
1663. May 19. Christopher Storr & Ellis Marshall. Married.
1665. Oct. 4. James Marshall filius James Marshall. Bapt.
1665. April 14. Richard Marshall. Buried.
1665. June 10. Eliza. Marshall. Buried.
1667. Sept. 1. John Marsh *(sic)* filius Thomas Marshall. 13 (years of age). Buried.
1667. Oct. 31. James filius James Marshall. 2 (years of age). Buried.
1667. Nov. 20. Henry Sotham & Marshall widd. Published.
1667. July 5. John filius James Marshall. Whitby. Bapt.
1668. May 10. Alice Daugh. of Thomas Marshal. Whitby. Bapt.
1668. Oct. 6. Mary Dau. of James Marshall. Whitby. Bapt.
1669. Nov. 10. Allicia filia Tho'æ Marshall. Whitby. Buried.
1671. Oct. 29. Elizabetha [filia] Johannis Marshall. Bapt.

HOLY TRINITY, HULL.

1662. Feb. 17. Henry s. of Wat. Marshall. Buried.
1663. Nov. 15. James so. of Thomas Marshall joyner. Bapt.

1663. Nov. 24. Henry Marshall. Buried.
1664. Nov. 3. Richard Marshall & Elizabeth Wickham. Married.
1664. March 22. Faith da. of George Marshall. Born.
1665. Aug. 7. John Marshall & Hannah Smith. Married.
1665. July 26. John s. of Richard Marshall. Bapt.
1665. April 2. James s. of Thomas Marshall pinner. Buried.
1666. Sept. 21. John s. of John Marshall. Bapt.
1667. May 14. John Hodshon & Elizabeth Marshall. Married.
1667. June 2. John Ellis & Sara Marshall. Married.
1667. July 24. Isack Marshall & Hannah Lockwood. Married. (See *ante*, p. 51.)
1667. Oct. 27. Leonard Marshall & Catherine Sandy. Married.
1667. Dec. 8. George s. of Leonard Marshall. Bapt.
1667. Sept. 14. Frances w. of George Marshall. Buried.
1667. Jan. 25. Christopher Marshall. Buried.
1668. Jan. 25. Robert Williams & Elizab. Marshall. Married.
1668. March 10. John s. of John Marshall. Bapt.
1668. July 6. William Marshall. Buried.
1670. March 8. George Marshall, soldier. Buried.
1670. May 19. Thomas Bellard & Hannah Marshall. Married.
1670. Aug. 21. William son of John Marshall. Bapt.
1671. June 5. John son of Richard Marshall. Buried.

FOSTON.

1662. March 2. John Marshall of Flaxton in the parish of Bossall and Grace Bell of Flaxton in the parish of Foston weir married.
1663. Feb. 28. Margret the daughter of John Marshall of Flaxton was baptized.
1663. March 8. Grace the wife of John Marshall of Flaxton was buried.
1663. March 12. Margrett the daughter of John Marshall of Flaxton was buried.

SS. JOHN AND MARTIN, BEVERLEY.

1662. April 10. Alice uxor Thomæ Marshall. Buried.
1665. Aug. 2. Thomas fil. Martini Marshall. Bapt.
1666. Sept. 29. Thomas fil Martini Marshal. Buried.
1667. Dec. 8. Marg. fil. Martini Marshall. Bapt.
1669. Oct. 30. Thomas Marshall marit'. Buried.
1670. March 12. Martin Marshall fil. Martini. Bapt.
1670. Jan. 14. Martin Marshall maritus. Buried.
1671. Nov. 7. Frances Marshall ux. Tho. Buried.

BARDSEY.

1661. June 29. John the sonn of Tho. Marshall, jun. Buried.
1661. Oct. 5. Edward the sonn of the sd Thomas Marshall. Buried.

1661. Oct. 26. Ann the daughter of Tho. Marshall, jun. Bapt.
1662. March 2. William Mawd and Dorothy Marshall. Married.
1666. Dec. 9. Elizabeth the daughter of Thomas Marshall junor. Bapt.
1666. April 30. Mathew Marshall & Alice Scott were married.
1667. Nov. 28. Robert Marshall and Alice Squire were married.
1667. Jan. 14. Mathew Marshall was buried.
1668. Oct. 9. Isabella the daughter of Robert Marshall. Bapt.
1669. Oct. 23. William the sonne of Robert Marshall. Bapt.
1669. Oct. 11. Robert Marshall the elder was buried.
1669. Oct. 30. Alice the wife of Robert Marshall the younger was buried.

Warmfield.

1661. Sept. 22. Daniell the sonne of John Marshall of Sharleston. Bapt.
1662. Aug. 27. The Male Childe of John Marshall being vnbaptized. Buried.
1664. Dec. 28. Jaine the Daughter of John Marshall of Sharleston. Bapt.
1667. Sept. 4. Mathew the sonne of John Marshall of Sharleston. Bapt.
1667. Sept. 5. Mathew ye sonne of John Marshall of Sharleston. Buried.

Aston.

1663. June 9. Mary the daughter of Thomas Marshall was baptised.
1664. June 26. Mary the daughter of Thomas Marshall was baptized.
1666. March 11. Mary the daughter of Thomas Marshall was buryed.
1667. May 13. William the sonne of Thomas Marshall of the Parke-yate was buryed.
1667. May 16. Alice the daughter of Thomas Marshall of Aughton was buryed.
1668. Feb. 2. Thomas Marshall of Aughton was buryed.
1669. Nov. 10. William Rushby and Margaret the Relict of Thomas Marshall were marryed.

Otley.

1661-2. Jan. 18. Francis son of John Marshall of Clyfton. Bapt.
1662. Nov. 5. Mercie dau. of Jeremiæ Marshall of Burley. Bapt.
1665. May 4. Alice dau. of Jeremya Marshall of Burley woodhead. Bapt.
1665. Dec. 4. Ephram son of Ephram Marshall of Eshold. Bapt.

1665. Jan. 7. Ellinger wiffe of John Marshall of Clyfton. Buried.
1666. April 21. Christoffer son of John Marshall of Clifton. Bapt.
1667. Oct. 30. Richard Hill of the pish of Leathley and Dyna Marshall. Married.
1667. Sept. 29. Christoffer Marshall of Menston. Buried.
1667. March 5. Mary wiffe of Robert Marshall of Bramhopp. Buried.
1668. Sept. 26. Richard son of John Marshall of Clifton. Bapt.

Settrington.

1662. Sept. 28. Elezabeth Marshall daughter of Symon Marshall. Bapt.
1662. Jan. 18. Elizabeth Marshall daughter of Henry Marshall. Bapt.
1665. Jan. 14. William Marshall the son of John Marshall. Bapt.
1665. March 11. Aylse Marshall the daughter of Henry Marshall. Bapt.
1666. April 8. Isabell Marshall the daughter of Thomas Marshal. Bapt.
1666. June 24. Cicily Marshall the daughter of Symon Marshall. Bapt.
1666. Aug. 20. William Marshall the sonne of John Marshall. Buried.
1666. Aug. 27. John Marshall the sonne of Symond Marshall. Buried.
1667. June 16. Margaret Marshall the daughter of John Marshall. Bapt.
1667. Feb. 23. William Marshall the sonne of Henry Marshall. Bapt.
1668. March 20. Will. Marshall the sonne of Henry Marshall. Buried.
1669. Nov. 7. Isabell Marshal ye dag. of Simon Marshal. Bapt.
1669. March 13. Henry Marshal ye sonne of Henry Marshal. Bapt.
1671. Nov. 14. Lawrence Marshall and Thomasin Key of Settrington. Married.

Thorp Arch.

1665. Sept. 13. Elizabeth ye daughter of John Marshall. Bapt.
1665. Sept. 13. Elizabeth ye wife of John Marshall. Buried.
1665. Nov. 28. Robert Marshall had a child stillborne buryed.
1665. Feb. 18. Elizabeth ye daughter of John Marshall. Buried.
1666. Nov. 27. John Marshall and Sarah Hill. Married.
1667. Jan. 19. Anne ye daughter of John Marshall. Bapt.
1669. Sept. 18. Elizabeth the daughter of John Marshall. Bapt.

Felkirk.

1660. May 3. Rich. Crosley & Easter Marshall. Married.
1660. Aug. 30. Rich. Marshall was baptized.
1661. Nov. 7. John Marshall & Anne Marshall. Married.
1663-4. Feb. 18. Eliz. Marshall was bapt.
1664. Sept. 15. Rob't Hutchinson & Sarah Marshall. Married.
1664. Nov. 3. Will'm Kay & Sarah Marshall. Married.
1664. Jan. 3. Jane Marshall. Bapt.
1664. Jan. 13. Joseph Marshall & Anne England. Married. (See Vol. i., p. 81).
1665. April 27. Richard Marshall was buried.
1665. Oct. 15. Jonathan Marshall sone of John. Bapt.
1665. Nov. 11. Jonathan Marshall sone of John. Buried.
1667. Oct. 10. Anne Marshall daugh. of Jo. was baptiz.
1668. Nov. 12. Anne Marshall daught. of Jo. was baptiz.
1669. April 10. Richard Tilney & Easter Marshall. Married.
1669. March 21. Sarah Marshall daughter of John. Bapt.

Bradford.

1661. June 18. A Child of Will'm Marshall's of Heaton. Buried.
1665. April 30. Sarah daughter of William Marshall of Thornton. Bapt.
1665. Nov. 10. William son of William Marshall of Heaton. Bapt.
1666. May 9. Samuell Marshall of Heaton. Buried.
1667. May 7. Edward Marshall & Sarah Hawle. Married.
1667. Nov. 12. Edward Marshall & Ann Hutton. Married.
1667. Aug. 19. Ann Wife of Edward Marshall of Heaton. Buried.
1668. May 1. Edward Son of William Marshall of Heaton. Bapt.
1668. Aug. 28. Jeremiah Son of Edward Marshall of Heaton. Bapt.

Sheffield.

1664. Nov. 27. Thomas filius Thomæ Marshall. Bapt.
1664. Dec. 25. Emanuell filius Phillippi Marsha *(sic)*. Bapt.
1664. Jan. 22. Ruth filia Henric' Marshall. Bapt.
1664. April 20. Maria filia Richard' Marshall. Buried.
1666. Oct. 7. Joh'es filius Philippi Marshall. Bapt.
1667. Aug. 11. Maria filia Thomæ Marshall. Bapt.
1667. Sept. 12. Thomas Marshall et Alicia Barber. Married.
1667. Oct. 27. Gulielmus Marshall et Anna Stevenson. Married.
1667. Nov. 12. Ric'us Marshaw. Buried.
1668. Aug. 2. Sara filia Gulielmi Marshall. Bapt.
1669. May 2. Samuel filius Phillippi Marshall. Bapt.
1669. Sept. 29. Joh'es Pearson et Anna Marshall. Married.
1669. May 13. Samuel fil. Phillippi Marshall. Buried.

Flamborough.

1662. June 2. Mary the Daughter of Richard Mershall. Bapt.
1663. April 7. Timothy the sonne of George Marshall, Gent. Bapt.
1663. Aug. 21. Christian ye Daught^r^ of Mrs Elezab. Mershall. Buried.

Moor Monkton.

1666. Sept. 12. Ann Marshall buried.
1666. Sept. 12. Henry Barker and Elezabeth Marshall. Married.
1666. Oct. 18. Katherine Marshall buried.
1666. Feb. 18. Richard Marshall sonn of Bryan Marshall. Bapt.
1667. July 27. John sonn of Richard Marshall. Bapt.
1667. Dec. 8. Guy the sonne of Richard Marshall. Buried.
1667. April 5. Thomas the sonne of Thomas Marshall. (? Buried.)
1668. Feb. 8. John sonne of Richard Marshall. Buried.
1669. Sept. 11. Bryan the sonne of Bryan Marshall. Bapt.
1669. Feb. 15. Richard sone of Rich. Marshall. Bapt.
1669. March 8. John sone of Richard Marshall. Buried.

Kellington.

1669. Aug. 11. Rob'tus filius Jacobi Marshall de Whitley. Buried.
1669. Dec. 18. Susanna uxor Gulielmi Marshall de Whitley. Buried.
1670. Sept. 11. Gulielmus filius Petri Marshall de Whitley. Bapt.
1670. Nov. 8. Jacobus filius Jacobi Marshall de Whitley. Bapt.
1670. Sept. 29. Gulielmus filius Petri Marshall. Whitley. Buried.

Egton.

1663. May 24. Mary filia Henerici Marshall. Bapt.
1663. May 20. Christopherus Marshall. Buried.
1663. June 19. Elizabetha Marshall. Buried.
1666. April 27. Ann filia Henry Marshall. Bapt.
1668. Jan. 3. Jana Marshall sepult.
1668. Jan. 29. Martha Marshall sepult.
1671. June 20. John Biggin and Elizabeth Marshall. Married.

Etton.

1664. July 24. Thomas Marshall and Elizabeth Watson. Married.
1664. Nov. 17. John Marshall. Buried.
1665. Oct. 22. John Marshall sonne to Thomas Marshall. Bapt.
1666. March 7. Anne Marshall widdow. Buried.
1668. Oct. 1. Margret Marshall daughter to Thom. Marshall. Bapt.

1668. Oct. 1. Anne Marshall wife to Thomas Marshall. Buried.
1669. Jan. 4. William Marshall sonne to Thomas Marshall. Bapt.
1669. Jan. 10. William Marshall sonne to Thom. Marshall. Buried.
1670. Dec. 23. Thomas Marshall sonne to Thom. Marshall. Bapt.
1670. Dec. 23. Thomas Marshall sonne to Thom. Marshall. Buried.
1670. Feb. 22. Jane Marshall wife to Thomas Marshall. Buried.
1671. Feb. 20. Thomas Marshall and Catherine Robinson. Married.

GUISELEY.

1661. Nov. 24. Christopher son of Christopher Marshall of Guiselay. Bapt.
1661. Nov. 7. Jeremy Marshall and Jane Beeane. Married. (Cf. Vol. i., p. 286.)
1661. May 19. Samuell Marshall of Horsforth. Buried.
1661. Aug. 1. Sarah Marshall of Eshould. Buried.
1661. Sept. 5. Ellen Marshall of Horsforth. Buried.
1662. Sept. 11. John son of Jeremie Marshall. Bapt.
1662. Dec. 4. Marie doughter of Joseph Marshall. Bapt.
1662. March 30. John son of Richard Marshall. Bapt. at Horsforth.
1662. May 17. Ruth Marshall of Yeadon. Buried.
1662. Oct. 12. Elisabeth Marshall of Rawdon. Buried.
1662. Nov. 10. Susan Marshall of Eshalld. Buried.
1663. John sonne of John Marshall of Yeadon Borne June the first 1660 and Bap. the 13th day of Aprill, 63.
1663. Judeth doughter of John Marshall Borne September the 20th and Baptized the 13th day of Aprill, 1663.
1663. Jan. 3. Elizabeth dovghter of Grace Marshall. Bapt.
1663. April 3. Samvell Marshall of Yeadon. Buried.
1663. Aug. 10. Marie Marshall of Rawdon. Buried.
1663. Oct. 6. Abraham Marshall. Buried.
1663. March 17. Margrett Marshall of Guislay. Buried.
1664. Dec. 8. Sarah dovghter of Josias Marshall. Bapt.
1664. April 16. Abraham Marshall. Buried.
1664. Oct. 27. Susanha Marshall of Eshould. Buried.
1664. Nov. 8. John Marshall of Yeadon. Buried.
1664. Feb. 24. Jodeth Marshall. Buried.
1665. May 14. William sonne of Richard Marshall. Bapt.
1665. Sept. 24. Hannay Doughter of John Marshall. Bapt.
1665. Oct. 29. Abraham sonne of Christopher Marshall. Bapt.
1665. Jan. 21. Sarall *(sic)* dovghter of Joseph Marshall. Bapt.
1665, Feb. 1. Luke Marshall. Buried.
1665. Feb. 5. Anne Marshall. Buried.
1665. April 25. Christop' Rhodes and Mearcy Marshall. Married.
1665. June 26. Thomas Sugden and Issabell Marshall. Married.
1666. Aug. 20. Josias sonne of Josias Marshall. Bapt.

1666. July 22. Gennett Marshall. Buried.
1666. Feb. 16. William Marshall. Buried.
1666. Feb. 25. Samuell Marshall. Buried.
1667. March 16. Suzan daughter of John Marshall. Bapt.
1667. Nov. 7. Thomas Marshall & Rebecka Ratstrick. Married.
1667. Oct. 27. Alice Marshall. Buried.
1667. March 2. Mercy Marshall. Buried.
1668. April 26. William sonn of Thomas Marshall. Bapt.
1668. Aug. 29. Anne dovghter of Josias Marshall. Bapt.
1668. July 6. Thomas Marshall of Yeadon. Buried.
1668. Feb. 16. A child of Thomas Marshall. Buried.
1668. May 6. Henrey Pollan and Mearcy Marshall. Married.
1668. July 8. Thomas Marshall and Mearcy Marshall. Married.
1669. June 30. A yonge child of Christopher Marshall. Buried.
1669. Oct. 29. A yonge child of Ann Marshall of Rawdon. Buried.
1669. Sept. 9. John Marshall and Marie Simpson. Married. (See Vol. i., p. 82).

ROYSTON.

1661. June 27. Ann daughter of William Marshall of Notton. Bapt.
1661. July 7. Ann daughter of William Marshall of Notton. Buried.
1661. Jan. 27. George Scholey of Roiston and Elizabeth Marshall widdow of Notton. Married.
1662. Sept. 11. Elizabeth daughter of William Marshall of Notton. Bapt.
1662. Aug. 20. Elizabeth wife of Robert Marshall of Notton. Buried.
1663. Feb. 27. Margaret daughter of William Marshall of Notton. Bapt.
1663. Dec. 22. Robert Marshall of Notton. Buried.
1666. April 10. Dorothy daughter of William Marshall of Notton. Bapt.
1666. June 22. Margaret daughter of William Marshall of Notton. Buried.
1668. Feb. 11. Gulielmus filius Emmitt' Marshall viduæ de Notton. Bapt.
1668. Aug. 27. Gulielmus Marshall de Notton sepultus fuit.
1669. March 19. Peter Marshall of Ferry Moore. Buried.

EASINGWOLD.

1661. Jan. 26. Anne the daughter of Richard Marshall. Bapt.
1663. Dec. 29. Elizabetha Filia Richardi Marshall Baptizata erat.
1667. Nov. 9. John son of Richard Marshall. Bapt.
1667. Feb. 19. Will. Marshall was buried.
1667. March 17. Mr George Marshall was buried.

1668. Aug. 28. Elizabeth daughter of Mr Marshall widdow was baptized.
1669. July 18. Hanna fil. Rich'i Marchall. Bapt.
1671. Sept. 18. Anna fil. Richardi Martiall. Buried.

Linton.

1662. May 22. Christopher son of Thomas Marshall of Griston [Grassington] Buried.
1663. Aug. 6. Robert the son of Will'm Marshall of Griston. Bapt.
1665. July 8. Anne wife of Will'm Marshall of Griston. Buried.

Darfield.

1661. Oct. 13. Samuel Marshall & Elizabeth Durham both of Darfield. Married.
1664. April 24. Mary daughter of Samuel Marshall of Darfield. Bapt.
1666. Jan. 6. Anne daughter of Samuel Marshall of Darfield-bridge. Bapt.
1666. May 3. Joshua Northfolke and Rosamund Marshall. Married.

Scarborough.

1661. Sept. 5. John Marshall and Elizabeth Thompsonne. Married. (See Vol. i., p. 81.)
1663. Jan. 18. Christopher son to Mr John Marshall borne, and baptized 29th.
1663. April 22. Marie Marshall, widow. Buried.
1669. Dec. 9. Duke Marshall. Buried.
1671. Nov. 30. Mathew Brauiner & Marie Marshall. Married.

Aldborough. (Vol. i., p. 238.)

1662. May 7. Elizabeth Marshall ye daughter of John Marshall. Bapt.
1663. Aug. 18. Thomas the sonne of John Marshall. Bapt.
1665. Aug. 22. Robertus Marshell filius Johañis. Bapt.
1667. Oct. 12. John Marshall. Buried.
1667. Dec. 5. Joan Marshall, widdow. Buried.

Birdsall.

1661. April 23. Francis Marshall son of John. Bapt.
1661. June 5. Anne Marshall daugh. of Thomas. Buried.
1661. June 20. George Marshall son of Tho. Buried.
1662. Feb. 3. Michaell Bell & Mary Marshall. Married.
1663. May 28. Johannes Marshall filius Johannis Marshall. Bapt.

STOKESLEY.

1661. Nov. 8. Robert the son of John Marshall of Stoxley buried.
1663-4. March 1. John ye sone of John Marshall of Stoxley. Bapt.
1666. Jan. 11. Francis Marshall of Newby. Buried.

PANNALL OR HUTTON PANNALL.

1662. July 17. Thomas Marshall. Buried.
1664. Dec. 25. Bilham. Bernard sonne to Bernard Marshall. Bapt.
1664. July 19. Bernard Marshall & Katharine Py .... of Bilham. Married.
1665. June 22. Bernard sonne to Bernard Marshall of Bilham. Buried.
1666. April 15. Bernard Marshall of Bilham. Buried.
1666. Aug. 19. Bilham. Mary daughter to vid. Marshall. Bapt?
1669. June 17. Bilham. Mary Daughter to Bernerd Marshall. Buried.

GATE HELMSLEY.

1662. Aug. 27. Anna filia Richardi Marshial. Bapt.
1667. March 1. Martha the daughter of Richard Marshall. Bapt.
1669. Feb. 27. Georgius Marshall filius Richardi Marshall, Carleton. Bapt. Buried 24 *(sic)* Feb., 1669. } *Helmsley.*

LEDSHAM.

1662. Nov. 29. Richard Marshall et Maria Ward coniuncti sunt.
1664. May 29. Maria Marshall fillia Richardi Marshall de Ledston. Bapt.
1669. Nov. 24. Georgius Dawson et Elizabetha Marshall. Married.

DUNNINGTON.

1662. Elizabeth Marshall dyed the 18th of may.
1665. April 19, Jacobus et Maria Gemini Infantes Jacobi Marshall. Bapt.
1665. April 26. Maria Marshall altera de Gemellis sepulta.
1665. April 30. Jacobus Marshall alter' de Gemellis sepultus.
1665. Oct. 24. Johannes Marshall alias Sharr spurius baptizat.

BRIDLINGTON.

1663. Jan. 24. Raiph ye son of Richard Marshall. Bapt.
1665. Nov. 21. A child of Richard Marshalls. Buried.
1666. Oct. 28. Anne ye daught' of Rich'd Marshall. Bapt.

1666. Nov. 27. John Michison & Catherine Marshall. Married.
1669. Aug. 8. Mary ye daught' of Richard Marshall. Bapt.

Thorner.

1661. April 6. Debery the daughter of Miles Marshall of Shadwell. Bapt.
1664. April 17. Sara ye Daughter of Miles Marshall. Bapt.
1667 (? 1666). April 1. Miles Marshall. Buried.
1671. Jan. 10. Maire Marshill was Buried.

North Cave.

1664. June 26. Thomas Marshall of South cliffe the son of Thomas. Bapt.
1664. July 9. Thomas Marshall the son of Thomas. Buried.
1664. Feb. 17. Isabell Marshall the daughter of Thomas. Buried.
1665. Oct. 1. Richard Marshall the son of Thomas. Bapt.
1666. March 10. Timothy Marshall the son of Thomas. Bapt.
1669. Dec. 26. Anne Marshall the daughter of Thomas. Bapt.
1669. Oct. 26. Catharine Marshall. Buried.

High Hoyland.

1664. March 15. Gulielmus Mashall de Clayton. Buried.
1665. Aug. 6. Franciscus Marshall de Parke-mill. Buried.
1665. Dec. 31. Maria filia Johannis Marshall de Clayton. Bapt.
1667. June 1. Elizabetha filia Johannis Marshall de Parke-mill. Bapt.
1667. Feb. 15. Anna Marshall vid. de Parke-mill. Buried.
1668. May 11. Thomas Michill et Anna Marshall. Married.
1668. Feb. 28. Franciscus filius Joañis Marshall. Bapt.
1669. July 29. Josephus Marshall de Emley et Anna Copley huius pochiæ. Married.
1669. Sept. 7. Johannes filius Richardi Marshall. Buried.
1669. January 11. Alicia Marshall vid. de Clayton. Buried.
1671. Aug. 17. Anna filia Joannis Marshall. Bapt.

Middleton.

1661. April 4. Willielmus Marshall and Anne Hardin. Married.
1661. March 12. Guliellmus Marshall. Buried.
1662. June 1. Anna fillus *(sic)* Guliellmi Marshall. Bapt.
1664. August 14. Jane Marshall. Buried.
1666. May 1. Richardus Jog et Gratia Marshall. Married.
1667. April 16. Thomas Marshall et Maria Clarke coniugati fuerint.
1667. January 22. Jane filia Thomæ Marshall. Bapt.
1667. August 18. Thomas Marshall sepult'.
1667. January 14. (*sic* but ? February.) Jane filia Thomæ Marshall sepult'.

MIRFIELD.

1663. Oct. 19. John Marshall & Sary Haye Marryed.
1664. Oct. 16. Sara daughter of John Marshall baptized.
1665. March 11. John the Son of John Marshall. Bapt.
1668. June 7. William sonn of William Marshall. Bapt.
1668. March 21. Grace the Daughter of John Marshall. Bapt.

WATTON.

1665. Oct. 17. Mary Marshall. Buried.
1668. January 25. Elisabeth the daughter of John Marshall. Bapt.
1670. June 27. Elisabeth ye doughter of John Marshall. Bapt.

SCALBY.

1661. July 8. George Stevenson and Ellis Marshall were married.
1661. Oct. 6. William the son of Thomas Marshall was buried.
1664. January 23. Xpofer the son of Xpofer Marshall was buried.
1665. March 10. William Marshall was Buried.

In the following the parish is written SCAUBEY but I suppose it is the same.

1666. Sept. 20. Jane ye daughter of Gorge Marshall. Bapt.
1666. July 31. Will: Whitwell & Jane Marshall, married.
1666. January 10. Jane ye daughter of George Marshall, buried.
1667. Nov. 10. Ralph ye sonne of George Marshall was baptized.
1667. May 17. Anne ye daughter of Will: Marshall was buried.

THORNTON NEAR PICKERING.

1663. January 10. Will'm Marshall senio^r^. Buried.
1664. April 17. James fil' Graciæ Marshall. Born.
1664. April 23. Jacobus fil' Graciæ Marshall mort'.
1665. Nov. 14. Will'm Marshall and Jane Birdsall. Married.
1665. May 28. Mary daughter of Ann Marshall vid'. Buried.
1666. Nov. 13. Christian fil' Will'mi Marshall. Bapt.
1666. March 9. Elizabeth wife of Rich: Marshall, mort'.

The following entries are marked THORNTON only:—

1667. June 17. Tho. fil. Gra. Marshall. Bapt.
1667. January 14. Rich: Marshall et Eliz: Awbray. Married.
1668. March 31. Will. Read and Ann Marshall widdow. Married.
1668. Sept. 6. Ann daughter of Rich. Marshall. Bapt.
1668. Feb. 28. Ann daughter of Will. Marshall. Bapt.
1670. Nov. 13. William son of Richard Marshall. Bapt.
1671. Oct. 29. William son of William Marshall. Bapt.
1671. January 3. William son of Richard Marshall. Buried.
1671. Feb. 7. Ann a child of William Marshall. Buried.

Cayton.

1667. May 6. William Marshall the sun of William Marshall. Bapt.
1668. March 12. Elizabeth Marshall the Daughter of Richard Marshall. Bapt.
1668. Feb. 1. George Backer was Married with Ann Marshall.
1669. June 6. Elizabeth Marshall ye Daughter of Will'i Marshall. Bapt.

Lofthouse.

1667. April 14. Loft. Boreal. Gulielmus Fi. Guilmi Marshal. Bapt.
1667. Oct. 10. Walpley. Georg' Colthirst & Jana Marshall. Married.
1667. April 25. Lofthouse Borealis. Guilielmus Fil' Gulielmi Marshal. Buried.
1668. April 30. William son of Wm Marshall. Bapt.

Brandsby.

1665. July 2. Gulielmus Marshall filius Johannis Marshall. Bapt.
1666. Oct. 14. Will. Marshall filius Johannis Marshall. Bapt.
1667. Dec. 8. Jacobus Marshall filius Johannis Marshall. Bapt.
1668. July 1. James Marshall. Buried.
1670. Oct. 3. Mary Marshall daughter of John Marshall. Bapt.
1671. Aug. 5. Marie Marshall ye daughter of John Marshall. Buried.

Penistone.

1665. Joh': Rich: Marsha: 8: Octo: Bapt.
1666. January 14th Richard Marshall. Buried.
1668. Nov. 14. Tho. Marshall. Buried.
1668. January 15. Aña vx. Richa. Marshall. Buried.
Thomas Marshall, a churchwarden this year.
1669. April 22. Richardus Marshall. Buried.

Leven.

1666. March 14. Marie daughter of Will'm Marshaile. Bapt.
1666. June 8. Will'm Marshaile and Dinah Fenby. Married.
1666. March 13. John Marshaile, Infant. Buried.
1667. Dec. 5. Marie Marshaile, Infant. Buried.
1668. Oct. 4. Peter soñe of Will'm Marshaile. Bapt.

Catton.

1666. Joannes Marshall de Parochiâ $S^{tæ}$ Trinitatis in Vico vulgo dicto Micklegate in Ebor. et Elizabetha Penrose de Kexby in Parochia Cattonensi Connubio juncti die tertio Octobris.

1667. Sept. 27. Joannes filius Joannis Marshall de Kexby. Bapt.
1669. Sept. 14. Margarett the daughter of John Marshall of Kexby. Bapt.

1667. April 10. Will. Marshall buryed.
1669. June 12. Ann Marshall buryed.
1669. Oct. 12. Henry Marshall & Elizabeth Pinder maryed. } *Appleton.*
1668. May 2. James Robinson of Berkin & Margret Marshall of Beale in the pish of Kellington were marryed at Ferry freiston. *Ferry Fryston.* See Vol. i., p. 82.
1669. January 24. Edward Marshall buryed. *Kirkella.*
1669. Feb. 23. Mary Marshall buried. *Burstwicke.*
1668. June 1. Robert Lee and Elizabeth Marshall were married. *Whitkirke.*
1666. April 22. Ruhamah Daughter of George Marshill of Brafford. Bapt.
1667. Aug. 30. Ruhamah daughter of George Marshall of Riplingham. Buried.
1667. January 14. George Marshall of Riplingham. Buried. } *Rowley.*
1666. May 27. Thomas ye son of Edward Marshall of Brighton. Bapt.
1669. Aug. 29. John ye son of Edward Marshall of Brighton. Bapt.
1669. Sept. 24. Thomas ye son of Edward Marshall of Brighton. Buried.
1669. Dec. 5. Edward Marshall of Brighton. Buried.
1671. Feb. 20. John ye son of Edward Marshall of Brighton. Buried. } *Bubwith.*
1665-6. March 23. Francis Marshall was Buried.
1667. June 11. Anthony Marshall son of David. Bapt. } *Badsworth.*
1667. Aug. 31. Mary the daughter of Mr Marshall. Buried. *Horbury.*
1665. Feb. 13. George Walton & Jane Marshall. Married. *Womersley.*
1665. March 26. . . . . . fil. Majoris Martiall de Stansf. Bapt.
1665. Feb. 4. Maria fil. Abrah'i Marshall. Stāsfeild. Bapt.
1669. Oct. 14. Major [son of] Major Marshall. Stansfield. Bapt. } *Heptonstall.*
1668. Dec. 17. Jane Marcell, spincer, buried.
1669. May 9. An the daughter of William Marshall. Bapt. } *Hutton Bushell.*

1666. May 26. Will'm Marshal illegitimate son of Maud Marshall. Buried.
1666. Sept. 20. Thomas Hutton and Elizabeth Marshal. Married.
1669. June 27. Ellin daughter of Brian and Elizabeth Marshall. Bapt.
1670. Nov. 23. Elizabeth wife of Brian Marshall. Buried.
Kirkby Overblows.

1661. July 27. John the son of Robert Marshall. Bapt.
1662. Nov. 28. John the son of Robert Marshall. Buried.
Kirk Heaton.

1662. April 20. Israell the sonne of Martin Marshall glazier. Bapt.
1668. May 8. Joh'es Tesh & Anna Marshall. Married.
St. Mary, Beverley.

1662. Aug. 17. Robert son to Robert Marshall. Bapt. *Westerdale.*

1660. Feb. 19. Ann the wife of Stephen Marshill. Buried. *Holme in Spaldingmoore.*

1661. Nov. 20. Mathew Marshall of Sutton Marryed to Elizabeth Tomlinson of Elvington.
1661. June 1. Ellin Marshall wife of Mathew Marshall buryed.
Sutton upon Derwent.

1662. Dec. 19. Ann Infant of Thomas Marshall Esqr was buried. *Maltby.*

1661. Jan. 20. Huge Emet of West Cottinwerth and Sary Marshall of Aughton. Married. *Aughton.*

1660. April 27. Elizabeth daughter of Mr Christopher Marshall. Bapt.
1662. Oct. 16. Elizabeth doughter of Mr Christopher Marshall. Buried. (See vol. i., p. 281.)
Woodchurch.

1660. Jan. 23. Sarah ye Daut of Will. Marshall. Buried.
1661. June 19. Eliz. ye Daut. of Will. Marshall. Bapt.
1664. Aug. 14. Catherine ye Dau. of Roger Marshall. Bapt.
Thorne.

1661. July 14. Robert Winterskalls & Deborah Marshall. Married. *Sprotley.*

1662. Feb. 23. Mary Marshill buryed. *Kilnsea.*

1661. Feb. 5. Will'm Ledum and Barberay Marshall. Married.
1661. May 22. Jaine wife of Phillipp Marshall was buried.
1667. Nov. 3. Esabell Marshall Daughter to John Marshall. Buried.
Ryther.

1661. Sept. 20. Henry Marshall. Buried. *Kilham.*

1662. Feb. 23. James Barmby & Jane Marshall both of New Malton. Married. *St. Michael's, New Malton.*

1662. April 8. Elizabeth Marshall. Buried.
1663. Nov. 8. Anna Marshall filia Thomæ Marshall. Bapt.
} *North Dalton.*

1660. July 4. Edward ye sonne of Jo. Marshall. Bapt.
1662. Aug. 17. Margaret daughter of William Marshall. Bapt.
} *Northallerton.*

1661. April 28. Christopher the son of Marke Marshall. Bapt. *Little Driffield.*

1662. July 1. Henrie Lazenbye and Dorrithy Marshall. Married. *Escrick.*

1662. June 22. James ye sone of Rich. Marshall & Philippa his wife was baptized. *Old Byland.*

1661. June 25. Robert Marshall the son of Robert Marshall of Thorpe. Bapt. *Barnby upon Dun.*

1663. Nov. 17. William Darrill & Mary Marshall. Married. *Thorganby.*

1663. Aug. 11. Myle^{d} Dayle & Ann Marshall. Married. *Fylingdales.*

1663. Oct. 11. Elizabet' Marshall filia Thomæ Marshall. Bapt. *Hinderwell.*

1663. July 2. Elin Marshall vid. Buried.
1665. Nov. 3. Johan's Marshall et Jana Hill. Married.
} *Danby with Glaisdale.*

1663. Nov. 23. William Pearson and Alce Marshall. Married. *Lyth.*

1663. Aug. 18. John Hancocke and Faith Marshall. Married. *Norton (East Riding).*

1663. April 5. Mary Marshall ye Daug. of Geo. Marshall of . hel . . [? Shelfe]. Bapt. *Felixkirk.*

1664. Dec. 25. Mercy d. of John Marshall. Bapt.
1667. Aug. 17. John s. of John Marshall. Bapt.
} *Wakefield.*

1664. Nov. 3. Thomas Marshall & Mary Box. Married.
1666. April 11. Thomas son of Thomas Marshall. Bapt.
1668. March 29. Elizabeth daughter of Thomas Marshall. Bapt.
1668. Feb. 10. Thomas son of Thomas Marshall. Buried.
1668. Feb. 24. Anne Marshall. Buried.
} *Treeton.*

1663. Feb. 4. Josias *Marshall* (?) & Ann Wilkinson. Married. *Baildon.*

1663. Jan. 24. Eliz. f. Will. Marshall de Farttowne. Bapt.
1666. Nov. 27. Eliz. f. Will. Marshall de Farttowne. Buried.
1666. May 6. Sarah f. Will. Marshall de Farttowne. Bapt.
} *Huddersfield.*

1666. April 15. William the sonne of Willi. Marshall. Bapt.
1668. Jan. 31. James the sonne of William Marshall. Bapt.
1669. Nov. 23. Thomas Woodaiell and Hester Marshall. Married.
} *Winteringham.*

1664. March 19. Elizabeth the daughter of James Marshall. Bapt. *Lastingham.*

1663. Aug. 31. Johannes Marshall de Castley sepult' fuit.
1663. Dec. 4. Vidua Marshall sepulta fuit.
1663. Dec. 21. Johannes Suttell et Vidua Gratia Marshall matrimonio copulati fuerunt.
1667. Oct. 29. Rich. Hill et Dinah Marshall Matrimonio Contract'.
} *Leathley.*

1669. May 4. John Appleby and Katherine Marshall. Married. *South Kilvington.*

1664. June 14. Anne Martiall ye daughter of Thomas of Rytō. Bapt.
1664. Jan. 23. Matthew Martiall of Ryton buryed.
1665. Oct. 27. Thomas Martiall ye son of Thomas of Kirkby misptō. Bapt.
1665. Feb. 11. Christopher Martiall ye son of Thomas of Ryton. Bapt.
} *Kirkby Misperton.*

1664. Nov. 14. Marya fillia Joh'ni Marshall. Buried.
1669. Jan. 30. Elizabethe filia Josephi Marshall et Anna uxor' eius. Bapt.
} *Emley.* See p. 34 *ante.*

1664. Oct. 20. Mary Daugh. of Rich. Marshall of Colton. Bapt.
1667. Sept. 11. John sonn of Henry Marshall of Wollas. Bapt.
1667. Feb. 12. Ellizab. Dough. of Rich. Marshall of Colton. Bapt.
1670. April 14. Henry Marshall of Bilborough & Jane Bell of Ap: were maried.
} *Bolton Percy.*

1662-3. March 19. John Son of John Marshall of High Paul & Mary his wife. Bapt.
1662. May 1. John Marshall of Paul & Mary Chadwell of Thorn widow. Married.
} *Paull.*

1664. May 26. Thomas Marshall son of Thomas. Bapt.
1664. June 19. Samuell Marshall son to John. Bapt.
1665. Oct. 5. John Marshall son of Thomas. Bapt.
1665. April 16. John Marshaw *(sic)* wife. Buried.
} *Sherburn.*

1663. April 12. Mathew son of Mathew Marshall. Bapt. 1663. April 16. Mathew son of Mathew Marshall an infant. Buried. 1664. July 19. Mathew Marshall housholder. Buried. 1665. Dec. 2. Thomas Cleaueland and Elizabeth Marshall both of this Towne. Married.	*Sutton upon Derwent.*
1663. Jan. 10. Mathew sonn of John Marshall. Bapt. 1666. Feb. 6. John Marshall. Buried. 1669. Dec. 25. Mary Marshall. Buried. 1669. Jan. 30. Thomas Marshall. Buried.	*Willerby.*
1664. Sept. 4. Joane Marshall the daughter of Francis Marshall. Bapt. *Mydleton cum Hilton.*	
1664. Oct. 11. Tho. son of Thomas Marshall. Bapt. 1666. Jan. 6. John son of John Marshall of Staningley. Bapt. 1667. May 1. Sam. Marshall & Ann Stansfeild. Married. 1668. March 21. Wm Son of John Marshall of Staningley. Bapt. 1669. Nov. 3. Sarah D^{tr} of Sam. Marshall of Idle. Bapt.	*Calverley.*
1666. Nuptiæ Celebratæ Inter Johañem Hall et Franciscam Marshall decimo septimo Maii. *Ilkley.*	
1664. Oct. 9. Maria Marshall filia Michaelis. Bapt. *Langton.*	
1664. Sept. 20. Dorith Marshall was Buried. *Elvington.*	
1665. Dec. 23. Isabel Marshall. Buried. 1665. March 14. Ann Marshall. Buried.	*Skirpenbeck.*
1667. Charles Taylour and Elizabeth Marsill. Married. *Overton.*	
1668. June 28. Christopher Waddington servant of John Rayley of Swinkil and Deborah Marschil of Cranswick both of Huton pish maried. *Hutton Cranswick.*	
1668. Dec. 4. Thomas, Tho. Marshall de Etton. Buried. *Routh.*	
1667. January 12. Elizabeth the daughter of William Marshall, dier. Bapt. 1668. January 27. Mary the daughter of William Marshall. Bapt. 1669. July 2. Elizabeth the daughter of Warshall *(sic)* dier. Buried.	*Doncaster.*
1664. Hester Marshel sepulta erat Nono die Maii. *Rillington with Scampston.*	
1664. May 7. Isbell the doughter of John Marshall. Bapt. 1666. Aug. 29. Mary the doughter of John Marshall. Bapt. 1666. Oct. 8. Mary the doughter of John Marshall. Bapt.	*Welwick.*

1666. Feb. 7. Jonathan Rawson of this parish and Alice Martiall of the parish of Calverley, 3 tymes published, married by our vicar. *Bingley*.

1666. Oct. 11. Elliz: daughter of Rich: Marshall. Bapt.
1669. August 28. Katherine daughter of Richard Marshall. Bapt.
— *Wath*.

1671. August 13. Jacobus filius Jacobi Marshall. Bapt. *Lastingham*.

1671. March 3. Jane wife of Tho. Marshall. Buried. *Cockan*.

1671. Dec. 24. . . . . the son of Richard Marshall. Bapt. *Skipsea*.

1671. Nov. 12. Anna Marshall vidua sepult' erat. *Bainton*.

1670-1. March 7. Robert Drinkraw and Darkas Marshall. Married. *St. Mary, Kingston upon Hull*.

1669. Nov. 11. Richard Marshall and Cesily Lenlay Marrid.
1671. March 13. David the son of William Marshall was baptized.
— *Guisborough*.

1671. Aug. 17. John Richardson and Sarah Martiall. Married. *Westow*.

1667. Dec. 16. Tho. son of Tho. Marshall. Buried.
1671. April 16. Tho. Marshall of Bramley was buried.
— *Braithwell*.

1669. May 16. Tho. Marshall Blacksmith of Wansford was buried. *Nafferton*.

1668. Nov. 30. Thomas Marshall & Aña Ashman. Married. *Fishlake*.

1668. May 19. William Hardesty of Newall & Katerane Marshall was Married with a lycence. See Vol. i., p. 271.
1669. Dec. 5. Mary ye Daughter of William Marshall. Bapt.
— *Tadcaster*.

1665. July 13. Edwardus filius Edwardi Marshall. Bapt. *Pontefract*.

1667. May 19. Dorothea filia Edovardi Marshall.
1668. March 14. Elizabetha filia Edouardi Marshall.
1668. Burials in Pontefract Parish Church. Aug. 1. Jane Marshall.
— *Chapel of St. Giles, Pontefract*.

1665. January 24. Thomas Marshall sonne of Richard Marshall of Colton. Bapt.
1665. Oct. 22. Mary ye Doughter of Richard Marshall of Colton. Buried.
— *Boolton.* Bolton Percy.

1667. Sept. 1. Leonard Marshall. Buried.
1669. June 29. Christopher Wilkinson & Mary Marshall. Married
1671. July 7. John Marshell. Buried.
— *Sherriff Hutton*.

1669. Nov. 27. Will'm Kitching and Ellen Marshall were marryed. *Topcliffe*.

1669. Oct. 20. Thomas the sonne of Mr Marshall. Buried. *Hovingham.*

1667. Nov. 2. John Richardson and Elizabeth Marshall of Bestecar. *Cantley.*

1669. May 30. Ann Martiall ye daughter of Anthony Martiall. Bapt. *Hutton Bonvill.*

1663. Feb. 28. Richard' filius Richardi Marshall de Linton. Bapt.
1664. Oct. 8. Rich. fil. Rich'i Marshall de Newton. Buried.
1667. Sept. 11. Thomas son of Richard Marshall of Linton. Bapt.
1667. Dec. 17. Thomas ye son of Richard Marshall of Linton. Bapt.
1668. Sept. 4. Will'im son of Richard Marshall of Linton. Buried.
Newton upon Ouse.

1664. January 18. Anne daughter of Tho. Marshall. Bapt. *Bramley (?).*

1665. Feb. 3. Peter Marshall. Buried. *St. Leonard's, New Malton.*

1665. Nov. 19. William Tipladie and Hellen Marshall. Married.
1668. Nov. 23. Emmote the wife of Lancelote Merchaell. Buried.
Brotton.

1668. January 19. Robert Williamson & Isabell Marshall. Married. *Seamer.*

1667. January 26. Guillelmus Marshall de Barton sepultus erat.
1668. Nov. 14. Isabel vxor Stephani Marshall de Barton. Buried.
Barton le Street.

1667. May 1. Christopher Ingledue & Margrett Marshall marryed. *Stainton.*

1666. June 25. Mary Daughter to Thomas Marshall of Burton. Bapt. *Burton Agnes.*

1666. January 20. Dorithe Marshall & John yates buried. *Cawthorne.*

1666. July 5. Will'm Beeford of Snainton in ye parish of Brompton and Anne Marshall of Wickam in ye parish of Old Malton, spinster, were married. *Brompton.*

1666. January 12. John ye son of John Marshall. Bapt.
1668. Sept. 11. Richard Webster & Jane Marshall. Married.
Flaxton.

1666. Aug. 26. Mary daughter of Joseph Marshall. Bapt.
1667. Sept. 5. Mary Marshall daughter of Joseph Marshall. Buried.
1668. June 14. Mary the daughter of Joseph Marshall. Bapt.
Adwick le Street.

1666. Sept. 20. Mary Marshall Daughter of Will'm Marshall was buryed.
1666. Feb. 22. Hellen Marshall was buryed.
Bilborough.

1668. Dec. 27. Añe Marshall vid. Buried. *Hessle.*
1666. Nov. 13. Richard Marshall and Anna Haine. Married. *Ellerburne.*

1666. June 16. Elizabetha Marshall filia Thom̄ Marshall. Buried.
1667. May 26. Elizabetha Marshall filia Thomæ Marshall. Bapt.
} *Hinderwell.*

1668. March 21. Eliz. filia Georgii Marshall. Bapt.
1668. May 28. Georgius Marshall et Anna Milnes. Married.
1671. June 12. Maria filia Georgii Marshall. Bapt.
} *Danby.*

1668. Dec. 13. Henry Mersell. Buried.
1671. April 29. Jana Marshall vid' ætat' 64. Buried.
} *Wykeham.*

1666. Nov. 14. Henry Sharp and Ann Marshall. Married.
1668. Oct. 18. Richard the sonn of John Marshall. Bapt.
} *Methley.*

1668. Dec. 15. Mr Will'm Marshall of the pish of Tadcaster & Mris Elizabeth Fletcher of the pish of Saxton. Married. *Saxton.*
1671. May 18. Immanuell Shepheard & Jane Marshall. Married. *Roos.*

1664. April 6. William Marshall buried.
1664. Aug. 11. Petronella wife of Marmaduke Marshall. Buried.
} *St. Mary's in Roos.*

1663. April 24. Will'm Marshall pat. fam. sepul' fuit.' *Chapelry of Righton (Reighton).*
1668. May 6. Wilfred Couke and Fransis Marsill. Married. *Keyingham ?*
1667. April 3. Robert Marshall buried. *Worsborough ?*
1667. January 23. Lawarenc Marshall and Helena Spicor. Married. *Santon (? Saxton.)* Sancton.

1667. May 26. Sara ye doughter of Will'm Marchall. Bapt.
1669. July 11. Sussanna dought. of John Martiall. Bapt.
} *Haitfeild, (? Hatfield).*

1661-2. March 24. Edward son of William Marshal. Buried.
1662-3. March 3. Richard son of Richard Marshall. Bapt.
} *Wentworth Chapel.*

1668. Sept. 27. Ann Daugh. of Tho. Marshall of Ap. Bapt. *Appleton in Bolton Percy parish.*
1661. Dec. 4. Bryan Marshall of Moore Muncton and Elliner Busterd of the parish of Bramham. Married. *Bramham.*
1662. Aug. 24. John Marshill & Marie Marshill was married. *North Ferriby.*

1661.	April 15. Grace the daughter of Robt Marshall baptized.	*Spofforth.*
1661.	April 28. Ann, Sarah, and Christian the daughters of Robt Marshall baptized. See Vol. i., p. 243.	
1666.	April 22. Walter ye son of Robert Marshall of Follifoot. Bapt.	
1662.	July 9. Isabell and Marie doughters of Thomas Marshall. Bapt.	*Stillingfleet.*
1662.	July 16. Isabell and Marie doughters of Thomas Marshall. Buried.	
1663.	Jan. 1. Stephen the sonn of Thomas Marshall of Akaster. Bapt.	

EXTRACTS FROM TRANSCRIPTS OF NOTTINGHAMSHIRE REGISTERS.

TUXFORD.

1666. 22 April. Hester dau. of Thomas Marshall and Jane his wife. Bapt.
1666. 16 Sept. Elizabeth wife of George Marshall, sen^{r}. Buried.
1668. George Marshall Junior buried June 9.
1668. Ann the Daughter of Mary Marshall, widow, was buried September 23.
1668. Thomas son of Georg Marshall bu. Februarie 12.
1669. Mary Marshall daughter of widow Marshall buried March 30th.
1669. Isabell Marshall widow buried Aprill 7th.
1670. George the son of Thomas Marshall & Mary his wife buried Aprill 16th.
1670. Thomas Marshall Blacksmith bu: October 5th.
1693. Elizabeth Marshall, widow, June ye 5th. Buried.
1704. Abraham son of Edward Marshall, June 13. Bapt.
1704. Abraham son of Edward Marshall, Aug. 21. Buried.
1704. Mary Marshall, Oct. 25. Buried.
1705. Sept. 3. Elizabeth daughter of Edward Marshall, joiner. Bapt.
1706. April 17. Thomas son of Edward Marshall, farmer. Bapt.
1707. Oct. 20. Edward son of Edward Marshall. Bapt.
1707. Dec. 3. Anne wife of Edward Marshall ye joiner. Buried.
1708. Dec. 7. Edward son of Edward Marshall. Bapt.
1712. Dec. 2. Abraham ye son of Edward Marshal, joiner. Bapt.
1712. Feb. 8. James ye son of James Marshall & Anne his wife. Bapt.
1714. Nov. 13. Martha the daughter of John Marshall & *Anne (?)* his wife. Bapt.
1714. Feb. 22. Mary the daughter of James Marshall and Anne his wife. Bapt.
1714. April 6. James the son of James Marshall was buried.

Sutton on Trent.

1668. Francis the sonne of Thomas Marshall & Anne his wife was Baptized Ap. 4th.
1668. Jane the Daughter of Thomas Marshall & Anne his wife was Buried May 10th.
1668. Anne the wife of Skillen Marshall was Buried August the 24th. See p. 63 *ante*.
1669. William the Son of Wm Marshall was baptized November the 13th.
1669. Will'm Marshall & Elizabeth Gee was Married August the 10th.
1669. Xpofer Marshall was buried March the 27th.

Clifton near Nottingham.

1669. William Marshall the sonne of John Marshall & of Mary his wife was baptised ye 18th day of Aprill.
1669. William Marshall the sonne of John Marshall and of Mary his wife was buried ye 12th day of June.
1670. Anne Marshall the daughter of John Marshall and of Mary his wife was baptised the 20th day of November.
1670. Elizabeth Marshall the daughter of John Marshall and of Mary his wife was baptised the 20th day of November.
1670. Elizabeth Marshall the daughter of John Marshall & of Mary his wife was buried ye 29th of November.

Kirton.

1669. Alice the daughter of Robert Marshal & Elizabeth his wife was baptized Feb. the 10th. *Kirton.*
1705. Jan. 4. Robert Marshall senr. Buried.
1706. Aug. 28. Richard son of Robert Marshall & Eliz. his wife. Bapt.
1709. Aug. 11. Mary Marshall. Bapt.
1712. Dec. 23. Elizabeth daughter of Robert Marshall & Elizabeth his wife. Bapt.
1697. May 6. Elizabeth wife of Robert Marshall. Buried.
1697. Dec. 16. John Marshall. Buried.
1697. April 18. William Hopkinson & Elizabeth Marshall. Married.
1699. May 23. Robert Marshall & Elizabeth Upton. Married.
1699. July 25. Joshua Roberts & Jane Marshall. Married.
1700. May 26. Joseph Quibell & Alice Marshall. Married.
1701. March 10. Robert Marshall. Bapt.
1703. Feb. 13. John Marshall. Born.

Worksop.

1641. Jan. 17. Robert Marshall. Buried.
1695. Dec. 20. Lydia ye Daug. of James Marshall. Bapt.

1699. April 20. Tho. Marshall & Sarah Barker. Married.
1707. March 20. Hen. Marshall, Labourer. Buried.
1708. May 1. Mary ye Dau. of James Marshall Junr. Bapt.
1709. March 3. James son of James Marshall. Bapt.
1710. Births. Penelope ye Daught^{r} of Isaac Marshall, Oct. 10th.
1710. Births. Penelope ye Daught^{r} of Isaac Marshall, Oct. 9th. (*sic.*)
1712. Nov. 29. John ye Son of James Marshal Junr. Bapt.
1713. Aug. 9. Anne ye Daughter of Isaac Marshall. Bapt.

Mattersey.

1670. Aña filia Francisci Marshall & Mariæ vx. ejus bapt. Sep^{t} 1°.
1695. Sept. 24. Will. Marshal & Abig. Godfrey. Married.
1699. April 16. Densill son of Wm Marshall. Bapt.
1701. Aug. 10. Elizabeth Daughter of Wm Marshal. Bapt.
1701. June 18. Densill son of Wm Marshall. Buried.
1703. April 25. Mary Daughter of William Marshall. Bapt.
1704. Jan. 7. William son of William Marshall. Bapt.
1707. June 22. Anne Daught^{r} of Wm Marshall. Bapt.
1709. Dec. 18. Hannah Daught^{r} of Wm Marshall. Bapt.
1711. March 9. Densill son of William Marshall. Bapt.
1714. June 13. Abigail Daughter of William Marshal. Bapt.
1714. Oct. 19. Abigail Daughter of William Marshall. Buried.

1703-4. Jan. 2. William Rodwell & Mary Marshal. Married. *Rossington.*

1700. April 24. Tho. ye son of Tho. Marshall. Bapt.
1704. Aug. 20. Sarah ye Daughter of Tho. Marshall. Bapt.
1704. Oct. 15. Sarah ye Dau. of Tho. Marshall. Buried.
1704. Feb. 26. John ye son of Tho. Marshall. Buried.
1708. Sept. 26. Jonathan son of Tho. Marshall. Bapt.
1709. Jan. 6. Jonathan ye son of Thomas Marshall. Buried.
West Drayton.

1709. Jan. 15. John Marshall & Sarah Farnsworth. Married.
1713. April 10. George Short and Anne Marshall. Married. (See pp. 46-7 *ante.*)
1713. April 28. Robert Marshall and Anne Vessey. Married.
1714. July 16. Robert son of Robert Marshall. Bapt.
Cuckney.

1669. William ye sonne of William Marshall and Alice his wife was baptized the 26 of September.
1669. William ye sonne of Will'm Marshall Octr 19th. Buried.
Weston.

1669. Thomas Marshall the sonne of Henry Marshall and Frances his wife babtysed November 20th. *North Collingham.*

1669. John the sonn of Robert Marchall & Margrett his wife Baptized feb. 11th. *Ratcliff on Trent.*

1641. Aug. 8. Abrahã Marshall the son of Hen. (?) Marshall and Bennitt his wife was bapt. *Selston.*

1641. Feb. 13. John Marshall son of Tobias Marshall and of Elizabeth his wife. Bapt. *Clifton cum Glapton.*

1670. Johannes Marshall sepult' Jan. 4to
1670. Elizabetha Marshall sep. Feb. 24to
Saundby.

1666. Nov. 4. Richard Marshall. Buried. *Owston.*

1666. July 15. Mary dau. of John Marshall. Bapt. *Whatton.*

1666. July 26. Martha dau. of John Marshall. Buried. *Mansfield Woodhouse.*

1668. Geo. ye son of Richard Marshall & Elis: his wife was bapt. Jan. 24. *Thorney.*

1666. July 15. Elizabeth dau. of Thomas and Anne Marshall. Bapt. *Flintham.*

1666. Jan. 14. Elizabeth Marshall of North Marnham, widow. Buried.
1668. William Marshall of Sutton sup Trent & Elizabeth Gee of North Marnham were Marryed November 19th.
Marnham.

1641. March 27. Gabriell Marshall senex sepultus fuit. *Ansley.*

1641. Oct. 14. Richard Marshall sonne of Thomas Marshall and of Joane his wife. Bapt.
1666. July 24. John Marshall of Basceford [Basford] and Mary Fallowell of Thorpe. Married.
Lowdham.

1615. Oct. 30. Richard Marciall & Agnes Craftes were maried. *Gotham.*

1667. Robert the sonn of John Marshall of Normonton was buried the Eighte daye of March. *Laxton.*

1670. John Marshall was Buryed August 29.
1670. Margery Marshall widdowe was Buryed March 11.
Beeston.

1713. Dec. 26. Sarah daughter of Thomas Marshalls. Bapt. *East Drayton.*

1714. June 24. William Marshal & Frances Greensmith. Married. *Sutton on Lound.*

1697. June 26. Lidya ye dau. of Daniel Clay, jun. Bapt. *Mansfield.*

1669. Jone ye doughter of John Marshall was buryed december ye 12th. *Barton in the Beans.*

1699. April 13. William Wagstaffe of Harworth & Añ Marshall. Married. *Bawtrey.*
1705. Aug. 30. Widdow Marshell buried. *Bawtry.*
1705. May 18. Elizabeth Daugh. of Wm Marshall. Bapt. } *Harworth.*
1706. Dec. 13. Sarah Daughter of William Marshall. Bapt. } *Harworth.*
1708. March 13. Wiliam ye sone of James Marchal. Bapt. *Elksley.*
1669. Oct. 25. Richard Burrowes of Snenton & Sarah Marshall of Plumtree. *Plumtree.*
1666. June 29. Roger son of Will. Marshall & Elizebath his wife. Bapt. *Tithby.*
1668. Rodger ye sonne of William Marshall of Tythby was buried May ye 27th. *Tythby.*
1669. John ye sonn of William Martiall & Elizabeth his wife was baptized February ye 20th. *Tythby.*
1703. March 21. Denshall Marshall. Buried. } *Sturton cum Fenton.*
1704. June 15. Wm Marshall & Margerett Machin. Married. } *Sturton cum Fenton.*
1702. Feb. 10. Benjamin Marshall & Sarah Lane of Doncaster by Lycence. *Ordsall.*
1698. Jan. 4. Geo. son of Jo. Marshall. Bapt. } *East Retford.*
1699. June 8. Mary the dau. of John Marshall. Bapt. } *East Retford.*
1668. John Marshall was buried June 19. *North Clifton.*
1670. Dec. 13. Tho. Marshall of South Clifton buried. *North Clifton.*
1692. May 29. William ye Son of Jo. Marshall. Bapt. } *Clarborough.*
1694. July 11. John the son of John Marshall. Bapt. } *Clarborough.*
1696. Aug. 13. Gervas ye son of John Marshall. Bapt. } *Clarborough.*
1701. April 24. Sarah Daugh. of John Marshall. Bapt. } *Clarborough.*
1703. May 3. Edward ye Son of John Marshall. Bapt. } *Clarborough.*
1695. Nov. 26. Francis Morton & Mary Marshall married. *Clarborough.*
1696. James Marshell Buried June 20, de Budby. *Edwinstowe.*
1698. July 3. John Loversale & Elizabeth Marshal married. *North Wheatley.*
1695. May 24. Tho. Lilly & Anne Marshall. Married. *Everton.*

CRAYFORD, CO. KENT.

1561. John Hethe & Juliana Marshall widow mar. 28 April.
1565. Silvestra dau. of Henry Symons *alias* Marshall bapt. 7 June.
1568. Henry son of Henry Symons *alias* Marscall bapt. 25 April.
" died the son of Hugh Marshall 6 June.

1583. Henry Simons *alias* Maschall buried 17 Sept.
1588. Johanna Maschall widow buried 6 Aug.
1635. Richard son of John Marshall & Margaret bapt. 26 Aug.
1640. Margaret dau. of John Marshall & Margaret bapt. 4 April.
1651. Ann wife of John Marschall buried 28 . . . .
1652. John son of John Marshall bapt. 28 May.
1663. Anne dau. of Christopher Marshall bapt. 29 Dec.
1664. John son of John Marshall buried 16 Oct.
1665. Christopher son of Christopher Marshall bapt 8 Oct.
1667. Dorothy dau. of Christopher Marshall bapt. 15 March.
1668. Christopher Marshall buried 7 Nov.
1671. Anne dau. of Jane Marshall buried 9 May.
1672. Jane Marshall buried 12 April.
1675. . . . . y[e] dau. of Richard Marshall bapt 17 Decr.
1680. Richard son of John Marshall bapt. 9 April.
1680. M[r] John Marshall buried 29 April.
1680. M[r] Richard Marshall buried 14 May.
1681. Anne wife of John Marshall buried 17 April.[1]
1724. Marshall dau. of John Williams bapt. 23 Aug.
1755. Stephen son of Stephen Marcshall bapt. 24 March.
1759. ,, ,, ,, ,, ,, 17 June.
,, Mary dau. ,, ,, buried 11 March.
1761. Hannah Bellow dau. of Stephen & Mary Marchall born 18 Apl. bapt 17 May.
1763. Mary Anne Browne dau. of Stephen & Mary Marshall born 7 Oct. bapt. 6 Nov.
1767. John Lewin, son, and Elizabeth, dau. of Stephen & Mary Marshall born 26 Jan., bapt. 27th same, both buried 16 Feb. same year.

Campsall, co. York.

1632. May 1. John Ambler & Joane Marshall. Married.
1695. Nov. 11. Anthony Marshall of Norton & Anne Lake of Campsall. Married.

MISCELLANEOUS NOTES OF WILLS AND ADM'ONS.

(Continued from Vol. ii., part i., p. 101.*)*

Robert Atkinson of Southwark, Feltmaker, in the parish of S[t] Olaves. Undated. To Thomas Marshall dwelling in Tunbridge parish my best gowne. Proved in P.C.C., 4 Feb., 1603. (14 Harte.)

William Marshall of the City of Bristol, gentleman. Dated 28 Feb., 1765. Kinsman John Leake. Friends William Bacon the younger of Markfield, co. Leicester, Hosier, James Bates [after-

[1] Cf. *Mar. Lic.*, p. 113 *ante.*

wards spelt Beates] of Woodhouse in the said county, Baker, and John Hartwell of Bristol, Malster, devisees in trust of messuage in Moyntague Street, Bristol, and also executors. Sister Mary Leake wife of William Leake, of Mount Sorrell, co. Leicester. Kinsman William Leake son of the said William Leake. Kinswoman Elizabeth Beates wife of the said James Beates. Kinswoman Ann Harding, widow. Kinswoman Mary Leake. Kinswoman Hannah Leake. Sister Ann Chamberlain. Elizabeth Smallbone of Hobingham, co. Berks. Proved in P.C.C., by William Bacon and James Bates, 23 June, 1768. (251 Secker.)

Anne Sumner of Marden, widow of Thomas Sumner. Dated 31 Jan., 1624. Elizabeth Marshall the daughter of Robert Marshall. My daughter Elizabeth Marshall and her two daughters. Robert Marshall a witness. Proved in P.C.C., 15 Feb., 1624. (13 Clarke.)

Emme Sharpe of London, Widow. Dated 11 Dec., 1623. George Marshall my son in law. Proved in P.C.C., 27 May, 1624. (44 Byrde.)

Edward Croft of the City of York, Mercer. Dated 9 June, 1612. Wife Alice sole executrix. Adm'on in P.C.C., 11 Dec., 1656 to William Marshall husband and administrator of Alice Marshall *alias* Croft deceased to administer goods left unadministered by her. (259 Berkley.) See Vol. i., app. p. 12.

John Ellison of Doncaster, co. York, Draper. Dated 1 Oct., 1603. Father Roger Ellison. Brother in law William Marshall of Doncaster, alderman, an executor, & he to have tuition of my daughter Jane Ellison. He proved in P.C.C., 13 Feb., 1603-4. (22 Harte.) See Vol. i., app., p. 8; Vol. ii., part i., p. 64.

Francis Marshall of Abbots' Salford,[1] co. Warwick, yeoman. Dated 29 January 1693. Desires to be decently buried amongst his Relations. To his deare Cosen and God Daughter Alice Marshall a bed etc., in ye farther Chamber. To Cosens Anne Marshall and Eliz^th Marshall to each of them a pair of fine flaxen sheets. To Cosen Tho. Marshall my best gloves. To my Cosen Nicholas Marshall my little Bed-stead with all the goods that came from Radford.[2] Residue to my wife Elioner Marshall, my sole executrix, and she to have the surplusage of my estate both Reall and Personall in the parish of Salford and Studley. Witnesses, William Bartholomew, and Elizabeth Andrews. Inventory taken 8 Feb., 1693. Will proved at Worcester 23 April, 1694.

Thomas Lynde, citizen and goldsmith of London. Dated 13 Dec., 1603. To loving cosen William *(sic)* Marshall 10^s, to be paid unto her *(sic)* within one month after my decease. Testator afterwards calls her "the said widowe Marshall my cosen." Adm'on in P.C.C., 16 Feb., 1603; and probate 5 May, 1612. (27 Harte.)

1 Abbots' Salford is in parish of Priors' Salford. 2 In the parish of Rous Lench, co. Worcester.

John Ruggle of Glemsford, co. Suffolk, Butcher. Dated 27 Feb., 1593. Mentions sister Elizabeth Firmin and her children Edward Firmin, Ann Tanner, Margaret Marshall, and Katherine Marshall. Proved in P.C.C., 6 Feb., 1594. (16 Scott.)

Joan Galland of South Cave, co. York, widow. Dated 16 June, 1651. To William Marshall 12[d] To grandchild Richard Marshall £12 which said William Marshall oweth me. Appoints Richard Marshall executor. He proved in P.C.C., 14 July, 1654. (485 Alchin.) See Vol. i., p. 81.

John Harvye of Elme in the Isle of Ely. Dated 24 March, 1652. Mentions his four grandchildren John Marshall, Edward Marshall, Dorothie Marshall, and Elizabeth Michell—£5 apiece to be paid them at their ages of 16. Proved in P.C.C., 30 Sept., 1653, by Elizabeth Harvye his relict. (379 Brent.) See Vol. i., p. 130.

Elline Moore of Hertford, spinster. Dated 30 Sept., 1652. "Vnto backside Joane Marshall widdow" 12[d]. Proved in P.C.C., 20 July, 1653. (378 Brent.)

George Marshall of Shipston upon Stower, co. Worcester, yeoman. Dated 11 March, 1658. To wife Judith £8. To eldest son William Marshall £8. To son John Marshall £8. To son Thomas Marshall £8. To daughter Elizabeth £3. To daughter Christian £8. To daughter Margery £8. To daughter Sisley Chamberlyn £8. To son George Marshall £8. To son Edward Marshall £8. Makes sons William, John, and Thomas Marshall executors. Proved in P.C.C. by Thomas Marshall 29 March, 1659, and power reserved to the other executors. (56 Pell.) See his burial, Vol. i., app. p. 39.

1659. May 20. Adm'on in P.C.C. of Thomas Marshall of Ringstead, co. Essex, to Alice Marshall his relict.

1659. Sept. 29. Adm'on in P.C.C. of Ambrose Marshall of Deptford, co. Kent, to Sarah Marshall his relict.

Anthony Watson, Minister of the church of Attenborough, co. Nott[m]. Nuncupative. Mentions William Marshall of Ashby, co. Leicester. Adm'on with will annexed in P.C.C. to Elizabeth Watson his relict, 17 Feb., 1657. (57 Wotton.)

Margaret Smith of East Retford, Widow. Dated 20 January, 1657. Mentions sister Anne Marshall. Brother in law M[r] John Marshall an executor. Adm'on with will annexed 30 Aug., 1658, in P.C.C. (434 Wotton.)

Nathaniell Billiald of Normanton upon Trent. Dated 9 May, 1658. Mentions Alice Marshall the daughter of Edward Harpham. Proved in P.C.C., 22 June, 1659. (352 Pell.)

Elizabeth Fletcher of Prescott, co. Lancaster, spinster. Dated 10 August, 1658. To Margaret Marshall of Prescott, widow, £3. To John Marshall of Prescott, Mercer, £3. To Elizabeth daughter of Richard Marshall of Prescott 20[s]. My brother in law Henry Marshall and William Marshall and Elizabeth Marshall his son and daughter. Makes said Henry Marshall sole executor. He proved in P.C.C., 6 January, 1658. (21 Pell.)

Thomas Randall of Colston Bassett, co. Nott^{m}, Labourer. Dated 7 May, 1658. To Thomas the son of Roger Marshall of Colston, six pence. Proved in P.C.C. by Katherine Randal his relict, 16 July, 1660. (146 Nabbs.)

Walter Byrd of Curborow, co. Stafford. Dated 11 June, 1642. To son in law Thomas Marshall and Anne his wife £5. Thomas Marshall their son. Proved in P.C.C., 7 Sept., 1642, by Margaret, Byrd his relict. (111 Campbell.)

John White of Sheere, co. Surrey. Dated 22 Sept., 1642. Mentions Nicholas Norwood son to Alexander Norwood of Leaphooke, co. Southampton, Innholder. Sister Mary Palmer wife of John Palmer of Horley, co. Surrey. My brother Thomas Norwood. My sister Alice Marshall wife to Thomas Marshall of the parish of Croydon, co. Surrey, husbandman. Proved in P.C.C., 20 *(sic)* Sept., 1642. (109 Campbell.)

Roger Dutton, the elder, Citizen and Salter of London. Mentions daughter Mary Marshall. Proved in P.C.C., 1642. (47 Campbell.) See Vol. ii., part i., p. 20.

Thomas Coe of Kenford, co. Suffolk. Mentions grand-daughter Mary Marshall. Proved in P.C.C., 1642. (15 Campbell.)

William Est of Rislip. Dated 24 March, 1616. Mentions sister Marshall. Proved in Commissary Court of London, 9 April, 1617. (Vol. 23, fo. 26.)

Henry Marshall of the Parish of St George in the county of Middlesex, tide-waiter. Dated 1 July, 1755. To son Henry Marshall 1^{s}. To daughter Susannah Marshall 1^{s}. Residue to wife Jane and makes her sole executrix. She proved in Commissary Court of London, 9 July, 1755. (Vol. 78.)

Nuncupative will of Jane Marshall *alias* Battie, of St Sepulchre's, London, widow. Dated 11 June, 1664. She gave all her estate to Mary Hughes, wife of Thomas Hughes of the said parish, desiring she would give something out of it to Sarah, Elizabeth, and Henrie Ferribie, and appointed said Mary Hughes executrix. She proved in Commissary Court of London, 31 January, 1664. See Vol. i., p. 195.

Adm'on in Commissary Court of London, 4 Dec., 1694, of Antony Marshall of St Benet, Pauls Wharf, to Anne Marshall, widow. See Vol. i., p. 194.

Elizabeth Marshall of the parish of St Mary Islington, co. Middlesex, widow. Dated 13 Oct., 1665. To sister in law Anne Marshall 12^{d}. Residue to brother John Roberts, and makes him sole executor. He proved in Commissary Court of London, 19 Oct., 1665. John Marshall is one of the witnesses. See Vol. i., p. 196.

Margaret Norton of Crosyates in the parish of Whitkirk. Dated 1 March, 1632. Mentions daughter Susanna Marshall. Makes Christopher Marshall executor. He proved in Exchequer Court at York, 9 May, 1633. (Vol. 42, fo. 179.)

Thomas Ellis of Doncaster, gentleman. Dated 4 April, 1562. Mentions wife Elizabeth. Sister Margaret Fulwood wife of Thomas Fulwood, alderman. Margaret Lewis daughter of Robert Lewys of Marr. To Elizabeth wife of John Marshall household stuff in the house of John Thwaytes in Doncaster, and a house and lands there, etc. (She evidently had no children then.) Thomas son of Robert Lewis, under age. Francis Frobisher, Esqr and Robert Lewys of Marr, yoman, executors. Both proved in Exchequer Court at York, 2 Dec., 1562. (Vol. 17, fo. 133.)

Francis Marshall of St Helens parish in Worcester, clothier. Dated 12 January, 1690. To my son 10^{s} to buy him a ring. Wife Mary sole executrix and residuary legatee. Daughter Mary. Witnesses, Tho. Shewringe, Tho. Pixell, and George Wilson. Proved at Worcester 22 July, 1706. Inventory dated 18 July, 1706.

John Baggitt. Will nuncupative. Dated 23 April, 1664. Appoints kinsman Richard Marshall executor. Anne Marshall, a witness. Proved in Consistory Court at Lincoln, 30 April 1664. (Vol. for 1664, fo. 668.)

Robert Castell of Woodham Walter co. Essex, Esq. Dated 4 Nov. (signed 6 Nov.), 1637. Brother Sir Edward Allen, Bart. Brother Stephen Marshall,[1] minister and preacher of Gods Word at Fynchfield. Proved in P.C.C., 10 Oct., 1638. (119 Lee.)

Robert Blacker of Shafton, yeoman. Dated 2 March, 1627, proved at York 14 March following. Mentions William Jenkinson of Shafton. William Reane. John Emley. David Marshall. Residue to daughter Isabel wife of Thomas Marshall. Richard Marshall a witness. See *Notes and Queries*, 6 Ser. iii., 366.

The following administrations are from the Probate Court at Ipswich:—

1643. April 24. John Marshall of Framlingham, adm'on to William Marshall his father.

1681. Feb. 4. Thomas Marshall of Butley, adm'on to Rebecca his widow.

1685. Aug. 5. John Marshall of Ipswich, adm'on to William Marshall his father.

1695. Oct. 19. William Marshall late of Ipswich but deceased in the ship called the "Devonshire" in the King's service, adm'on to Anne his widow.

Mary Townshend wife of John Townshend of Horstead, co. Norfolk, butcher. Sons John and Edward Roath. Sister Alice wife of John Marshall of Nottingham, shoemaker. Dated 3, and proved at Norwich, 12 March, 1714.

Grace Marshall of Denby in the parish of Peniston, widow. Dated 14 Nov., 1632. To Henry Marshall 6^{d}, to his wife 6^{d}, and to every one of his children 4^{d}. To my son Robert Marshall 12^{d}, to his wife 12^{d}, and to every one of his children 2^{s} 6^{d}. To Richard

1 See his will, Vol. i., p. 120.

Snydall my grandchild 40^s. To John Snydall my son in law 3^s 4^d and to my daughter Dorothy his wife 3^s 4^d. John Snydall and Francis Snydall my grandchildren. My sister Jennett Ouldam. My son Richard Marshall. My son Thomas Marshall, and my daughter Francis Marshall. Son Richard Marshall ex'or. He proved in Exchequer Court at York, 15 Feb., 1632. (Vol. 42, fo. 48.)

John Marshall of Leeds, Clothier. Dated 30 March, 1633. To be buried in parish church of Leeds. Wife Margaret. John Beason my sisters son. Edith wife of the said John Beason. John Beason his son. Robert Metcalfe and Katherine his wife. Richard Lapitch my cousin and Mary his wife. Margaret Noble my cousin wife of Ambrose Noble. Mathew Funtance and his wife. Jennet Fauntance. Richard Funtance my brother in law and his son in law William Todd. Alice Todd my cousin and her child. My sister in law Elizabeth Lawe, John Lawe her son and his wife. Dorothy Ealbecke my cousin. Mr Alderman Browne of Norwich, and his bedfellow Mrs Browne, Mr Jay of Norwich his son in law and his wife, Mrs Browne his daughter that is unmarried. Mr Edward Cutbert the elder, and Mr William Cutbert his brother of Owndale in Northamptonshire, and Mr Cawthorne their brother in law. Mr Edward Cutbert the younger. Mr Everell Hudson of Peroth. Mr Skneath, Draper. To the poor of Kirkbye Wharfe where I was born 10^s. Mentions a house standing under the Call brow belonging to the Free school of Leeds,—gives tenant right in said house to Grace Fletcher and her children and George Pease and his wife and children, to either of them their own parts wherein they now dwell. To every spinner I have 6d. apiece. John Benson my cousin. Richard Lapitch and Margaret Noble his sister. 10^s a year to poor of Leeds for ever. Calls John Benson "my nephew" and makes him sole ex'or. He proved in Exchequer Court at York, 17 June, 1633. (Vol. 42, fo. 105.)

John Marshall of Yeadon in parish of Guiseley. Dated 7 April, 1633. Son Thomas Marshall. Son Samuel Marshall. Son Joseph Marshall. Daughter Mercy Marshall. Daughter Mary Ive. Son William Marshall's children. Son Robert's children. Richard Foster's children. William Ive's children. Son Samuel Marshall, and son in law Abraham Marshall joint executors and residuary legatees. Both proved in Exchequer Court at York, 9 May, 1633. (Vol. 42, fo. 179.)

John Marshall of Robinhood Bay. Dated 11 July, 1634. To be buried in church or church yard of Filingdailes. My wife [no christian name given.] Every one of my sisters. To my son Richard the silver buttons of my leather doublet. My brother John Bigginge. Margaret Lawnd. My uncle Peter Marshall. My cousin John Marshall. Henry Spendley. Lands to son Richard when 21. Daughter Vrsuley Marshall, son Peter, and my wife executors. George Conyers sen^r a supervisor. Proved in Exchequer Court at York by Vrsula Marshall, Peter Marshall, and . . . . . *(sic)* Marshall widow and relict, 16 April, 1635. (Vol. 42, fo. 459.)

Peter Marshall of Pattrington in Holdernes. Dated 1 April, 1635. Gives tuition of sons William and John Marshall, and of daughter Isabell Marshall to Mary my wife their mother. Appoints them all executors. Proved by Mary Marshall the relict in Exchequer Court at York and power reserved to the other executors, 1 July, 1635. (Vol. 42, fo. 547.)

James Marshall of Bradford. Dated 22 April, 1634. Mentions four daughters and two sons (no names given) all under age. Makes wife (no name) executrix. She proved (no name given) in Exchequer Court at York 1 Oct., 1635. (Vol. 42, fo. 666.)

William Marshall of Weston, co. Nottingham, husbandman. Dated 8 March, 1611. To be buried in churchyard of Weston. Thomas Marshall and Elizabeth Marshall the children of my son William Marshall. My brother Robert Marshall. Thomas Marshall son to my said brother. Son William Marshall and Katherine his wife residuary legatees, and said son William executor. He proved in Exchequer Court at York, 6 March, 1616. (Vol. 34, fo. 393.) See Vol. i., pp. 108, 221.

Edward Marshall of Nether Yeadon. Dated 16 July, 1616, nuncupative. My sons Michael, William, and Abraham Marshall. My daughter Jenet. My late son Edward Marshall deceased six of his youngest children. Jane my wife. Jenet late wife to my said late son. Samuel Marshall my grandchild son of late son Edward. Wife Jane and grandson Samuel executors. Christopher Marshall a witness. Proved in Exchequer Court at York 9 July, 1617, by Jane Marshall and power reserved to Samuel. (Vol. 34, fo. 592.) See Vol. i., p. 282.

Thomas Marshall of Moore Allerton, yeoman. Dated 13 August, 1613. To be buried in Parish church of Leeds. To wife Anne messuage in Chapel Allerton called Crofts farm. John Thwates my son in law. Anne Marshall my daughter. To Thomas Marshall my son reversion of the said farm. My two sons in law John Battie and John Thwaite. William Marshall my son. The capital messuage of Mooretowne where I now dwell. Thomas and George Marshall my two younger sons under age. Wife Anne sole executrix. She proved in Exchequer Court at York, 30 June, 1614. (Vol. 33, fo. 148.)

Anne Marshall died 3 June, 1627. Her will is registered in Vol. 39, fo. 225. For further notices of this family, see *Notes and Queries*, 6 Ser. vi., p. 387.

Ann Marshall of Moreallerton, widow. Dated 24 May, 1627. To be buried in the parish church of Leeds. Son William Marshall, and recites decease of Thomas Marshall his father. John Battie my grandchild. Elizabeth Battie, Sara Battie, Timothie Battie, and Rebecca Battie, children of John Battie my son in law. Robert Myers my grandchild son of Thomas Myers. Mary Myers daughter of the said Thomas Myers. Dorothie Battie my daughter wife of John Battie. Jane my daughter wife of John Thwaits. My daughter Ann wife of the aforesaid Thomas Myers. My son William Marshall his wife. My son George Marshall his wife.

To my son Thomas Marshall £30. My son George Marshall. Ann Marshall daughter of my son William Marshall. The rest of my son William Marshalls children, to wit, Hellene, Elizabeth, and Edith. To Ann Marshall daughter of William Marshall younger my goddaughter one ewe and a lamb. To Alice . . . . . daughter of William Marshall late of Leeds deceased and now wife of . . . . of Leeds 40^{s}. Sons Thomas and George executors. Proved in Exchequer Court at York by Thomas Marshall and power reserved to George Marshall, 14 July, 1627.

Richard Marshall of Thorpe Arch, husbandman. Dated 10 March, 1616. Son Robert Marshall. Marie my wife. Sister Alice Marshall. Robert Fearne's children. William Scotte's children. Robert Stable's two children. John Fallis' children. Robert Dickonson and William Scott supervisors. Son Robert and wife Marie executors, wife to be tutor to said Robert during his minority. Will'm Marshall the elder a witness. Proved by relict 9 July, 1617, in Exchequer Court at York. (Vol. 34, fo. 591.)

Susanna Marshall of Everthorpe ~~[? Etherthorpe~~ in parish of ~~Darfield.]~~ co. York, spinster. Dated 30 July, 1712. Roger Wilson my brother. Thomas Wilson my nephew. Hunter Wilson my nephew. Philipp Constable. Robert Wilson my nephew. Ann Hoal my neice. Ann Wilson my neice. Susanna Wilson my neice. Catherine Talboy. Jane Weedley. Thomas Wilson and Roger Wilson my brother's executors. See probate Vol. i., p. 300.

Thomas Marshall of Farmedale, co. York, weaver. Dated 4 Feb., 1712. Son William Marshall. Daughter Jane Marshall. Jane my wife sole executrix. See probate, Vol. i., p. 300.

Thomas Marshall of Pontefract, Merchant. Will dated 21 August, 1645. Mentions neice Jane Marshall and her sister Mary. Adm'on with will annexed to Jane Marshall *alias* Hancocke now wife of William Hancocke, in Exchequer Court at York, 7 Sept., 1646.

James Marshall of Linton upon Owse, co. York, farmer. Dated 16 April, 1687. To be buried at the parish church of Nuton [Newton upon Ouse.] Cousin Thomas Marshall. Cousin Elizabeth Marshall. Uncle Thomas Marshall. To Marie Scott sons £3 that thare mother oweth me. Uncle Thomas Limbfont. Ann Carterett. Thomas May. Catheran Bradlay. Helling Marshall. Uncle Calluart and Ant eather of them 12^{d}. Uncle Thomas Marshall and his sun Tobyas Marshall executors. Proved in Exchequer Court at York by Thomas Marshall, 26 Nov., 1687. Bond annexed of Thomas Marshall of Moore Mounton, husbandman, Elizabeth Marshall of the same, widow, and Robert Hare of the same, husbandman. This will is among the Vacancy Wills.

Abraham Marshall of Tuxford, co Nott^{m}, blacksmith. Dated 28 Oct., 1686. My four children now living namely Ane, Elizabeth, Jane, and Edward. Daughter Ane to have farm and to pay the others their portions as they shall be 21 or marry, and to put son Edward to a trade if he desire to go. Brother William Marshall of Ratcliffe and brother Fran. Turner of Tuxford to be supervisors.

Adm'on with will annexed to Anne Marshall his daughter 29 Dec., 1686. This will will be found amongst the Vacancy Wills in the Probate Office at York. See Vol. i., p. 117; Vol. ii., part i., p. 75.

Ellis Marshall of Wellam Morhouse. Dated 9 Sept., 1583. To the church of Clareboroughe 2s. Richard Marshall of East Waytton (? Drayton) my brother. Rychard Nycolsone of Hedon my brother in law. Isabell my sister wife of the said Richard. My brother Thomas Marshall. Robert Marshall my brother. Henry Marshall my brother. William Bellame of East Retford, executor. He proved in the Exchequer Court at York, 1 Dec., 1583. (Vol. xxii., fo. 464.)

(Original Will.) Bernard Marshall of Horsforth, co. York, yeoman. Dated 26 March, 1635. To be buried in the parish church of Giesleye. To every one of my grandchildren except William Thornton 10s. To said William Thornton 32s. To Bernard Powell my grandchild one blacke cow. Residue to Bridgitt Miers, Agnes Lambert widow, and Elizabeth Powell, my three daughters, and appoints them executors. Thomas Fetheer a witness. Proved in the Exchequer Court at York by said executors 15 Oct., 1635.

Robert Marshall of Blith. Dated 4 April, 1522. To be buried in the church of saynte peter in Blith. Mentions—Alexander Kokkett. Sir George Tyas. Sir John Mirfyne. Sir Henry. John Pullen. John Sheperd. Robert Belby. John Semar. Jenett my maidyn. John Donston. Jane Adamson. Thomas Walker. William Kendall. Wife Elizabeth executrix. Sir Nicolas Kendall supervisor. Proved by relict in Exchequer Court at York, 15 May, 1522. (Vol. 9, fo. 230.)

William Marshall of Malton. Dated 3 March, 1527. To John Walker my curate for my tithes 3s 4d, and 20d to pray for my soul. "Lego d'no Will'o Marshall canonico filio meo xiijs iiijd. Wife Alice and sons Richard Marshall and Thomas Marshall residuary legatees and executors. George Marshall a witness. Proved in the Exchequer Court at York by the within named executors, 19 March, 1527. (Vol. 9, fo. 389.)

Richard Marshall of Moregaite in the pishe of Claireburghe. Dated 5 March, 1544. To be buried in the churchyard there. To Jennette my basterde doughter xxs besides xxs which I the saide Richarde owe unto her. Johã Marshall my daughter. Residue to Elyne Marshall my wife and Johañ my daughter and makes them executrixes. Proved by relict in Exchequer Court at York, and power reserved to Johane 9 Oct., 1545. (Vol. 13, fo. 82.)

Edward Marshall of Eland, co. York, clothier. Dated 30 January, 1596. Mentions a suit depending between himself and one William Marshall of Eland for £200 as appears by an obligation in the custody of the Justices at Westminster, and that Mr John Savill of the Newe Hall, Esquire, hath a letter of attorney under my hand and seal for to prosecute the suit for me. My brother John Marshall. Wife Grace Marshall. Appoints John Savill, Esqr, sole executor. He proved 23 June, 1597, in Exchequer Court at York. (Vol. 27, fo. 4.)

Robert Marshall of Stanthrop in the parish of Sutton upon Trent, co. Nottingham, in the presence of Henrie Kinge and William Okes,—nuncupative. Dated Saturday, 1 October, 1597. To daughter Anne Marshall £10. To my brother Henrie, meaning said *(sic)* Henrie Okes my house that John Jay dwells in—for life. Young William Marshall my brother's son. To my Mayden Nan Flintham a little browne Cowe. My wife. Robert Marshall Thomas Marshall's childe. Proved in Exchequer Court at York 11 January, 1597, by . . . . . . *(sic)* the relict and power reserved to Anne Marshall the daughter. (Vol. 27, fo. 123.)

Will'm Martiall of Sutton upon Trent in the co. of Nottingham, husbandman. Dated 26 Dec., in the 40th yeare of our Queene [Elizabeth]. To be buried in the parish church of Sutton aforesaid. Son William Martiall. Elizabeth my wife. Richard Theaker. Will'm Wilson. Son William Marshall executor. He proved in Exchequer Court at York, 22 March, 1597. (Vol 27, fo. 207.)

Richard Marshall of the parish of Rowsbie, [*i.e.* Roxby.] Dated 24 Sept., 1597. To be buried in the churchyard of Rawsbie. To the eldest daughter of John Roger of North Lofthows one close presser. Robert Petch of Rowsbie. Son William Marshall and daughter Jane Marshall executors. Proved in Exchequer Court at York by said William and power reserved to Jane, 20 June, 1598. (Vol. 27, fo. 305.)

Richard Marshall of Doncaster, alderman. Dated 26 March, 1586. To be buried in parish church of Doncaster. To wife Anne Marshall house at Doncaster in which James Porter now dwelleth. To my daughter Alice £120, and the goods given to her by her late mother my wife now deceased. My brother in law Robert Jefferesone of Barwicke in Ellmyt to have the education and bringing up of my said daughter till she shall be married or come to lawful years. Said Robert Jefferesone's children, Henry J., William J., Effame J., and Anne J. To Thomas Barmbie my sister's son 5[s]. Thomas Kytchine and his wife. Thomas Croft. Fraunces Croft my maid. Residue to son William Marshall and appoints him executor. "My verie frend John Lewis of Marr esquire." If son William dies without issue testator devises his lands and tenements to his (testator's) daughter Anne, with remainder to my brother John Marshall and his heirs males, remainder to Henrie Marshall one other of the brothers of me the said Richard Marshall, remainder over to right heirs. Adm'on in the Exchequer Court at York, with will annexed 21 April, 1586, to Robert Jeffrason during the minority of William Marshall the son and executor. (Vol. 23, fo. 192.)

(Original Will.) Peter Marshall[1] of Marton in Holderness, co. York, yeoman. Dated 21 July, 1636. To Lord Viscount Dunbar and his good Lady my grey colt whose use he will prove the better ether for double or single gelding. To John Constable, Esq., my

[1] See his wife mentioned, Peacock's *List of Roman Catholics in co. York*, p. 125.

master, son and heir of the said Lord Viscount Dunbar, my bay stoned colt and my grandchild Peter Marshall, whom I pray God may prove an honest and faithful servant to him and his as I have hereto been one to his grandfather before him. To Mr Mathew and Mr Henry Constable my sorrell young mare. To my nephew John Marshall his children 10s among them. To my brother Christopher Marshall his children 10s among them. My sister Jane Watson her children. My sister Agnes Goudams her children. My sister Anne Marsingale her children. To my neece Jane Marsingale being now my servant £3. Residue to Henry Marshall my son and heir and to his children now borne equally among them, provided that if my son John Marshall do come again and demand anything my will is he shall have half of the goods unbequeathed. Richard Dearing and Robert Moore of Marton, supervisors. Proved in the Exchequer Court at York, 19 January, 1636-7, by Henry Marshall of Marton.

(Original Will.) Marie Marshall of Linton upon ows [Ouse], co. York, weedow. Dated 10 March, 1685. To son George £5 that his uncle George Browne left him at his death. Residue to James Marshall and George Marshall, and if one die before he come to lawful age his part to go to his brother. To sister Alse Wykelef 5s. To John Bell 5s. To sister Elizabeth Crouder 5s. No ex'ors appointed. Adm'on with will annexed to Thomas Marshall to use of James Marshall, under age, the universal surviving legatee, 30 Oct., 1686.

John Marshall, clerk, Vicare of South Kyrkbye, co. York. Dated 20 January, 1567. To be buried in the church of South Kyrkbye. Sister Edythe. Brother Thomas sole executor. Elizabeth wife of John Cramwell of South Kirkbye. Susanne Cramwell daughter of John Cramwell aforesaid. The children of Lawrence Tusson whom he had by my sister. Janet Syvor. Lawrence Rawson my brother in Lawe. John Thurleston master of the free Gramer Scole at Hymsworthe. Proved 31 March, 1568, by Thomas Marshall, sole executor. *Archbishop's Book*, "*Younge and Grindal*," at York, fo. 46b. See Hunter's *South Yorkshire*, Vol. ii., p. 449.

In *Archbishop's Book*, "*Holgate and Heath*," fo. 165, will be found the will of Elizabeth Marshall of Ackborough (? Aldborough), proved 18 January, 1554.

Richard Marshall, Vicar of Fishlake. Mentions his brother Robert Marshall. Proved at York 5 Feb., 1505. (*Archbishop's Book* at York, "*Savage*," fo. 184.) See Vol. i., p. 131; and Hunter's *Deanery of Doncaster*, Vol. i., p. 193.

Roger Marshall of the Trinities, Pontefract, clerk. Dated 18 July, 1569. To be buried in the church of All hallows in Pontefract among my brethren. To my brother Thomas £4. To Katherine Buckle 20s. To the poor of Massam 20s, and to the reparation of the church of Massam 3s 4d. To cousin Wells at the Moreside 2s, and to each of her children 2s. To William Foster and his wife 40s. Margaret his mother. James Nycolson and his wife, and Thomas Nycolson his son. Peter Rogers. Alice Fewston. Margaret Russell. To the poor of Pontefract 20s. To every one of the brethren and sisters of the Trinities in Pontefract and to either of their madenes xiijd. Christopher Easbye's wife. To Lionel Marshall 3s 4d. William Johnson and Christopher Easby, executors and residuary legatees. Witnesses and supervisors, Sir Richard Rigeall, Sir John Soresbye, John Squire, schoolmaster of Pontefract. Proved at York, 5 Oct., 1570. (Vol. xix., fo. 57.)

Densal Marshall of Sturton in the co. of Nottingham, yeoman. Dated 2 June, 1697. Mentions Mary Birket and Anne Birket my grandchildren natural and lawful children of William Birket of Egmanton, yeoman, and then calls William Birket "my son in law." Mary Booth my grandchild, daughter of Andrew Booth of Sturton, my son in law. To Elizabeth Booth my grandchild, daughter of Andrew Booth, £100. Said Andrew Booth residuary legatee and sole executor. *Original Will (at York).* See Vol. i., p. 309.

From Dickering Act Book at York.

1648. Dec. 28. Probate of the will of George Marshall of Fallingfosse to Elizabeth Marshall his relict and sole executrix.

1651. Feb. 14. Adm'on of William Marshall of Burniston to Isabell Marshall, widow, and Ellis Marshall, spinster, of the same.

1667. May 31. Probate of the will of John Marshall of Staxton to Sarah Marshall his relict and sole executrix. See Vol. i., p. 276.

1668. Sept. 25. Adm'on of Robert Marshall of Foxholes to Daniel Todd "ejus *nepoti*."

1668. Oct. 22. Probate of the will of Sarah Marshall of Staxton to Thomas Marshall her son and sole executor. See Vol. i., p. 276.

From Ainstie Act Book at York.

1597. April 23. Adm'on of George Marshall of Nun Appleton to Anne his relict.

1598. Dec. 5. Probate of the will of Maud Marshall of Rawdon to Christopher her son, and power reserved to Jane and Johanna her daughters.

1598. March 30. Adm'on of George Marshall of Walton to Jane his relict.

1598. Oct. 4. Probate of the will of Katherihe Marshall of Tadcaster to Edward Marshall.

1602. Dec. 1. Probate of the will of Thomas Marshall of Birkin to Isabel his relict.

1603. May 12. Adm'on of John Marshall of Sherburne to Margaret Morgan *alias* Marshall wife of Hugh Morgan.[1]

[1] Hugh Morgan's will was proved by Margaret his relict, 7 Aug., 1619.

1604. Oct. 25. Adm'on of William Marshall of Leeds to Richard Marshall and John Watson for Alice and Christopher his children.

1605. June 11. Adm'on of Mercie Marshall of Scots-hall in the parish of Leeds to Thomas Barnby her brother. ? de bonis non. See Vol. i., p. 257.

1605. Oct. 22. Probate of the will of Robert Marshall of Tadcaster to James Barker to sole use of Katherine Marshall testator's daughter, a minor and sole executrix; and care of the said Katherine according to her voluntary election committed to the said James. A caveat was entered 1 July previous.

1606. Jany. 27. Adm'on of Alexander Marshall of Street Houses in Bilborough to Leonard Harpham of Bilborough, for Thomas, Mary, Margaret, and Alexander his children.

1607. May 22. Adm'on of Edward Marshall of Tadcaster to Thomas his son.

1611. Sept. 27. Adm'on of Elizabeth Marshall of Thorp Arch to Richard Marshall.

1614. May 6. Probate of the will of William Marshall of East Rigton to Beatrice and Richard Marshall.

1615. Aug. 18. Probate of the will of John Marshall of Hessay to Alice his relict, for Thomas, Elizabeth, Helen, Margaret, John, Jannet, and Elizabeth *(sic)* the children.

1616. April 18. Probate of the will of George Marshall of Thorp Arch to Alice his relict.

1616. Oct. 3. Adm'on of Edward Marshall of Nether Yeadon, with tuition of John, William, Jeromy, Elizabeth, Joseph, and Mercy, his children, to Jane Marshall of Yeadon, widow. See Vol. i., p. 282.

1616. Nov. 26. Probate of the will of Richard Marshall of Hessay to Thomas Marshall, William Winter, and William Adcock, tutors of Brian, Helen, Thomas, Agnes, and Jane, children of deceased.

1617. March 20. Probate of the will of John Marshall of Bolton (Percy) to Edward Marshall for Dorothy Marshall daughter of deceased.

1619. June 23. Adm'on of Jane Marshall of Rawden to Sibel Grimshaw, widow.

1621. July 3. Probate of the will of Thomas Marshall of Hessay to Anne his relict and Thomas Marshall his son.

1621. Dec. 20. Probate of the will of William Marshall of Aketon to Dorothy his relict.

1621. Dec. 20. Adm'on of Barnard Marshall of Bramhope to Anne his relict.

1623. Feb. 6. Probate of the will of Richard Marshall of Colton to Mary his relict, Henry Newarke and Henry Doughty co-executors having renounced.

1623. May 22. Probate of the will of Christopher Marshall of Kirkdighton to John Dunwell, Margaret his relict having died before she proved.

1623. May 22. Probate of the will of Margaret Marshall of Kirkdighton, widow, to John Dunwell sole executor.

1624. Aug. 4. Adm'on of Peter Marshall of Fareburn to Alice his relict.

1625. Feb. 25. Adm'on of Christopher Marshall of Bramham to Jane his relict.

1625. April 20. Probate of the will of John Marshall of Cawood to John Marshall his son, and power reserved to Robert Marshall co-executor.

1625. Nov. 4. Adm'on of William Marshall of Tadcaster to Mark his son and Anne his relict.

1633. May 9. Adm'on of Mary Marshall of Colton to Dulcibella Marshall her daughter.

1635-6. Jan[y] 15. Probate of the will of John Marshall of Clifton to John Marshall, Francis Marshall, and Hugh Yates, executors.

1637. Sept. 7. Adm'on of Isabella Marshall, widow, of Yeadon in parish of Guiseley to Ralph Dixon of Leeds, mercer, her brother, to use of Jane Marshall, Elizabeth, and Mary Marshall her children.

1637. Sept. 11. Probate of the will of Thomas Marshall of Shereburn to Mary Marshall his relict and sole executrix.

1637. Sept. 5. Probate of the will of John Marshall of Rawden to Edward Marshall and Abraham *Grymeshawe* co-executors. (This corrects note of adm'on Vol. i., p. 293).

1638. April 6. Adm'on of Robert Marshall of Yeadon to Margaret Marshall his relict.

1638. April 6. Adm'on of John Marshall of East Keswick to William Marshall of the same.

1638. March 28. Adm'on of Leonard Marshall of Tadcaster to Isabella Marshall his relict. Cf. Vol i., pp. 116, 263, 270.

Vol. i., p. 267, *note* 5. Add to this, "1640. Oct. 5. Probate of the will of Edward Marshall of Tadcaster to William Marshall of the same, yeoman, to the use of Margaret, Elizabeth, and Anne Marshall, his children, Elizabeth Marshall the widdow and relict of the testator having renounced, and the same day tuition of Margaret Marshall and Anne Marshall children of the said deceased was committed to Robert Sainter of Tadcaster, yeoman."

FROM CRAVEN WITH RIPON ACT BOOK AT YORK.

1670. Feb. 16. Probate of the will of Jane Marshall of Felbeck house to William Pullan sole executor. See Vol. i., p. 115.

1671. Aug. 16. Probate of will of George Marshall of Grantley to Peter Marshall one of the executors. See Vol. i., p. 280, where for "said executors" read "Peter Marshall."

1671. Oct. 3. Probate of the will of Christopher Marshall of Clifton to Henry Marshall sole executor.

1677. April 2. Probate of the will of William Marshall of Waddington to Margaret his widow and sole executrix. See Vol. i., p. 295.

1691. June 2. Probate of the will of John Marshall of Grisington [in parish of Linton] to Elizabeth Marshall, widow, sole executrix.

1691. March 15. Probate of the will of John Marshall of Skipton to Thomas Gawthorpe sole executor.

1709. Aug. 1. Adm'on of Hanna Marshall *alias* Mortin late wife of William Mortin of Bewerley to her said husband.

From Prerogative Act Book at York.

1635. Nov. 23. Probate of the will of James Marshall of Donnington to John Marshall, and Anne Smeaton, widow. See Vol. ii., part i., p. 53.

1643. Feb. 10. Probate of the nuncupative will of Roland Marshall of Gate Helmsley to Emot Marshall universal legatee.

1645. Sept. 13. Probate of the will of Anthony Marshall of Branthwate, co. Cumberland, to John Marshall and William Marshall.

From Holderness Act Book at York.

1650. Augt. 23. Probate of the will of Thomas Marshall of Pattrington to Jane Marshall his relict.

1677. Augt. 27. The will of Catherine Marshall of Otteringham, is in a bundle marked "reinfecta." See Vol. ii., part i., p. 113.

From Cleveland Act Book at York.

1684. Nov. 22. Adm'on of George Marshall of Glesedale to Ellis Marshall his relict.

1685. Sept. 3. Probate of the will of Ellitia [Ellis] Marshall of Gleasdaile to Richard Marshall sole executor.

1688. Feb. 19. Probate of the will of Henry Marshall of Egton to John Marshall sole executor. See Vol. i., p. 274.

1694. Jany. 24. Probate of the will of Margaret Marshall of Burreby to Henry Ripley sole executor.

1705. April 18. Adm'on of Francis Marshall of Carleton to John Marshall, James Marshall, Thomas Scarth, and Richard Fairweather.

1708. May 21. Probate of the will of Margaret Marshall of Oakebridge Holme in the chapelry of Egton to Paul Marshall sole executor. See Vol. i., p. 274.

From Pontefract Act Book at York.

1661. Dec. 16. Probate of will of Peter Marshall of Whitby to Peter Marshall his son. See Vol. i., p. 273.

FROM RETFORD ACT BOOK AT YORK.

1547. May 5. Adm'on of Walter Marshall of Grove to Anne Marshall his relict.

1560. May 2. Adm'on of William Marshall of West Cottam to Alice his relict.

1560. May 2. Adm'on of William Marshall of Carleton in the parish of Snayth to Alice his relict.

1615. Aug. 23. Adm'on "Malsami" Martiall of Norton Cuckney to Isabella Marshall, widow.

1619. Oct. 7. Adm'on of Thomas Martiall of Carlton in Lindrick to Mary Martiall his relict.

FROM NEWARK ACT BOOK AT YORK.

1608. Sept. 17. Adm'on of John Marshall of Newark on Trent to John Marshall his son.

1612. May 7. Adm'on of William Marshall of Scarnethorp to Gabriel Tailor.

THE FOLLOWING ARE FROM A BOOK IN THE EXCHEQUER COURT AT YORK, ENTITLED, "CURATIONES, 1592—1638."

15 Jan^{y}., 1608. Care of Mary Marshall, daughter of Andrew Marshall late of the City of York, deceased, to Miles Fawcet of the City of York, tanner.

14 May, 1611. Care of Tobias Marshall, son of William Marshall late of the City of York, deceased, aged 14, to William Marshall his brother.

11 April, 1614. Care of Elizabeth Marshall, daughter of Andrew Marshall late of the City of York, deceased, aged 12, to Thomas Spence of York, tanner.

31 Oct., 1619. Care of Dorothy Marshall, daughter of John Marshall late of Bolton Percy, to Richard Marshall her uncle on the father's side.

19 July, 1617. Care of John Marshall, son of Andrew Marshall late of the City of York, aged 15, to Thomas Spence, tanner.

21 June, 1623. Tuition of Mary Marshall, daughter of Richard Marshall late of Appleton, to Katherine Dawson of Nunmounckton; and again 29 Sept., 1623, to Thomas Dobson of Nunmonkton.

29 Nov., 1634. Tuition of George Marshall and Thomas Marshall, sons of Thomas Marshall of Flamborough, co. York, gent., one of the adm'ors of Alice Creyke,[1] spinster, late of Branton in the province of York, to the said Thomas Marshall their father.

[1] The will of Alice Crake, dated 27 Oct., 1634, was proved in the Exchequer Court at York, 18 Nov. following. (Vol. 42, fo. 342). I made the following note of it:—

Where as my portion is and remayneth in the hands of Mr Gregory Crake my brother, amounting to £500. To Mrs Anne Marshall [see her *Mar. Lic.*,

1 March, 1635. Care of Mary Marshall, daughter of Christopher Marshall of the City of York, aged 16, to Jonas Spacy of York, Innholder.
Care of Anne Marshall, daughter of same, aged 16, to Jonas Spacy, 9 January, 1637.

9 Feb., 1637. Tuition of Sara, daughter of John Marshall late of Worrall, to Thomas Sampson of Worrall; and 6 March, 1637, tuition of same to Thomas Taylor of Wadsley, yeoman.

THE FOLLOWING ARE IN A VACANCY ACT BOOK OF THE EXCHEQUER COURT AT YORK, CONTAINING ACTS FROM 1559—1561.

"Mem. that no man be admitted to adm'on of the goods of William Marshall of the parish of Kyrkelethome deceased intestate until such time as Robert Marshall his brother be called for his interest, etc." Adm'on of William Marshall of West Cottam (West Coatham in parish of Kirkleatham) to Alice Marshall his relict, 2 May, 1560.

Adm'on of William Marshall of Carlton in the parish of Snayth to Alice Marshall his relict, 2 May, 1560.

THESE ADM'ONS WERE GRANTED DURING THE VACANCY OF THE SEE.

1687. March 3. Adm'on (de bonis non) of Richard Marshall of Linton on Ouse (not yet administered by Mary Marshall his relict, deceased) to Thomas Marshall his brother. Bond of same date, in which Thomas Marshall of Moore Mounton, agricola, and Hellen Marshall of the same, spinster, are bound in £100. See Vol. i., p. 308.

1687. March 13. Adm'on of John Marshall of Thorne Gumbald to Mary Featherstone, widow, of the parish of Paghill, *alias* Paul, his mother.

John Bingham, of Marnham. Dated 18 January, 1657. "I give Robert Marshall' Sonne Selvester Marshall Tenn shillings." To Elizabeth Marshall 10s. Proved in Exchequer Court at York. (Vol. 43, fo. 592).

Joseph Marshall of Doncaster, co. York, gentleman. Dated 5 Sept., 1757. Friend Mary Storrs, daughter of Caleb Storrs late of Stockport in the co. of Chester, deceased. Cousin Joseph

Vol. i., p. 80] my mother £50. To Mrs Christian Crake my sister £50, and all my lands in Sewerby. To Mr Raiphe Crake £10, and my silver castinge bottle. To the other six children of Gregory Crake my brother, every one of them £30. To Mr Gregory Crake my brother £50, and to my sister Ursula his wife £20. To my neice Mrs Frances Tankerd £40. To George Marshall £10. To Thomas Marshall younger £5. To every one of my uncle Robert Crake's children 40s, my aunt Margaret his wife. To the Lady Wharton 40s. To the Lady Wentworth 20s. To Mrs Catherine Wharton wife of Mr Michael Wharton 20s. To Mrs Margaret Constable wife of John Constable 10s. There are many other legatees. Sir George Wentworth and Mr John Wright, executors.

Potter of Gainsborough, chandler. Cousin John Potter of the same. Cousin Mary Potter, spinster. Cousin Rebecca, the wife of William Jalland, sister of the said Joseph Potter. Cousin Jane Sargent widow of John Sargent late of Hull. Cousin Thomas Green of London, nephew to the said Jane Sargent. Money to quakers at Gainsborough and Warmsworth. Mary Storrs, executrix, and Joseph Hobson of Macclesfield, co. Chester, yeoman, executor. Proved in Exchequer Court at York. (Vol. 102, fo. 65).

Benjamin Marshall of Holbich-drove, co. Lincoln, yeoman. Mentions James Marshall and William Marshall. "My wife" sole executor. Dated 15 March, 1722-3. Then mentions James Frankes and Robert Nobell. Witnesses, Thomas Noble and Ann Brown. [This note is from the original will in the Consistory Court at Lincoln. There is no record of date of probate.]

Thomas Marshall of Thorpe in the county of Lincolne, Labourer. Dated 12 May, 1697. To son John Marshall £10 at his age of 21. To daughter Anne Marshall £10 at her age of 18. If wife "be bigg with child" £10 to said child. Mentions his brother and sister, but not by name. Nephew William Simson son of William Simson of Thorpe, 10s. Wife Rose sole executrix. She proved in Consistory Court at Lincoln, 30 July, 1697. (Vol. for 1697-8, fo. 64.)

NOTES OF DEEDS.[1]

Grant of tenement, etc., in Pleasley by Robert Marshall to William Bardall, clerk, and Thomas Hewes. Dated on feast of St Lucy, Virgin, 1 Edward IV. [1462.]

Deed Poll. Be it known unto all men, etc. Bridget Rowe of St Mary Savoy in co. Middlesex, spinster, appoints welbeloved friend John Marshall of Steple Morden in co. Cambridge, yeoman, her attorney to enter into tenements which came to Mary Rowe my mother, and Anne Nelson her sister, in Ridware, Yoxhall, Morrey, Longdon, and Bancrofte, co. Stafford, by the death of Nicholas Aldridge their brother, and to all tenements which came to said mother by the death of her sister Anne Nelson in the said towns, and to deliver my deed of sale of the said premisses bearing date with these presents to William Marshall of St Mary Savoy aforesaid, Grocer, and Rebecca his wife. Dated 16 May, 1637.

Covenant to pass a fine. Indenture made 10 January, 1637, between William Marshall, Citizen and Grocer of London, and Rebecca his wife one of the daughters and coheirs of Mary Rowe, widow, deceased, and Bridgit Rowe, spinster, another of the daughters and coheirs of the said Mary Rowe of the one part, and Lawrence Davis of London, gent., and James Martyn, Citizen and Draper of London, of the other part. William Marshall and Rebecca his wife covenant with Lawrence Davis and James

[1] In possession of George W. Marshall.

Martyn to levy a fine to them of two messuages in Bancrofte, co. Stafford, in the tenure of Edward Hall, with their appurtenances in Bancrofte, Sandborrowe, and Hampstall Ridware, and messuage in Bancrofte in the tenure of Ciceley Knowles, widow, and messuage in same occupation of John Gretton, being four messuages, four gardens, seventy acres of land, 10 acres of meadow, one hundred and twenty acres of pasture, and fifty acres of moor.

Signed. Lawrence Davis. (Seal gone.) James Martin. (Seal. Three birds within a bordure.)

Marriage Settlement. Endorsed "19 June, 1642. Marriage Articles. William Marshall and Jane Scrogge. For securing Her a jointure of £60 per annum out of Bancroft, Longdon, etc." Indenture made 19 June, 17 Charles, between William Marshall[1] Cittizen and Merchant Taylor of London of the one part, and Humfry Fishe of Norhill in the co. of Bedford, Esq., William Dowman of Uffington in the Co. of Lincoln, Esq., and Humfry Terricke one of the Procters of the Arches, London, and Jane Scrogges one of the daughters of William Scrogges, Esq., deceased, of the other part. Whereas it is agreed that a marriage shall be solemnized between William Marshall and Jane Scrogges—in consideration of £600 paid to him for the marriage portion of the said Jane he agrees to levy a fine to the said Humfry Fishe and said Humfry Terricke of two messuages in Bancroft, co. Stafford, in the tenure of Edward Hall, and other lands there, and of messuage in Longdon co. Stafford now or late in the tenure of Isaac Walton, and other lands at Longdon, Bancroft, Sandborrow, Hampstall Ridware, Yoxall, Morrey, and Longdon, to the use of him the said William Marshall and Jane his intended wife for their lives, and to the survivor of them, with remainder to the right heirs of said William Marshall, and said William Marshall grants the said premises, excepting an annuity of £25 to Bridget Cole wife of William Cole, citizen and embroiderer of London, to the said Humfry Fishe and William Dowman,—provided always if the said William Marshall shall convey lands of the yearly value of £60 to the said trustees the estate limited in this indenture shall cease, and then the said lands shall come to the heirs of the said William Marshall by Rebecca his late wife.[2] Further grant of messuage in St Mary le Strand in trust for William Marshall's children (if any) by said Jane Scrogges.[3]

Indenture dated 5 June, 1732, between John Marshall of Pickering, co. York, Webster, of one part, and Francis Nickelson of Pickering and Ann his wife of the other part. John Marshall sells to Francis Nickelson for £14 10 0 a close in the North Field of Pickering. Covenant to bar dower of Ann now wife of John Marshall.

1 See Vol. i., App. p. 3. His original Will is in my possession, sealed with, Arms. Three bars and canton. Crest. A demi man holding a baton.

2 Mentioned above as daughter and coheir of Mary Rowe.

3 See her Will, Vol. i., p. 101.

Indenture dated 1 May, 1678, between William Marshall of Cayton, co. York, yeoman, of the one part, and William Marshall of Cayton, yeoman, son of the said William Marshall, of the other part. William Marshall the father in consideration of 5s and of the natural love and affection which he beareth unto his said son, sells him messuage and garth at Cayton now in tenure of said William Marshall the son. Memm of Livery and seizin witnessed by Ingram Orwain, Frances Moore, and Richard Stevenson.

Lease for a year. Indenture dated 7 March, 1687, between Samuel Marshall of the Town of Cambridge, haberdasher, of the one part, and John Stanford of the Town of Huntingdon, gardiner, of the other part. Lease for a year at rent of a pepper-corn of two cottages, etc., in the parish of St John's, Huntingdon, in the tenure of John Corbit, Thomas Norris, and Elizabeth Moore, widow. Signed by Samuel Marshall. SEAL. Arms. A fess betw. 3 dolphins naiant. Crest. A dolphin as in the arms.

Indenture dated 8 October, 1634, between Richard Gregge of Killingbecke, in the Co. of York, yeoman, George Marshall of Buslingthorpe in the said co., yeoman, and Anne his wife of the one part, and Edward Brooke of Killingbecke aforesaid, yeoman, and Katherine his wife of the other part. Richard Gregge, George Marshall and Anne his wife sell part of a house in Killingbecke, two acres in occupation of Richard Gregge, three acres in Scarcroft, close late in tenure of Laurence Askwith, and John Gregge, father of the said Richard Gregge, etc., to Edward Brooke and Katherine his wife for £30.

Deed endorsed "Mr Marshall, his wife, Dr Hickes & wife, their Condicōnall Assignmt of ye lease of Bennett's house to Rayner for paymt of 103li the 11th of November, 1695. 26 August, 1704. Assignmt by Lingard, Rayner's Exr, to Jenkins."

Indenture dated 10 May, 1695, between John Marshall of St Margaret's, Westminster, in the co. of Middlesex, gent., and Tabitha his wife, and George Hicks, D.D., and Frances his wife, who was the relict and executrix of John Marshall, late citizen and cooke of London of the one part, and Robert Rayner of Southwark, co. Surrey, gent., of the other part. Whereas the Draper's Company by their indenture of lease, dated 26 November, 1669, leased a messuage in Philpot Lane in the parish of St Andrew Hubbard, London, then in tenure of Simon Hewson, Mealeman, for sixty-one years to said John Marshall, deceased, whose estate therein is come to John Marshall party hereto by his will and by deed poll dated 29 September, 1684, made by the said George Hicks to the said John Marshall party hereto. John Marshall and Tabitha his wife convey said messuage to Robert Rayner in consideration of £100.

Assignment endorsed on the deed of residue of term of 61 years, dated 26 August, 1704, by John Lingard, Citizen and Vintner, of London, executor of the will of Robert Rayner, in consideration of £100 to George Jenkins of the parish of St Bride's, London, gent.

The following pedigree shows the connection of the persons mentioned in this deed. See Vol. i., p. 145.

. . . . . . Marshall =

Richard Marshall. = Mentioned in his brother's will, 1677. Cf. Vol. ii., Part i., p. 47.

John Marshall, = Citizen and Cook of London. Will pro. in P.C.C., 1677.

Frances, dau. of Charles Mallory. Will proved in P.C.C., 1715. = George Hickes, D.D., Dean of Worcester. Will pro. in P.C.C., 1715.

William Marshall, eldest son. Devisee of land at King's Bromley in will of John Marshall, 1677.

John Marshall of St. Margaret's, Westminster. Under age 1677. Will pro. in P.C.C., 1713. = Tabitha, dau. of Thomas Nowell of Dover. Will pro. in P.C.C., 1732. See *Westminster Abbey Registers*, p. 338.

John Marshall of Milbank, Westminster. Will pro. in Commissary Court of London, 1712. =

Frances. Mentioned in her father's will, 1709.

Deed endorsed "The Deed leading the uses of a Recovery against Mr Lavigne wherein Mrs Tunstall is vouched." Indenture dated 1 Nov., 1697, between Peter Lavigne of the parish of St Paul, Covent Garden, in co. Middlesex, Grocer, of the first part, Elizabeth Tunstall of Brentford, in co. Middlesex, widow, of the second part, and Ralph Marshall late of the parish of St Paul, Covent Garden, and now of the parish of St Clement Danes, Esq., and Charles Marshall of London, Grocer, of the third part. Relates to Messuage in tenure of John Blow called Coleherne or Great Coleherne in the parish of Kensington, co. Middlesex, etc. Recites Indenture of Release, dated 2 February last past, [1696-7] between Peter Lavigne of first part, Elizabeth his now wife by the name of Elizabeth Alchorne, widow, of second part, and Ralph Marshall and Charles Marshall of third part.

Elizabeth Tunstall sealed with arms—A chevron between three tuns.

Indenture dated 4 July, 1741. Thomas Marshall of Seacroft, co. York, Butcher, and Frances his wife, in consideration of £100, grant House and Lands in Conisthorpe in the parish of Goldsborough to the Honble Richard Arundell of Allerton Mauliverer, Esq.

Indenture dated 19 March, 26 Elizabeth, [1583-4] between Raphe Marshall of Carleton within the parish of South Muskham in the co. of Nottingham, Esq., of the one part, and Anthony Haslame, of Newark upon Trent, in the co. aforesaid, mercer, of the other part. Lease of close of 110 acres in the parish of South Muskham called Cranckley in consideration of £85 to said Anthony Haslame for two years, except the first crop of five acres parcel of the said premisses now in the occupation of Mr John Leake, at the rent of one pound of pepper.

Deed endorsed "A deede of Anuitie made by John Marshall to the use of Thomas Elles and his heyres of xx m'ks a yere," etc. To all the faithful in Christ Thomas Ellys of Pawnton Magna in co. Lincoln, Esq., and Merchant of the Staple of Calais, and Henry

Stathum, clerk, send greeting in our Lord God everlasting. Recites that John Marshall of South Carleton in the parish of South Muskham juxta Newark, gent., and Merchant of the Staple of Calais did by his indenture dated 7 July, 34 Henry VIII. [1542] grant to Thomas Ellys and Henry Stathum half the manor of South Muskham which the said John Marshall lately purchased of William Pawlett, Knight, Lord S[t] John, and lands in South Muskham and Carleton which he lately purchased of said William Pawlett, Knight, and also his lands in Beesthorpe, co. Nottingham, on condition that they should demise the said lands to the said John Marshall and Anne his wife to the use of them and their heirs paying therefor annually 20 marks. Dated 9 January, 35 Henry VIII. [1544.] Livery of seizin endorsed dated 22 July; and also this memorandum, "Thys Tom̄ Ellis wasse blynd at the tyme, he subscrybyd & longe affore alsoe." Enrolled on Close Roll, and recognisance dated 9 May, 36 Henry VIII.

Indenture dated 9 June, 20 Elizabeth [1578], between Henry Marshall of South Carlton in the co. of Nottingham, Esq[r], of the one part, and Ralph Marshall of South Muskham, Gent., brother of the said Henry, of the other part. Witnesseth that said Henry Marshall hath to farm let to said Ralph Marshall a messuage and five oxgangs of land, etc., called Wandholte in Cranlkey, etc., for term of 21 years at two peppercorns. Signed by Ralph Marshall.

Indenture dated 6 August, 24 Elizabeth [1582], between Ralphe Marshall of Sowthcarleton in the co. of Nottingham, gent., of the one part, and Bryan Clarke of Stoke in the same County, yeoman, of the other part. Witnesseth that said Raphe Marshall hath to farm letten unto the said Bryan Clarke one farm now in the tenure of Nicholas Irelonde situate in Sowthcarleton aforesaid and three oxgangs, etc., in the town fields of South Muskham and South Carleton now in the tenure of William Yonge of Muskham, also lands in Cranley in occupation of Gregory Roxton for term of twenty-one years at rent of 46[s] a year. Covenant by Bryan Clarke to fetch "two loades of Coales and one loade of woode" yearly, and also to "plowe three seu'all daies," and "lead Corne or hey one daie yerely" during said term, also to be "contributory, etc., as concerninge the warres." Signed, Bryan Clarke.

Indenture made 14 July, 38 Elizabeth [1596], between Roger Gregory the younger, son of Roger Gregory the elder of East Stockwith, co. Lincoln, gent., of the one part, and Raphe Marshall of South Carleton in the co. of Nottingham, Esq., of the other part. Whereas the said Ralph by his indenture of lease dated 20 May, 32 Elizabeth [1590], for the sum of £600 did demise to Humfrey Litleton[1] of Colmers in co. Worcester, gent., one capital messuage called the old Hall in South Carleton, with certain lands, from the 24th of March then last past for the term of twenty-seven years, at the yearly rent during the first ten years of 12[d], and £4 1 0 during the residue of the said twenty-seven years, in which said indenture there is a covenant on behalf of the said Ralph that

1 He was buried at Naunton, near Pershore, 1624. See *Genealogist*, Vol. iii., p. 99.

Henry Marshall of South Carlton, Esq., father of the said Ralph, should upon request after three months next after his return from beyond the seas into England, execute unto the said Humfrey Litleton any act for confirming the said indenture of lease, and whereas the said Humfrey Litleton by his indenture of assignment dated 30 October, 33 Elizabeth [1591], did assign the said term of years to the said Roger Gregory the elder, and whereas the said Henry Marshall in performance of the above mentioned covenant of him the said Ralph in the said indenture contained, did by his indenture dated 15 March, 35 Elizabeth [1593], confirm to the said Roger Gregory the elder as well the same first mentioned indenture made by Ralph Marshall to Humfrey Litleton and the said indenture of assignment dated 30 October, made by said Humfrey Litleton unto the said Roger Gregory the elder. To have and to hold all the said demised premises expressed in the said indentures of 20 May and 30 October, unto the said Roger Gregory the elder, from the day of the date of the said last indenture made by Henry Marshall unto Roger Gregory the elder, dated 15 March, 35 Elizabeth, for term of years then unexpired contained in said former indenture dated 20 May, and whereas the said Raphe Marshall by another indenture of Covenants of marriage, dated 23 December, 34 Elizabeth [1592], made between him the said Ralph Marshall of the one part, and said Roger Gregory the elder of the other part, in consideration of £900 to him by the said Roger paid did covenant that he the said Ralfe Marshall and Frances his wife should levy a fine unto William Gregory, Gent., Roger Gregory the younger, William Whalley, gent., and Charles Yarburgh, gent., of all that the Manor of South Muskham and Carlton to such uses as said first recited indenture dated 23 December declared. He the said Henry Marshall did by his indenture dated 15 March, 35 Elizabeth [1593], in consideration of £133 6 8 paid by Roger Gregory the elder, allow to him the said indenture and fine, and whereas the said Roger the elder by his deed of assignment of concurrent date hath released to his son Roger Gregory the younger the messuage mentioned in the indenture of 15 March, 35 Elizabeth, and whereas the said Ralph by his indenture of bargain and sale dated 14 July instant, hath sold to the said Roger Gregory the elder and his heirs all that capital messuage called Burntewicks farm in South Muskham, late in the tenure of Charles Yarburghe, now in the tenure of John Wilkinson, and farm in the occupation of Henry Webster, a close in tenure of John Bristow, a close called Hareholme late in the tenure of Robert Marshall, and also a messuage, etc., late in the tenure of Ralph Marshall, gent., uncle to the said Ralph Marshall party to these presents, now in the tenure of the said Robert Marshall, and other lands in Muskham and Carlton. The said Roger Gregory the younger covenants with the said Ralph Marshall party to these presents, that he the said Roger the younger and the said Roger the elder will not during so long as the said Roger the elder shall peaceably enjoy the said lands, take any use of the messuage, &c., called the old Hall specified in the indenture dated 15 March, 35 Elizabeth. Signed, Raffe Marshall.

Indenture dated 13 July, 40 Elizabeth [1598], between John Rotherham of Seymers, in the parish of Great Marlow, co. Bucks., Esq., one of the six clerks of the High Court of Chancery, of the one part, and Henry Marshall of South Carlton, in the parish of South Muskham, Esq., and Ralph Marshall the younger, of South Carlton, aforesaid, son and heir apparent of the said Henry, of the other part. Witnesseth that John Rotherham doth grant to said Henry Marshall and Ralph Marshall two annuities, one to the said Henry Marshall of £144, and one to said Ralph Marshall of £156, out of manors of South Muskham and South Carlton, until the year 1604, the annuity to Henry Marshall to be paid in the Chapel of the Rolls, London, and the annuity to Ralph Marshall to be paid at the south porch of the parish church in Newark upon Trent. Covenant that after John Rotherham shall have paid £400 to Roger Gregory the elder, a portion of the above annuities shall cease. Covenant by John Rotherham that Raphe Marshall the younger shall be at liberty to remove goods, &c., till Pentecost, 1604, if *the said (sic.)* £5,600 be not in the meantime fully paid. "And likewise that the said Raphe Marshall the younger shall upon reasonable warninge and demaunde have fortye Couple of silver heared Conyes forth of the warren w^thin the above mencyoned p^rmisses, whereof Thirtie Couple to be Does, yf they be there to be had." Also 100 young apple trees and 20 Walnut trees. And lastly the said Henry Marshall, and Raphe Marshall the younger shall not "by the libertye aforesaid of removeinge theire moveable goods deface, dymynishe, or ympayre any p'te of the premisses herein mencyoned to be bargayned & solde by unglaseinge unwaynescottinge or impaleing of any p'te or p'ts of the premisses, etc., exceptinge only the armes in the wenscott and armes in the glasse wyndowes." Signed, Henry Marshall. Rapfe Marshall.

Deed endorsed "Marshall's Release of p'te of two annuities & of p'te of the £5,600. £800 of the debt discharged & £40 of the yerely anuitie." To all Christian people, etc., Henry Marshall, late of South Carleton, Esq., and Raphe Marshall the younger, Esq., son and heir apparent of the said Henry Marshall send greeting in our Lord God everlasting. Whereas John Rotherham of Seamers, in the parish of Great Marlow, co. Bucks., Esq., by indenture dated 13 July, 40 Elizabeth [1598], is to pay at Whit Sunday, 1604, to said Henry Marshall £5,600, and whereas he has paid £800 part of the said sum, and whereas by the said indenture he granted to the said Henry and Ralph annuities of £144 and £156, said Henry and Ralph release £40 out of the said annuities. Dated 9 November, 1598.

Close Roll. 5 Anne, Part 8, No. 21. Indenture dated 10 May, 1706, between William Marshall of Theddlethorpe, co. Lincoln, Gent., John Marshall, and William Marshall, his two sons, and Catherine Marshall his daughter, and William Doweswell of Humberston, co. Lincoln, Gent., and Susanna his wife of the one part, and Mathew Humberstone of the City of London, Esq., of the other part. The Marshalls sell to him a messuage in Humberstone. See Vol. i., p. 13.

Close Roll. 17 Car. II., Part 7, No. 8. Indenture dated 16 Feb., 17 Car. II. [1665-6], between Edmond Marshall of Newcastle upon Tyne, co. Northumberland, Draper, of the one part, and Francis Rogers of Netherthorpe in the parish of Thorpe Salvin, co. York, Esq., of the other part. Edmond Marshall for £110 sells to said Francis Rogers two ninth parts of the manor of Leeds. Covenant by Edmond Marshall and Frances his now wife for further assurance. Edward Marshall acknowledged this Indenture 21 Feb., in said year.

Close Roll, 1653, Part 21, No. 42. Indenture dated 13 April, 1653, between the Right Honble Sir Thomas Pope, Bart., and Earl of Downe in Ireland, Edward Twyford of Burford, co. Oxon, Gent., and Lancelott Grandger of Witney in the said co., Gent., of the one part, and Ralph Marshall, the younger, of Chawford, in the said co., yeoman, of the other part. Grant of lands in parish of Enston, now or late in the occupation of widow Marshall which were before granted to Nicholas Marshall, deceased, and to Nicholas Marshall his son by copy of court roll of the manor of Enston.

MISCELLANEA.

Notes of Fines.

Notts. 5 Henry VI. [1426-7]. Between Wiiliam Marshall of Southmuskham, William Besewyk, Vicar of Southmuskham, and John Marshall of Southmuskham, junior, plaintiffs, and Thomas de Leek of Holme, next Newerk, and Margaret his wife, defendants. Thomas and Margaret receive 100 marks for land in Southmuskham, etc.

Notts. Michaelmas, 21 Car. II. [1669]. Between Silvester Lawrence, gent., plaintiff, and Thomas Marshall, gent., and Anne his wife, and Henry Cam and Alice his wife, defendants, of two messuages, etc., in Newark. Consideration, £100.

Notts. Hillary, 27 and 28 Car. II. [1676]. Between Edward Marshall, gent., and Thomas Cliffe, gent., plaintiffs, and William Sawer and Elizabeth his wife, and Samuel Cookson and Millicent his wife, defendants, of two messuages, ten acres of land, ten acres of meadow, ten acres of pasture, and common of pasture in Girton and East Stoake. Consideration, £60.

Notts. Trinity, 34 Car. II. [1682]. Between Lawrence Oliphant, gent., and Robert Heron, gent., plaintiffs, and Thomas Marshall, Esq., and Anne his wife, Walter Fawnt, gent., and Anne his wife, defendants, of messuages and lands in Stirroppe, Oulcoats, North Collingham, South Collingham, and Sutton on Trent. Consideration, £500.

Notts. Hilary, 5 William & Mary [1693]. Between Thomas Marshall, gent., plaintiff, and Rebecca Wellard, widow, and Samuel Kelley, gent., and Dorcas his wife, defendants, of messuage in Newark upon Trent. Consideration, £100.

Notts. Trinity, 6 William and Mary [1694]. Between Francis Burton and John Myuuett plaintiffs, and Paul Jackson and Mary his wife, and Nicholas Marshall and Frances his wife, defendants, of a cottage, etc., in West Markham and East Drayton. Consideration, £60.

Lincolnshire. Michaelmas, 1653. Between Thomas Marshall the younger, William Palmer. gent,, and John Thorpe, gent., plaintiffs, and Thomas Marshall the elder, John Baynes the elder, John Baynes the younger, William Baynes, Thomas Day, gent., and Mary his wife, John Atkinson and Katherine his wife, Thomas Easterby and Justine his wife, William Williamott and Elizabeth his wife, and William Ostler and Susan his wife, defendants, of two cottages, fifty-three acres of meadow, fourty-four acres of pasture, etc., in Gresby, Huttoft, Sutton, Mablethorpe, and North Somercoats. Defendants acknowledge the said lands to be the right of Thomas Marshall the younger, as also those which they have of the gift of Thomas Marshall the elder. Consideration, £100.

Inquisitions Post Mortem.

Inq. post mortem. Chancery Inquisitions, 3 and 4 Philip and Mary, Part 1, No. 32:—Inq. taken at Stratford Langthorne, in co. Essex, 15 Oct., 3 and 4 Philip and Mary, on the death of Ralph Marshall. He died 21 March, 2 and 3 Philip and Mary. Nicholas Marshall is his son and heir, and was aged five years and more at his father's death. See Vol. i., p. 88.

Inq. Post Mortem. Chancery Inquisitions, 5 Car. 1. Virtute officii, No. 17. Inquisition taken at Kirbymoreside, co. York, 28 Sept., 5 Car. 1. [1629], on the death of Henry Marshall of Eskdaileside in co. York. He died 20 August, before the taking of this inquisition, and was seized in fee of a messuage, etc., and close called the broad Inge, and piece of land called Longe tonge, etc., etc., in Eskdaile-side, and Margaret now wife of Bartholemew Ableson, aged 27, and Anne now wife of Richard White, aged 25, are his daughters and next heirs. See Vol. i., p. 266.

Marriage Allegations.

Surrey. Faculty Office:—1688, April 19. Willm Symons of Weibridge, bachr, aged about 27, and Jane Marshall of Mickleham, spinster, aged about 22, to marry at Mickleham.

At Gloucester:—1703, May 9. Atwood Finch of Oxenton, aged 22, bachelor, and Mary Marshall of Elmston Hardwick, aged 22, spinster.

At Ipswich:—1640, Sept. 25. Robert Marshall to marry Mary Spatchett, widow, of St. Margaret's Ilketshall. 1681, June 24.

William Marshall to marry Hannah Onewright, both single, and of Ipswich. 1685, April 23. Edward Marshall of Debenham, single, to marry Sarah Punchard of Bedingfield, widow.

Monumental Inscriptions.

In churchyard belonging to St. Dunstan's in the West, in Breams Buildings :—

Here sleeps ovr babes in cilence heav'ns thaire rest
For God takes soonest those he loueth best.
Samewell Marshall the 2[d] sonne of
Edward Marshall & of Anne his wife
dyed May 27, 1631, aged two yeares.
Anne Marshall their first dav. dyed 21th
of Jvne, 1635, aged one yeare 9 moneths.
Nicholas Marshall their third soñ dyed
Decem. 5th, 1635, aged 5 yeares 6 moneths.

See Vol. i., app. p. 24.

At Lancing, co. Sussex :—

In Memory of Jane wife of John Marshall, who died Nov[br] 12th, 1878, aged 34 years. (Headstone, south-west of church).

At Howden, co. York :—

William Marshall, Baliffe of Howden Shire interred the 24th day of April, 1694. Gerard Marshall his Grandchild interred the 31th day of August, 1694. (Flat stone in nave).

At Swanscombe, co. Kent :—

The following inscriptions correct account at Vol. i., p. 14. See also Vol. ii., p. 82. On a ledger in the north aisle :—

Rev[d] Charles Robert Marshall died 12th April, 1823. Aged 58 Years.

On white marble tablet on north wall of north aisle near to the above ledger :—

In a vault beneath are deposited the remains of The Rev[d] Ch[s] Rob[t] Marshall, B.D. Rector of Cold Hanworth, Lincolnshire, Vicar of Exning, Suffolk, and youngest son of W. Marshall, Esq[r], of Thedlethorpe, Lincolnshire. He died 12th of April, 1823, aged 59 years. This tablet was erected by his widow Sarah only daughter of J. Parfett, Esq[r], of Putham, Hampshire.

On a headstone in Worlingworth churchyard, co. Suffolk :—

This spot of earth is Sacred to the remains of John and Phebe Marshall of this parish, who lived together half a century an honest and inoffensive life and in death were not divided. John Marshall departed this life April 6th 1850, Aged four score. Phebe his wife followed him July 6th 1850, Aged three score and ten.

In Parish Church, Huddersfield :—

In Memory of The Rev. John Marshall, B.A., Curate of Sidbury, Salop, who died at Manchester, Feb. 20, 1835, aged 39, on a journey to visit his now surviving parents, Thomas and Betty Marshall, of Thorpe, Almondbury. Also of Betty, wife of Thomas

Marshall, Esq., of Thorpe, near Almondbury, and mother of the above Rev. John Marshall. She died on the 11 Feb., 1842, aged 77 years. Also of Thomas Marshall, Esq., of Thorpe, near Almondbury, who died on the 19th Day of December, 1847, aged 85 years. Also of Jonas Hobson Marshall, last surviving son of the above Thomas and Betty Marshall, who died on the 20th day of January, 1849, aged 50 years. Also of Martha, daughter of the above Thomas and Betty Marshall, who died August 4th, 1859, aged 74 years.

Public Record Office. Bill Book, Vol. x., Trin. 25 Car. ii., No. 57:—

Edward Greathead, clerk, *v.* William Marshall as to Rectorial tythe of West Bridgford, co. Notts.

Patent Roll, 6 Edward iv.:—

Roll i., memb. 10. Richard Marshall of Scawton, co. York, yeoman,—pardon for outlawry.

Roll ii., memb. 14. Johanne Marshall of Kytelyngton, in co. Nottingham, gentlewoman,—general pardon, dated 5 Novr. Per Rex ipse.

Exchequer Lay Subsidy $\frac{141}{20}$:—

Joh'es Marchall, Taillour, per annum, lvij . viij.
Rob'us Marchall', per annum, . . Ciij . iiij.

Exchequer Lay Subsidy, 3-4 Car i. Notts., $\frac{160}{268}$:—

East Draiton. Anna Marshall, vid' in ter' xxs—iiijs.
Rampton. Will'us Marshall in ter' xxs—iiijs.

Exchequer Lay Subsidy, 18 Jac. i., $\frac{160}{279}$:—

East Drayton. Ric'us Marshall in boñ iijl—iijs.

From a MS. Vol. of Miscellaneous Collections by Gregory King, Rouge Dragon, in the possession of Walter Rye, Esq.:—

In pedigree of Turner, fo. 1081. Sarah, eldest daughter of Jacob Turner, married Thomas Marshall of Halden, co. Kent, gent.

College of Arms, Visitation of Nottinghamshire, 1662, MS., C 34, fo. 16:

John Dand (son of John Dand, born 1554) died in his father's lifetime having married . . . . daughter of . . . . Marshall of Tidwall, [co. Derby].

Add note to Vol. i., p. 67:—

Edward Marshall was Vicar of Maltby, 1730-1779, and was instituted on the death of Samuel Pickering, clerk, 24 Feb., 1729. Patron King George ii. See book *Blackburn* in Consistory Court at York, fo. 93. Probate of the will of his wife Rebecca (Stead), to whom he was married at Nottingham, 8 Oct., 1741, was granted to him 18 Nov., 1778, in Exchequer Court at York, he being sole executor and residuary legatee.

MARSHALL OF LOUTH, CO. LINCOLN, ETC.

John Marshall had issue, John Marshall, of Greystonegill, co. York, who died at Menwith Hill, in Hempsthwaite, near Harrowgate, 16. . . He had issue :—

1. John Marshall, Curate of Slaidburn.

2. Henry Marshall, Rector of Orby and Salmonby, co. Linc., obiit 1741; married at West Theddlethorpe, co. Lincoln, 1694, Mary, daughter of — Bottomley, of Louth, and had Joshua, born 21st June, 1695, curate of Orby, 1725, died 1729, unmarried, and buried at Orby; and Mary, married at East Theddlethorpe, 1726, as his second wife, the Hon. Charles Bertie, son of Robert, 4th Earl of Lindsey, who died, *s.p.* and was buried at West Theddlethorpe, 1727. (See M.I. *Gent. Mag.*, Vol. 78, pt. i., p. 20). She was buried there in 1746. His first wife was Dame Margery Newcomen, relict of Nicolas Newcomen, died 1725.

3. Thomas Marshall.

4. Leonard Marshall.

1. Mary.

John Marshall, Curate of Slaidburn from 1687-1701, when he was made Vicar of Mumby, where he died 30th October, 1702, having married in 1687, Hellen, daughter of — Yeadon, of Sledburn, and left issue :—

1. John Marshall son and heir, surgeon in the army temp. Queen Anne, was at the storming of Port Royal, Nova Scotia, under the command of Genl. Nicholson. He afterwards settled and practised at Louth, of which town he was warden four times. He died 17th April, 1759, and was buried at Louth, æt. 68 (see M.I., Vol. i., p. 312), having married 1715, Jane, second daughter of Christopher Hilyard, of Kelstern, by whom he had issue; and secondly, Sarah, second daughter of John Sopford, R.N., of Utterby, she died 29th November, 1760, *s.p.*

2. Henry Marshall, born 1699, Curate of Salmonby, and afterwards Rector and patron of that benefice. He died 1778. Married Katherine, daughter of —, died 1797, buried at Salmonby, and had one son, Henry, Rector of Salmonby 1779, died 1812, buried in the chancel of Salmonby.

1. Elizabeth, born 1692.

2. Mary, born 1702.

3. Hannah, wife to Thomas Elmhirst, of Lusby and Stixwold, ob. 1764.

4. Isabella, wife to — Salmon, of Stepney, surgeon, living 1778.

John Marshal above named had issue by Jane (Hilyard) his wife :—

1. Jane, born 1716, wife to Charles Newark, Alderman of Grimsby.

2. John Marshall, born 1717, ob. infans.

3. Ann, born 1718, ob. infans.

4. Christopher Marshall, born 1720-1, a surgeon in the Royal Navy, married and had issue.

5. Dorothy, born December 15th, 1721.

6. Hilyard Marshall, Alderman, a surgeon of Grimsby, born at Louth, 29th February, 1724, where he died, and was buried 13th March, 1797. He married Mary Bowis. She died 1812, aged 73, and was buried at Grimsby. They had, 1, Jane, born 1757, ob. *s.p.* 2, Mary-Anne, daughter and co-heir, born at Grimsby, 4th July, 1769, died 11th April, 1818, and buried at Grimsby. Married 10th June, 1800, to the Rev. J. C. Leppington, and had issue. 3, Mary, wife of T. Tomlinson, of Humberston.

7. George Marshall, born 1st December, 1726, died *s.p.*

8. Henry Marshall, born 5th March, 1727. Surgeon in the Royal Navy on board the Capstan; was at the capture of Minorca by the French. Died at Gibraltar 2nd August, 1756.

EXTRACTS FROM VARIOUS REGISTERS.

(Continued from page 50.)

SOUTH MUSKHAM, CO. NOTT^M.

Baptism.

1590. Sept. 6. John son of Robert Marshall.

Marriages.

1701. March 5. John Marshall and Esther Brown.
1702. Aug. 26. Thomas Taylor and Mary Marshall.
1710-11. Feb. 7. George Marshall and Mary Blow both of Sutton-on-Trent.

Burials.

1603-4. Jan. 31. Bridget wife of Robert Marshall.
1603-4. March 5. Charles son of Robert Marshall.
1604. April 6. Robert Marshall.
1610. Dec. 7. Raffe Marshall.
1612. April 19. Frances, wife of Raffe Marshall, Esq.
1787. Aug. 4. Revd John Marshall, found drownded, aged 41.
1792. Feb. 26. Mary Marshall, died the 24th, aged 56.

SHELTON, CO. NOTT^M.

Francis Marshall, Gent., and Dorothie Hartopp married May 31st, 1604.

John fforster, Gent., and Anne Marshall married on Shrove Sunday, 1607.

William Mearing, Gent., and Mrs Isabell Marshall married on Shrove Sunday, 1607.

Ralph Marshall, Gent., buried December the 10th, 1617.

Mr. Ralph Martiall and Katherine Breedon married Jan^ry, the 24th, 1633.

Ralph Marshall buried March 17th, 1636-7.

NEWARK, CO. NOTT^M.

Baptisms.

1599. May . . .* John, son of William Marshall.
1599. Sept. 16.* Thomas, son of John Marshall.
1599. Octr 11.* Robert son of Mr Raphe Marshall, Esqr.
1661. Augt. 24. Elizabeth dau'r of Mr Thomas Marshall.
1662. April 18. Michaell son of Thomas Marshall.
1663.* Sept. 14. Richard son of William Marshall.
1663.* Nov. 26. Isabella dau. of Thomas Marshall.
1665.* May 2. Ann dau. of William Marshall.
1665-6.* March 1. Henry son of Thomas Marshall.
1666-7.* Jany 30. Thomas son of William Marshall.
1669.* April 25. Francis Marshall son of Thom.
1674. Aug. 9.* Edward Marshall son of William.
1689-90.* Feb. 13. John son of John Marshall. Buried 28 Feby.
1691.* Aug. 2. Francis, son of John Marshall.

Marriages.

1599. Octr 30.* William Walker and Margaret Marshall.
1624 (?). Septr 4. Mr Gabriel Savell and Dorothy Marshall.
1688. July 26.* John Wilson and Anne Marshall.
1689. April 23.* John Marshall and Eliz. Hoyes.
1800. Jan^ry 14. George Marshall and Shady Bower both of Newark, by banns.

Burials.

1599. Augt 19.* Elizabeth Marshall, æt. 2.
1599, Septr 18.* Thomas son of John Marshall, infant.
1624. Aug. 2. "Mr Francis Marshall departed." [Buried at South Muskham, 3 Aug^t., 1624, Francis Marshall.]
1655. Decr 22. Mrs Frances wife of Mr Thomas Marshall.
1662.* Aug. 11. Michael Marshall son of Thomas.
1668.* Jany 22. Thomas Marshal son of Thomas.
1669.* Feb. 6. Rob't Marshal son of Thomas.
1683.* July 15. Anne wife of Mr Thomas Marshall.
1683.* Septr. 5. Mr Thomas Marshall.
1748-9. March 4. A child of Mr John Marshall.
1753. Jan^ry 1. Mr Marshall sen^r.
1772. Decr 27. Mr John Marshall.

SOUTHWELL, CO. NOTT^M.

Marriages.

1594. June 2. Nicholas Godfrey and Agnes Martiall.
1723. Sept. 17. Edward Bettinson of Upton and Elizabeth Marshall of Southwell.

* Those entries marked with an asterisk are from the transcripts at York.

Burials.

1627. March 26. John Martiall gent.
1628. April 27. Katherine dau'r of Katherine Marshall.
1682-3. Feb. 12. Martha wife of Mr John Marshall.
1685. June 21. Webster son of Mr John Marshall.
1689-90. Feb. 20. Isaac and Rebecca children of Richard Laughton. (Transcript.)
1699. May 26. John Marshall.
1776. Nov. 21. Mr Gervase Marshall.
1781. Feb. 26. John Marshall of Newark.

SUTTON ON LOUND, CO. NOTTINGHAM.

1566. Sept. 29. Sutton. John Marshall of Whitwell & Margarett Throop were maryed.
1613. April 28. Lound. Edward Marshall & Mary Portor were maryed.
1614. Dec. 27. Lound. Joahne Marshall the wife of Oliu'. Buried.
1614-15. Jan. 30. Lound. Oliu' Marshall and Alice Kirkby. Married.
1615. Nov. 19. Lound. Libius Marshell soone of Oliver Marshell. Bapt.
1619. May 19. Lound. Thomas son of Oliver Marshall. Bapt.
1625. June 23. Sutton. Richard Hibberson and Alice Marshall. Married.
1626. Dec. 27. Elizabeth dau. of same. Bapt.

BLOXHAM, OR BLOXHOLME, CO. LINCOLN.[1]

Baptisms.

1605. Aug. 15. Wm the sonne of Wm Marshall.
1608. March 12. Anne the daughtr of Wm Marshall.
1612. Dec. 14. Elizabetha filia Wmi Marshall.
1615. March 2. Thomas fili' Wmi Marshall.
1620. June 1. Christopherus Marshall.
1632. William Marshall, gardianus.
1633. Dec. 12. Sara Marshall filia Johannæ illigitima.
1635. June 18. Thomas Marshal filius Thomæ Marshall.[2]
1649. Jan. 17. Robert soñe of Xp̃r Marshall & ffriswyd his wife.
1663. May 20. Nicolis Marshall.
1685. Robert Marshall was churchwarden.
1687. March 26. Esther the supposed Daughter of Nicholas Marshall and Helena Truman. Buried April 11 following.

Burials.

1640. June 15. Wiłłus Marshall sen. sepultus fuit.
1672. June 25. Widow Marshall was buried.

From these entries and the Abstracts of Wills at Vol. i., p. 218, I have drawn out the following pedigree :—

[1] From the Transcripts at Lincoln. [2] Son of Thomas Marshall who removed to this parish from Marston about this date.

William Marshall of Bloxholme, sen., Church-warden, 1632. Buried there, 15 June, 1640. ═╤

William Marshall. Bapt. at Bloxholme, 15 August, 1605. Ment^{d} in will of his sister Jone, 1644.	Thomas Marshall. Bapt. at Bloxholme, 2 March, 1615. Ment^{d} in will of his sister Jone, 1644.	Christopher Marshall of Bloxholme, Co. Linc., labourer. Bapt. there, 1 June, 1620. Ment^{d} in will of his sister Jone, 1644. Will dated 5 Oct., proved 30 Nov., 1667. ═	Frideswide. Ex'x to her husband, 1667. Buried at Bloxholme, 25 June, 1672. Will dated 23 June, proved 12 July, 1672.	Jone. Will as of Bloxholme, Co. Linc., spinster, dated 21 Sept., 1644. Reg^{d} at Linc. in Vol. for 1643-4, fo. 233. ═ Sarah. Bapt. at Bloxholme, 12 Dec., 1633. Ment^{d} in her mother's will, 1644.	Anne. Bapt. at Bloxholme, 12 March, 1608. Ment^{d} in will of her sister Jone, 1644.	Elizabeth. Bapt. at Bloxholme, 14 Dec., 1612. Ment^{d} in will of her sister Jone, 1644.

Issue of Christopher Marshall and Frideswide:

Robert Marshall of Bloxholme, yeoman. Bapt. there, 17 Jan., 1649. Ment^{d} in his father's will, 1667, in his mother's will, 1672, and in will of his brother Christopher, 1687. Will dated 18, pro. 27 Oct., 1692.	William Marshall of Rouston, Co. Linc., yeoman. Mentioned in his father's will, 1667, in his mother's will, 1672, and pro. will of his brother Christopher, 1687. Pro. will of his bro. Robert, 1692. Will dated 2 Dec., 1700, pro. 26 Sept., 1702. ═	Hester. Ment^{d} in will of Robert Marshall, 1692. Pro. her husband's will, 1702.	Kellam or Kenelm Marshall. Ment^{d} in his father's will, 1667, as under 16, in his mother's will, 1672, in will of his brother Christopher, 1687, and in will of his brother Robert, 1692.	Christopher Marshall of the City of Lincoln, gent. Ment^{d} in his father's will, 1667, and in his mother's will, 1672. Will dated 5 May, 1687, pro. 10 June, foll^{g}. Buried at St. Swithin, Linc., 8 May, 1687.	Nicholas Marshall. Bapt. 20 May, 1663. Mentioned in his mother's will, 1672, in will of his bro. Christopher, 1687, and in will of his brother Robert, 1692.	Martha. Ment^{d} in her father's will, 1667, and in her mother's will, 1672. Married John Paxton of Gosberton, Co. Linc. Both ment^{d} in will of Christopher Marshall in 1687, and in will of Robert Marshall, 1692. ═ ↓	Grace. Ment^{d} in her father's will, 1667, and in her mother's will, 1672.

Issue of William Marshall and Hester:

Barbara. Ment^{d} in will of Christopher Marshall, 1687, in will of Robert Marshall, 1692, and in her father's will, 1700.	Hester. Ment^{d} in will of Christopher Marshall, 1687, in will of Robert Marshall, 1692, and in her father's will, 1700.	Elizabeth. Ment^{d} in will of Christopher Marshall, 1687, in will of Robert Marshall, 1692, and in her father's will, 1700.	Anne. Ment^{d} in will of Robert Marshall, 1692, and in her father's will, 1700.	Sarah. Ment^{d} in will of Robert Marshall, 1692, and in her father's will, 1700.

HOUGH ON THE HILL, CO. LINCOLN.[1]

1586. May 15. Miles harvie [and] Eline Marshall, married.
1590. Oct. 3. Alex. Marshall. Bapt.
1590-1. Jan. 20. John Marshall. Bapt.
1590-1. Feb. 17. John Marshall. Buried.
1593. Barnardus Marshall sepultus Aprilis ix^{o}.
1597. Elisabeth Marshall vicesimo tertio Junij, baptisat'.
1603. Nov. 18. Richardus filius Augustini Marshall. Bapt.
1604. Augustine Marshall was churchwarden.
1606. April 17. Vid. Marshall. Buried.
1606. Sept. 16. Elenor filia Augustini Marshall. Bapt.
1607. June 16. William Marshall. Buried.
1608. May 6. Jana filia Augustini Marshall. Bapt.
1611. May 5. Thomas filius Augustini Marshall. Bapt.
1615. Thomas Allen and Winiferd Marshall the xxijth of May, nupt.
1624-5. Feb. 3. Robert Seamer, yeoman, & Elisabeth Marshall, singlewoman. Married.
1663. March 29. The wife of Alexander Marshall, buried.
1666. June 29. Allexander Marshall of Brandon, buried.

MARSTON, CO. LINCOLN.[1]

1585. Dec. 19. Thomas Marshall sonn to Myles Marshall. Bapt.
Miles Marshall was churchwarden in 1598.
1594-5. Jan. 18. Mary Marshall daughter to Barnard Marshall. Bapt.
1615. Dec. 7. Elizabeth the wife of Thomas Goodburne was buried.
1616-7. Jan. 4. Gervase the sō of Tho. Marshall. Bapt.
1619. March 31. Alice the daughter of Thomas Marshall. Bapt.
1624. May 23. Beniamin Marshall sonne to Tho. Marshall. Bapt.
1625-6. Jan. 18. Anne Goodborne wife to Thomas, buryed.
1628. April 15. Marie ye doghter of Thomas Marshal. Bapt.
1632. Aug. 26. Richard ye sonne of Thomas Marshall. Bapt.
1636. March 16. Susanna Marshall was buried.

For the evidences upon which the following pedigree is based refer to Vol. i., 74, 78, 80, 97-99, 224, 242, 244, 246, 278, 305, 323, 325, 327; App. 7, 8, 9, 12, 44; Vol. ii., Part i., 50, 59, 61, 65, 78, 80, 98, 108, 113; Part ii., 80. *Notes and Queries*, 6 Series, vii., 123. *The Visitations of Lincolnshire*, 1634, (C. 23, Index i., fo. 73), *and Yorkshire*, 1666, (C. 40, fo. 133), the portions of the pedigree proved by these records and E.1. are printed in italics.

ARMS.—Sable, three bars argent, a canton ermine.

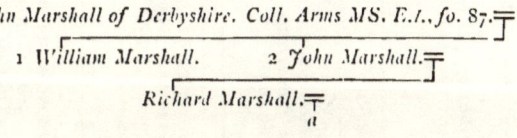

John Marshall of Derbyshire. Coll. Arms MS. E.1., fo. 87.=

1 *William Marshall.* 2 *John Marshall.*=

Richard Marshall.=

a

[1] From the transcripts at Lincoln.

a

John Marshall of Brandon in the parish of Hough, Co. Lincoln. Will dated 21 Dec. 1529, proved in Consistory Court at Lincoln, 7 May, 1530. = *Margaret.* Executrix to her husband, 1529.

Johan dau'r of John Loughborow of Folkingham. 1 *wife.* = *Miles Marshall.* Mentd as "eldest son," in his father's will, 1529, then under age. Mentd in his brother's will, 1542. = *Isabel dau'r of Hugh Burdet of Brandon.* 2 *wife.*

Hugh Marshall of the par. of Hough. Mentd in his father's will, 1529. Will dated 22 Sept., 1542. Registered in Consistory Court at Lincoln, Vols. for 1545-6, Book ii., fo. 129. = ... dau'r of Alexander Burder. Ex'or to Hugh Marshall.

Elizabeth. Mentd in her brother's will, 1542.

Margaret. Mentd in her brother's will, 1542.

Jennet. Mentd in her brother's will, 1542.

Agnes. Mentd in her brother's will, 1542.

John Marshall. called eldest son in Visitation of Lincolnshire, 1634. ? an error for Thomas.

Ellen dau'r of Edmond Burdet of Brandon. 1 *wife.* = *Thomas Marshall of Brandon.* Will dated 17 May, 1570, proved in Consistory Court at Lincoln, 16 June following. *Eldest son.* = *Katherine, dau'r of John Bye of Hough.* Pro. her husband's will, 1570. 2 *wife.*

Margaret. Mentioned in her father's will, 1570; and in will of her brother, William Marshall, 1607.

Barnard Marshall. Mentd in will of his brother, Thomas Marshall, 1570. Pro. the will of his sister, Isabell Marshall, 1590. Buried at Hough, 9 April, 1593. 2 *son.* = *Elizabeth, dau'r of . . . . Menesforde of Hough.* Will pro. in Consistory Court at Linc., 5 August, 1606.

Elizabeth. Married Robert Menesford of Hough.

Miles Marshall of Marston, Co. Lincoln. Mentd in will of his brother, Thomas Marshall, 1570. Churchwarden of Marston, 1598. Will dated 8 Aug., pro. in Consistory Court at Lincoln, 7 Oct., 1620. = *Suzan, dau'r of Dennis Spendluff, of Hougham, Co. Linc.* Pro. her husband's will, 1620. Buried at Marston, 16 March, 1636. 1

Isabell. Will of 6 Feb., 1590, pro. in Consistory Court at Lincoln, 5 Mar. following. 2 *dau'r.*

Alice. 3 *dau'r.*

Margaret. 4 *dau'r.*

Augustine Marshall of Brandon, called eldest son in his father's will, 1570. Churchwarden of Hough in 1604. Pro. the will of his brother, William Marshall, 1607. Will dated 21 Jan., 1612, and codicil dated 11 Sept., 1616, proved in Consistory Court at Lincoln, 13 Nov., 1616; and in P.C.C., 18 Feb., 1624 (25 Clark.) = Margery. Mentd in will of Willm Marshall, 1607. Pro. her husband's will, 1616, and again in 1624. Will dated 17 June, 1638, pro. in Consistory Court at Linc., 17 *Nov.?* 1638.

a

Miles Marshall. Mentd in his father's will, 1570, then under age. Mentd in will of his brother, William Marshall, 1607.

William Marshall. Mentd in his father's will, 1570. Bur. at Hough, 16 June, 1607. Will dated 11 June, 1607, pro. in Consistory Court at Lincoln, 24 June following.

Parnell. Mentd in her father's will, 1570; and in will of her brother, Augustine Marshall, 1612.

Mary. Mentd in her father's will, 1570; and in will of her brother, Willm Marshall, 1607. ? Married 12 Oct., 1589, to Francis Walcot or Walker of Fryston, in par. Cathorpe, and had issue Ellen. See Vol. i., p. 99.

b

a — b

Augustine Marshall. Ment^{d} in will of William Marshall, 1607. Called eldest son in his father's will, 1612.

Alexander Marshall. Bapt. at Hough, 3 Oct., 1590. Ment^{d} in will of William Marshall, 1607. Called 2nd son in his father's will, 1612. Buried at Hough, 29 June, 1666. = His wife. Bur. at Hough, 29 Mar., 1663.

Edward Marshall. Ment^{d} in will of William Marshall, 1607. Called 3rd son in his father's will, 1612.

Richard Marshall of Brandon. Bapt. at Hough, 18 Nov., 1603. Ment^{d} in will of William Marshall, 1607. Called 4th son in his father's will, 1612. = Elizabeth, dau'r of Thomas Shipman of Scarrington, Co. Nott^{m}. Bapt. there 16 Feb., 1605. Married there 9 May, 1627. See *Genealogist*, New Series, Vol. iii., p. 156.

Thomas Marshall. Bapt. at Hough, 5 May, 1611. Called youngest son in his father's will, 1612. Ment^{d} in his mother's will, 1638.

" Anne, wife of Mr. Thomas Marshall," bur. at Newark, 15 July, 1683. ::: Thomas Marshall, admitted at St. John's College, Cambridge, 19 May, 1648, then aged 18. Admo'r to his father, 1653. Living at Maltby, Co. York, 1664, and at Stirrup, Co. Nott^{m}, in 1678. See Exchequer Lay Subsidy, York, $\frac{210}{393}$, and Close Roll, 31 Car. II., Part ii., No. 32. Thoroton's *History of Nottinghamshire*, Vol. iii., p. 424. Buried at Newark, Co. Nott^{m}, 5 Sept., 1683. Adm'on granted in Exchequer Court at York, 23 Sept., 1683, to his daughter Frances, wife of Timothy Ellis. = Frances, dau'r of Robert Saunderson of Serlby, Co. Nott^{m}, See Thoroton's *History of Nottinghamshire*, Vol. iii., p. 427; Raine's *History of Blyth*, p. 75. Bur. at Newark, 22 Dec., 1655.

Elizabeth. Bapt. at Hough, 23 June, 1597. Ment^{d} in will of William Marshall, 1607, and in her father's will, 1612. ? Mar. at Hough, 3 Feb., 1624-5, to Robert Seamer.

Ellinor. Bapt. at Hough, 16 Sept., 1606. Ment^{d} in will of William Marshall, 1607, and in her father's will, 1612.

Mary. Ment^{d} in will of William Marshall, 1607, and in her father's will, 1612.

Joane. Bapt. at Hough, 6 May, 1608. Ment^{d} in her father's will, 1612.

Thomas Marshall. Bapt. at Blyth, Co. Nott^{m}, 22 March, 1668-9. Buried there 3 May following.

Ann, died an infant. Buried at Maltby, 19 Dec. 1662.

Frances. Administered to her father's estate, 1683. = Timothy Ellis of Newark.

Thomas Marshall of Marston, son and heir. Bapt. there 19 Dec., 1585. Churchwarden of Marston in 1620. Ment^{d} in his father's will, 1620. Entered his pedigree in Visitation of Lincoln. 1634. *Of Bloxholm, Co. Lincoln, in* 1634. *Died* 22 *January*, 1653. = *Mary, dau'r of George Baynes of Lincoln. (Called Thomas Banes in Visitation of Yorkshire*, 1665.)

a

Winifred. Married at Hough, 22 May, 1615, to *Thomas Allen of Colcby, Co. Lincoln, clerk.* [2]

Anne.

Mary. Married Thomas Goodburne of Marston. Ment^{d} in her father's will, 1620.

Isabell, wife of Edward Downer of Great Ponton, Co. Linc. Ment^{d} in her father's will, 1620.

a

Gervace Marshall, *clerk*, *son and heir*, *aged* 18 *in* 1634. *Of Whatton in the Vale*, *Co. Nottingham*, 1665. Bapt. at Marston, 4 Jan., 1616-17. Instituted to the Vicarage of Whatton, 11 Sept., 1662. Buried there 21 March, 1675-6. Will dated 18 March, 1673, pro. in Consistory Court at York, 10 July, 1676. = Elizabeth, dau'r and co-heir of William Mundy of Bellow Park in the parish of Bilsthorpe, Co. Nott^m^. Ment^d^ (as also her husband) in her father's will, dated 18 June, 1648, proved in Exchequer Court at York, 3 Jan. following. Buried at Whatton, 30 November, 1663. [3]

Benjamin Marshall of Doncaster, *Co. York*, *aged* 41, 14 *Sept.*, 1665. Bapt. at Marston, 23 May, 1624. Entered his pedigree in Visitation of Yorkshire, 1666. Mayor of Doncaster, 1669. Bur. there 16 Nov., 1669. Will dated 9 Oct., 1669, pro. in Exchequer Court at York, 26 November following. [4] = *Elizabeth*, *dau'r of John Farnley of Thornhill*, *Co. York*, *and widow of William Maddocks of Doncaster*. Married there 17 Oct., 1661. Pro. her husband's will, 1669. Buried at Doncaster, 30 Oct., 1687. [5]

Richard Marshall. Bapt. at Marston, 26 Aug., 1632.

Thomas Marshall. Bapt. at Bloxholme, Co. Linc., 18 June, 1635. *Citizen of London*, 1665.

Alice. Bapt. at Marston, 31 March, 1619. Buried at Doncaster, 5 March, 1683. Will dated 16 June, 1681, proved in Exchequer Court at York, 24 April, 1684. = *Obadiah Martin*, Mayor and Innholder *of Doncaster*, 1668. Buried there 2 Aug., 1678. Will dated 26 Mar., 1678, proved in Exchequer Court at York, 15 August following.

Elizabeth. Buried at Doncaster, 3 Sept., 1666, then a "widow." = *Robert Walcot of Scredington*, *Co. Linc.* Buried at Doncaster, 1666. See Jackson's *History of St. George's Church*, *Doncaster*, app., p. 87.

Mary. Mentioned in will of Benjamin Marshall, 1669. Living at Doncaster in 1678, then a spinster, made affidavit that Obadiah Martin, who she therein calls "mye uncle," was buried in woollen. See Hatfield's *Historical Notices of Doncaster*, 1st Series, p. 360.

Mary. Bapt. at Marston, 15 April, 1628.

Gervase Marshall. Bapt. at Whatton, 19 Oct., 1648. Bur. there, 30 April, 1670.

Anne, dau'r of . . . . . Flower. Married at Whatton, 9 Feb., 1673-4. Bur. there, 18 October, 1678. = Thomas Marshall. Bapt. at Whatton, 22 Jan., 1649-50. Pro. his father's will, 1676. Buried at Scarrington, Co. Nott^m^, 4 Dec., 1707. Will as of Scarrington, husbandman, dated 1 Dec., 1707, pro. in Exchequer Court at York, 19 Dec. following. [6] = Winifred. Pro. her husband's will, 1707.

William Marshall. Ment^d^ in will of his brother, Thomas Marshall, 1707.

John Marshall of Grantham, barber, Ment^d^ in will of Thomas Martin, 1688; and in will of his brother, Thomas Marshall, 1707. Adm'on in Consistory Court at Lincoln, 3 Oct., 1711. = Hester Rowes or Rouse. Mar. at Grantham, Co. Linc., 27 April, 1694. Administratrix to her husband 1711. Adm'on to Robert Rouse of Grantham, in Consistory Court at Linc., 20 April, 1714.

Robert Marshall. Buried at Whatton, 7 May, 1671.

Mary. Bapt. at Whatton, 12 Jan., 1662-3.

b

Children of Thomas Marshall and Anne:

Thomas Marshall. Bapt. at Whatton 7 Dec., 1676. Bur. there, 6 Jan., 1683-4.

John Marshall. Born at Whatton. Bur. there, 18 Oct., 1678.

Elizabeth. Bapt. at Whatton, 14 Feb., 1674-5. [? Married William Bush, who is ment^d^ in will of Thomas Marshall, 1707. Bur. at Scarrington, 7 Apl., 1708. Had issue a dau., Sarah, bapt there, 16 Apl., 1697.]

a

a — *b*

Thomas Marshall. Bapt. at Whatton, 1 May, and bur. there, 26 August, 1688.

Gervase Marshall. Bapt. at Whatton, 21 Dec., 1692. Mentd in his father's will, 1707. Care of person of Gervase Marshall, son of Thomas Marshall of Scarrington, granted according to his election in Exchequer Court at York, to Mathew Hall, 23 April, 1709. (Nottm cum Bingham Act Book.) ═

Thomas Marshall. Bapt. at Whatton, 19 March, 1694-5. Mentd in his father's will, 1707.

Benjamin Marshall. Bapt. at Scarrington, 20 Oct., 1698. Mentd in his father's will, 1707.

Martin Marshall. Bapt. at Scarrington, 21 Nov., 1703. Mentioned in his father's will, 1707. Will as of St. Giles in the Fields, London, baker, dated 25 June, 1763, proved in P.C.C., 6 Sept. following. (440 Cæsar.) ═

Hanna. Bapt. at Whatton, 3 June, 1683. Mar. Mathew Hall. Buried at Scarrington, 18 Aug., 1728. ═

- **Thomas Hall.** Bapt. at Scarrington, 22 March, 1702-3.

Mary. Bapt. at Whatton, 1 Apl., 1684. Mar. at Scarrington, to John Caunt of Bridgford, 25 Nov., 1706.

Jane. Bapt. at Whatton, 20 Sept., 1690. Mentd in her father's will, 1707.

Winifrid. Bapt. at Scarrington, 7 March, 1700-1.

Gervase Marshall of Westminster, and of St. George's, Bloomsbury, London, baker. Mentd in Chancery Suit, 1753.[7]

William Marshall. Mentd in his father's will, 1763.

Winifred. Mentd in Chancery Suit, 1753. Proved her father's will, 1763.

Thomas Martin of Doncaster, gent. Pro. his mother's will, 1684. Bur. there, 5 Feb., 1688. Will dated 17 Jan., 1688, proved in Exchequer Court at York, 24 May 1690. (Vol. 61, fo. 246.) See Jackson's *Doncaster Charities*, p. 42; *Historical Notices of Doncaster*, 2nd Series, p. 134.

Robert Martin. Died s.p.

Alice. Married at Doncaster, 1 May, 1681. Mentd in will of her brother, Thomas Martin, 1688; and in her husband's will, 1715. Died 14 and bur. 16 August, 1728, at Doncaster, aged 76. ═ **John Cowley** of Doncaster, gent. Died 5 Feb., 1716-17, and bur. there. Will dated 2 Feb., 1715, proved in Exchequer Court at York. (Vol. 71, fo. 274.) ↓

Mary. Died s.p.

Penelope. Bapt. at Doncaster, 24 Oct., 1660. Mar. at Harworth, Co. Nottm, 6 Oct., 1687. Mentioned in will of her brother, Thomas Martin, 1688; and in her husband's will, 1722. ═ **Henry Rutter** of Worksop, Co. Nottm, mercer. Will dated 26 April, 1722. Adm'on in P.C.C., 4 March, 1734. (59 Ducie.) ↓

---

1 Called Anne dau'r of Robert Spendola of Dene, Co. Northampton, in Visitation of Yorkshire, 1666.

2 Marriage Licence at Lincoln. 1615. 8 April. Thos. Allen of Colby, clerk, æt. about 36 and Winifride Marshall of Hough æt. about 26, daūr of Miles Marshall of Marston, yeoman. His parents deceased; her father consents.

"Mr William Layng Vicar of Colbie, buried, Septr 26, 1614."—*Coleby Register*. He must have been succeeded by Thomas Allen, who is first mentioned in Coleby Register at the burial of a servant of his in 1616. The following entries in Coleby Register relate to him and his wife:—

Winifred Allen the wife of Thomas Allen, Vicar of Colebie, was buried the 10th day of March, 1643. Mr Thomas Allen Vicar of Colbie buried the xviij day of August, 1644.

Will of Thomas Allen of Colebie in the co. of Lincolne, Clark. Dated 27 June, 1644. To be buried in the Quiere under the blew stone neere to my wife. My sister Richardson and her four daughters. My land to William Allen my kinsman. John Allen my brother and his children. Makes said brother and his son William executors. Administration with will annexed to John Allen of Knighton, co. Leicester, brother of testator, in Consistory Court at Lincoln. (Vol. for 1643-4.) The testator omitted to sign the will, hence the administration.

3 Chancery Proceedings before 1714, "Whittington," Bundle 467. Marshall *v.* Munday. Bill of Complaint, exhibited, "17° die Maij 1650." "Humbly Complaineing sheweth vnto yor Lordshippes yor daylie Orato^rs^ Gervas Marshall of Whatton in ye Countie of Nottingham Clarke and Elizabeth his wife daughter and heire of Wittm Munday of Bellowe Parke in ye Contie of Nottingham yeoman deceased and Administratrix of ye goods and Chattles of Margrat Munday deceased yor Oratrixes sister late ye wife of [*blank*] Dauson alsoe deceased That whereas Anne Munday late of Bellowe parke aforesaid widd was in her life tyme possessed of a greate ꝑsonall estate to ye value of fiue hundred pounds at ye least and being thereof soe possessed she the said Anne Munday did make her last will and Testam^t^ in writing and thereby amongst other things did giue as followeth vizt That whereas by one deede or writinge by her formerly made she hadd giuen vnto Wittm Munday ye sonne of Wittm Munday of Bellowe Parke aforesaid ye sum̃e of fortye pounds of good and lawfull monie of England her will then was that Twentie pounds thereof should be and remaine vnto her God daughter Anne Munday in ye said will before named and ye other Twentye pounds thereof should be and remaine vnto Margrat Munday and yor Orato^r^ Elizabeth by the name of Margarett Munday and Elizabeth Munday sisters of ye said Wittm Munday deceased equally to be diuided betwixt them and of her said will she ye said Anne Munday widd did make ye said Wittm Munday of Bellowe parke aforesaid her sole Executo^r^ and shortly after That is to say in or about ye yeare of our Lord One Thousand six hundred Twentie and fiue ye said Anne Munday of Bellowe parke aforesaid widd dyed possessed of ye said great ꝑsonall estate by and after whose decease ye said Wittm Munday ꝓued ye said will and tooke vppon him ye execucõn thereof and possessed himselfe of ye said ꝑsonall estate And also receiued and possessed himselfe of ye said fortie pounds appointed to be raised by ye said deede and shortly after he ye said Wittm Munday did marrie and take to wife Judith But neũ ye lesse ye said Wittm Munday did not paie vnto yor Oratrix Elizabeth and her said sister Margrat nor to eyther of them ye said Twentie pounds nor anie ꝑte thereof but did alledge y^t^ yor Oratrix Elizabeth and her said sister Margrat being then w^th^in age could not giue vnto him ye said Wittm Munday a sufficient dischardge thereof And ye said Wittm Munday ye Executo^r^ being likewise seised in his demesne as of ffee of and in diũs Messuages Lands Tenem^ts^ and Hereditam^ts^ in Lenton Edenstowe and Kersall in ye said Countie of Nottingham and in other lands in ye Countie of ye Towne of Nottingham And being alsoe possessed of all or ye most ꝑte of ye said ꝑsonall estate left vnto him by ye said Anne Munday widd and haueing in his hands and Custodie ye writings Euedences Escripts and minnem^ts^ touchinge and concerninge ye said lands he ye said Wittm Munday did make his last will and Testam^t^ and thereof did make and ordeyne ye said Judith his wife his sole Executrix and about [*blank*] yeares sithence dyed possessed of ye most ꝑte of ye said ꝑsonall estate left vnto him by ye said Anne Munday and of a good ꝑsonall estate of his owne And also dyed seised in his demesne as of ffee of and in ye said lands and p^r^misses in Lenton Edenstowe and Kersall in ye said Countie of Nott̃ and in ye said Countie of ye Towne of Nottinghã leaueing yor Oratrix Elizabeth his sole daughter and heire." (Judith, the widow, having a (life?) interest would not pay. Margaret, the sister, had died intestate, and without issue.)

4 In the original Visitation, this note of the authority on which the arms were allowed is given: "For proofe of coat Mr Marshall shewed me part of a pedigree in a parchment Roll signed by R. Chester Herald a° 1562." I suppose "R" to have been Robert Cooke, afterwards Clarenceux.

5 William Maddox was of Doncaster, Innholder, married at Pontefract in 1641. Buried at Doncaster, 8 Aug., 1660. Will dated 4 Aug., 1660, proved by his relict in Exchequer Court at York, 29 May, 1661.

6 He probably had three wives, as there is a Marriage Allegation in Archdeaconry of Nottingham, 24 July, 1680, for Thomas Marshall of Aslocton, husbandman, widower, and Hannah Wilcock of Whatton, spinster, aged 23. Some information as to this Thomas and his father, Gervase Marshall, Vicar of

South Muskham, co. Nottingham.

The following entries in this register should be added to those given at p. 79 *ante*.

1590. Oct. 1. Rauffe Marshall the sonne of Rob't Marshall. Bapt.
1591. Sept. 15. Fraunces Marshall the daught. of Rauffe Marshall. Bapt.
1592. Aug. 8. Fraunces Marshall the daught of Rauff Marshall. Bapt.
1593-4. Jan. 22. Robert Oglethorpe a Yorkshire gent., and Anne the daughter of Henrie Marshall. Married.
1593. Nov. 3. William Marshall son of Ralph Marshall. Bapt.
1594. Dec. 15. Margaret dau. of Ralph Marshall. Bapt.
1595. Dec. 19. Alice dau. of Ralph Marshall. Bapt.
1597. March 26. Brigett dau. of Ralph Marshall. Bapt.
1606. July 6. Richard Browne of this parish and Joane Marshall of the parish of Newarke upon Trent. Married.

There are several Marshalls connected with South Muskham, to whom I am unable to assign places in the following pedigree. The adm'on of Robert Marshall, who died in 1604, will be found in Vol. ii., Part 1, p. 102. He appears to have been related to persons of the name residing at Staveley Woodthorpe, co. Derby. See pages 44-46.

Francis Marshall, who died at Newark, and was buried at South Muskham, 3 August, 1624, may have been a son of Ralph Marshall, who died in 1617. It will be noticed in the pedigree that he had two daughters, both named Frances, and they are entered as "daughter" in the parish register. It is not improbable that the word "daughter" in one of these cases has been written in error for "son." The will of Francis Marshall "of Newark upon Trent, Esq.," is dated 29 July, 1624, and was proved by his sister Bridget Marshall, 4 May, 1626. He gives "to Dorothie Marshall my wife the bed whereon I lie." (Vol. i., p. 265.) I find a Dorothy Marshall marrying at Newark, 4 Sept., 1624, to Gabriel Savill. He was buried there 26 March, 1625. Her will, dated 3 April, 1625, was proved at York, 4 May, 1626 (Vol. i., p. 305). The same day be it noted as that of her first husband, Francis Marshall. She was buried at Newark, 4 April, 1625. I cannot vouch for the accuracy of these dates.

Whatton, will be found in the Public Record Office, from suits relating to the tithes of Whatton, Bill Book, Vol. x., Hilary, 23 and 24 Car. II., No. 49; and Mich., 21 Car. II., Bill Book, Vol. xii., Mich., 25 Car. II., No. 58; and Trinity, 29 Car. II., No. 75.

7 Chancery Proceedings, 1714-1758, Winter, 590. Marshall *v.* Marshall. Bill of Complaint, exhibited 6 Nov., 1753, of Gervas Marshall, of Westminster, Co. Midd'x, Baker, also of parish of St. George, Bloomsbury. "One Martin Marshall your orators uncle dealing in meal and flour." Winifred Marshall, one deft., under age of 21, by her father, the said Martin, of St. Giles in the Fields, Co. Midd'x, Baker.

Grant of Crest to Henry Marshall.

To all and singuler aswell Kinges Heraldes & officers of Armes as Nobles Gentilmen and others which these presents shall see or here William Heruye otherwise called Clarencieulx Principall Heralde and King of Armes of the southe Easte and West partes of England from the Ryuer of Trent sendeth due comendations and greatynge. For as moche as auncientlie from the begynynge ye valiaunt and vertuous actes of excellent parsons haue bene comended to the worlde with sondry monuments and remembrances of their good deserts Emonges the which one of the chefiste and most vsuall hath ben the bearinge of signes & tokens in shildes called Armes the which ar none other thinges than euidences and demonstraco͠ns of prowes & valour dyuerslie distributed accordinge to the quallities and deserts of the parsons that such signes and tokens of the dilligent faythfull and cowragious might apere before the negligente cowarde and ignorant and be an efficient cause to moue stirre and kyndle the hartts of men to the imytaco͠n of vertue and nobleness Euen so hath the same bene and yet is continuallye obserued to thyntent that such as haue don comendable service to theyr Prince or Contrey eyther in warr or peace may both receyue due honor yn their lyves and also deryue the same successiuelie to theire posteritie after them And whereas Henry Marshall of Carleton in ye Counte of Nottinghame esquyer is descended of ye right line of the Marshalls of ye said Counte of Nottingham and he not certeyne how to deryue hym selfe theryn hath ynstantlie required me the say^d Carencieulx King of Armes to make searche yn the Registers and recordes of myne office for the trew and parfect descent to him belonginge and so to sett forth suche armes as is to him incident and lawfull to be used and borne whiche accordinglie I did accomplishe and founde the said Henry Marshall to be ye sonne and heire of John Marshall sonn and heire to Thomas Marshall which Thomas was sonne and heire to Ralph Marshall of Carlton in the parishe of Muscam in the said Counte esquyre and so fyndinge the trew and perfecte dissent of the said Henrye coulde not without his greate iniurye but sett forth such Armes as was incident to him from his Auncestors That is to saye he beareth Sables three barres argent a canton ermyn. And forasmuche as I founde no Creaste belonginge to ye saide armes as comonlie to all auncient armes ther belonged none I haue giuen unto hym by waye of encrease for his Creaste and Cognisaunce vppon a wreathe argent and sables A man of Armes from the weaste vppwarde armed in an Armoure of percell gilte his beauer open with a plume of fethers of dyuers collers on his helme wearing a scarfe bawdrickwise with a staff gold in his hand, mantled gules doubled argent as more playnelie aperith depicted on this margent, which Armes and Creaste I the saide Clarencieulx Kinge of Armes by powre and auctorite to myne office annexed and graunted under the greate seale of England haue ratefied and confirmed geuen and graunted and by theise p^rsent' do ratefye and confirme geue & graunte unto and for the saide Henry Marshall esquyre and to his posterite to use beare and shew for euer more in shilde cote armoure or otherwise and therein to be reuested at his and their libertie and pleasure without ympediment lett or interupco͠n of any person or persons. In witnes wherof I ye said Clarencieulx Kinge of Armes haue signed theise pntes w^t my hande and putt thereunto ye seale of myne office & ye seale of myne Armes. Yeuen at London ye firste of June yn ye yeare of the reigne of owre most dread souereigne Ladye Elizabeth by the grace of god Queene of England Fraunce and Ireland deffendor of the fayth, &c.

W. heruy al's clarencieulx
King of Armes.

The original patent was in the hands of John Bird, Scrivener, in Warwick Lane, London, on the 18 January, 1639. He was probably a descendant of the grantee. See *Note* 2 to the following pedigree.

Pedigree of Marshall of South Carlton,

co. Nottingham.

For the evidences upon which this pedigree is based, see Vol. i., 2, 229, 265, 323, 326; Vol. ii., Part i., 14, 16, 56, 100, 101; Part ii., 70-73, 79, 80. College of Arms MSS., Philpot 30, fo. 109^b;

Derby and Notts. M.P. Vis I., fo. 58; EDN. 10, fo. 64. (*Visitation of Lincolnshire*, 1592, signed "Thomas Marshall," "Richard Marschall.") The portions printed in italics are from the latter MS. Thoroton's *History of Nottinghamshire*, Vol. iii., p. 151.

Will'm Marshall of Carleton, Co. Nott. 1 = *Katherin d. to Thomas Leeke.*

John Marshall. = *Eliz. d. to Raufe Bingham.*
Thomas Marshall.
Robert Marshall.
Jone.

Rauffe Marshall of South Carlton in the par. of South Muskham. Died 20 Sept., 1505. Inq. p. m. dated 16 Nov., 1505. = *Katherin d. to Tho. Neville of Rowleston.*
Richard Marshall.
Agnes wife to Laurence Hatfeilde.
Eliz. wife to Jo. Burton.
Elline wife to Thomas White.

Thomas Marshall of South *Carleton.* Aged 40 at date of his father's Inq. p. m. Died 22 Jan., 1523-4. Inq. p. m. dated 16 Sept., 1524. = *Ann d. & heire to Willm Hunston of Calles.* Should be Agnes d. and h. of William Muston of Calais.
Richard Marshall. ? Mar. Catherine dau. of Anthony Staunton. See Coll. of Arms MS., C. 34. Thoroton's *Notts.*, Vol. i., p. 316.
Agnes wife to Thomas Ellis of Swineshead and Great Ponton, Co. Linc. He died 28 April, 1545. Inq. p.m. =

Alice wife to Andrew Garnon. Harleian Soc. Vol. iv., p. 135. =
Isabell wife to Thomas Huett. Should be "Hunt." Harleian Soc. Vol. iv., p. 167. =
Elizabeth wife to James Ward.

John Marshall of South Carlton, Merchant of the Staple of Calais. Aged 25 at the date of his father's Inq. p.m. Party to an indenture dated 9 Jan., 1544. Claimed part of the Manor of South Muskham, 34 Henry VIII., 1542-3, and 4 and 5 Philip and Mary, 1557-8. Purchased half the Manor of South Muskham of Sir Wm. Paulett, Knt., Lord St John. 2 = *Ann d. to Henry Cave.* Living 22 July, 1544.
John Marshall. *2nd son.* 3

1 *Will'm Marshall.* Died s.p. before 1562.

2 *Henry Marshall* of South Carlton, Esq. Claimed part of the Manor of South Muskham, 2 Eliz., 1559-60. Had grant of a crest, 1 June, 1562. Mentd in will of his brother, John Marshall, 1582. In parts beyond the seas, 14 July, 1596. Party to an indenture dated 9 Nov., 1598. = *Mawde, d. and heir of Will'm Scrimser, son of Rich. son of Tho. son of Will'm son of Geoffry, which Geffrey mar. the d. & heire to . . . Muschampe, by Eliza. d. & coheir to Nicho. Midleton.*

3 *Raufe* Marshall. Had lease of a farm from his brother Henry, 1578, then of South Muskham. Mentd in will of his brother, John Marshall, 1582. Proved will of his brother, Francis Marshall, 1606. Buried at South Muskham, 7 Dec., 1610. Will dated 4 Dec., 1610, pro. in Peculiar Court of Southwell, 7 May, 1611. =

Robert Marshall. Mentd in will of Francis Marshall, 1606; and in his father's will, 1610.
Anne. Mentd in will of Francis Marshall, 1606; and in her father's will, 1610. Mar. . . . . Askew.
Mary. Called "the elder" in will of Francis Marshall, 1606. Mentd in her father's will, 1610.

a *b*

a — b

4 *John* Marshall of South Carlton. Will dated 13 Nov., 1582, pro. in Peculiar Court of Southwell, 28 May, 1583. = ... dau'r of Richard Athelstan, Proved her husband's will, 1583.

5 *Francis* Marshall of North Muskham. Ment[d] in will of his brother, John Marshall, 1582. Will dated 27 April, 1606, proved in Peculiar Court of Southwell, 22 Oct. following.

Dorothy.

Katherin. (? Wife of . . . . Mering.)

Children of John Marshall:

- Henry Marshall. Ment[d] in his father's will, 1582, then under age.
- Ellinor. Ment[d] in her father's will, 1582.
- *Raph* Marshall, merchant of the Staple of Lincoln, and of Muskham and Carlton. Ment[d] in will of John Marshall, 1582. Party to indentures dated 14 July, 1596, and 9 Nov., 1598. Buried at Shelton, Co. Nottingham, 10 Dec., 1617. [4] = Frances, dau'r of Robert Markham. Marriage articles dated 23 Dec., 1591. Ment[d] in indenture dated 14 July, 1596. Buried at South Muskham, 19 April, 1612. *Genealogist*, Vol. iv., p. 252.
- *William* Marshall. Ment[d] in will of John Marshall, 1582.
- *Henry* Marshall.
- *Elizabeth.*
- Anne. Mar. at South Muskham, 22 Jan., 1593-4, to Robert Oglethorpe, of Bramham, Co. York. [5]

Children of Raph Marshall and Frances:

- Ralph Marshall. Bapt. at South Muskham, 1 Oct., 1590. Bur. at Shelton, 17 March, 1636-7. = Katherine, dau'r of . . . . . Breedon. Mar. at Shelton, 24 Jan., 1633. ? assessed to Subsidy in 1642. Pub. Rec. Office, Subsidy, Notts., $\frac{160}{303}$
- William Marshall. Bapt. at South Muskham, 3 Nov., 1593.
- Robert Marshall. Bapt. at Newark, 11 Oct., 1599.
- Frances. [6] Bapt. at South Muskham, 15 Sept., 1591.
- Frances. [6] Bapt. at South Muskham, 8 August, 1592.
- Margaret. Bapt. at South Muskham, 15 Dec., 1594.
- Alice. Bapt. at South Muskham, 19 Dec., 1595.
- Bridgit. Bapt. at South Muskham, 26 March, 1597.

---

[1] In Harleian MSS., 1550, fo. 24[b], and 1484, fo. 17, he is stated to have died *sine prole*.

[2] 13 Jan[y], 1558. Adm'on granted in Exchequer Court at York, to Henry Marshall and John Marshall to the use of John, Francis, Dorothy, and Katherine Marshall, minors, the children of deceased. —*Newark Act Book*.

[3] MS. M.P. Vis. I., fo. 68, reads "2 sons," which is probably correct, the word *sons* having been miswritten *John* by some transcriber.

[4] He probably had another daughter besides those here mentioned. John Bird, of Ashton, afterwards of London, married Maud, da. of Raffe Marshall, of Carlton, co. Notts.—*Visitations of Northamptonshire*, edited by W. C. Metcalfe, p. 166.

[5] Mar. Lic. (Paver's *Collections*), 1593. Rob't Oglethorpe, of Bramham, gent., to marry Anne Marshall, of Holme, co. Nott[m].

[6] Query if one of these children was wife of Peter Roos, of Knesall.—Thoroton's *Notts.*, Vol. iii., p. 207.

ALTHORPE, CO. LINCOLN.

1677. May 8. John Marshall and Ellin Knowelson of Amcoats was marryd. May 8.
1677. May 23. Elenor wife of Edward Marshall of Amcoats buried.
1679. April 13. Ann daughter of John Marshall of Amcoats christened.
1679. Nov. 27. John son of John Marshall of Amcoats baptised.
1683. May 11. Edwarde Marshall the younger and Elizabethe Knowlton both of Amcoats marryd.
1684. July 13. Elizabeth daughter of John Marshall of Amcoats and of Ellin his wife bapt^d.
1685. Oct. 5. William sonne of Edwarde Marshall of Amcoats and Elizabeth his wife baptised October ye 5. 1685.
1686. Dec. 5. Luke son of Edward Marshall of Amcoates and Elizabeth his wife bapt^d.
1687. April 21. Luke son of Edward Marshall of Amcoats buryed.
1688. April 29. Clemence Daughter of John Marshall of Amcoats and of Ellin his wife baptised April 29. Ye same daye Thomas son of Edward Marshall of Amcoats and Elizabeth his wife baptised.
1690. Dec. 14. Benjamin son of Edward Marshall of Amcoats and Elizabeth his wife bapt.
1694. Dec. 3. Edward sonne of Edwarde Marshall and Elizabeth his wife of Amcoats baptised.
1697. Jan. 2. John son of Edward and Elizabeth Marshall of Amcoats bapt.
1701. Dec. 21. Elizabeth daughter of Edward and Elizabeth Marshall of Amcoats baptised.
1703. March 24. Elizabeth daughter of Edward Marshall of Amcoats buried.
1709. Aug. 14. Thomas son of William and Mary Marshall of Amcoats baptised.
1712. April 27. William son of William and Mary Marshall of Amcoats baptised.
1714. Dec. 26. Mary Daughter of William and Mary Marshall of Amcoats baptised.
1717. Jan. 5. John son of William and Mary Marshall of Amcoats baptised.
1720. Sept. 23. Edward son of William and Mary Marshall of Amcoats baptised.
1722. Jan. 31. Edward Marshall of Amcoats buryed.
1725. July 23. Ann daughter of William Marshall buried.
1725-6. Jan. 7. Edward son of William and Mary Marshall buried.
1726. Nov. 17. John Butterwick of Whitgift and Clemence Marshall of Amcoats married.
1728. April 15. Hannah daughter of John and Hannah Marshall baptised.

1728. Feb. 23. Hannah wife of John Marshall[1] buried.
1735. Oct. 22. John son of John and Jane Marshall baptised.
1738. April 26. Jane daughter of John and Jane Marshall of Amcoats baptised.
1740. Sept. 19. Thomas son of John and Jane Marshall baptised.
1746. Nov. 7. Edward son of John and Jane Marshall baptd.
1751. Oct. 4. Mary daughter of John and Ann Marshall baptised.
1753. July 20. Ann daughter of John and Ann Marshall baptised.
1740. Sept. 19. Thomas son of John and Jane Marshall of Amcoats buried.
1742. Feb. 2. Benjamin son of John Marshall of Amcoats buried.
1746. March 4. William Marshall of Amcoats buried.
1755. Nov. 28. Elizabeth daughter of John and Ann Marshall buried.
Edward Peart of Owston marryd to Hannah Marshall ye 6 February.
John Ross and Ruth Marshall mard.
1757. Benjamin Robinson and Ann Marshall widow mard.
1759. Nov. 23. William Marshall of Althorpe husbandman and Mary Godfrey married.
1755. Dec. 2. John Marshall and Anne Belton by license.
1770. Richard Marshall and Mary Lidgard mard.
1773. May 23. John Eastwood and Mary Marshall schoolmistress marryed.
1798. Feb. 20. Richard Horner and Mary Marshall mard.
1804. Jan. 10. John Smith and Jane Marshall married.
1756. June 15. "John Marshall parish clerk buried."
1757. Jan. 3. Mary wife of William Marshall of Amcoats buried.
1760. Sept. 14. William son of William and Mary Marshall of Amcoats baptised.
1762. July 11. "Thomas son of William and Mary Marshall baptised one July 11."
1764. Sept. 7. Jane wife of John Marshall of Amcoats buried.
1765. Jan. 20. "Mary daughter of William and Mary Marshall of Amcoats baptised *at Amcoats Chapel*."
1766. Jane daughter of William and Mary Marshall of Amcoats baptised privately June 28, publicly July 14.
1771. Jan. 12. Elizabeth daughter of William Marshall farmer and Mary his wife of Amcoats buried.
1771. Jan. 13. Edward son of John Marshall steward and the late Jane his wife buried.
1771. Feb. 15. William Marshall farmer of Amcotts buried.
1773. John son of John Marshall steward of Amcots (? Buried).
1770. Elizabeth daughter of William Marshall and of Mary his wife bapd.
1785. Jan. 29. Jane wife of John Marshall of Stockwith buried.
1794. Jan. 4. Thomas son of Thomas and Sophia Marshall baptized. (Died unmarried, killed by a fall from his horse, August 1877, will proved 1878; lived at Althorpe).

1 Vol. II. of the Register beginning 1729 is signed by Mr. Godfrey, curate, and by "John Marshall, clerk of Althorpe Church, 1748."

1795. Oct. 4. William son of Thomas and Sophia Marshall baptised.

From the foregoing extracts, and information kindly supplied by Mr. W. N. Marshall, I am able to give the following pedigree:—

Edward Marshall of Amcotts in the parish of Althorpe had issue by his wife Elenor, buried 23 May, 1677:—

Edward Marshall of Amcotts, married Elizabeth Knowlton, 1683, and had William, b. 1684, d. 1746, married Mary . . . . who died 1757, of whom presently; Luke, b. 1686, d. 1687; Thomas, b. 1688; Benjamin, b. 1690; Edward, b. 1694; John, b. 1697; and Elizabeth, b. 1701, d. 1703.

William and Mary had, Thomas, b. 1709; William; Mary, b. 1714; John, b. 1717, parish clerk of Althorpe 1748, d. 1756, his son John is called Steward of Amcotts; Edward, b. 1720, d. 1725; Ann, d. 1725. William, the second son, of Althorpe, b. 1712, d. 1771, married 1759 Mary Godfrey, and had issue, with three daughters, Mary, b. 1765, Jane, b. 1766, and Elizabeth died an infant, two sons, William, b. 1760, lived at Epworth and died there,[1] and Thomas, b. 1762, d. August 1850, married Sophia Millson of Messingham, by whom he had:—

1. Thomas, of Althorpe, Draper and Farmer, b. 1794, killed by a fall from his horse, 31 August, 1877.
2. William; see below.
3. Jane.
4. James Millson, of Butterwick, buried at Messingham, 1886.
5. Stephen, of Hull, died August 1868.
6. Hannah, married James Horberry of Gunthorpe, co. Nottingham, living without issue, 1888.
7. Sarah, married John Watkin of Wintringham, and died 1877, leaving two daughters.

William Marshall, the second son, was of Wintringham. Died 16 Sept., 1883. Settled at Wintringham in the year 1826. Married 1st, Ruth Glew of Derrythorpe, by whom he had—1. William, died an infant. 2. Mary, died an infant. 3. Sophia, married Rev. James Knaggs of London, and died in 1855, leaving issue a son, William, now at the Cape. He married secondly, Dinah Rack of South Ferriby, of an old Quaker family, and had issue by her:—

1. Ellen Elizabeth, born 1835, died s. p. 1860.
2. Dinah, married Henry Nicholson of Hull, and has issue William, born 1876, living 1888.
3. Thomas Rack, born Jan. 1837, died 3 Aug., 1876, unm.
4. Mary Jane, married John William Goodwin, of Winterton, farmer, and has issue.
5. William Nettleship Marshall, of Wintringham, born June 11, 1841, married Dec. 16, 1877, Anne Elizabeth, daughter of John Boast of North Dalton, co. York, and has issue:—

[1] Had two sons, both clergymen, one, William, was vicar of St. Matthew's, Sheffield.

i. Nellie, died an infant May 1879.
ii. Katherine Mary, born 29 May, 1880.
iii. Hugh, born 3 Aug., 1887.

FROM TRANSCRIPTS AT LINCOLN.

1628. Dec. 30. ,Elizabeth Storry. Buried.
1629-30. Jan. 16. Edward Storry & Jonne Marshall. Married.
1629-30. March 23. Edward Storry. Buried.
1671. May 30. William Marshall son of Thomas. Buried.
1684. Sept. 10. Judith Marshall. Buried.
} *Horsington co. Lincoln.*

1587-8. March 20. Mris Wenefrid Marshall. Buried. *Honington, co, Lincoln.*

1635, June 9. William Marshall and Susan Orson were married. *Hougham, co. Lincoln.*

1670. Abraham the base son of Jane Marshall baptized March 19.
1698. Nov. 7. John Dutton of this parish & Jane Marshall of Kirton were married.
1702. Jan. 17. James Marshall of Mansfield, Taylor, and Mary Rogers of Walesby were married.
} *Register of Walesby, co. Nottm.*

LIST OF BIOGRAPHICAL NOTICES OF MARSHALLS.

SAMUEL. Captain R.N. Died at Gosport, April 1768. Charnock's *Biographica Navalis*, vi., 51.

THOMAS. Captain of "Thomas and Elizabeth" Fireship. Charnock's *Biographica Navalis*, i., 242, ii. 277. Commission dated 3 April, 1689, Addl M.S. (Brit. Mus.) 31,242.

ALEXANDER, M.D. A Scotsman. *Gentleman's Magazine*, lxxxiii., i. 483.

CHARLES. Lieut. R.N. Died at Havant, aged 65, 28 Dec., 1803. *Gentleman's Magazine*, lxxiii., 1261.—MI., which gives his Arms as, *Barry of* 6 *Sable and Argent, a canton Ermine*, in Longcroft's *Account of Bosmere*, 58.

CHARLES. The Rev., M.A., Rector of Harpurhey. Died 1884. *Liverpool Daily Post* of 2 August, 1884.

JOSEPH. Of Heslerton Hall, son of James[1] of the Bierley Iron-works, near Bradford. Died 17 Oct., 1880, aged 77. *Malton Gazette*, 23 Oct., 1880. *Times*, 23 Oct., 1880.

JAMES, SIR. Knighted 1882. Chief Justice of the Gold Coast Colony. *Times*, 10 June, 1882.

CUTHBERT, D.D. Buried in York Minster, 25 Jan., 1549-50. Cooper's *Athenæ Cantabrigienses*, vol. i., pp. 97, 538.

THOMAS. Abbot of St. Werburgh's, Chester, attainted 22 Jan., 1538-9. Cooper's *Athenæ Cantabrigienses*, vol. i., p. 70.

EDMUND. Reverend. Died 8 May, 1797. *Gentleman's Magazine*, vol. 67, p. 446.

THOMAS. Rector of Lincoln College, Oxford, and Dean of Gloucester. Died 1685. *Gentleman's Magazine*, vol. 63, p. 323.

JAMES. Killed in action, Lt. R.N. Buried at Deal, 18 July, 1805. *Gentleman's Magazine*, vol. 75, p. 775.

1 His father was overseer of the poor at Huddersfield. He himself was an ironmonger at Bradford, and had two brothers, Thomas who was buried at Huddersfield, and Jeremiah, who had John, Joseph, Thomas, a machine maker, and a dau. married to Overy Johnson. John had three sons, and two daughters, and was a rich yeoman and a great character.

NOTES OF CHANCERY SUITS.[1]

Marshall v. Godarth.—Whittington I., 447.

12 January, 1669.

Complainant.—Benjamin Marshall of Doncaster, co. York, and Elizabeth his wife, late the relict of William Maddox, late of Leeds, deceased, and executor of his last will.

Defendant.—Joseph Godarth and Cicely his wife.

One Thomas Dent was in his lifetime indebted to William Maddox £40. Upon dying, Cicely his wife administered his estate but did not pay William Maddox his £40. She afterwards married Joseph Godarth. Defendants now refuse to pay complainant the £40.—Vol. ii., part ii., p. 86.

Marshall v. Williamson.—Collins III., 571; Whittington I., 36.

12th Feb., 1649, — May, 1649.

Complainant.—Thomas Marshall of Norwich, gentleman, administrator of the goods of Henry Marshall, gentleman, deceased, complainant's cousin.

Defendant.—Anthony Williamson of Tilney in Marshland in co. Norfolk.

Henry Marshall, deceased, lived for three years or more with the defendant, and last Christmas died in his house, intestate. Complainant being next of kin to the said Henry Marshall, took out letters of administration. Deceased must have had at least £1000 in his possession at time of his decease, but defendant has hidden away the greater part of this.

Marshall v. Marshall.—Collins II., 18.

15th May, 1653.

Complainants.—Mary Marshall, widow and executrix of John Marshall, late of Horton Kirby, co. Kent, yeoman; Humphrey Dixon,[2] of the same, gentleman, Elizabeth his wife, and Mary Marshall, the last two daughters of the said John Marshall, deceased.

Defendant.—John Marshall of Horton Kirby, co. Kent.

John Marshall the elder, about the 23 September, 1652, made his will bequeathing to Mary his wife £20 a year, and after some other legacies were satisfied, among which was an annuity of £10 per annum to his son John, the residue of his estate. Since his death John Marshall the younger has taken possession of the will and probably burnt it, and now claims what the law allows him as next heir.

The defendant says he believes that a messuage possessed by his late father in Horton Kirby, was entailed on him, and it was not in the power of his father to will it away from him. It is true he took his mother's keys, and opening her trunk took from thence two sheets of paper, bound together, and burnt them; but, except that his mother asserted so, he has no reason to believe these were his father's will, as he never read them.

[1] The reference at the end of some of these notes indicates the preceding page of this book at which further information will be found relative to the parties to the suit.

[2] 1650. May 16. Humfre Dixon of Tunbridge, Kent. and Elizabeth Marshall of Horton Kerbey, Kent. Married. *Register of St. Bartholomew the Great, London.*

Reynardson Depositions, 993.

Deposition taken at Horton Kirbie, co. Kent, 12 July, 1653. Witnesses examined on behalf of Mary Marshall, widow, complainant, against John Marshall, defendant.

John Marshall in bill named was at time of his death seized of a messuage in Horton Kirbie. John Marshall is late husband of Mary, complainant. John, defendant, is son of John, deceased.—Vol. i., p. 114.

Marshall v. Marshall.—Hamilton I., 235, 14.

27th July, 1709.

Complainant.—Petronell Marshall, relict and sole executrix of Nicholas Marshall the elder, late of parish of St. Mabyn, co. Cornwall.

Defendant.—Susannah Marshall and Nicholas Marshall her son, an infant.

An indenture was made between Nicholas Marshall the elder and Nicholas Marshall the younger on the 27th Jan., 1697, by which it was agreed that Nicholas the younger (in consideration of £100) conveyed to Nicholas the elder one house called the Hall, and an orchard adjoining, being in Trevilder in parish of Egloshayle, co. Cornwall. This property was to remain in the hands of Nicholas Marshall the elder and his descendants (leaving Nicholas the younger and his heirs out of account) during the lives of Nicholas the elder and Honor and Elizabeth Marshall, sisters of Nicholas the elder, after which it might be redeemed on payment of £100. Nicholas the elder died, making his will 26th March, 1699, leaving said property to Petronell Marshall (the complainant) his wife. Nicholas the younger, who survived both Honor and Elizabeth, died in 1708, leaving Susannah his wife and Nicholas his son. Susannah and Nicholas have entered into the property and refuse to pay the £100.

Whittington II., 396.

The answer of Susannah Marshall, widow, and Nicholas Marshall, infant, by the said Susannah, his mother and guardian, to the will of Petronell Marshall, complainant.

They say that Petronell Marshall of the parish of St. Mabyn, co. Cornwall, widow, executrix and late wife of Nicholas Marshall, deceased, out of her love for her son Nicholas Marshall, father of defendant, the father since deceased, did give to the said Nicholas her son all her land, etc., in Egloshaile, co. Cornwall, and this ought by right to descend to defendant.—Vol. i., p. 197.

Marshall v. Rogers.—Collins II., 196.

5th June, 1671.

Complainants.—Daniel Marshall of St. Andrew's, Holborn, co. Middlesex; Mary Marshall, daughter of Matthew Marshall, deceased; Martha Marshall, spinster, sister of said Daniel; Samuel Marshall of Huntingdon, co. Huntingdon; Philip Marshall of Eltesley, co. Cambridge; Benjamin Chatteris and Mary his wife, daughter of John Long, deceased, and Margaret his wife; Philip Marshall of London, blacksmith; Anthony Marshall of Cherry Orton, co. Huntingdon, last two being sons of Matthew Marshall, deceased; and Richard Smith of Cambridge.

Defendants.—Richard Rogers and Rebecca his wife and others.

John Marshall of the Inner Temple, gent., did on the 15th December, in the 20th year of his now majesty, publish his will as follows:—"My body to be buried in the Temple Church by my late wife, Martha. To my kinsman John Marshall of the Inner Temple, my silver basin. To Rebecca Rogers, wife of Richard Rogers, and daughter of my late brother, Edward, all my messuages, etc., in or neare Temple Bar, called the greene cushin and .... now in occupation of Robert Britten, carpenter, and Thomas Porter, bricklayer. To Mary and ..... the two daughters of Mathew Marshall, son of my late brother, Philip Marshall, my property situate in Hemingby near Hornecastle, co. Lincoln. To Mary Marshall, widow, relict of my said brother Philip, £50. To Daniel Marshall, son of my late brother Miles Marshall, those three messuages situate in Sheirlane, co. Middlesex. To Martha Marshall, sister of said Daniel, my other two messuages in Sheirlane. Item to Thomas Marshall, Taylor, who lives about St. Giles in the fields (and who calls himself my brother) £20. All property I hold of the Archbishop of Canterbury, lying near Dover, co. Kent, to Samuel Marshall, son of my late brother Philip. To Philip Marshall, son of late brother Philip, of Eltisley, co. Cambridge, the lease of the Parsonage of Leesdown in the Isle of Shepey, co. Kent. To Mary, daughter of John Long and Margaret (my late sister, deceased), my property in Long Acre, in parish of St. Martin's in the fields, co. Middlesex, and £100 in money. To Anthony and Philip Marshall, sons of my late brother Matthew, my right to property in Brower's Yard in the Strand. To Richard Smith, my late wife's brother's son, my property in Southwark, co. Surrey. To Joane, wife of Richard Gynn, daughter of my late brother Philip, £20. To Mary, wife of Moses Burton and daughter of my late brother Matthew, £20. Item to Elizabeth Isaac, daughter of my sister Joane Isaac, £40. To the rest of the children of my said sister Joane, £20 each. To the two daughters of my late sister Mary Naull, £20. To the children of Samuel Burdett by Anne, my wife's kinswoman, £50. To children of Elizabeth, now wife of John Bentley, late wife of Peter Frisby, £50. To the children of John Smith by Mary, my late wife's kinswoman, £50. To Martha Mayfield, a jewel. To Miles Marshall, my late brother's widdow, £10. To Mary, relict of my late brother Edward, £30. To Mary, daughter of my sister Margaret Long, my pewter, etc. My presidents to John Warter. I forgive Mr. Killingworth what he owes me. To the poor of Parish of St. Bride's, £5. My kinsman Mr. Robert Marshall, £20. To my cousin Samuel Gabry, £5. I nominate Moses Burton and John Gabry executors. The rest to my sister's nephews and neices, to be divided. Dated 15th December, 1688." The said John, testator, shortly after died. The defendants have got into their hands a false will, and are molesting complainants.

Marshall v. Gabry.—Collins II., 194.

30th June, 1671.

The answer of John Gabry, one of the defendants, to the Bill of Daniel Marshall, Mary Marshall, Martha Marshall, Samuel and Philip Marshall, Benjamin Chatteris and Mary his wife, Philip and Anthony Marshall, and Richard Smith.

He says he doubts if John Marshall, deceased, was in sound mind when he made his will, but he has never interfered in the management of the estate. He will give up an old will in his possession if the Court thinks fit.—Vol. ii., p. 21.

Marshall v. Guilman.—Whittington I., 467.

17 May, 1658.

Complainants.—Mary Morden by John Marshall her guardian and others.

Defendants.—Joseph Guilman and others.

Mary Morden inherited some money from her father, William Morden. Joseph Guilman is one of the executors, and will not pay her.

Marshall v. Morden.—Hamilton II., 237, 106.
26th Nov. 1669.

Complainant.—Cristopher Marshall of Southwark, co. Middlesex, and Elizabeth his wife, administratrix of the goods of Robert Gell her father.

Defendants.—Anne Morden and Robert Morden, an infant, by said Anne his mother.

John Morden was indebted to Robert Gell £100, and died without having paid the debt. Robert Gell is also dead, and Anne, wife of John Morden, ought to pay complainant the £100, she being administratrix of her father's goods.

Marshall v. Morden.—Hamilton III., 485.
21st March, 1670.

The further answer of Anne Morden, widow, and Robert Morden, infant, to the Bill of Cristopher Marshall and Elizabeth his wife.

After the death of John Morden, Anne's late husband, she had an inventory made of his goods, and the total worth of them amounted to £218 19*s.* 6*d.* See "Marshall *v.* Wallett."

Marshall v. Wallett.—Hamilton III., 498.
26th Nov., 1670.

Complainants.—Cristopher Marshall of Southwark, co. Middlesex, and Elizabeth his wife, daughter of the late Robert Gell, late of St. Mary Aldermary, London.

Defendants.—William Wallett, Katherine Wallett, and others.

John Morden, in co. Cambridge, was in his lifetime, that is in 1660, indebted to Robert Gell £100, and never paid it. John Morden also in 1645 promised for valuable considerations an annuity for life to oratrix of £12. John Morden died worth £500 in personal property, and holding lands in Lincoln and elsewhere. But now Anne, his relict, confederating with William Wallett and Katherine Wallett and others, refuse to pay said sums.

Marshall v. Thompson.—Mitford II., p. 294, 107.
3rd May, 1678.

The answer of Anthony Thompson, one of the defendants, to the Bill of Cristopher Marshall and Elizabeth his wife, and Elizabeth Morden.

He believes that John Morden the younger, sometime of co. Cambridge, did become indebted to Robert Gell in the Bill named, in sum of £100. He does not know if John Morden entered into a bond with Elizabeth Morden, complainant, by which it was agreed that he should pay the said Elizabeth £12 per annum. He says complainants never told him they were owed anything by Anne Morden, relict of the said John Morden. Defendant says he was executor of the said Anne's will. John Morden had lands in Lincolnshire and Cambridgeshire.

Marshall v. Appleyard.—Hamilton III., 528.

Complainant.—Cristopher Marshall of Southwark, co. Surrey, and Elizabeth his wife.

Defendant.—Anne Appleyard.

The late John Appleyard, who was husband to Anne the defendant, borrowed certain sums of money from Robert Gell, father of Elizabeth Marshall the oratrix. Elizabeth Marshall is administratrix of the goods of the late Robert Gell, and has applied to Anne for payment of the debts. Anne will not pay.

Marshall v. Marshall.—Reynardson VI., 277.

23 Jan., 1690.

Complainant.—Elizabeth Marshall of Barnes, co. Surrey, relict of Cristopher Marshall, junior, son of Cristopher Marshall, senior, Dyer, of London.

Defendants.—Cristopher Marshall, senior, of London, and Isaac Delillers.

The two Cristopher Marshalls—father and son—were in partnership for nearly twenty years selling and dyeing cloth. At the death of Cristopher Marshall, junior, one Isaac Delillers owed the firm a considerable sum of money, which upon his death should have by right descended to oratrix. But the two defendants, confederating together, endeavour to keep complainant out of her just rights.

Marshall v. Marshall.—Collins II., 319, 448.

15th March, 1699, 10 June, 1700, and 6 June, 1701.

Complainants.—Sarah Marshall, Rebecca Marshall, Elizabeth Marshall, in behalf of themselves, and Robert Marshall and Ellen Marshall, infants, by said Sarah their next friend.

Defendants.—Gell Marshall, Cristopher Marshall, and others.

Elizabeth Marshall, deceased, late mother of complainants, was daughter of Robert Gell, doctor of divinity. She married Cristopher Marshall, father of complainants, and brought him about £7000. This sum was nearly all the said Cristopher had, and he bought land with it. He made no will before his death, and Gell, his eldest son, came by right into nearly all his estate. Elizabeth Marshall had, however, some land in Cambridgeshire, at Pampisford, Bringes, Duxford and Brightes Closes, and this land she intended to leave to her younger children. She, too, never made a will, but often told Gell in the presence of different people that she did not intend to leave him anything. Gell now confederating with his brother Cristopher endeavours to keep complainants out of their rights.

Gell says his father left a life interest in the Manor of Hinxton, Cambridge, to Elizabeth defendant's mother; also ditto on a copyhold estate in parish of Wandsworth, co. Surrey. He never heard his mother say she intended to leave him nothing.

The further answer of Cristopher Marshall, one of the defendants, to the Bill of Complaint of Sarah Marshall, Rabecca Marshall, and Elizabeth Marshall, on behalf of themselves, and of Robert Marshall and Ellen Marshall, infants.

He says he does not know what lands his late mother died seized of in Brings or Bright's closes, only he knows that one Robert Stubbins was tenant to his late mother for some lands she held at a place called Brings. The defendant, Cristopher Marshall's brother Gell Marshall instructed John Hughes to act for him. This John Hughes, his brother has told him, was a perfect cheat or one of the worst of men, and he never asked him to draw any articles for him.

The answers of Elizabeth Marshall, Robert Marshall, and Ellen Marshall, by their Guardian Sarah Marshall, to the Bill of Gell Marshall.

They say it may be true that Gell Marshall is the eldest son of Cristopher Marshall, deceased, late of London, and that he, the late Cristopber, held lands in Cambridgeshire, Lincoln, and Surrey, but these estates were purchased with his wife's money. It is not true that these defendants or John Hughes ever made complainant sign the articles referred to in his bill.

Marshall v. Marshall.—Mitford, III., 456, 46.
24th April, 1700.

Complainant.—Cristopher Marshall of London, apothecary, administrator of the goods of Elizabeth Marshall his mother, deceased.

Defendants.—Sarah Marshall, Rebecca, Elizabeth, Robert, and Ellen Marshall, the last two infants.

Elizabeth Marshall, complainant's late mother, was the only daughter of Robert Gell, who by his will left her worth £10,000 or more, which came to Cristopher Marshall, father of complainant, upon his intermarriage with her. After the death of both Cristopher and Elizabeth his wife, complainant, together with his brother Gell, intended administering the estate, and fearing the evil purposes of John Hughes, who married Sarah Marshall, and the other defendants, he locked the door of his mother's room. The defendants have broken this open and taken away all the jewels and valuables contained in it.—Vol. I., App. p. 33.

Marshall v. Marshall.—Whittington I., 77.
17 Dec., 1664.

Complainant.—Edmond Marshall of Newcastle upon Tyne.

Defendants.—Thomas Marshall and John Marshall.

Thomas Marshall's Defence.—He does not believe it to be true that William Marshall, late of More Allerton, was indebted to Sir Charles Hussey of Hunnington, co. Lincoln, kt. He believes the complainant was due that amount to him, and got defendant to stand surety for him among others.

Marshall v. Marshall.—Whittington I., 77.
1st July, 1664.

The answer of George Marshall, one of the defendants, to the Bill of Edmund Marshall.

He says it may be true William Marshall, father of defendant and complainant, made a will dated 22 April, 1662, but he also made a will on the 9th July, 1662, cancelling all former wills.

Marshall v. Marshall.—Reynardson I. and II., 408.
11th Nov., 1670.

Complainants.—Edmund Marshall of Newcastle upon Tyne, Robert Brook, John Sharp, etc.

Defendant.—George Marshall.

William Marshall had a debt which he could not pay, and Edmund Marshall and George, sons of William, entered with others into a bond for its payment. William is since dead, and George, who is his eldest son and has inherited all his estate refuses to pay his share of the debt, alledging that his father gave him a counter bond cancelling his share.

Marshall v. Marshall.—Hamilton I., 237, 78; Whittington I., 75.
21st Jan., 1664, 24 Oct., 1664.

Complainant.—Edmund Marshall of Newcastle upon Tyne.

Defendant.—George Marshall of Moore Allerton, co. York.

William Marshall, the father of both complainant and defendant, being in want of £200, borrowed it from Sir Charles Hussy. George and Edmund, together with Richard Midgely and Henry Rhoades, entered into a bond also insuring the payment of this. William the father died without paying the debt, and George, before he died, got him to enter secretly into making a counter bond relieving him (George) from all risk.—See Interrogatories to be administered on behalf of George Marshall, gent., one of the defendants, to Bill of Edmund Marshall, woollen draper.—Hamilton, Depositions, II., p. 275.

Marshall v. Marshall.—Whittington II., 100.
10th May, 1665.

Complainant.—John Marshall of city of London, surviving executor of the last will of William Marshall, his late brother.
Defendant.—Edmund Marshall.

William Marshall of More Allerton, co. York, deceased, father of complainant and defendant, was in his lifetime anxious to give Edmund his second son a piece of land in a village called Woodhouse. But not thinking this would be fair to his other children, he made Edmund enter into a bond by which he had to pay £100 in a given time to his (Edmund's) brother William. William the father died, and William the son (not knowing in his lifetime about this bond) also died beyond seas. John is executor of William's will, and Edmund nevertheless refuses to pay him the £100.

Marshall v. Marshall.—Whittington II., 96.
22nd Nov., 1666.

Complainant.—Thomas Marshall of London, merchant, son of William Marshall of Moor Allerton, Leeds, Yorkshire.
Defendants.—Edmund Marshall, George Marshall, etc.

William Marshall, about the 22 April, 1662, made his will. By this he gave to his son Edmund and his friends Edward Birckby and Timothy Rayner and their heirs all his water mills called Woodmilne, in Chappell Allerton, also his messuage, etc., in Kirkgate. This messuage, etc., to be sold, and £600 out of proceeds to pay his debts. Also he bequeathed to Edmund his son, Birckby, and Timothy Rayner his dwellinghouse in Moor Allerton, in trust for his wife Elizabeth. To his son William, £100. To his son, Thomas Marshall, £100. To his wife's daughters Francis and Mary Hodgson, £10. The residue of his estate to be divided between Elizabeth Lambe, wife of William Lambe,[1] Mary wife of Robert Brooke, Gertrude wife of Henry Wilden, Edmund, William, Robert, John, and Thomas, his sons. Since the making this will both William and Robert Marshall are dead. The trustees will not administer the said estate, and George and Edmund, confederating together, pretend another will exists.

Marshall v. Marshall.—Hamilton III., 538.
26th Jan., 1678.

Complainants.—Edmund Marshall of Moor Allerton, co. York, son of William Marshall of Moor Allerton, co. York.
Defendants.—Katherine Marshall, widow, George Marshall, an infant, by Katherine his mother.

William Marshall was in his lifetime seized of lands and tenements in Moor Allerton. He being anxious to make provision for his children—George his eldest son being about to marry—made his last will and did by it bequeath to complainant, Edward Birkby of Scoldcroft, co. York, Timothy Raner of Galberston, co. York, all that water corn mill called Wood Milne, in the lordship of Chappell Allerton, co. York, also a messuage and tenement in Leeds Kirkgate. These were to be sold and £600 of the profits to be applied to payment of the testator's debts. Also he devises the dwelling house in Moor Allerton, where he dwelt, to be given during three years to Elizabeth his wife; after that the house to go to George, testator's elder son, he paying £300 to Martha, Mary, and Elizabeth Brooke, daughters of Robert and Mary Brooke (Mary Brooke

1 William Lamb was of Coulston, co. Gloucester, and died *circa* 1675.—See *Visitation of Gloucestershire*, 1683.

being sister of complainant and said George). George in his lifetime would not suffer complainant to perform the will, but brought forth another which he said was genuine, and they had several law suits, in which George lost. Now Katherine Marshall, relict of said George, and George her son, pretend that by a deed William Marshall the father gave George his son the messuages declared in the will to be sold in payment of debts.

Marshall v. Marshall.—Whittington II., 139.
23rd Oct., 1680.

Complainant.—Katherine Marshall, widow, administratrix of goods, etc., of George Marshall her late husband, and George Marshall an infant by said Katherine his mother. George the infant is grandson of William Marshall of Moor Allerton.

Defendants.—Frances Marshall, William Marshall, Edward Birkby, Robert Brooke, etc.

George Marshall is heir to some property through George his father from William his grandfather, but Frances the relict of Edmund son of William, and William son of Edmund and grandson of William, claim it through said Edmund.—(See Depositions 914 for Interrogatories.)—See Vol. i., p. 136; ii, Part ii., p. 56, etc.

Marshall v. Brooke.—Mitford Dep., 681.
9th April, 19 James I.

Examination of Nicholas Reyner, of Stubley, co. York, for George Marshall and Agnes his wife, and John Whittaker, against Thomas Brooke and Margaret Brooke and others.

He says he knew Edmonde Brooke, father of Thomas Brooke, and Jennett his wife. He says he has heard it reported that Jennett had the old house at Stanley settled upon her, and that Agnes, one of the complainants, lived therein.

Marshall v. Brooke.—Whittington II., 100.
10th May, 1665.

Complainant.—John Marshall of London, executor of the will of his late brother William Marshall of Moore Allerton, co. York.

Defendant.—Robert Brooke.

William Marshall, late of Moore Allerton, complainant's father, left Edmond his second son some land in a village called Woodhouse. This he thought too large a legacy, so he made Edmond become bound to William, Edmond's brother, in a bond of £200. William the brother died over seas. Now Edmond, combining with Robert Brooke, will not pay the £200, pretending to have paid the same and producing a forged receipt.

Marshall v. Brooke.—Hamilton III., 531.
5th July, 1677.

Complainant.—Edmond Marshall of Moore Allerton, parish of Leeds, co. York, son of William Marshall, late of Moore Allerton.

Defendants.—Robert Brooke, Martha Brooke, and others.

On the 22 April, 1662, the late William Marshall published his will, and among other legacies left to Edmond his son, the complainant, to Edward Birkby of Scolecroft, and to Timothy Reyner the woodmilne in the manor of Chappell Allerton, co. York. He also left £300 to defendants, and made orator executor. Orator paid defendants their legacy, but they now pretend they have never received it.

Marshall v. Rodes.—Whittington II., 99.

24th Oct. 1664.

Complainant.—Edmund Marshall of Newcastle upon Tyne, woollen draper.

Defendants.—Henry Rhodes, Richard Midgeley, and others.

William Marshall, late of Moore Allerton, co. Yorke, borrowed some money from Sir Charles Hussey, and George Marshall, his eldest son, and Edmund Marshall, the complainant, together with defendants, became bound with him to the said Sir Charles Hussey. Now defendants (William being dead) try to make complainant meet the whole sum.

Marshall v. Lambe.—Reynardson III., 49.

6th July, 1666.

Complainant.—John Marshall of Moore Allerton, co. Yorke.

Defendant.—William Lambe, George Marshall, and others.

The answer of William Lambe.

He says he believes that Edmund Marshall did about the time mentioned begin a suit in the Common Pleas against George Marshall in the Bill named. The complainant and defendant became bail for the said George Marshall. The said George is supposed to have become bound to Edmund in trust for William Marshall the father.

The answer of George Marshall.

He believes that William Marshall his father held lands in Moore Allerton. He made his will the 19th July, 1662, as follows. His body to be buried in the Parish Church at Leeds. To George Marshall, my eldest son, my water corn-mill and fulling mill, called Woodmill, and houses belonging, being in Chapel Allerton, also my house in Leeds Kirkgate, on condition he pay to Thomas Marshall my youngest son £250, and to the three daughters of Robert Brooke my son-in-law, Martha, Elizabeth, and Jane. To Elizabeth my wife household goods. To Robert Brooke and Mary his wife my Smithy Mill. To Mary Duffield my grandchild, £10. Ann Duffield my grandchild. To Elizabeth my eldest daughter, wife of William Lambe, £40. Whereas there are £50 owing to me by my son Edmund Marshall I give £10 thereof to his son William Marshall, £10 to Mary his daughter, and £10 to Frances his wife. All the rest of my goods to George my son and Elizabeth my wife, whom I make my executors. Defendant believes before the making of this will another will was made, but this will revokes the former one.

Marshall v. Blake.—Whittington II., 123.

6th Feb., 1673.

The answer of William Blake to the Bill of John Marshall, executor of William Marshall, deceased.

He says he believes William Marshall was a merchant trading in the East Indies. He had a letter from the said William, ordering him to look after his goods, which he faithfully did, and all goods intrusted to him he has faithfully returned.—See also, Hamilton, II., 236.

Marshall v. Bridges.—Hamilton III., 510.

19th June, 1674.

Complainant.—John Marshall of London, salter, executor of the last will of his brother William Marshall of Hughley, in the East Indies, merchant.

Defendant.—Shem Bridges.

Shem Bridges resided in Hughley, East Indies, at the time of William Marshall's death, and complainant desired him to make an inventory of and look after the personal estate of his brother. He took possession of the said estate but has never properly accounted for it.—Vol. i., p. 136.

Marshall v. Marshall.—Whittington I., 486.

30 Nov., 1677.

Complainants.—John Marshall of London; Henry Barwell of the Borough of Leicester, co. Leicester, and Sara his wife; John Day of the same and Mary his wife; John Marshall, Sara, and Mary, being daughters of John Marshall, of Leicester, blacksmith.

Defendants.—Susannah Marshall, relict of William Marshall (who was brother to John Marshall the elder), and Tobias his son and heir.

John Marshall died about 1655, when complainants were under age, and William administered his estate. He also died shortly after, and Susannah his widow and Tobias his son came into possession of not only his estate but also the estate of John Marshall. Defendants will not now give complainants their due.—Vol. i., App., p. 17.

Marshall v. Marshall.—Mitford IV., 588.

24th May, 1699.

Complainant.—Samuel Marshall of Eshold, co. York.

Defendant.—Joseph Marshall.

Edward Marshall of Yeadon, co. York, grandfather of complainant and defendant, married Jennett, daughter of William Womersley, and by so doing became proprietor of certain lands, etc., in Horsforth, which the said Jennett inherited from her father. By Jennett, Edward Marshall had issue, Samuel (the eldest), father of complainant; Abraham (the second), father of defendant; William, Joseph, Jeremy, Elizabeth, and Mary. Samuel Marshall, the complainant, should come into this property, being eldest son of the eldest son of Edward Marshall. But defendant will not allow him to do this, pretending that Jennett conveyed the said property to his father Abraham, by a deed dated 14th May, 1628.—Vol. i., p. 282.

Marshall v. Marshall.—Whittington III., 353.

21st April, 1697.

Complainant.—Richard Marshall, the elder, of Longhope, co. Gloucester, son of late William Marshall of Longhope.

Defendant.—Anne Marshall, widow.

William Marshall, owing some money, got orator to pay it for him, and promised to return it. In November 1670, he died, leaving great sums of money, and his wife Elizabeth administered the estate. Elizabeth also died, making Thomas, orator's younger brother, executor, and shortly after Thomas also died, making his wife Anne executor. Anne will not pay orator his debt.

Marshall v. Marshall.—Whittington II., 279.

15th Nov., 1690.

Complainant.—Cristopher Marshall of Masham, co. York.

Defendant.—Mary Marshall, relict of Arthur Marshall.

Arthur Marshall, on the 28th February, 1690, died intestate, leaving some real estate in Carleton, Masham, Fearby, and elsewhere, which orator, being next heir, should inherit, but Mary Marshall, his relict, will not allow this.—Vol. i., p. 83—ii. Part ii., p. 100.

Marshall v. Burges.—Collins III., 544.

9th May, 1687.

Complainant.—Thomas Marshall of Whitchurch, co. Southhampton, and Jane his wife.

Defendant.—Anne Burges.

Richard Burges of Lurgarshall, co. Wilts., blacksmith, left certain messuages to his son William Burges, on condition that his said son would pay £20 to Jane his sister and now wife of complainant. William died before fulfilling his father's orders, and now Anne his wife refuses to do so on sundry pretexts.

Marshall v. Parlby.—Bridges II., 173.

4th Dec., 1693.

Complainants.—William Marshall of Scalford, co. Leicester, gent., administrator of the goods of John Marshall, late of Scalford, his father; and Elizabeth Wilcocks of Melton Mowbray, co. Leicester, widow, executrix of the will of Richard Willcocks, late of Melton Mowbray, her husband.

Defendants.—Hugh Parleby and Margaret his wife.

George Dixon, junior, late of Statherne, co. Leicester, being in need of money, came to John Marshall, deceased, and borrowed money from him. John Marshall lent it to him and entered into an agreement dated 7th December, 1675, by which it was agreed that the money should be returned with interest in or before May next ensuing. Richard Willcocks also entered into a similar agreement with George Dixon. George Dixon, being unable to pay on the agreed day, delivered into Richard Wilcock's hands an indenture of feoffment or deed of purchase of land lying in Statherne, which the said Richard Willcocks and John Marshall were to keep until the moneys were returned. George Dixon died, and the land descended to Margaret, wife of Hugh Parleby, who refuses to acknowledge complainant's right to it.—Vol. i., p. 154.

Marshall v. Marshall.—Mitford V., 318.

15th July, 1663.

Complainant.—Henry Marshall of Egton Banks, in the parish of Lyth, co. York, son of Ralph Marshall of Oakbar Holme, co. York.

Defendant.—Margaret Marshall, relict of William Marshall, eldest son of Ralph, also complainant's father.

On the 19th July, 1643, Ralph Marshall died intestate. William, his eldest son, came into the real estate lying in Oakbar holme and Egton Banks. About three weeks after the said Ralph's death Jane his wife also died intestate. Both Ralph and Jane were possessed of a large personal estate which should in part have come to complainant. But complainant being not then of age, William administered the estate and never gave complainant his share, though he was always promising to do so. About four years since William died, and now Margaret his relict refuses to acknowledge complainant's claim.

Marshall v. Agar.—Mitford II., 112.

12th Feb., 1652.

Complainants.—Henry Marshall of the Lordship of Egton, co. York, yeoman, and Mary his wife.

Defendant.—William Agar.

Peter Agar, son of William Agar, married oratrix, and said William promised to give him a certain sum of money on his marriage. Peter died before he received this, and now William will not give it to oratrix, his relict. Mary, oratrix, is now wife of Henry Marshall, and is daughter of John Keld, late of Harwood Dale, co. York.—Vol. i., p. 274.

Marshall v. Maddison.—Hamilton III., 464.

17th Nov., 1662.

Complainant.—Thomas Marshall of Kingston upon Hull, co. York, marriner.

Defendant.—Robert Maddison.

Thomas Robertson of Humberston, co. Lincoln, and Elizabeth Hansard, mother of said Thomas, or one of them, were seized of some land in parish Trusthorpe and a close called South Somerhead, in co. Lincoln. This property they or one of them sold to William Marshall, complainant's uncle. William died about 22 years since, and the property went to Ralph his brother. Ralph sold the same to orator, who is Ralph's son. But Robert Maddison claims the property by right of descent through Thomas Maddison his grandfather, and William Maddison his father.

Marshall v. Marshall.—Hamilton IV., 638.

19th March, 1707.

Complainant.—John Marshall of Thedlethorpe, co. Lincoln, eldest son and executor of the will of William Marshall, late of Thedlethorpe, co. Lincoln.

Defendant.—William Marshall and Katherine Marshall (now Odlinge), brother and sister to complainant.

William Marshall made his will on the 21st August, 1706, leaving certain sums of money to William and Katherine, his two younger children, an annuity of £40 per annum to Grace his wife, and the residue of his estate to complainant, his eldest son. At the time of his father's death complainant was with his regiment, he being a lieutenant, and also for some little time after. When he got home he found his brother and sister had been selling a great deal of his personal estate (that left him by his late father), and with the help of Thomas Odlinge of Hammersmith, whom Katherine Marshall married, committed other fraudulent practices.—Vol. i., p. 13.

Marshall v. Barnard.—Collins II., 231.

6th Nov., 1677.

Complainants.—William Marshall of Thedlethorpe, co. Lincoln, and Grace his wife, sole daughter of William Smyth, late of Humberstone, co. Lincoln.

Defendants.—Thomas Barnard, Anthony Allenson, and others.

William Smith, father of the defendant Grace, about 1672 made his last will and left her the bulk of his estate, which she was to receive on her majority or marriage. He made Anthony Allenson and others executors thereof. Also John Smith made his will in 1668, this John Smith being Grace's grandfather, and left oratrix £50, which she was never paid by her father William, who was John's executor. The defendants will not account for the personal estate of the late William, Grace's father, nor give her her due.

Marshall v. Marshall.—Hamilton I., 233, 25.
16th Jan., 1713.

Complainant.—William Marshall of Braybrooke, co. Northampton, one of the sons of Richard Marshall of Braybrooke, deceased.
Defendants.—Susannah Marshall, widow, and Robert Marshall, an infant, by Susannah his mother.

Richard Marshall in his lifetime was seized of sundry closes, lands, and hereditaments in Braybrook and upon the 4th February, 1703, made his will, leaving complainant a legacy of £100, and shortly after died. After his death Thomas Marshall his eldest son took possession of his property, and some time after, without having paid complainant, died, leaving Robert, his eldest son. Complainant has applied to Robert for his legacy, but Robert, confederating with his mother Susannah, refuses to give it to him.

The defendants in answer say Thomas Marshall, in Bill named died leaving Robert his son and Hannah his daughter and Susannah his wife. Defendant's have never refused to pay complainant his legacy.—Vol. i., p. 312.

Marshall v. Marshall.—Mitford IV., 574.
1st May, 1696.

Complainant.—William Marshall of Wray, co. Lancaster, son of John of Wray.
Defendant.—Thomas Marshall, who married the sister of John Marshall, complainant's father.

John Marshall had an estate in Wray, and in June, 1676, died, leaving complainant, his only son, then aged eight years, and one daughter named Jennett, since married to one Robert Fletcher of Melling. Upon pretext of relationship, Thomas Marshall, the defendant, took out letters of administration and administered John Marshall's estate. He has, however, cheated complainant.—Vol. ii., pp. 33, 34.

Marshall v. Marshall.—Hamilton Depositions, II., 275;
James I. Mitford I., 72.

Complainant.—Robert Marshall.
Defendant.—Alice Marshall, widow.

John Marshall, deceased, was husband to Alice, defendant, and lived at Exeter. Robert, the complainant, is brother to John Marshall, deceased, the younger. The dispute is in connection with money left by John Marshall to his brother.--Vol. ii., p. 10.

Marshall v. Payne.—Mitford V., 330.
3 Dec., 1677.

Complainant.—Jael Marshall, relict of James Marshall, late of City of Exeter, deceased.[1]
Defendants.—Hugh Abell, Cristopher Payne, Andrew Stavicke, and others.

James Marshall, in consideration of a marriage between oratrix and him did by indenture grant certain lands he had in St. Olave and elsewhere, within the City of Exeter, to her after his death. The defendants have now entered into possession, and pretend the property was mortgaged to them for considerable sums of money.

1 He was of Exeter, Brewer, in 1665.—See Marshall v. Tucker.—Hamilton III., 470.

Marshall v. Stavicke.—Mitford II., 216.

3rd Dec., 1677.

Complainant.—Jael Marshall, relict of James Marshall, late of the City of Exeter, and daughter of William Mercer.

Defendants—Andrew Stavicke and others.

The late James Marshall had some land in the Parish of St. Olave, and also some in the north part of the City of Exeter. The last mentioned land was by indenture conveyed to oratrix on John Marshall's death, in consideration of a marriage portion given to said James Marshall by William Mercer. But one Hugh Abell, combining with Andrew Stavicke and others, have taken possession of the premises.—Vol. ii., p. 13.

Marshall v. Heather.—Bridges V., 627.

27th Jan., 1700.

Complainant.—John Marshall of Sharlston, co. York.

Defendant.—Samuel Heather of London, apothecary.

The complainant was settled with his wife and family at Selby, when Samuel Heather, brother of complainant's wife, urged him to remove with his family to Sharlston, and take a farm there belonging to the said defendant. This farm was in bad repair, but Heather promised to put it in good repair if complainant would take it on a lease for three years. This complainant did, but defendant will not perform his part of the bargain.—Vol. i., p. 309, etc.

Thomas Marshall.—Reynardson I. and II., 431.

28th Nov., 1699.

Complainant.—Thomas Marshall, eldest son of Humfrey Marshall, deceased, late of Combes Head, co. Derby.

Defendant.—Humfrey Marshall the younger, 4th son of Humfrey Marshall the elder.

Humfrey Marshall the elder and his heirs had conveyed to them land lying in Chapel le Frith, co. Derby, by Thomas Month and Anne his wife. To the use of Humfrey Marshall for life, then to orator for life, then to George, second son of Humfrey the elder, then to Godfrey, third son of the said Humfrey, and after to the use of any other sons of the said Humfrey. Orator married the daughter of Roger Worthenton. Defendant pretends the said premises belong to him by deed, being conveyed to him by Humfrey the elder, Humfrey the elder being dead.

Marshall v. Marshall.—Whittington III., 535.

13 May, 1703.

Complainant.—Thomas Marshall of Hinckley, co. Leicester.

Defendants.—Nathaniel Marshall and Elizabeth Flavil, both children of Elizabeth Marshall, orator's mother.

Thomas Marshall being in debt conveyed to his mother his house at Hinckley, and also some land at Earleshilton, co. Leicester, on the understanding that she (orator's mother) would pay orator's debts and leave said home, etc., to orator in her will. This she never did, leaving orator nothing, or next to nothing, and his brother and sister, the defendants, all.—Vol. i., pp. 231-3.

Marshall v. Marshall.—Mitford II., 116, 123.
26th May, 1652.

Complainant.—Anne Marshall of Little Tew, co. Oxford, executrix of the last will of John Marshall, her late husband, and of Edmund Marshall, son of the said John and Anne.
Defendant.—Ralph Marshall.

Anne Marshall before exhibited a Bill against Ralph Marshall the elder and Ralph Marshall the younger, his son, for the payment of certain sums of money intrusted to them for her use by her late husband. After the lawsuit, complainant and defendant agreed to submit unsettled differences to John Cary. But John Cary confederating with Ralph Marshall the elder is endeavouring to cheat complainant.—Vol. i., App. 10.

Marshall v. Marshall.—Mitford III., 473, 25.
29 Jan., 1705.

Complainant.—Anne Marshall, relict of Hezekiah Marshall, who worked for Government at Deptford, co. Kent.
Defendant.—Thomas Marshall, father of Hezekiah Marshall.

Thomas Marshall had left him a great number of valuables and a great deal of money by Hezekiah in trust for Anne, complainant, and will not account properly for them.—Vol. i., App. 34.

Marshall v. Corbett.—Reynardson IV., 86.
24th Oct., 1679.

Complainant.—Elizabeth Marshall of Westminster, relict of James Marshall of St. Martin in the fields, co. Middlesex.
Defendant.—Nicholas Corbett.

Robert Parsons of Waybridge, deceased, late husband of oratrix, by his will left some copyhold land held according to the custom of the manor of Cobham, co. Surrey, to Elizabeth the oratrix. After his death Elizabeth married James Marshall. James Marshall being in debt one Thomas Poole promised to relieve him on condition that Elizabeth would convey said lands to him. This Elizabeth did, but Thomas Poole promised that upon receipt of the money given to Elizabeth again he would return her the land. Nicholas Corbett has the land now, and refuses to give it up to oratrix.

Marshall v. Corbett.—Reynardson II., 416.
12th May, 1683.

Complainant.—Elizabeth Marshall of St. Margaret's, Westminster, co. Middlesex, widow, relict of James Marshall.
Defendants.—Nicholas Corbett and Thomas Poole.

Robert Parsons, late of Weybridge, co. Surrey, was in his lifetime seized of some lands in Surrey. These by his will he left to Elizabeth his then wife, and after her death to Symon Walter his uncle, the oratrix's late father. Both Elizabeth and Symon Walter are dead, and the lands should descend to oratrix. But defendants endeavour to defraud her of her rights.

Marshall, Richard.—Collins III., 542.
4th Jan., 1695.

Complainant.—Richard Marshall of London, cordweaver.
Defendants.—Alice Battin of Nuberry, co. Berks.; Michael Hullcupp of Baghurst, co. Southampton; and John Deane.

Thomas Hullcupp, deceased, was seized of land, etc., in the parish of Baghurst, co. Southampton, and being so seized married Jane Marshall, complainant's mother. Because of this marriage he settled the said lands on Jane and her heirs, if he should die without heirs. This he did, and complainant is entitled to the property, being next of kin to Jane, that is eldest son of Jane by her former husband John Marshall. But the defendants claim the said property and endeavour to oust orator.

Marshall v. Marshall.—Mitford V., 330, 51.

28th May, 1679.

Complainant.—Steven Marshall of Ashover, co. Derby.

Defendant.—Martin Marshall.

William Marshall, father of both complainant and defendant, was in his lifetime seized of land, etc., in Bradwall, co. Derby, and dying, about 1660, intestate, complainant should come into the property, being his eldest son. But Martin his (complainant's) younger brother pretends William the father, by a deed in his lifetime, conveyed the said property to him, and molests complainant.

Marshall v. Gray.—Whittington II., 95.

4th Oct., 1662.

Complainant.—Gilbert Marshall of Houghall, co. Durham.

Defendants.—Ralph Gray and Barbara his wife.

Complainant having occasion to borrow money went to one William Calverley, late of Newcastle, and got him to lend him some £700, and Richard Marshall of Gray's Inn, London, and himself became bound in the sum of £1000 for repayment, several other people standing security. But the said William Calverley, not thinking his money secure, asked orator to sell him his manor of Sellaby, which he did. Now defendants, who are the admistrator's of William Calverley, try to make orator pay the £1000, the bonds never having been cancelled as they ought.

Marshall v. Stamford.—Mitford II., 208.

14th Feb., 1675.

Complainants.—Richard Marshall of Gray's Inn, co. Middlesex, and Katherine his wife, and John Skinner.

Defendant.—Alice Stanford.

Katherine and John Skinner, orators, were executors of the will of Nicholas Skinner. Nicholas Skinner was owed £100 by Anthony Stanford and Alice his relict will not satisfy the said debt, though Anthony died worth a great deal of money.

Marshall v. Marshall.—Whittington III., 522.

19th Jan., 1670.

Complainant.—Gilbert Marshall, late of Houghall, co. Durham, deceased, son of Gilbert Marshall of same place.

Defendant.—Richard Marshall of Gray's Inn, London, uncle of complainant.

Gilbert Marshall, father of complainant, wanted to renew a lease of the manor of Heburne, co. Durham, and borrowed £600 from his brother Richard to do this. Richard now pretends the manor belongs to him.

Marshall v. Marshall.—Whittington II., 249.

27th Jan., 1698.

Complainant.—Richard Marshall of Gray's Inn, co. Middlesex.

Defendants.—Jane Marshall, and Gilbert Marshall her father.

Orator married one Jane Cannon, relict of Henry Cannon, and the said Jane by deed conveyed certain lands lying in Harpedon, co. Hertford, and some others lying in Luton, co. Bedford, to orator. She died, and her daughter Jane Cannon, married Gilbert Marshall, junior, son of Gilbert Marshall, orator's elder brother, Jane daughter of Gilbert Marshall, junr., and Jane his wife, now claims said property as heir to orator's wife Jane.

Marshall, Richard.—Reynardson I. and II., 435.
2nd Dec., 1696.

Complainant.—Richard Marshall of Gray's Inn, co. Middlesex.
Defendant.—Jane Marshall, daughter and heir of Jane Marshall deceased, late wife of Gilbert Marshall of Sellaby, co. Durham, daughter and heir of Jane Cannon.

Jane Cannon had lands, etc., in Harpedon, co. Hertford, and within the parish of Luton, co. Bedford. In the year 1662 orator married Jane Cannon, she having previously conveyed the said lands to him. Now the defendant pretends the lands should descend to her.—Vol. ii., p. 4.

Marshall v. Fossicke.—Hamilton III., 394.
11 Feb., 1650.

Complainant.—John Marshall of Wisbich in the Isle of Ely, co. Cambridge, son of John Marshall of the Isle of Ely, by Jackomye his first wife.
Defendants.—Alice Marshall, second wife of John Marshall the father; James Marshall and William Marshall her sons; and others.

John Marshall the father made a will in favour of Alice and Alice's children, but he revoked that will and made one favourable to complainant. The second will has got into defendant's hands, and they pretend the first was never cancelled. John Marshall the father died in June last past. No mention of Fossicke in the Bill.

The answers of Alice Marshall, widow, and William Marshall, gentleman, to the Bill of John Marshall.

They believe it to be true that John Marshall, gentleman, in the Bill named, late husband of the defendant Alice, and father of the defendant William, was seized of lands in Cambridge, North Notts., and Lincoln, also land in the Isle of Ely. The said John had issue by his former wife, complainant, and by the defendant Alice two sons (that is to say) this defendant William Marshall, and James Marshall, and four daughters now living. They never had any deeds other than those given them by the will of the late John Marshall.

Marshall v. Marshall.—Hamilton, Depositions I., 271.

Interrogatories to be administered to witnesses on behalf of John Marshall, gentleman, complainant, against William Marshall, gentleman, and Alice Marshall, widow, defendants.

John Marshall, father of complainant, had land in Marshland, co. Norfolk. He made his last will 21st April, 1650. William Marshall, defendant, is son of John Marshall the elder, and brother of complainant.

John Marshall the elder had complainant by Jacomy his first wife. Complainant married Alice.

Marshall v. Marshall.—Hamilton III., 434.

1652.

Complainant.—Frances Marshall of the Isle of Ely, co. Cambridge, one of the daughters of John Marshall of Wisbich, deceased, by Isaac Degge of London, her guardian.

Defendant.—William Marshall.

John Marshall before he died made William his son executor of his last will, and made him promise particularly to give oratrix £500 as stated in the will, and besides that a yearly sum, the amount of which orator knows not. William her brother has never yet fulfilled the trust reposed in him.—Vol. i., App. p. 13.

Marshall v. Lacy.—Collins II., 143, 216.

21st Oct., 1657.

Complainant.—William Marshall of Lincoln's Inn, co. Middlesex.

Defendants.—Thomas Lacy, John Mann, Thomas Scott, and others.

Complainant had certain marshlands and tenements in the Isle of Ely, co. Cambridge. These were useless, owing to the water. But lately the Earl of Bedford drained the land, and orator's property has become valuable. The defendants have unjustly taken possession.

Marshall v. Budd.—Collins II., 147.

1660?

The answer of John Budd, defendant, to the Bill of John Marshall, complainant.

He says it is true William Budd, the complainant, John Marshall's grandfather, and this defendant's father was seized of property in the parish of Wellington, co. Somerset. It is true Edith, William Budd's eldest daughter, married John Marshall, complainant's father. He denies that his father ever made a deed giving certain property called Roegreene to the complainant's father.

Marshall v. Cowlam.—Mitford V., 318.

24th Oct., 1660.

Complainant.—Charles Marshall of Great Limber, and heretofore of Little Limber, co. Lincoln.

Defendant.—William Cowlam.

Complainant, Charles Marshall of Kirmingtonne and William Cowlam entered into a Bond with Sir Edward Rosseter, which has become due. William Cowlam will not pay his share of this, nor will he pay other sums of money which he owes complainant.

Marshall v. Cowlam.—Whittington I., 63.

22 Nov., 1661.

Complainant.—Charles Marshall of Crowston (late of Little Limber) co. Lincoln.

Defendant.—William Cowlam.

Complainant was tenant to Sir Edward Rossiter of Somerby, co. Lincoln, and could not pay his rent. William Cowlam lent him money to do so, said money to be repaid on a certain date. Complainant could not do this, and defendant first took his stock, and then wanted full payment of the Bond.

Marshall v. Ellis.—Hamilton III., 560.

24th Jan., 1681.

Complainant.—John Marshall an infant by Jonathan Coulam of London, dyer.

Defendant.—Richard Ellis.

John Marshall the complainant is the only son of John Marshall, who was the eldest son of Charles Marshall, late of Kirmington, co. Lincoln, yeoman, who married Mary King, the eldest daughter of John King, late of Wootten, co. Lincoln. John King had property in Wootten and Kermington and elsewhere, and this property should come to complainant, he being the legal heir, his grandfather Charles Marshall having married John King's daughter Mary King. But one Richard Ellis claims to be nearer and has entered into possession. Vol. i., p. 113.

Marshall v. Unett.—Hamilton II., 239, 119.

13 Jan., 1662.

Complainant.—Richard Marshall the younger of Longdon, co. Stafford.

Defendants.—Alice Unett of Longdon, widow, and others.

John Unett of Longdon and Robert Shipton in February, 13th Charles II., sold two copyhold closes in the manor of Longdon, to Richard Marshall, Elizabeth his wife, and their heirs, and afterwards died. The defendants now try to force complainant from the premises, pretending they belong to them on account of a former lease.

Marshall v. Lycett.—Hamilton II., 240, 88.

22 Nov., 1647.

Complainants.—Hugh Marshall of Longdon, co. Stafford, and Margaret his wife, daughter of John Browne, late of Longdon, deceased.

Defendants.—Henry Lycett, William Clerke, and others.

The defendants had some land called Sandy Glades in Longdon left them in trust for Richard Brown by the late John Brown, upon this condition, that if the said Richard did not, within a certain time, pay £40 to oratrix then the land was to go to her. Richard did not pay the money in the given time, and the land ought to come to oratrix.—Vol. i., App. pp. 2, 3.

Marshall v. Watson.—Whittington II., 139.

Complainant.—Anthony Marshall of Kirby Kendall, co. Westmoreland.

Defendants.—Henry Watson and James Watson.

Complainant married Jennett, daughter of Henry Watson, and niece of James Watson. The said Henry and James promised a marriage portion with her of £80 which they will not now pay.

Marshall v. Kniveton.—Hamilton III., 416.

29th Nov., 1652.

Complainant.—John Marshall of London, draper, son and heir of George Marshall, late of Diseworth, co. Leicester, and Katherine his wife, said George being son and heir of George Marshall of Diseworth, co. Leicester, and Margaret his wife.

Defendants.—Joseph Kniveton and Anne his wife.

Certain lands in Diseworth, Leicester, were in possession of George the grandfather, from him they descended to George the son, then to George the grandson (orator's brother), and then to Rebecca, daughter of George the grandson. All these people being dead the lands should come to orator, but defendants having got hold of certain deeds endeavour to defraud orator of the premises.

Marshall v. Stowe.—Whittington II, 114.

22nd Nov., 1673.

Complainant.—Sarah Marshall, relict of John Marshall, late of Diseworth, co. Leicester.

Defendant.—William Stowe.

Complainant should by law have a third part of the property of her husband. But defendant will not allow her to enjoy this, pretending the late John Marshall owed him money.

Marshall v. Trentham.—Collins II., 168.

20th June, 1664.

Complainant.—John Marshall of Diseworth, co. Leicester, gent.

Defendants.—James Trentham, James Abney, and others.

Complainant's wife being sister to one James Abney, late of Loughborough, co. Leicester, complainant with James Trentham backed a bill for the said James Abney; in other ways, James Abney and James Trentham (who is James Abney's stepson, being the son of his now wife by a former husband) became indebted to complainant, and now they confederate to defraud him.—Vol. i., pp. 144, 233.

Marshall v. Shelford.—Hamilton III., 399.

18th May, 1652.

Complainant.—Samuel Marshall of Much Waltham, co. Essex.

Defendant.—Robert Shelford.

Samuel Marshall married Elizabeth, daughter of William Shelford. William promised said Samuel, complainant, £80, as Elizabeth's marriage portion. William Shelford died before it was paid, and Robert his son will not pay it.

Marshall v. Chiborne.—Mitford I., 6.

16th Oct., 1605.

Complainant.—William Marshall of Orsett, co. Essex.

Defendants.—Cristopher Chiborne, William Hurte, and others.

Complainant should have some land in the manor of Orsett as great grandson of Richard Hurte, but Christopher Chiborne and the other defendants who are trustees for the property endeavour to defraud him of it.

Marshall v. Cowell.—Hamilton III., 457.

17th June, 1654.

Complainant.—John Marshall of Queenborough, marriner, and Elizabeth his wife, daughter of Thomas Smith, late of Feversham, co. Kent.

Defendants.—Jonas Cowell, and Francis Smith, an infant.

Thomas Smith left Elizabeth, wife of John Marshall, a legacy of £50, which defendants will not give her.

Marshall v. Cowell.—Collins II., 170.

5th July, 1655.

Complainant.—John Marshall of Milton, next Sittingborne, co. Kent.

Defendants.—Jonah Cowell, William Evans, and others.

Orator's wife, Elizabeth, is the daughter of Thomas Smith, late of Feversham, and should receive certain legacies in the shape of debts which were due from the defendants to Thomas Smith at the time of his death. But defendants will not pay their debts.

Marshall v. Rowe.—Whittington I., 496.

18 July, 1682.

Complainant.—Philip Marshall of Crediton, co. Devon.

Defendants.—John Rowe and others.

Philip, complainant, intermarried with one Agnes Lee, and upon said marriage put £200 in John Rowe's hands in trust for the said Agnes during her life. Agnes is dead, and now John Rowe pretends the £200 belongs to him.

Marshall v. King.—Whittington I., 33.

12 May, 1652.

Complainant.—Thomas Marshall of Abbott Ripton, co. Huntingdon.

Defendant.—Thomas King.

John King by his will made 28 August, 1633, left £60 apiece to his three children, Mary, James, and Robert. If any of these died the survivors to divide the legacies. He made Thomas King his second son executor of his will. Mary King married complainant, and on her coming of age received her legacy. Shortly after she died, but before her death James died under age. Complainant therefore claims a moiety of James's legacy.—Vol. i., App. p. 11.

Marshall v. London.—Mitford I., 60.

1st June, 1644.

Complainant.—John Marshall of Wimbish, co. Essex, brother of Stephen Marshall of Walden, co. Essex.

Defendant.—William London and Martha his wife, sister and administratrix of the goods of the late Stephen Marshall.

On the 8th of April, 1643, Stephen Marshall made his last will, and left everything to John Marshall, complainant, and his children. But Martha, the defendant, had letters of administration granted to her without right, and keeps all Stephen's estate.

Marshall v. Marshall.—Bridges II., 206.

26th May, 1699.

Complainant.—Richard Marshall of St. Clement's Danes, Middlesex, butcher.

Defendants.—Samuel Marshall a minor by Edward Stanton the elder his guardian and Rebecca his wife, Michael Bennett and Lydia his wife.

Hannah Marshall, late wife of orator, about two years since possessed herself of certain household valuables of orator's. The said Hannah, having done this, employed the said valuables in trade. On the 24th February, 1698, Hannah died when orator was away from home. On orator's return he found nearly all his valuables had been removed by Samuel Marshall his son, Mansell Bennett of St. James's, Westminster, and Lydia his wife, and Edward Staunton of St. Marten's in the fields. The confederates pretend they have removed nothing, and will not give the valuables up because complainant does not know what they are.

Michael Bennet and Lydia answer that they received some trifles from Hannah upon her deathbed, in return for £4 lent to Hannah by Lydia, who was her sister. They believe Hannah owned herself the things they received.

Edward Stanton says Hannah Marshall separated from her husband because of his mistreatment, and excepting the house which she had left her by her mother, Sarah Rolph, she had at that time nothing in the world. Edward Stanton and Rebecca his wife helped her in her poverty, but complainant never did, nor had Hannah any of his goods at her death.

Marshall v. Barker.—Bridges III., 282.

4th Feb., 1692.

Complainants.—William Marshall of London, baker, and Elizabeth his wife, and Anne Barker an infant by the said William Marshall her guardian. Elizabeth and Anne are daughters of Richard Barker of Rotherith, co. Surrey.

Defendants.—Richard Barker and others.

William Barker, grandfather of oratrix, had certain property called the Bell and the Little Custom House. This he left to his wife Elizabeth, and after her death to descend to his eldest son, and after to the children of his eldest son. Both he and his wife died, leaving two sons, Richard and George. Richard died some time since, and oratrices ought to have come into possession. But George the son of William the grandfather, taking advantage of oratrices' infancy, took possession of the property and shortly after died. Richard his son is now in possession and will not leave.

Marshall v. Pritchard.—Bridges IV., 422.

9th May, 1662.

Complainant.—Symon Marshall of Dedington, co. Oxford, executor of the last will of Elizabeth Gilkes, late of Dedington, his grandmother.

Defendant.—William Pritchard.

About 1652 Elizabeth Gilkes gave William Pritchard £200 in trust for her daughter Elizabeth Marshall, since deceased, and late wife of Edward Marshall of Dedington. Should Elizabeth Marshall die it was understood that that £200 should descend to orator, and failing orator, to his infant son Symon. But now William Pritchard, confederating with persons unknown, refuses to give up the money.

The defendant says the money was left in trust with him for Symon, complainant's son, and therefore refuses to give any account of the money to complainant.

Marshall v. Roberts.—Mitford II., 130.

18th May, 1658.

Complainants.—Isaac Marshall, Anne Marshall, and Martha Marshall, children of Margaret Marshall and infants, by Ann Shewell of Greet, parish Winchcombe, co. Gloucester, widow, sister to their mother.

Defendants.—Thomas Roberts, William Reeve, and others.

The infants' late grandfather, Giles Roberts, left to Margaret Marshall and her heirs an annuity of £100. The defendants now endeavour to defraud complainants of their right to this money, the will of the said Giles Roberts having been lost.

Marshall v. Love.—Mitford II., 102; Hamilton I., 237, 99. 27 November, 1650.

Complainants.—Erasmus Marshall of East Rudham, co. Norfolk, and Dorothy his wife.

Defendants.—Henry Love of Cranworth and Mary his wife.

Thomas Walpole was seized of some lands in Cranworth, in co. Norfolk, which he sold to defendants for £210. Shortly after this Thomas Walpole died intestate. Dorothy the complainant being his next heir claims £300, but defendants combining with others refuse to give her the money, pretending that Thomas Walpole has a son living.

Marshall v. Crofte.—Whittington I., 42.

12 Feb., 1699.

Complainants.—Robert Marshall and Anne his wife, daughter of Robert Croft, deceased, co. York.

Defendant.—Jennet Croft, widow.

James Croft, uncle of oratrix, was seized of lands in the parish of Leeds, and of a great personal estate. He died about 1643, and in his will left £20 to oratrix, besides other legacies, notably to Robert Croft, eldest son of Robert, oratrix's father, and Anne Croft, daughter of Thomas Croft, oratrix's uncle and testator's brother. But now Jennet Croft, relict of the late James Croft the testator, and his executrix, will not pay the £20 legacy.

Marshall v. Hodgson.—Hamilton I., 238, 108.

13th Feb., 1651.

Complainant.—John Marshall of North Allerton, co. York, grocer.

Defendants.—James Hodgson and Margaret his wife.

Complainant upon his marriage with Phillis Fossicke got a promise of a certain marriage portion from Lancelott Fossicke, Phillis' father. Before he was paid this both Lancelott and Phillis died. Now James Hodgson and Margaret his wife, daughter of said Lancelott and executrix of his will, refuse to pay the marriage portion.

Marshall v. Harrison.—Mitford I., 47.

30th Nov., 1697.

Complainants.—John Marshall of North Allerton and Elizabeth his wife and others.

Defendants.—John Harrison, Robert Thorpe, and others.

John Harrison and other defendants have through some means got hold of a great deal of the personal estate of the late John Scott, oratrix's father, and will not give it up to oratrix his next heir.

Marshall v. Fairfax.—Hamilton I., 221, 41; 229, 46; 234, 9; 235, 43; Collins, Dep., 128.

3rd Feb., 1708.

The answer of Thomas Lord Fairfax, Baron of Cameroon, in that part of Great Britain called Scotland, to the Bill of Henry Marshall, complainant.

He believes his father Henry Lord Fairfax, did borrow of William Marshall, the complainant's grandfather, £500. He believes Thomas Lord Fairfax, in the Bill named, deceased, was in his lifetime seized of the manor of Rigton. Henry Marshall's father was William Marshall and his grandfather was William.—Vol. i., p. 317.

Marshall v. Saunders.—Reynardson III., 3.

17th May, 1642.

Complainant.—Ingram Marshall of Newington, co. Kent, brother of Thomas Marshall, both sons of Thomas Marshall.

Defendants.—John Saunders and Alice his wife.

Thomas Marshall, complainant's brother, on the 26th January, 1618, made his will, and by it gave complainant all the lands left him by his late father, Thomas Marshall, in Newington. To Alice Marshall his wife £50, also £25 now in the hands of David March his father in law. To Alice Marshall his daughter £50, to be paid when she is eighteen years old. He made complainant executor, and gave him the residue of his goods. The defendants pretend the said will is not genuine.—Vol. i., p. 121.

Marshall v. Saunders.—Mitford V., 314.

14th Feb., 1649.

Complainant.—Elizabeth Marshall of Great Wytley, co. Worcester, spinster, administratrix of the goods of Elizabeth Marshall, late of Inchberrowe or Inclerowe, co. Worcester, widow.

Defendant.—Anne Saunders, relict of John Saunders.

William Marshall, deceased, had property called Cockhay, situate in Oddingley, co. Worcester, and died so seized. His son John entered into the premises and died without issue. One Elizabeth Marshall also died with a great personal estate. Oratrix is heir to both John and Elizabeth, and should inherit their estates. But Anne Saunders, whose husband owed the late Elizabeth £20, will not pay, and confederating with others also keeps from her certain deeds.—Vol. i., App. p. 10.

Marshall v. Mabyn.—Bridges I. 7.

25th May, 1650.

Complainant.—Thomas Marshall of Pomiestocke, co. Cornwall, and Honor his wife; Robert Webb of the same parish and Phillipe his wife, the daughters of one John Mabyn late of Pomiestock, deceased.

Defendant.—Andrew Mabyn, son of Alexander Mabyn, brother of John.

One Alexander Mabyn being possessed of some property called the Souther Beare Ball, Easter Beare Ball, and Norther Beare Ball, did about 1611, in consideration of a marriage between John Mabyn (his son and oratrice's father) and Anne Mill, daughter of Diggory Mill, convey the said property to the said John. Afterwards John being in need of money, regranted the said property to his father as security for the payment of certain sums of money lent to him by his father at that time. Shortly after this John died, and Alexander came into the said property. He also died, and Andrew Mabyn his son refuses to give up the property to oratrixes, who are entitled to it.

Marshall v. Prees.—Mitford II., 134.

23 June, 1658.

Complainant.—Thomas Marshall of Leomster, co. Hereford, yeoman, and Sybell his wife, and James Phillips of Southericke, ? Southwark, co. Surrey, gardener.

Defendants.—James Preece, William Preece, and William Webb.

John Morris, deceased, of Kinnersley, had in his lifetime certain lands in Kinnersley. He settled these on himself for life, then on Margery his wife, and afterwards on their heirs. John and Margery had issue, Walter, Elizabeth, and Johan, and they both shortly after died. Walter then entered the premises and married Katherine, daughter of Oliver Preece. Elizabeth, daughter of said John Morris, married and had issue Sybel, oratrix. Johan married John Phillips and had issue James Phillips, orator. Walter, the said son of late John Morris died, and Katherine his wife took possession. She has sold the property aforesaid to defendants, which she had no right to do.

Marshall v. Price.—Collins II., 235.

20th June, 1679.

Complainant.—Sybell Marshall of Leominster, co. Hereford, relict of —— Marshall.

Defendants.—James Price, Thomas Price, and William Webb.

John Morris, of the parish of Kinnersley, co. Hereford, oratrix's late grandfather, had some land in Kinnersley. John Morris died 60 years since, leaving Walter Morris his son, who died without issue, and Elizabeth his daughter, oratrix's mother. Oratrix ought to inherit this land as her mother's heir, but the defendants, who had a lease of it from John and Walter Morris, pretend it is theirs.

Marshall v. Price.—Collins II., 152.

The several answers of James Price, William Price, and William Webbe, defendants, to the Bill of Thomas Marshall and Sybil his wife.

They say they are willing to pay Sybil the £15 due to her as being daughter of Elizabeth, who was daughter of John Morrice.

Marshall v. Stephens.—Mitford II., 155.

Complainant.—Thomas Marshall of Oakesey, co. Wilts., and Margaret his wife.

Defendants.—Henry Stephens and Henry Blanford.

Margaret, oratrix, is the daughter of the late Thomas Earle. This Thomas Earle left her £80 in his will, and made his wife Margaret executrix thereof, and defendants overseers. Margaret has paid the £80 to defendants, but they will not pay oratrix.

Marshall v. Earle.—Mitford V., 319.

28th Nov., 1665.

Complainant.—Thomas Marshall of Oakesey, co. Wilts., and Margaret his wife, daughter of Thomas Earle, late of Kemble, co. Wilts.

Defendants.—Mary Earle, relict of Thomas Earle, and Henry Blandford the elder, of Poole, and Henry Stephens of Kemble.

About twenty years ago Thomas Earle made his last will and left oratrix £80. This money he put into defendants' hands as trustees for oratrix, and now they will not pay.

Marshall v. Coventry.—Hamilton I., 239, 60.

5th April, 1687.

Complainant.—Frances Marshall, widow, administratrix of the goods of William Wakelyn, late of Cashalton, co. Surrey.

Defendants.—Francis Coventry and Dame Elizabeth Hoskyne *als.* Coventry.

William Wakelyn was in the service of Dame Elizabeth, both before and after her marriage with Frauncis Coventry. At divers times he lent her money, in all amounting to £200. William Wakelyn is dead and defendants refuse to pay oratrix the sum.

Marshall v. Waterer.—Whittington II., 151.

Dec., 1684.

The answers of Frauncis Coventry and Dame Elizabeth Hoskins to the Bill of Frances Marshall, widow, complainant, also the answer of Margaret Waterer.

Margaret Waterer says she never took any of the goods of William Wakelyn, which she had not a right to.

Marshall v. Jeffreys.—Bridges, Depositions, Chas. II., 400.

Interrogatories.

Do you know complainants, Thomas Marshall and Anne his wife, William Bouner and Douglas his wife, and defendants, Herbert Jeffreys and Susannah his wife and William Palmer? Did you know Sir Henry Vaughan, knight, late grandfather of the said Anne and Douglas? How long is it since he died? Did you know John Vaughan, son of Sir Henry and father of the said executrices? How long is it since he died? Did you know Douglas, widdow of the said John Vaughan, deceased, and Frauncis and Henry Vaughan, deceased, sons of the said John? Do you know the manor of Kirkham? Did not it belong first to Sir Henry Vaughan, then to Francis (John dying before his father), then to Henry? Did not Henry mortgage the said property to Lady Rockingham, and did not Thomas Marshall and the other complainants redeem the same? Witnesses were examined at Blyth, co. Nottingham.

Marshall v. Jeffreys.—Whittington, Depositions, 807.

23 Sept. 1675.

Depositions taken on behalf of Herbert Jeffreys and Susanna his wife, defendants, to the Bill of Thomas Marshall and Anne his wife, William Bonner and Douglas his wife, taken at the house of Cristopher Conyers, in Stonegate, city of York.

Thomas Langley of the city of York, says, he knew Sir Henry Vaughan, Francis Vaughan, and Henry Vaughan, but did not know John Vaughan, but he believes the said John died before Sir Henry, and knows Sir Henry died in 1655, and that Francis Vaughan and Henry Vaughan are also since dead. The complainants Anne and Douglas, and the defendant Susanna, are sisters and heirs of the said Henry, who was brother and heir of Francis, who was son and heir of John, who was son and heir of Sir Henry. Knows the manor of Kirkham.—Vol. ii., part i., p. 107.

Marshall v. Glossoppe.—Collins V., 278.

25 Nov., 1681.

Complainant.—Gilbert Marshall of Banketopp, in the parish of Hope, co. Derby, and Margaret his wife, late relict of Edmond Glossoppe of Offerton, in the said parish of Hope.

Defendant.—Richard Glossoppe.

Robert Glossoppe of Ryeley, in parish of Hope, had lands in the said parish and left them to Margaret the complainant, his mother. Margaret entered into possession, but now Richard Glossope, testator's elder brother, tries to oust complainant.

Marshall v. Glossopp.—Collins, Depositions, 124.
25 April, 34 Chas. II.

Interrogatories to be administered on behalf of Gilbert Marshall and Margaret his wife and William Glossopp, infant, against Ralph Glossopp, defendant.

Did you know Edmund Glossopp late of Offerton, in the parish of Hope, co. Derby? Did you know Robert Glossopp, second son of the said Edward?

Marshall v. Crooke.—Collins II., 209.
13th Nov., 1672.

Complainant.—Thomas Marshall of Denby, co. York, yeoman, brother and heir of Richard Marshall, clothier, of Penistone, co. York, deceased, who died without issue about 1670. Richard's mother is Joane.

Defendant.—John Crooke, clerk.

Richard and his mother Joan borrowed some money from John Crooke, father of defendant, mortgaging to him some land lying in Showbread, also some land called Shacklerowes (? Thacker Rowes). If the interest and principal of said loan were not paid by a certain date the lands were to go to John Crooke. John Crooke, Joan, and Richard died. Now John the son tries to force the orator (who inherited the lands from his brother) to give him the land, though he is willing to pay both principal and interest of the debt.

Marshall v. Crooke.—Collins II., 209.
24 Feb., 1672.

The answer of John Crooke, clerk, to the Bill of Complaint of Thomas Marshall.

It was agreed between the parties that if Richard and Joan his mother or their heirs should fail to pay John Crooke, father of this defendant, or his heirs, the agreed sums upon the agreed dates, that then upon John Crooke or his heirs paying £18, they should have the property for ever.—Vol. i., p. 277.

Marshall v. Burward.—Bridges I., 33.
16th May, 1657.

Complainant.—John Marshall of St. Lawrence in Ilketshall, co. Suffolk, tayler, and Elizabeth his wife, formerly the wife of William Cullingforthe of Mettingham, co. Suffolk.

Defendants.—William Burward and Frauncis Burward.

William Burward, father of Elizabeth the oratrix and Frauncis her brother, did upon her marriage with William Cullingforthe promise her £100. This was never paid in the life of the said William Cullingforthe, and now the defendants refuse to satisfy the debt.

Marshall v. Emsworth.—Collins II., 118.
28th Sept., 1648.

The answer of Henry Emsworth, one of the defendants, to the Bill of John Marshall, complainant.

Anne Parkhurst was sister to Katherine Stedd. He married Katherine with the approval of Anne Parkhurst. Complainant was executor of Anne Parkhurst's will and defrauded defendants and Anne, daughter of Katherine, of their inheritance.

Marshall v. Stedd.—Bridges I., 26.

23 Jan., 1656.

Complainant.—John Marshall of St. Bride's, London.

Defendants.—Robert Stedd, Katherine his wife, and Anne Stedd his daughter, infant.

Anne Parkhurst of Southwark, co. Surrey, cousin of orator, did at her death leave him some money. This money Katherine Stedd, wife of Robert Stedd and sister of the late Anne Parkhurst, pretends should belong to Anne her daughter.

Marshall v. Sparke.—Whittington I., 34.

11th Nov., 1646.

Complainant.—Anthony Marshall of Howden, co. Yorke, and Jeane his wife, late relict of Edward Musgrave, and others.

Defendant.—Robert Spark and others.

Edward Musgrave gave defendants a messuage in settlement of a debt, but now defendants claim the debt from complainant Musgrave's heirs.

Marshall v. Fanshawe.—Collins II., 105.

11 June, 1649.

Complainant.—Frauncis Marshall, citizen of London.

Defendants.—Thomas Fanshawe and Katherine his wife.

Thomas Knighton was in his lifetime seized of the manor of Bayford, co. Hertford, He had two sons, Thomas and John, and he settled Bayford on John his younger son. At his death John entered into possession. John had issue George and Ralph (who had issue Anne, who is orator's mother). George had issue John, who died without issue. The property ought therefore to come to orator through Anne. But Thomas Fanshawe, son of Sir Thomas Fanshawe and Katherine his wife, pretend some right to the estate.

Marshall v. Sheere.—Hamilton I., 220, 28.

6 June, 1653.

Complainant.—Anne Marshall, widow, relict of Henry Marshall, late of Hackney.

Defendant.—Mary Sheere, widow.

John Knighton, esq., deceased, was in his lifetime seized of lands in co. Hertford. Upon his death the same came to his son Sir George Knighton, who died without issue. It then descended to Ralph, brother to Sir George, and he had one daughter, namely oratrix. But now Mary Sheere, confederating with others, pretend oratrix has no right to the property.

Marshall v. Gardiner.—Collins II., 130.

1656.

Complainant.—Anne Marshall, widow.

Defendant.—Mary Gardiner, widow.

The defence of Mary Gardiner.—She denies that upon the death of John Knighton, son of Sir George Knighton, deceased, the manors of Little Amwell and Renetts Hall should by right have descended to complainant, as John conveyed them away in his lifetime.

Marshall v. Stevenson.—Mitford II., 136.

31st Oct., 1660.

Complainant.—Richard Marshall of London and Susan his wife.
Defendant.—John Stevenson.

Roger Stevenson, who married Katherine Page, aunt of Susan, oratrix, owed Susan some money which now John Stevenson his son, his father being dead, will not pay.

Marshall v. Cholmeley.—Reynardson I., 408.

10th Nov., 1634.

Complainant.—William Marshall of Aslabye, co. Yorke.
Defendant.—Henry Cholmeley.

William, complainant, because his unmarried brother Thomas Marshall was very poor, intended to give him a close called Wrelton close. Thomas died on the 27th May, 1633, before the deed conveying this property was signed. Now Henry Cholmeley and John Armitage endeavour as trustees of the said property, to keep it for Thomas's heirs. William Marshall's wife is Alice.—Vol. i., p. 22.

Marshall v. Dawes.—Collins II., 243.

21st Oct., 1682.

The several answers of Drew Dawes, Anne his wife, and Elizabeth Nicholson, to the Bill of John Marshall.

Drewe Dawes says William Nicholson, late of Tuddington, co. Middlesex, was in his lifetime possessed of the lands in Bill mentioned. He was father of Anne and Elizabeth, defendants. The complainant never purchased the said lands from defendants, who came into a part thereof, but he may have purchased the parts which descended to Mary and Rebecca, sisters of the defendants.

Marshall v. Ward.—Collins II., 247.

10 Oct., 1683.

Complainant.—Richard Marshall, second son of John Marshall of Tuddington, co. Middlesex, infant, by his said father.
Defendant.—John Ward.

Richard Marshall, late citizen of London, complainant's uncle, was in his lifetime possessed of lands and houses in Prince's Street and Drury Lane. About the 6th October, 1679, he gave the said property by will to Elizabeth his wife. Elizabeth shortly after by will gave the said estate to Richard, her nephew. But now defendant who administered her goods, tries to defraud complainant of the same.—Vol. i., App., pp. 9, 32.

Marshall v. Beinton.—Collins II., 275.

20th Oct., 1682.

Complainant.—Edward Marshall of Worcester, son of John, infant, by Thomas Giles, guardian.
Defendant.—Richard Beinton.

Edward Marshall, father of John Marshall, and grandfather of complainant, had some lands in Worcester which ought to have descended to complainant upon the death of John Marshall, his father, which happened in May, 1677. But defendant, who is complainant's tutor, endeavours to defraud orator.—Vol. i., App., p. 27.

Marshall v. Whetstone.—Bridges I., 17.

1655.

Complainant.—Martha Marshall of St. Sepulchre's, London, spinster.

Defendants.—William Whetstone the younger, and Simon Marshall and his wife.

William Whetstone the elder, late of High Holborne, baker, about 1648 borrowed £25 from oratrix. Shortly after he died, and his son William the younger refuses to pay oratrix, declaring that William the elder died without any estate. But he has paid other debts, such as a debt to Simon Marshall and Martha his wife, daughter of William deceased.

Marshall v. Sacheverell.—Depositions, Bridges, 396.

4th Oct., 17 James I.

Interrogatories to be answered.

Do you know Thomas Marshall, complainant. and do you know Francis Marshall, complainant's father, and Thomas Marshall, his grandfather? Do you know the farm in Barton? Did Thomas the grandfather buy the same from Elizabeth Bougham?—Vol. i., p. 276.

Marshall v. Rudd.—Depositions, Bridges, 396.

5th Oct., 3rd James I.

Interrogatories to be answered.

Do you know the complainant, John Marshall, and the defendant, Matthew Rudd? Do you know Alice Brett was owner of the messuage in question, and the wife of William Hull? Did not Agnes Hull, daughter of William Hull, marry Richard Marshall of Chelmessed, and had she not a right to the said messuage? What issue had Richard Marshall and his wife?

Answer.

Four sons, viz.: (1) Thomas, (2) Richard, (3) John, (4) William, and two daughters, (1) Alice, (2) Agnes. Thomas died without issue, and Richard had John the complainant.

Marshall v. Cooper.—Reynardson I. and II., 408.

12th Feb., 1660.

Complainant.—Robert Marshall of Stradewood, parish Netherbury. co. Dorsett, son of Robert Marshall of Bowood, co. Dorsett.

Defendants.—Henry Cooper and Anne his wife, and William Marshall.

Robert Marshall the elder did about 1641 make his last will, and by it, besides certain legacies to his daughters, did leave orator £100 to be paid by William Marshall, eldest son of Robert the elder, out of lands called Pomehayes in Netherbury, which Robert the elder left him. He also made Anne his wife responsible for his (complainant's) education. Anne and William were executors of the said will, but they have never paid complainant his legacy. Anne has lately married Henry Cooper.

Marshall v. Fettiplace.—Collins II., 113.

Nov., 1651.

Complainants.—Oliver Marshall of Bowe, co. Middlesex, and Jane his wife, Cristopher Newland of Farnham, and Elizabeth his wife, and John Branch of Horsham, co. Sussex, and Ann his wife.

Defendants.—William Fettiplace and Anne Best, widow.

The three oratrices were the three daughters of Nicholas Best, late of Horsham, deceased, Elizabeth Ede was grandmother of the said oratrices. She died in 1625, leaving £40 each to the said oratrices. But now William Fettiplace and Anne Best try to defraud them of their rights.

Marshall v. Crompton.—Collins II., 139.

2 Nov., 1637.

The answer of Thomas Crompton, one of the defendants, to the Bill of William Marshall and Anne Marshall.

He believes that John Procter in the Bill named did make a former conveyance to Sir Richard Weston, kt., of property mentioned in the Bill.

Marshall v. Proctor.—Collins II., 139.

Complainants.—Anne Marshall of Ridgly, co. Stafford, widow, executrix of last will of George Marshall, her husband, deceased, and William Marshall an infant, by Anne his mother.

Defendants.—John Proctor, Timothy Rawlyns, and others.

John Proctor, late of Stone, co. Stafford, held some tenements, etc., in Bradley, in the manor of Alton, co. Stafford. This land, because of a marriage between George Marshall, complainant's father, and Elizabeth the daughter of John Proctor, was conveyed to the said George Marshall. Elizabeth, George Marshall's first wife, died, and his second, Anne, the oratrix, had issue, William the orator. John Proctor and others endeavour to keep this land from him.

Marshall v. Procter.—Mitford, Depositions, 678.

28th Feb., 1659.

John Davenport of Stafford examined on behalf of William and Anne Marshall.

He did know George Marshall, deceased, and Elizabeth Procter his first wife, and daughter of defendant, John Procter.

On the marriage of said couple, John Procter agreed to give the said George Marshall his lands and tenements in Bradley in the manor of Alton, co. Stafford, and to the heirs of the said George and Elizabeth. Failing issue, the lands of George and also of William Marshall, George's father, to go to Anne Procter, Elizabeth's sister.

Marshall v. Weston.—Collins II., 138.

The replication of William Marshall by Anne Marshall his mother, to the several answers of Sir Richard Weston, kt., Thomas Crompton, John Proctor, and others.

They say that the deed mentioned by Sir Richard Weston as having been indented previously is a false one. Elizabeth, wife of George Marshall, was daughter of John Proctor.

Marshall v. Weston.—Collins II., 139.

17th Feb., 1637.

The answer of Sir Richard Weston, kt., to the Bill of Anne Marshall and William her son.

He says it is true John Proctor in the Bill named by deed indented 8th September, in the third year of his now majesty, covenants to George Marshall and Elizabeth his then wife, all property in Bill mentioned. He had, however, covenanted it to defendants for certain purposes previously.

Marshall v. Cudmore.—Collins II., 123.

11th Feb., 1653.

Complainant.—Elizabeth Marshall, relict of Alexander Marshall, late of Loxbeare, co. Devon, for herself and Hugh her son, infant.

Defendants.—Zacharie Cudmore, gentleman, Edward Grave, and others.

One George Southcote granted the advowson of the church of Loxbeare, co. Devon, to the late Alexander Marshall, Hugh Marshall his eldest son, and their heirs for ever. Now defendants endeavour to keep Hugh out of his inheritance.—Vol. i., p. 109.

Marshall v. Smith.—Collins II., 131.

12 Feb., 1649.

Complainant.—John Marshall, citizen of London, sometime Queen's Bailliff on the then manor of Croyland, co. Lincoln.

Defendant.—Walter Smith.

Edward Smith of Market Deeping, deceased, got orator to lend him some money in April, 1631. This orator did, but Edward Smith, who was orator's uncle, put off the repayment of the debt, and gave out he was going to make orator his heir. This he never did, and Walter Smith, his executor, also refuses to pay the debt.

Marshall v. Langdon.—Collins II., 194.

30th June, 1699.

Complainants.—Alexander Marshall of Neither Stowey, co. Somerset, gentleman, and Anne his wife, daughter of John Crosse, late of Burlescombe.

Defendants.—John Langdon and Anne his wife.

Anne Cogan, grandmother of oratrix, did on the 15th January, 15th year of the King that now is, make her will and by it leave oratrix £70. She made Anne Langdon, her daughter, sole executrix. John and Anne have never paid oratrix her legacy, nor made an inventory of the late Anne Cogan's estate.

Marshall v. Langdon.—Collins, Depositions, 121.

Interrogatories to be administered on behalf of Alexander Marshall and Anne his wife, complainants, and John Langdon and Anne his wife.

What personal estate had Anne the complainant upon her marriage with Alexander Marshall? What personal estate did the said John Crosse die possessed of? Was not Dorothy Crosse, complainant's aunt, one of the executors of his will?—Vol. i., p. 77.

Marshall v. Francis.—Collins II., 202.

31st May, 1671.

Complainant.—Elizabeth Marshall, infant daughter of John Marshall, deceased, who was son of Thomas Marshall of Wellesbourne, co. Warwick, by Richard Wilson, her father-in-law.

Defendant.—John Frauncis and Elizabeth his wife.

Thomas Marshall the grandfather made his will 20th April, 1653, leaving certain property t6 John his son. Shortly after his death Elizabeth his relict married John Frauncis and took possession of the property unjustly. John, oratrix's father, dying soon after Thomas his father.

Marshall v. Francis.—Hamilton II., 240, 5.

29th Feb., 1675.

Complainant.—Elizabeth Marshall, infant daughter of John Marshall and granddaughter of Thomas Marshall, both deceased, by Elizabeth Wilson, her mother.

Defendants.—John Francis, Elizabeth his wife, and George Francis.

Thomas Marshall the grandfather held lands in Bradwell, co. Gloucester, and did about 1653, appoint, that Elizabeth his second wife, now wife of John Francis, of Wellsborne, should have the profits of said lands during the minority of his son John. The defendants pretend that John Marshall conveyed the said lands to them in his lifetime.—Vol. i., App. p. 4.

Marshall v. Perrot.—Reynardson IV., 101.

3rd Dec., 1686.

Complainants.—John Marshall of Warboys, co. Huntingdon, and Mary his wife, daughter and heir of Richard Perrot, late of Gamlingay, co. Cambridge, who was next brother and heir to Robert Perrot, late of Warboys.

Defendant.—George Perrot of Warboys.

Richard Perrot, father of oratrix had three brothers Robert, George, and Edward Perrot. Robert died intestate, and George took out letters of administration of his goods. But the real estate of the said Robert should have descended to Richard and then to oratrix, instead of which defendant has taken the rents and profits thereof.—Vol. i., p. 198.

Marshall v. Brackley.—Reynardson IV., 100.

1st April, 1687.

Complainant.—John Marshall of the Inner Temple, London, son of John Marshall and brother of Richard Marshall, who died intestate and without issue.

Defendants.—Richard Brackley and John Brackley.

One Luke Cordwell was to pay £900 for some lands in the parishes of St. Mary's and All-hallowes to Richard Brackley. £500 of this was in trust, however, to the use of Anne Marshall, wife of John Marshall, complainant's father, and her heirs for ever. Anne and John, also Richard, complainant's brother, are dead, and complainant should have the £500, but defendant will not give it to him.

Marshall v. Kirke.—Mitford III., 390.

13th Feb., 1687.

Complainant.—Isabel Marshall of the parish of St. Giles in the fields, co. Middlesex.

Defendant.—Elizabeth Kirke, widow.

The late Thomas Kirke of the parish of St. James, Clarkenwell, co. Middlesex, did by his last will leave Isabel Marshall, complainant, his daughter, a legacy of £35. He made Elizabeth Kirke his wife sole executrix, and she will not pay oratrix her legacy.

Marshall v. Capell.—Mitford III., 403.

10th May, 1687.

Complainant.—Richard Marshall of Brayles, co. Warwick, executor of the last will of Susannah Oakley, daughter of Humphrey Oakley, late of Brayles.

Defendant.—Henry Capell and others.

Susannah made orator sole executor of her will, and died with a great personal estate, chiefly in jewels and money. The defendants have taken possession of this estate, and will not give it to complainant.—Vol. i., p. 46.

Marshall v. Halford.—Mitford, Depositions, 679.

9 Jan., 1590.

Depositions taken at Shipton upon Stowre, co. Worcester, on behalf of George Marshall and Christian Marshall, complainants, against Henry Halford and Christian his wife, defendants. Richard . . . . . of Barcheston, co. Warwick, examined.

Henry Halford entered into an obligation of £100 with William and Jean Marshall, son and daughter of John Marshall, the condition being that the said William and Jean should enjoy all their lives the lands in Shipton upon Stowre, now in occupation of George Marshall.—Vol. i., App., p. 38.

Marshall v. Younge.—Mitford, Depositions, 681.

13th August, 32 Eliz.

William Marshall of the city of York, about 66 years old, was examined on the part of Richard Marshall against James Hobson, John Scott, Elizabeth Bainbridge, Jane Younge, and others.

He says he knows Richard Marshall, of London, haberdasher. He also knew Richard Marshall of Wakefield, complainant's father. Richard the father had some property in the city of York. He put the said premises into the hands of the trustees for the use of himself and Margaret Ellys whom he afterwards married, for their lives, and after to their heirs.

Marshall v. Morton.—Whittington I., 39.

14th April, 1649.

Complainant.—William Marshall of Stannington, co. York, and Anne his wife, one of the daughters of Richard Hoyland, late of Stannington.

Defendants.—Godfrey Morton and Anne his wife.

Anne, one of the defendants, is relict and executrix of the will of Richard Hoyland. In this will he left Anne, complainant, a legacy, of which defendants endeavour to defraud her.

Marshall v. Mostyn.—Reynardson IV., 116.

31st May, 1688.

Complainant.—Edward Marshall of East Greenwich, co. Kent, glazier, and Elizabeth his wife, sister and heir of Edward Crumpton.

Defendants.—Roger Mostyn and others.

Elizabeth, as heir to Edward Crumpton, should have come into some property in the parishes of Wrexham, Bromboe, and Pennly, co. Denbigh, but complainants being very old and living far away, the defendants have defrauded them of their property.

Marshall v. Hatt.—Mitford II., 94.

2 April, 1650.

The answer of Thomas Hatt, one of the defendants, to the Bill of Anne Marshall, widow.

He believes the said John Goodrich, father of complainant, was in his lifetime seized of a messuage situate in St. Edmonds Bury, and that he made his will, leaving his eldest son John Goodrich sole executor. He married Martha Goodrich, sister of complainant. He does not believe the said Martha owed Anne Marshall any money.

Marshall v. Burton.—Collins II., 154.

Feb. 1636.

Complainants.—George Marshall and Susan his wife, William Watson and Jane his wife, Richard Coward and Anne his wife, and Jeane Lewis.

Defendant.—Sir Henry Burton, knight.

John Lewis, deceased, had some property in the parish of St. Phillips in the city of Bristol. This property should by right descend to the complainants, the four daughters of John Lewis, deceased, but Sir Henry Burton has unwarrantably taken possession.

Marshall v. Newcombe.—Whittington I., 467.

23rd June, 1658.

Complainant.—Edward Marshall of Tadcaster, co. York, infant, by Mary Taylor his mother, late wife of Edward Marshall who was son of Edward Marshall.

Defendants.—Tobyas Newcombe and Elizabeth his wife, and William Marshall.

Edward Marshall, grandfather of Edward Marshall, complainant, had certain lands and tenements in Tadcaster, also the grandfather was heir to certain lands, then in possession of Anne Sainter his mother and orator's great grandmother. The grandfather's property descended to Edward, complainant's father, when in his infancy, and under the guardianship of one William Marshall, who was no kinsman of his, but whose wife was. Now the said William, combining with Tobyas Newcombe, endeavour to keep back the property from complainant, Edward the father being dead.—Vol. i., p. 116.

Marshall v. Pitt.—Collins II., 275.

6th Feb., 1681.

Complainant.—Joseph Marshall of Hackney, co. Middlesex, son of Joseph.

Defendant.—James Pitt, infant, son of Thomas Pitt, deceased, by his mother, Mary Pitt.

Joseph Marshall, complainant's father, lent Thomas Pitt, defendant's father, some money. The interest on this loan defendant could not pay, so he gave over some houses he had to Joseph the father, and told his tenants to pay their rent to him. The rent did not amount to the interest due. Since Thomas Pitt's death his son James unjustly claims the premises. Vol. i., p. 196.

Marshall v. Towerson.—Collins II., 297.

4 June, 1685.

Complainant.—Thomas Marshall and Isabell his wife, both of the town and county of Kingston upon Hull, she being sole executrix of the will of Joseph Towerson of the same place.

Defendant.—Nicholas Towerson.

Joseph Towerson entered into a bond of £200 with Nicholas Towerson his brother. This bond Lawrence Towerson, their father, commanded in his will should be cancelled. Isabell, oratrix, was wife to the said Joseph, and is now executrix of his last will. And now Nicholas the defendant endeavours to get the £200 from defendant.

Marshall v. Williamson.—Bridges IV., 525.

Complainant.—Edward Marshall of the parish of St. Dunston's, London, executor of the last Will of Robert Burton, late of the parish of St. Andrew, Holburne, Middlesex.

Defendant.—William Williamson of the city of York.

Robert Burton had certain property at his death in the name of William Williamson. Upon the death of Robert Burton, orator, who was his executor, went to him and asked him to give up the property, but he will not, and pretends it is his.

The answer of William Williamson to the Bill of Edward Marshall.

He says for several years he has lived near the city of York, whereas Robert Burton lived near the city of London. He has had no business dealings with him whatever, and has certainly no property belonging to him in his name.

Marshall v. May.—Hamilton I., 237, 65.

29th Nov., 1654.

Complainants.—James Marshall, Peter Marshall, Jean Marshall, sons and daughter of John Marshall, late of St. Evall, co. Cornwall.

Defendant.—Humphrey May.

John Marshall the father was possessed of sundry lands called Trehar, in the parish of St. Evall, and about twelve years since sold the same to John Robins for £150. He had other personal estate besides the purchase money for the said estate, and died about eleven years since, leaving all his property to Humphrey May in trust for orators. Humphrey May will not pay complainants their due, although they are all of age long since.

Marshall v. Midgeley.—Reynardson III., 16, 18.

15th June, 1654.

Complainants.—Arthur Marshall of Ayslaby, co. York, and Elizabeth his wife, daughter and heir of John Myers of the city of York.

Defendants.—William Midgeley, William Mellish, and others.

One William Garbut owed John Myers great sums of money, and in payment thereof conveyed his lands in Sowerby, Bagby, and Thirske to John Myers. Defendants now pretend they have a prior right to the premises on account of a debt owing to them from the said William Garbut.—See *Marshall v. Garbut*, Reynardson III., 18, dated 15 June, 1655.—Vol. I., p. 19.

Marshall v. Hutchinson.—Whittington V., 232.
12 May, 1684.

Complainants.—William Marshall of Bolling, in the parish of Bradford, co. York, labourer, and Alice his wife, administratrix of the goods of Edward Sowden the younger, son of Edward Sowden, late of Eccleshill, co, York, and Martha his wife.

Defendants.—George Hutchinson, and Margaret Hutchinson, widow.

Edward Sowden the elder died leaving his son most of his property. Edward Sowden the younger died shortly after intestate. Alice Marshall, oratrix, should come into the property of both Edward the elder and younger, being sister to Edward the elder and aunt to Edward the younger, but defendants endeavour to defraud her of her rights.

Marshall v. Ivey.—Whittington II., 233.
25 Jan., 1689.

Complainants.—John Marshall of East Dereham, co. Norfolk, and Martha his wife, relict of William Ivey.

Defendants.—Shadrach Ivey and others.

Thomas Ivey left certain lands in Yaxham and Westfields to William his eldest son. After William's death the said lands should come to oratrix his relict, but Shadrach Ivey, another son of Thomas Ivey, endeavours to get the same from oratrix.

Marshall v. Thompson.—Whittington I., 477.
31st Oct., 1667.

Complainants.—John Marshall of Scarborough, co. York, and Elizabeth his wife, daughter of Cristopher Thompson.

Defendants.—Sarah Thompson and others.

Cristopher left a legacy of £1660 to oratrix his daughter, which Sarah will not pay.

Marshall v. Walton.—Reynardson IV., 78.
26th Nov., 1679.

Complainants.—John Marshall of London, gentleman, and Nathaniel Purse of Worplesdon, co. Surrey.

Defendants.—Thomas Walton and others.

John Berry, late of Southwarke. left complainants legacies, which the defendants, executors of John Berry's will, do not settle.

Marshall v. Warkman.—Hamilton I., 222, 62.
11th Nov. 1706.

Complainants.—John Marshall of Priavin, co. Worcester, and Mary his wife, late Mary Day.

Defendant.—Thomas Warkman.

Thomas Day, complainant's father, had some copyhold land in Priavin, co. Worcester. This should by descent have come to oratrix, but Thomas Warkman pretends it belongs to him according to the custom of the manor.

Marshall v. Curtler.—Whittington II., 177.

17th May, 1675.

Complainant.—Lettice Marshall, widow, formerly wife of William Hereford, daughter of the late Thomas Lucy of St. James's, Clerkenwell.

Defendants.—Anne Curtler, widow, Robert Curtler, and others.

A dispute about the estate of the late Thomas Lucy, complainant's father.

Marshall v. Wood.—Whittington II., 234.

9th July, 1689.

Complainant.—Francis Marshall of London, mariner, son of Francis Marshall, late of Erith, co. Kent.

Defendants.—Elizabeth Marshall, relict of Francis Marshall the elder, and Richard Wood.

In 1688, Francis Marshall the elder died intestate, leaving Elizabeth his relict and seven children, viz., John, Elizabeth, Francis the orator, Robert, Dorothy, Sarah, and Edward. Elizabeth administered his goods, and confederating with Richard Wood will not give orator his share.

Marshall v. Levitt.—Whittington II., 166.

15 May, 1672.

Complainants.—Richard Marshall of Hinckley, co. Leicester, and Anne his wife, one of the daughters of the late Thomas Hodgkinson of Adderston, co. Warwick.

Defendants.—Edward Levitt and Elizabeth his wife.

Thomas Hodgkinson by his will left Anne the complainant, his daughter, £20, and made his wife Anne his sole executrix. Anne died without paying the legacy and made Elizabeth her daughter her executrix. Elizabeth, now wife of Edward Levitt, refuses to pay the legacy.

Marshall v. Gore.—Whittington II., 231.

9th June, 1687.

Complainant.—John Marshall of the parish of St. Andrew, Holborne, son of William Marshall of Lincoln's Inn Fields, and Frauncis his wife.

Defendants.—Humphrey Gore, Samuel Stevenson, and others.

William Marshall, orator's father, was owed sundry sums of money by defendants. He made his last will on the 22nd February, 1667, and in it left orator his debts. Defendants will not pay complainant—Vol. I., App. pp. 13-15.

Marshall v. Cooke.—Mitford II., 244.

30th May, 1661.

Complainant.—Nicholas Marshall of Taunton, co. Somerset, and Elizabeth his wife, daughter of John Smith, late of Taunton, deceased.

Defendant.—Ruben Cooke and his wife.

Elizabeth Marshall should by rights come into some messuages in Taunton, which formerly belonged to her father, but defendants have taken possession.

Marshall al's. Hall v. Marshall.—Collins II., 154.

13 May, 1648.

Complainant.—Humphrey Marshall *al's.* Hall, of Wood, in the parish of Hope, co. Derby.

Defendants.—Mary Marshall and Jane Marshall.

Complainant owed Anthony Marshall £10, which he paid. The obligation however was never cancelled, and Jane and Mary, daughters of Anthony, who is now dead, claim the money.

Marshall v. Marshall.—Mitford, Depositions, 678.

Examination of witnesses at Exeter in suit between Robert Marshall, and Alice Marshall, widow.

Edward Salter of Exeter says he knew John Marshall the elder, sixteen years before his death, and John Marshall the younger six months before his death. John the younger is brother to Robert, complainant, and John Marshall the elder is uncle to Robert, complainant, and John the younger. He does not believe John the elder has concealed any of the property of John the younger.

Marshall v. Ball.—Whittington I., 20.

25 June, 1653.

Complainants.—John Marshall of Fenetterie (? Feniton), co. Devon, gent., and Grace his wife.

Defendant.—John Ball.

Richard Stofford, late brother of oratrix, held some land in Ottery St. Mary, co. Devon. Upon oratrix marrying with John Marshall the said Richard promised to leave the same to oratrix if he did not marry. He has since died unmarried, but John Ball and others have entered into the premises.

Marshall v. Marshall.—Mitford IV., 574.

1st May, 1696.

Complainant.—William Marshall of Wray, co. Lancaster, son of John Marshall of Wray.

Defendant.—Thomas Marshall.

John Marshall, complainant's father, was at his death seized of some land in Wray, in the Manor of Hornby, and a good personal estate. Being so seized, in June, 1676, he died, leaving orator his only son an infant, and one daughter Jennett, now married to Robert Fletcher of Mellinge. Thomas Marshall of Wray, who married the said John Marshall's sister, entered into possession of the real and personal estate of the said John in trust for orator. He will not now account for it. During his minority orator lived with Robert Marshall, his uncle, or father's brother.

Marshall v. Clarke.—Whittington III., 525.

2 Jan., 1697.

Complainant.—Roger Marshall of Lockton, co. York, and Grace his wife, daughter of Grace Clarke of Lockton, deceased.

Defendant.—William Clarke.

Grace Clarke, mother of oratrix, died in 1687, and left some money to oratrix. This money William Clarke, her brother, has in his possession and will not give up.

Marshall v. Woodwarke.—Whittington I., 497.

17 Dec., 1683.

Complainant.—Richard Marshall of Glaisedaile, co. York, son of George Marshall.

Defendant.—George Woodwarke.

George Marshall, by indenture dated 11th April last past, sold to defendant a parcel of ground called Ellercar Close, with proviso that if Richard the orator should wish to rebuy it within three years he might do so. Richard wishes to do so, but defendant will not keep to his bargain.

Marshall v. Marshall.—Whittington I., 36.

3rd July, 1650.

The answer of William Marshall, one of the defendants, to the Bill of George Marshall, executor of the last will of Elizabeth Cowper.

The defendant says George Marshall should not have the sum of £105 plus interest since the death of Elizabeth Cowper.

Marshall v. Hunton.—Whittington II., 149.

Nov., 1684.

Complainant.—John Marshall of Burstwicke in Holderness, co. York, executor of the will of John Hull of Holmpton in Holderness, his uncle.

Defendant.—Thomas Hunton.

Just before his death the said John Hull intrusted Thomas Hunton with two bags of money which he will not now account for.

Marshall v. Churchill.—Hamilton, 224, 71.

29 April, 1684.

Complainants.—Thomas Marshall of Ilminster, co. Somerset, physician, John Turner of Crickett, co. Somerset, Henry Backaller of Chard, co. Somerset, and others.

Defendants.—Margaret Churchill, John Speke, and others.

Margaret Prideaux of Whitelackington, relict of Edmund Prideaux, deceased, made her last will in 1683, and left complainants sundry sums of money. She appointed John Speke, her grandson, executor of her will, and he will not pay complainants their legacies.

Marshall v. Barnard.—Mitford II., 259, 66.

20th Nov., 1682.

Complainant.—Samuel Marshall of Stratford le Bowe, co. Middlesex, brewer, and Henry Quelch, and others.

Defendants.—Henry Barnard of London and Richard Greenwood.

Anne Chester, late of London, widow by her last will left the complainant legacies and made defendants executors thereof. Defendants have never paid complainants their legacies.

Marshall v. Izard.—Hamilton I., 223, 23.

26th May, 1693.

Complainant.—John Marshall of London, executor of the last will of John Bynold, son and heir of Henry Bynold of London.

Defendants.—Edmund Izard, William French, and others.

Wm Lord Marshall of England had yssue Wm. port gu. a bend of 5 fusills or.

Gilbert E. of Ogre & E. of Pembroke mar. & had yssue Richard. Ogre port arg. on a chiefe az. 3 [illegible] of the first.

Wm Marshall E. of Glouc. mar. the sister of Jervis Alaude & they had yssue Wm. Alaude port party p pale arg. & gu. 3 [illegible] counterchanged.

[illegible] Mackmur ruler of Ireland mar. & had yssue Eva his dau. & heire. Mackmur port sab. 3 garbes arg. [illegible]

Richard Strongbow E. of Pembroke mar. Eva the dau. & heire of Dermot Mackmur E. of Lienster & they had yssue Isabell their dau. & sole heire.

Wm Marshall E. of Glouc. & Worster mar. the dau. of the Lord Stafford & they had yssue 2 sonnes wch were both named William ye elder & younger. Stafford port or a cheveron gu.

Robt. Brusse King of Scotts mar. Isabell dau. & one of the heires of David E. of Angus & Galloway & they had yssue Wm Lo. Brusse.

Sr Wm Marshall Knight Lo. of Chepstow mar. Avicia dau. of Wakkinton & they had yssue Wm Marshall Knight. 1268.

Sr Tho. Empingham Kt covenanted and agreed wth Sr Wm Marshall Kt the younger brother to Wm Marshall E. of Pembroke for the mar. of [illegible] Wm Marshall his son wch was Lo. of Chepstow in the County of Monmouth & An the dau. & heire yt they should be mar. before the feast of Pentecost next ensuing. Anno 1263. Now yt this An nor [illegible] her father yt would not agree unto the former condition except yt Sr Wm Marshall Knight her husband now beare to Sr Wm Marshall Kt should name all her children begotten of her body Empingham after the name of her wife [illegible] & beare her name [illegible] but [illegible] such name but that there names should be named Marshalls so longe as the world endured & so they were both united & he by the right of this lady An his wife was seised [illegible] of the manor of Empingham to him & his heires for ever.

Wm Marshall the elder mar. Isabell the dau. & sole heire of Richard Strongbow E. of Ogre & they had issue 5 sonnes & 5 dau. wch sones were all E. successively & dyed wthout yssue temp. H. 3. 1226. Marshall quartereth Strongbow & Mackmur.

Wm Bruse Lo. of Gower mar. the dau. & heire generall of . . . & they had yssue . . .

Sr Wm Marshall Kt mar. An the dau. & heire of Sr Tho. Empingham Kt. Empingham port. Barry of 6 pieces arg. & sab. a canton ermyn.

Wm Ferrers E. of Darby mar. Sibill the 4th dau. of Wm Marshall E. of Pembroke. port vairy gu. & or.

Gilbert de Clare E. of Glocester mar. Isabell one of the dau. & heires of Wm Marshall E. of Pembroke, port or 3 cheverons gu.

Wm Marshall E. of Pembroke mar. the dau. of K. John & dyed wthout yssue. K. John port gu. 3 Lyons passant gardant or.

Warrante Lo. Mountchancy mar. Johan eldest dau. of Wm Marshall E. of Pembroke.

Roger Bygod E. of Norfolk mar. Maud 2nd dau. of Wm Marshall E. of Pembroke.

Wm Bruse Lo. of Gower mar. the first dau. of Wm Marshall E. of Pembroke.

Sr Adam Bruse 3d sonne of Wm Lo. of Gower unto whome he gave his manor of Bruse in Pickering he was married and had yssue Sr Adam Bruse of Pickering. Sr Adam port or a saltire engrailed gules, a chiefe indented per fesse of . . . . & [illegible]

Sr Wm Bruse 4th sonne of Wm Lo. Bruse to whome he gave his manor of Lurbee & Vearby in the County of Lincolne. Sr Wm port arg. a lyon rampt gu. crowned or between a semme of cross crossletts of the 2nd.

Sr Walter Hewicke Kt mar. the dau. of Sr Roger Bewick Kt & they had yssue Walter Hewicke esqr. Sir Walter port gu. a lyon rampt arg. the field [illegible] 1368.

Jo. Marshall sonn & heire of Sr Wm Marshall Kt mar. the dau. of Mr Hurden & they had yssue Wm Marshall. Hurden port paly of 5 pieces gu. & or.

Philip Bruse of Gower Brible & Bramber mar. Bertha 2nd dau. & heire of Milo E. of Herford & Constable of England & had yssue 3 dau.

Sr Robt Bruse Kt of whome Sr Thomas Moreton is discended.

Sr Adam Bruse Lo. the . . . . Pickering (?) married . . . . & had yssue Sr Will'm (?) . . . . his port arg. a border engrailed gu. & on a chiefe sab. 3 mulletts of the field.

Wm Marshall sonn & heire of Jo. Marshall mar. . . . . the dau. of Anthony Harrington & had yssue Jo. Marshall. Harrington port or a chiefe gu. a bend engrailed az.

Aline (?) mar. to . . . . called Constable of England & they had issue Humphrey.

Isabell eldest dau. of Philip L. Bruse & heire mar. to Lewllin Prince of Wales dyed wthout yssue. Lwellin port a canton quarterly, first or a lyon pas. gu. 2nd gu. a lyon passant or 3 as the 2nd the 4th as the first.

Eva mar. to Jo. L. Mowbray Duke of Norfolke & they had yssue Jo. & Elle.

Maud 2d dau. mar. to Roger Mortimer Lo. of Wigmore Meath & Ulster & they had yssue.

Ella 3rd dau. mar. to Wm Lo. Cantelupe & had yssue 2 dau.

Wm Bruse Kt sonn & heire to Sr Adam mar. the dau. & heire of Ralph Earle esqr & they had yssue Wm Bruse esqr. An mar. to Jo. Hastings Esq. Earle port az. a cheveron between 3 escallops or a border engrailed of the last.

Jo. Marshall was receiver to King H. 5. he mar. the dau. of Edward [illegible] in the county of Northumberland & they had yssue Wm & Jo. 1400.

Sr Jo. Hotham of Scorbrough L. of Wilton Moriane & Ganthy mar. An dau. of Sr Wm Bruse of Pickering Kt & they had yssue Sr Jo. Hotham Kt. Hotham port barry of 10 [illegible] on a chiefe or a [illegible] sab.

Wm Marshall Lo. of Empingham Wm [illegible] manor he [illegible] he mar. Katherine the dau. of Gregory Tunstall esqr & had yssue Jo. Marshall. Tunstall port arg. a [illegible] between 3 [illegible] heads erased sab. crested & wattled gu.

Wm Bruse esqr mar. the dau. & heire of Walter Hewicke & they had yssue Maud wch others & Mr Egglesfeild mar. the dau.

Jo. Marshall of Lincolne mar. the dau. of Leonard Crofe of Croftesike Esqr & they had yssue Ann. Crofe port vert & gu. on a bend indented or 3 [illegible] sab.

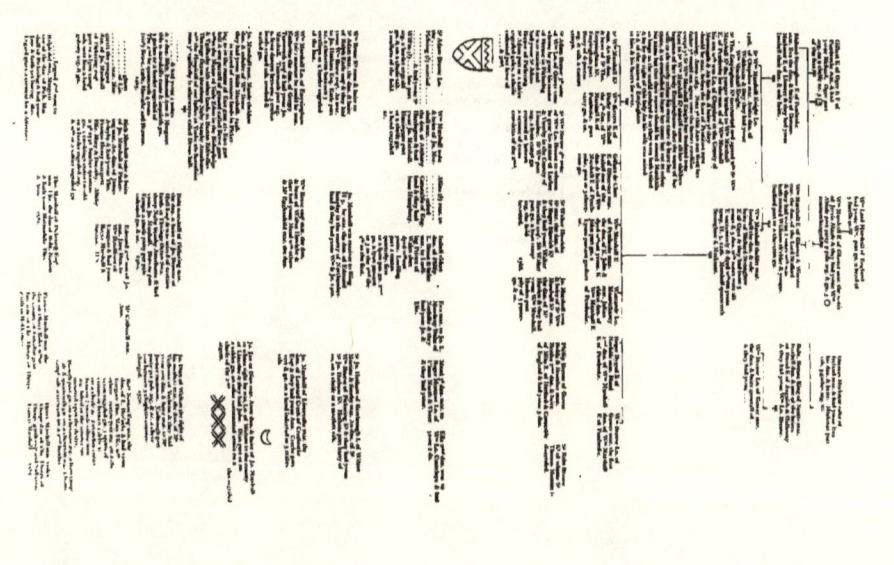

Jo. Marshall mar. Maude eldest dau. & coheire of Wm Bruse they had yssue Robt Marshall. 1448.
[illegible] seased of certaine lands in Pickering as in the manor of Bruse gate als Bruse gate [illegible] & one parcell of ground called Bruse garth [illegible] the Manor of [illegible] in the [illegible] & [illegible] with other lands in [illegible] Thornton [illegible] Sigsby [illegible] with the Hospitall of our ladie at Yorke [illegible] the said [illegible] is otherwayes called Bruse hall.

Jo. Jue or Dias mar. Anne dau. & heire of Jo. Marshall in whose right he was Lo. of Welton in the county of Lincolne & they had John. Dias port or on a saltire gu. [illegible] on a chiefe of the 2nd [illegible] argent.

[illegible]

. . . . & had yssue 2 sonnes & 2 dau. Robt, Edmund Ann & Margaret this is marshalls coate & impaleth gu. 3 garbes or a border engrailed of The 2nd he quartereth 4 coats [illegible] Bruse, Earle, Hewicke and Browne. 1483.

Robt Marshall of Pickering mar. the dau. & heire of Jo. Browne of Hull Esqr & was seised of certaine lands in [illegible] Sea. [illegible] & had yssue Jo. Marshall. Browne port [illegible] a chiefe party per pale indented gu. & az. 1560.

Jo. Dias of Welton the right of his mother mar. the dau. of Mr [illegible] & they had yssue one dau. & heire mar. to Mr [illegible]. [illegible] port party per pale arg. & az. a [illegible] between 3 [illegible] counterchanged. 1570.

. . . . [illegible] . . . . of Lin- . . . . mar. Margarett the yongest dau. of Jo. Marshall of Pickering esqr port or a lyon rampt sab. [illegible] gobony arg. & gu.

Rich Marshall sonne & heire of Jo. Marshall of Pickering mar. An. dau. of James [illegible] & had yssue Tho. Frances Henry margarett Elle. Mary & Dorothy. [illegible] a [illegible] quarterly gu. [illegible] on a border engrailed arg. & [illegible] engrailed gu.

Edward 2nd sonne of Jo. mar. Jane Dau. to Wm [illegible] of [illegible] & had yssue Roger Marshall & [illegible].

Mr Cathwell mar. Ann.

[illegible] Esqr mar. the dau. of [illegible] & had yssue [illegible]

. . . . Legard 2nd sonne to Ralph dyd mar. Margaret one of the dau. of Rich. Marshall of Pickering & had yssue Jane & [illegible] yet living. this Legard gives a crescent for a difference.

Tho. Marshall of Pickering Esqr mar. the dau. of Robt. [illegible] & hath yssue [illegible] Tho. & [illegible] 1581.

Frances Marshall mar. the [illegible]

Henry Marshall mar. [illegible] Francis Marshall [illegible]

Legard beareth next to his owne coate
arg. on a bend gu. 3 cressants or.
3^{ly} gu. a bend or. 4^{ly} arg. 3 water bougetts sab.

Rider quartereth wth Tunstall &
gu. a bend between 6 plates.

Thorp of Welwike Thorpe port 6 coats first arg. a lyon
rampt gu. 2^{ond} gu. 2 pales or on a
cheife arg. a fesse dancete az.
3^{d} nubuly arg. & sab. on a cheife of the
first 3 martletts in fesse of the 2^{ond}
4 or on a cheveron sab. 3 plates
5th or a cheveron betwene 3 mulletts gu.
6th gu. a cheveron or betwgen 3 mulletts
arg.

Henry Bynold had some property in Falkner's Alley in the parish of St. Sepulchres, Middlesex. This ought to have descended to John his son, and after John to different relations mentioned in his will. But now Edmund Izard, William French, and others, pretend to own the same.

Eliezer Marshall.—Collins III., 545.

28th June, 1672.

Complainants.—Eliezer Marshall of Ackwarr (? Wickwar), co. Gloucester, and Elizabeth his wife.

Defendants.—John North and Mary his wife.

Thomas Stephens, father of Elizabeth the oratrix, had some property at Winterburne, co. Wilts. He left by his will certain property to oratrix, and certain other to Mary, now wife of John North, his other daughter. Mary and John North try to defeat oratrix of her share.

Marshall v. Kent.—Bridges, 588, Miscellaneous.

10th Feb., 1707.

Complainant.—Benjamin Marshall of the parish of St. Bridgett, London; Henry Marshall of Cambridge, Edward Greene and Abigail his wife, and others.

Defendants.—Charles Kent, Thomas Blick and Katherine his wife, and others.

Benjamin and Henry Marshall and Abigail Greene are children of John Marshall the elder, who was brother of Katherine, wife of Nicholas Severne, they (Nicholas and Katherine) being grandparents of Charles Knight, late of Kingston, that is the father and mother of Isabel, late mother of the late Charles Knight. Samuel Marshall of Portsmouth, co. Southampton, is son of John Marshall the younger, who is son of John Marshall the elder. Charles Knight in his will left £2,000 to his poor relations in London. Complainants and defendants both claim.

MR. MARSHALL OF FLAMBOROUGH'S PEDIGREE.

The annexed folding table is an exact copy of a pedigree in the possession of Dr. Collins of York, which is probably a rough transcript of one of those old vellum rolls it was the fashion for almost every family to have made in the sixteenth century. The writing is of the end of that period.

My reason for printing it is, that, although evidently fictitious as to many of the statements it contains, it throws a light on the origin of the arms borne by the Yorkshire and other families of the name, nowhere else to be obtained. It will be noticed that it has mostly been written without the usual lines indicative of descent, and that in the one or two instances where an attempt to give them has been made they are wrongly drawn. In the first two instances it is plain that they indicate, not only the father, but the wife's father also, and in the third instance there should have been a break between Sir Wm. Marshall, Kt., and Wm. Ferrers Earl of Derby. So far as the Marshall line of descent is shown it is evidently intended to stand thus:—

William Lord Marshall of England.=

William Marshall Earl of Gloucester.= . . . . sister of Jervace Abtofte.

William Marshall Earl of Gloucester & Worcester.= . . . . dau. of Lord Stafford.

Sir William Marshall, Kt., Lord of Chepstow. Party to Marriage Settlement, 1263.=Avicia. dau. of Wolderane. | William Marshall THE ELDER, Earl of Pembroke. Married Isabel, d. and heir of Richard Strongbow.=

Sir William Marshall, Kt.=Anne, d. & heir of Sir Thos. Empringham, Kt.

John Marshall, son and heir.= . . . . . dau. of Mr. Harden.

William Marshall.= . . . . . dau. of Anthony Harrington.

John Marshall, Receiver to K. Henry V.= . . . . . dau. of Edmund Lamplugh.

William Marshall, Lord of Empringham, which manor he sold. 1408.=Katherine, dau. of Gregory Tamworth. | John Marshall. Mar. dau. of Leonard Creek.=

John Marshall, 1446.=Maud, eld. dau. and coheir of William Bruse.

Robert Marshall of Pickering, 1460.= . . . . dau. and heir of John Browne.

John Marshall.=

Richard Marshall.=Anne, dau. of James Aislaby. | Edmund Marshall.=Jane, dau. of William Dallison. | Anne, mar. . . . Catherall. | Margaret.

The reader should confer this with the pedigree given in Vol i., p. 1. It does not appear who the Mr. Marshall of Flamborough may have been for whom this pedigree was made. Possibly Thomas the eldest son of Richard Marshall, who married the daughter of James Aislaby. In some MSS. he is said to have been living unmarried in 1584, and in others to have married Elizabeth, the daughter of Robert Norton, and had issue Marmaduke and Thomas. Thomas Marshall of Flamborough married in 1624 Anne Creyke, widow, and in 1634 tuition of his two sons, George and Thomas, was granted to him as administrator of Alice Creyke or Crake, spinster, the daughter of his wife by her former husband.

In a MS. collection of pedigrees, etc., by Gregory King, Rouge Dragon, now in the possession of Walter Rye, Esq., there is a pedigree which appears to have been copied from this. It is described as "The copy of a paper in y[e] hands of Charles Marshall of London, Grocer, 8[o] Oct., 1689," and was evidently produced by him when he entered his pedigree in the last Visitation of London. It adds the following items to this pedigree :—

1. To the marriage of Thomas Marshall and Elizabeth Norton, 1583, "3 flower de luces."
2. Ralph Marshall, son of Francis Marshall, Esq., married Betteris Saule, the daughter of Robert Saule, and had issue six sons and two daughters. Saule is subsequently spelt Sale. This is no doubt an error, as his first wife was Beatrice ——, and his second Elizabeth Sale.

3. Francis Marshall, son and heir of Henry Marshall, married the daughter of Richard Browne, Esq., and had issue William, who died without issue, and Ralph. This information is new, as all the previous accounts only state that he was aged one and a half years in 1584. Perhaps the writer confused him with his *uncle*, Francis Marshall.

In speaking of the arms of this family, *Barry of six Argent and Sable, a canton Ermine*, I observed, Vol. i., p. 3, "This coat is doubtless the original bearing of most families of the name, at least if one may judge from several others, evidently variations of it, recorded by the Heralds. I am quite unable to explain its origin, and to show in what manner it may be deemed to be, as all early coats are, canting." The story told by this pedigree of the assumption of the Arms of Empringham in lieu of his own coat by Sir William Marshall who married the heiress of Sir Thomas Empringham, explains the whole matter by showing that the coat was not that of Marshall, but the Empringham coat assumed in lieu of change of name, which was the alternative condition in the settlement made in the marriage of Sir William Marshall with the daughter and heir of Sir Thomas Empringham. That the pedigree here set forth is not accurate in many of its statements is I think unquestionable, but this does not in my opinion in the least degree impair its trustworthiness as to the reason why the barry coat came to be used as the Arms of Marshall.

EXTRACTS FROM VARIOUS REGISTERS.

(Continued from p. 96).

BRANT BROUGHTON, CO. LINCOLN.[1]

1630. Alice Marshall was buried the xxvijth of July.
1635. Nicholas Marshall, churchwarden.
1687. Richard Marshall and Priscilla Clarke were married No. 10.
1688. Thomas, son of Richard Marshall and Priscilla his wife bap. Octob. 28. Thomas son of Richd Marshall was buried Decemb. 11.
1712-3. Feb. 1. Priscilla Marshall, bur.
1715. Richard Marshall churchwarden.
1715. May 8. Will'm Marshal and Mary Gold mar.
1715-6. Feb. 19. Mary Marshall dau. of Will'm & Mary bapt.
1716. April 10. Richard Marshall bur. (See his will, vol. i., p. 223).
1733. April 4. Mary the wife of William Marshall buried.
1733. July 5. William Marshall buried.

[1] From Transcripts at Lincoln.

FROM TRANSCRIPTS OF BINBROOK ST. GABRIEL'S REGISTER, DEAN AND CHAPTER'S TRANSCRIPTS AT LINCOLN.

1663. Maria Marshall fil• Stephen. et Earbie Marshall bapt. 13 Martii.
1666. Thomas Marshall the son of Stephen and Earbie Marshall was bapt. the 7 day of Oct.
1671. Frances dau. of Stephen and Earbie Marshall bapt. 11 June.
1679. Stephen Marshall, buried.
1686. Lancelot Marshall, adult, bapt.
1683. George Gibbon and Irby Marshall were marryed 9br ye 13th.

HOLY TRINITY, HULL.

1576. Elizabeth dau. of Symon Marshall, bapt.
1602. July 22. Mary dau. of George Marshall, bapt.

Marriages.

1566. May 13. John Marshall & Jane Harvy.
1570. John Marshall & Margaret Skinner.
1575. Symon Marshall & Cicely Foskett.
1591. July 14. Thomas Marshall & Elizth Adams.
1627. Abraham Marshall & Joan Baker.
1635. Nicholas Marshall. Buried.

ST. MARY'S, HULL.

1574. James son of John Marshall, Bapt.
1577. Margerie, wife of John Marshall. Buried.
1579. Robert, son of William Marshall bapt., & buried.
1581. James, son of Wm Marshall. Bapt.
1588. William Marshall, shipwright. Buried.

FROM TRANSCRIPT OF MOULTON REGISTER AT LINCOLN.

1591. John Webster and Betteris Marshall married, May 28.
1620. John Younger and Katherine Marshall, married, Feb. 18.
1630. John Marshall and Prudence Gaudge. Married. Dec. 16.
1631. Buried. Thomas filius Joh'is Yonger et Katherine Marshall, Martij 28o.
1675. Samuell filius Johan' Marshall et Elianor, bapt. Martij 24.

John Marshall was churchwarden in 1707.

FROM TRANSCRIPT OF WHAPLODE REGISTER AT LINCOLN.

1587. Rychard Marchall & Jone Awcrofte were maryed the 5 day of Octr.
1587. Ales Marshall the dau. of Thos Marshall was bapt. the vi. day of March.
1590. Adam the sonne of Thomas Marshall was bapt. the ixth daye of Aprill.
1616. Adam Marshall and Elizabeth Roberts maryed the 20 May.

1618. Robert the son of John Marshall, carpent', babt. 4 Oct.
1687. Eliz. f. John Marshall, bapt. Sept. 22.
1693. Robert Marshall, buried, August 31.

1633. Israel Marshall & Mary Thewlis. Married.[1] *Sculcoates, near Hull.*

1592. Symon Marshall & Maryon Young. Married. *Sutton, near Hull.*

1600. April 20. John Marshall and Jennet Pitt. Married. *Transcript of Felkirk Register at York.*

1739. Tho[s] Marshall of Bassingham and Mary Doubleday of Awburn marry'd May 3[d]. *Transcript of St. Swithin's Register at Lincoln.*

1638. John Marshall and Anne Everit were married the eight day of June. *Transcript of Whaplode Drove Register at Lincoln.*

1657. James Marshall, bach[r], of S[t] Mathew, Friday S[t], and Elizabeth Maddison spinster of this. Banns published in Cheapside Market, Nov. 4, 11, 16.

1655. June 22. John Marshall of S[t] Giles, Cripplegate, and Ann Halton of S[t] Botolph, Bishopsgate. Married. *Register of St. Bartholomew the Great, London.*

MISCELLANEOUS NOTES OF WILLS AND ADM'ONS.

(Continued from Vol. ii., part ii., p. 67).

Wills at Lichfield.[2]

William Marshall, senior, of Hilton, co. Derby, yeoman. Dated 9th Feb[y], 1713-14. My house & croft adjoining in liberty of Hilton to be sold at Discretion of my executrix. To my eldest son W[m] £1. My executrix to dispose of the lease I have from Duke of Devonshire. My children to have residue of my estate, viz., Dorothy, Sarah, Mary, Thomas, Eliz[th], and Liddia. Wife Ruth executrix, and friend Thomas Heacock of Ask overseer. Witnesses Thomas Heacock, Thomas Bankcraft. Proved 6th April, 1722. On another sheet is written, I W[m] Marshall son of W[m] Marshall of Hilton, co. Derby, renounce my right to personal estate of the said William and licence Ruth Marshall my mother-in-law to administer the same. Dated 19th Nov[r], 1720.

Adm'on of Mary Marshall of Dore, co. Derby, to Hannah Turner, of Dronfield, spinster, her daughter, and Joseph Parker, of Dronfield, Butcher, 3 Oct[r], 1723.

Mary Marshall of Dore, co. Derby, grants on 19th Feb[y], 1719, all her estate to her daughter Hannah Turner.

George Marshall of Whitwell, co. Derby, yeoman, dated 31 August, 1721. My house and land to my wife for life, and after to

[1] See Vol. i., p. 269, *Note.* [2] See Vol. ii., pp. 44-48.

my son John Marshall. To my two sons John and Matthew 12 pence each. To Eliz. Hoard, Mary my 2nd daughter, and Isabell Harrison, each 12 pence. Isabell Marshall my grandaughter. Residue to Joan my wife, and makes her sole executrix. Witnesses John Raynes, Richd Raynes, Thos. Major. Proved by Joan Marshall the relict 5 Octr, 1721.

Anne Marshall of Derby, widdowe. Dated 21 October, 1697. My body to be buried at discretion of my executors and of my son-in-law Ferdinand Low and his wife. Whereas Henry Walker, late of London, clerk, my late brother, left me a legacy of £200, about which there was a law suit in chancery which I won; I leave what remains of the same to my two grand children Anne and Francis Ward, and appoints them executors. Said Ferdinand Lowe, John Smith of Osgathorpe, co. Leicester, and my coz. John Daykeyne, overseers. Witnesses, John Welstrapp, Eliz. Kinop, John Dakeyne. Proved by Anne Hedges *als*. Ward, and Francis Ward, 16 April, 1703.

Richard Marshall of Salbridge, in Parish of Woolfhamcoate, co. Warwick, Shepeard. Dated 20 May, 1703. To my sisters Eliz. Marshall of Salbridge, and Hannah Yorke of Shawell, and my kinsman Thomas Goode of Flecknoe, son of my sister Sarah Goode, decd, my houses and lands in Flecknoe wherein Samuel Shirtland lives to be equally divided between them. These houses, lands, etc., were left to me by the Will of my kinsman Henry Tompkins, late of Flecknoe. To aforesaid Eliz. Marshall and Hannah Yorke that close in Flecknoe called Nicholas Close, now in occupation of Robert Chambers. To Elizabeth my new dwellinghouse in Salbridge. The residue to my sister Eliz. whom I appoint executrix. Witnesses, Thomas Quinney, John Adams. Proved by Eliz. Marshall, 14 Octr, 1703.

Thomas Marshall of Derby, co. Derby. Dated 27 January, 1682-3. To my wife and executrix my dwelling-house and all my personal estate on condition she pay my debts and give to my 3 sons John, Thomas, and Joseph, £7 each when they reach 14 years, and to my daughter Elizabeth £7 when she reaches 18 years. If my wife fail to do this I give power to Wm Brookehouse my friend and John Marshall my brother to sell my house and pay my legacies. Witnesses Benjamin Smedley, Wm Brookhouse, junr., Jonathen Marshall. Proved by Elizabeth his relict, 26 April, 1683.

Edward Marshall of Derby, carpenter. Dated 14 May, 1681. To my 5 children John, Eliz., Edward, Mary, and Ann, 5*s*. each. To my child which my wife now goes with 5*s*. if it live. The residue to Hannah my wife whom I appoint executrix. I appoint my friend Richard Hopkinson, and my loving brother Joseph Ma——? (Marshall) overseer. Witnesses, Francis Gilbert, Richard Hopkinson, Joseph Moore. Proved by Hannah Marshall, 22 Septr., 1681.

Richard Marshall, the elder, of Tansley, in the Parish of Crich, co. Derby, yeoman. Dated 26 January, 1679-80. My daughter

Eliz. Kilhare. Whereas Humphrey Marshall my son promised at his marriage to pay £20 to whomsoever I bequeathed it in my will, I bequeath it as follows; £6 to Richard Marshall my son, and £14 to my wife Eliz. To my daughter Eliz. Kilhares' two children, 20*s.* each. To my son Richard's four children, £4. To my son Humphrey's two children, 5*s.* To my son George Marshall, 5*s.* To my son Edward Marshall, 5*s.* To Mr Joseph Topham 20*s.* The residue to my wife, whom I appoint my executrix. Witnesses, Anne Pursglove, Henry Flint, Jos. Topham. Proved by Eliz. Marshall the relict, 23 March, 1679-80.

Wills proved in Court of Dean and Chapter of Lincoln.

Thomas Marshall a fellowe of Burghershe Chauntry in Lincoln Cathedral. Dated 5 May, 1539. To sister Cecile Est vj^s^ viij^d^. Proved 10 May 1539. Book A., fo. 78.

John Marshall of Owmby in Searby, husbandman. Dated 28 Aug., 1557. To be bur^d^ in Searby Church. Son Thos Marshall. To Poor of Grasby and Clixby. Daurs. Eliz^th^, Agnes, and Joane. House and lands at Owmby to son Thos Marshall with rem^r^ to son Henry Marshall. Supervisor John Wilkinson. Witnesses, Edmund Wymarke, vicar of Searby, and Edmund Good. Proved 8 Sept., 1557. Book A., fo. 177.

Johan Marshall, sp^r^, of Scredington. Dated 23 Dec., 1576. Brother Barth^w^ Marshall. Sister Eliz^th^ Marshall. Residue to father in law Geo. Stockdale and appoints him executor. Proved 9 Jan., 1576-7.

Thomas Marshall of Melton Ross. Dated 25 May, 1580. To son Robert Marshall a cottage, &c., at Kirmington, and £40. To youngest son Richard Marshall £40. Son Wm Marshall. Daurs Dorothy, and Ellen Marshall. Steven Richardson of Wotton and his wife Frances my daughter. Wife Elizabeth. Proved 9 June, 1580.

Henry Marshall of the Close of Lincoln, cooke. Dated 10 Dec., 1582. Gives all to wife Johan. Proved 8 Feb., 1582.

Joan Marshall of the Close of Lincoln, widow. Adm'on 7 March, 1613, to Elizabeth Osney *alias* Marshall and Isabella Kingston *alias* Marshall her daughters. Sureties, Ambrose Osney of Stainton by Langworth, yeoman, and Thomas Kingston of the Close of Lincoln, gent.

Richard Marshall of North Kelsey. Adm'on 28 June, 1616, to his widow Margaret.

Dean and Chapter's Wills, New Index.

1620-7. Christ^r^ Marshall of Dalbie, fo. 123.
1630-52. Robt Marshall of New Sleeford, fo. 104.
1630-52. Simon Marshall of North Kelsey, fo. 179.

Names of Marshalls in the Indexes to Inventories at Lincoln.

1528. Richard Marshall of Grantham.
1543. John Marshall of Spillesbie.
1546. Marion Marshall of Gosbertowne.
1547. Thos Marshall of Bostonne.
1566. *Marshall of Stepinge.
1567. *Marshall of Lincoln.
1588. *Marshall of Lednam. *Marshall of Sutton.
1590. *Marshall of Quarrington.
1591. *Marshall of Billingaie.
1592. Roger Marshall of Holbech.[1] *Marshall of Haltonne.[2]
1594. *Marshall of Hicame (? Hykeham).
1597. *Marshall of Lincoln.[3] *Marshall of Fishtoft.[4]
1604. Rob. Marshall of Conesby.
1607. Wm Marshall of Billingburgh.
1608. Thos Marshall of Marshchapel. John Marshall of Horncastle.
1609. *Marshall of Hackonbie. Rob. Marshall of Snelland.

The following in another volume of Index:—

1549. Marshall, John, of Pulham, 131. Marcyall, W^m, Sturton, 226.
1550. Marshall, Jo., Sturton, 142. Marshall, W^m, Spaldinge, 172. Marshall, John, Algarkirke, 236. Marshall, Rob., Billingaie, 267.
1552. Marshall, Alison, Boston, 184.
1553. Marciall, Cuthbert, Esterheale, 33.
1556. Marshall, Rob., Mumbie, 187.
1557. Marshall, George, Gouxill, 180. Marshall, Rob, Aslackbie, 376. Marshall, W^m, Billingaie, 563.
1558. Marshall, Marc [blank], 401. Marshall, Willm, Sedgbrook, 605. Marshall, Robert, Crowland, 692. Marshall, John, Rathbie, 949.
1569. Marshall, Stephen, Gunnerbie, 87.
1571. Marshall, Percival, Boston, 174.
1574. Marshall, Laurence, Lincoln, 137.
1580. Marshall, Thos, Clee, 259.
1583. Marshall, Thos, Canwicke, 31.
1591. Marshall, Thos, Carlton, 377.

*Christian Names not given in Index.

[1] 1592. June 9. Adm'on of Roger Marshall of Holbech, to Agnes his widow "in persona Will'mi Ingram" Inventory, £12 6*s*. 10*d*.

[2] 1592. Sept. 12. Adm'on of John Marshall of Halton to Joan his widow. Inventory, £63 14*s*. 8*d*.

On June 11 in this year Adm'on of Agnes Cade *alias* Marshall of Holbeach, was granted to her son William Cade "in persona Chr̃oferi Addington de Moulton." Inventory, £12 13*s*. 6*d*.

[3] 1597. April 16. Adm'on of William Marshall of Lincoln, to Isabella his widow.

[4] 1597. May 12. Adm'on of John Marshall of Fishtoft to Elizabeth his widow. Inventory, £13 6*s*. 8*d*.

1591. Marshall, Eliz^th, Gouxill, 435.
1594. Marshall, W^m, Luddington, 184.
1607. Marshall, W^m, Brandon, 59.

ADM'ONS (LINCOLN), 1637 AND 1638

1637. Marshall, John, Thedlethorp.
1638. Marshall, Tho., Tathwell.
1638. Marshall, W^m, Ashby.
1638. Marshall, W^m, Freiston.

FROM ADM'ON ACT BOOKS, LINCOLN, 1568 TO 1579.

1568. July 16. John Marshall of Edlington. Adm'on to Alice his widow. Inventory, £19 3*s*. 8*d*.

1571. Aug. 26. James Marshall. Adm'on to John Marshall of Tattershall, brother of dec^d. Inventory, 66*s*. 8*d*.

1573. Thomas Markall of Demelbie. Adm'on to Marg^t his widow.

FROM PROBATE AND ADM'ON ACT BOOK AT LINCOLN, 1611-1618.

1613. Nov. 26. Wm Marshall of Tidd St Mary. Adm'on to R^d Marshall his son. Inventory, £62 10*s*. 8*d*.

1615. Oct. 12. John Marshall of Londonthorp. Adm'on to his widow Margaret. Inventory, £70 6*s*. 8*d*.

1615. Nov. 17. Robert Marshall son of Robert Marshall late of Snelland dec^d. Adm'on to Suzanne Tointon *alias* Marshall wife of William Tointon of Snelland, mother of s^d Robert Marshall the son. Inventory, 30*s*.

1617. John Marshall of Bassingham. Adm'on to his widow Margery. Inventory, £44 1*s*. 8*d*. "The debtes exceed the goodes very muche.

FROM ADM'ON ACT BOOK AT LINCOLN, 1629-32.

1629-30. Jan. 29. Elizabeth Marshall of Goxhill, widow. Adm'on to her brother George Marshall. Inventory, £9 16*s*. 8*d*.

1630. May 22. Henry Marshall of St Katherine's without, Lincoln. Adm'on to his brother William Marshall of Sutton Bonington, co. Nott^m, lainus. Inventory, £35 14*s*. 6*d*. (Fol. 32.)

1631. Sept. 1. John Marshall of Holbech. Adm'on to his widow Isabella. Inventory, £13 4*s*. 0*d*.

1632. June 6. Christopher Marshall of Kirmington. Adm'on to Eliz. Foxe *alias* Marshall wife of Wm Foxe of Immingham, and daur. of deceased. Inventory, £125 13*s*. 6*d*.

1632. July 26. Thomas Marshall of the City of Lincoln. Adm'on to his widow Mary. Inventory, £5 5*s*. 8*d*. Debita excedunt bona.

FROM PROBATE AND ADM'ON ACT BOOK AT LINCOLN, 1665-1674.

1671. May 6. Richard Marshall of East Halton, yeom. Account of Eliz[th] Marshall widow and administratrix of the deceased. Inventory, £214 14*s.* 8*d.*

1674. Nov. 6. Elizabeth Marshall of East Halton, widow. Adm'on to Edward Legerd of Gresby testamentary guardian of Elizabeth Marshall daughter and executrix of deceased, a minor. £142 16*s.* 8*d.* See Vol. i., p. 220.

PROBATE AND ADM'ON ACT BOOKS, 1582-1594.

1584. Apl. 6. Adm'on of Reginald Marshall of Moulton to his father James Marshall. Inventory, £13 0*s.* 9*d.*

1587. July 4. Adm'on of Marg[t] Marshall of Brandon to Alice Winter *alias* Marshall her sister.

1587. March 28. Adm'on of William Marshall of Kingerbie to his brother Alexander Marshall.

1587. March 15. Adm'on of Anne Marshall of Sutton to Randall Borowe next of kin. Inventory, £xxi., xvi.

1587. Oct. 21. Adm'on of Margery Marshall of Gayton to Joanna Suttonne of Irforth next of kin. Inventory, 46*s.* 3*d.*

1587. Aug. 30. Adm'on of Margaret Marshall of Wrangle to her sister Eliz. Lee by her proctor John Lee to the use of W[m] Marshall and John Boston her children. Inventory, £13 16*s.* 10*d.*

1588. Feb. 21. Adm'on of Richard Marshall of Sutton S[t] Edmund to Joan his widow. Inventory, £19 12*s.* 6*d.*

1590. July 25. Adm'on of Jenett Marshall of Quarrington to Vincent Barton of Silk-Willoughbie to the use of Marg[t] and Edmund Marshall his children. Inventory, 46*s.*

1591. Oct. 4. Adm'on of R[d] Marshall of Billingaie to Agnes his widow. Inventory, £111 3*s.*

The Will of Robert Burton of S[t] Andrews, Holborne, co. Midd., cook. Dated 14 Dec[r], 1678. My body to be buried in Parish of S[t] Giles in the fields in the Church there. My mother Mary Burton. My uncle William Williamson. To my godson Robert Cooper son of John Cooper of St. Andrew's, Holborne, £10. To my friend M[r] Sam[l] Bishopp, 10*s.* To M[rs] Lydia Pierson 10*s.* The residue to my friend Edward Marshall of S[t] Dunstan in the West, London, Cooke, and appoints him executor. He proved 8 Dec[r], 1678, in P.C.C. (*Vide ante*, p. 132.)

Marmaduke Marshall of the City of Westminster, gentleman. Dated 15 June, 1661. My children and grandchildren shall be paid the sum of 12[d] each. Residue to wife Susannah Marshall, and makes her executrix. Elizabeth More a witness. Proved by relict in P.C.C., 8 July, 1661. (114 May). See Vol. i., 135.

Will of Paul Marshall of the Hamblett of Lymehouse in the parish of Stebunheath *alias* Stepney, yeoman, and late of the Ile Garnesey, being in the said Ile borne and brought up, and being bound on a voyage to the East Indies. Dated 13 January, 1654. John Grove of Lymehouse and Susan his wife universal legatees and executors. She proved, and power reserved to John Grove, 20 July, 1657, in P.C.C. 280 Ruthen.

FROM NEWARK ACT BOOK, AT YORK, 1558-1607.

1558. January 13. Adm'on of John Marshall of South Carlton, to Henry Marshall and John Marshall to use of John, Francis, Dorothy, and Katherine Marshall, minors, children of deceased. See *ante*, p. 91.

1577. Oct. 12. Probate of the will of Robert Marshall of Cromwell to Joanne his relict, and Elene his daughter. See Vol. i., p. 256.

1578. May 15. Probate of the will of Agnes Marshall of Newark to Edward Wilson. See Vol. i., p. 256.

1581. July 11. Probate of the will of Roger Marshall, clerk, "non beneficiati" to Thomas Gill. See Vol. ii., Part i., p. 55.

1591. June 23. Probate of the will of Elizabeth Marshall of North Collingham to Joan Thorpe. And same time probate of the will of Henry Marshall of North Collingham to Joan Thorpe. See Vol. i., p. 257.

1593. June 22. Probate of the will of John Marshall of North Collingham to John, James, and *Timothy* (?) Marshall his children. See Vol. i., p. 258.

1597. January 5. Probate of the nuncupative will of Robert Marshall of Sutton on Trent to Beatrice Marshall his relict, and power reserved to Anne his daughter, and tuition of the said Anne to Beatrice her mother. See *ante*, p. 59.

1605. April 25. Probate of the will of Elizabeth Marshall of Gresthorpe to Robert Marshall sole executor. See Vol. i., p. 260.

1605. Oct. 10. Adm'on of Robert Marshall of South Muskham to John and Oliver Marshall his brothers. Inventory under £40. Compare this with adm'on, Vol. ii., p. 101.

1605. Oct. 10. Adm'on of Simon Marshall of Newark to Alice Hatley *alias* Marshall wife of Michael Hatley and daughter of the said deceased. See Vol. i., p. 305.

CALENDAR OF WILLS IN COMMISSARY COURT, LONDON,

(Continued from Vol. i., p. 194.)

1761.	Marshall, Mary.	Middx.	March.	Will.
1763.	Marshall, Robert.	Pts.	April.	Adm'on.
1763.	Marshall, William.	Pts.	March.	Adm'on.
1771.	Marshall, William.	Pts.	March.	Adm'on.

1774.	Marshall, Robert.	Middx.	December.	Will.
1776.	Marshall, John.	Middx.	April.	Will.
1778.	Marshall, Mary.	Middx.	August.	Will.
1784.	Marshall, Ann.	Middx.	June.	Adm'on.
1786.	Marshall, Thomas.	London.	December.	Will.
1789.	Marshall, John.	Middx.	March.	Will.
1789.	Marshall, John.	Middx.	May.	Will.
1789.	Marshall, John.	Middx.	December.	Will.

Will of Elizabeth Franke of Godstone, co. Surrey. Dated 1688-9. Mentions sons Robert Marshall and John Marshall. Robert, John, John, Elizabeth, and Anne, children of said son Robert. Proved by Robert and John the sons 1690-1, in Archdeaconry Court of Surrey.

Will of Jane Tanner of Wandsworth, widow. Proved in Archdeaconry Court of Surrey, 1699. To grand-children George Marshall and Obadiah Marshall 5*s*. Residue to George Marshall, junior, my grand son in trust to educate his sister Lydia Marshall, and his brother Jasiell Marshall.

From Act Book for Deanery Court at York.

1704. Oct. 1. Probate of John Marshall, senior, of Pickering, to Elizabeth his widow, and John, and Thomas, his sons.

1706. Oct. 30. Administration of John Marshall of Kilham, to George Holdstock.

1716. June 15. Probate of Elizabeth Marshall of Pickering to Thomas Marshall her son.

Grants of Arms to Marshalls.

ARMS.—Barry of six Argent and Sable, on a canton Ermine an escutcheon also Sable.

CREST.—A demi man in armour proper, his helmet plumed Sable, over his armour a sash, and in his dexter hand a baton Or. *Camden's Grants*, iii., 18, describes it as "A demy man armed Or, feathers Sa., Caparison ppr, holding a trunchion Or."

Granted to Thomas Marshall of Michelham, co. Sussex, son of Edward Marshall of Hitchin. 2 Dec., 1612. *Camden's Grants*, ii., 37*b*, iii., 18. See Vol. i., p. 96., App., p. 6.

ARMS.—Barry of ten Ermine and Or, an Eagle displayed Azure, on a chief engrailed Gules three Goats' heads erased Argent.

CREST.—A Goats' head erased Ermine, armed Or, gorged with a chaplet of Roses Gules, in the mouth a branch of hop proper.

Granted to Charles Marshall of Cranbrooke, co. Kent, and of the City of London, Merchant, and James Marshall of Cranbrooke, his only brother, 3 January, 1821.

ARMS.—Azure on a pile between two Anchors in base Or an Anchor Sable.

CREST.—A female figure vested Argent, the right hand pointing to a rainbow above her head proper, and with the left supporting an anchor in front Sable.

Granted to George Marshall of Broadwater, co. Surrey, and his descendants, 14 December, 1850.

ARMS.—Per Saltire Or and Sable a saltire counterchanged, a woman's head couped at the shoulders proper, crowned with a ducal coronet of the first.

Granted to Elizabeth Burrows, widow of Walter Burrows, of Lambeth, co. Surrey, sole surviving daughter of Francis Marshall of Lambeth, 12 July, 1785.

ARMS.—Gules, two bars Argent between as many flanches Ermine, on each a cross-crosslet of the field.

CREST.—A man habited as a pikeman of the seventeenth century and in a corslet, holding in his dexter hand a cross-crosslet fitché Or, on his head in profile a morion proper plumed Gules.

Granted to John Marshall of Manchester and Ardwick and his descendants, 15 June, 1822.

ARMS.—Or, a heron Sable, a chief of the last thereon three Annulets Gold.

Granted to Sarah Marshall widow of John Marshall of Manchester and Ardwick, and daughter and coheir of James Earnshaw, and her descendants (as the arms of Earnshaw), 2 August, 1833.

ARMS.—Barry of six Argent and Sable, on a chevron engrailed Gules three pheons Or.

CREST.—A demi heraldic tyger Sable, gutté d'or, armed, crined, tufted, and gorged with a collar gemel also Or, resting the sinister paw upon an escocheon Gules charged with a pheon Gold.

Granted to Hubert Marshall, Col. in the Indian forces, Military Secretary to the Government at Madras, and his descendants, 5 Sept., 1863.

ARMS.—Or, on a chevron Azure between three Lions rampant Gules an anchor of the first surmounting a sword saltire ways proper, pomel and hilt gold, a chief wavy of the second, thereon a Naval crown Or between a representation of the Imperial Russian Military Order of St. George on the dexter, and a like representation of the Cross of the Royal Swedish Military Order of the Sword on the sinister each pendant from the respective ribbands of the said orders all proper.

CREST.—Upon a mount Vert in front of a Newfoundland dog sejant reguardant proper an escocheon Argent thereon in base waves of the sea and floating therein a naked man the sinister arm elevated also proper.

Granted to John-William-Phillips Marshall of Rochester, co. Kent, Capt. R.N., C.B., etc., and his descendants, 10 Feb., 1829.

MISCELLANEOUS NOTES.

Deed Poll. John Marshall of Worsoppe in com. Nottingham, yoman, in consideration of £12 sells to William Sanderson of Blithe in co. afs[d] gent. two acres of arrable in Blithe near a place called Briber-hill-yate abutting on the lands of George Chaulner, now in the tenure of Edmund Morton of Blithe. Dated 1 February, 10 James, 1612.

Bond by said John Marshall & Jane his wife, ... Marshall and Edwarde Marshall his sons to William Sanderson for further assurance by levying fine or otherwise. Dated 1 February, 1612.

Bond between John Marshall of Worksopp, yeoman, and William Saunderson of Blith abbey. Dated 3 Dec[r], 8 James, 1610. To perform covenants declared in one paire of Indentures bearing date with this obligation.—*Above in hands of Mr. Robert White of Worksop.*

Sunday, 12 March, 1619-20. Stephen Marshall, B.A., of Emanuel College, Cambridge, aged 24 or thereabouts, born at Godmingester [Godmanchester], co. Huntingdon, now curate of Wethersfield, co. Essex, ordained priest by Bishop of London. He was ordained deacon by same Bishop. *Bishop's Books at St. Pauls' Cathedral.* In the Vicar General's Books, Vol. 13, there is a licence to him to be a schoolmaster, in 1630.

Funeral Certificate of Nicholas Marshall.

Additional MS., 4820, fo. 21.

Nicholas Marchshall[1] *al's* Mareschall of Bedingham in the county of Suffolk, Esqr., departed this life at Bedingham hall aforesaid the . . . of Aprill 1621 in the 19th year of the reighn of King James. He was buried without any Escochons in the Chauncell belonging to the Parrish of Denny land in the County of Essex. He was the only Son of . . . . March Hall of Pretlewell in the said county of Essex, Esqr. He married for his first Wife Elizabeth the Daughter of S[r] John Browne of Hambird in the Parish of Norton in the s[d] County of Essex, Knt., and by her had one only Daught[r] sole heir call[d] Mary.

He married for his second Wife Alice the Daught[r] of George Brook of Aspall in th' Co͞m Esqr. but had no Jssue by her. He made the s[d] Alice sole executrix of last Will and Testam[t] which doe testifie the truith of this Certifft und[r] her hand being taken at Redinghall in the co͞m of Norfolk the 17th of Aprł 1622 by me Thomas Preston Deputy to Henry Chittinge Esq[r] Chest[r] Herrald.

1588. May 4. Nich[s] Becke of Wintringham and Margaret Marshall of same. *Marriage Licence Bond at Lincoln.*

1776. Nov. 28. John Marshall of Crowle, farmer and widower, aged 48, and Frances Jure of same, spinster, aged 42. Surety, Cornelius Peacock of same, gent. *Marriage Licence Bond at Lincoln.*

[1] See Vol. i., pp. 61, 77, 97.

The following entry on the De Banco Roll corrects the pedigree given in the Visitation of Yorkshire, 1584. See Vol. i., p. 4.

De Banco Roll, Michaelmas Term, A° 27 Henry VI. (1448-9), membrane 601.

"Ebor̄ *ss.* Wiłłs Eure ꝛ Wiłłs Moretoñ, clicus, sum̄ fuerunt ad respondend Rob̄to Ingiltoñ ꝛ Margarete vx̄i eius de ptito q̄d pmitant eos p̄sentare idoneam psonam ad eccłiam de Thornetoñ in Pykeryngliтh que vacat ꝛ ad suam spectat donac̄oem ꝛc̄."——"Et p̄dc̄i Wiłłs ꝛ Wiłłs p Ricm̄ Thornburgh Attorñ suū veñ Et defend vim ꝛ iniur̄ quando ꝛc̄ Et dic̄ q̄d p̄dc̄i Rob̄tus Ingiltoñ ꝛ Margareta Acc̄oem suam p̄dc̄am v̄sus eos manutenere non debent quia idem Wiłłs Eure dic̄ q̄d quidam Wiłłs Bruys, Chiualer, nup fuit sc̄itus de vno mesuagio, cum ptiñ, in Thornetoñ p̄dicт ad quod aduocacio eccłie p̄dc̄e ptinet ꝛ a tempore quo non extat memoria ptinuit ꝛ sic inde sc̄itus de mesuagio illo ad quod ꝛc̄ diu ante tempus quo p̄dc̄i Rob̄tus Ingiltoñ ꝛ Margareta p narrac̄oem suam p̄dc̄am suppoñ p̄fatum Rog̃um ad eccłiam p̄dc̄am p̄fatum Walt̃um p̄sentasse ad eccłiam illam p̄sentauit quendam Ricm̄ Maltoñ, Clicum suū, qui ad p̄sentac̄oem suam fuit admissus ꝛ institutus in eadem tempore pacis tempore dñi R nup Regis Angł sc̄di post conquestum et postea p̄dc̄us Wiłłs Bruys ante p̄dc̄am p̄sentac̄oem p̄fato Walt̃o in forma p̄dc̄a fc̄am decimo die Septembr̄ anno regni p̄dc̄i dñi R nup Regis vicesimo apud Thornetoñ p̄dc̄am dimisit p̄fato Rogero (Wandesford) mesuagiū p̄dcm̄, cum ptiñ, ad quod ꝛc̄ Hend sibi a p̄dc̄o decimo die Septembr̄ vsq, ad finem triginta annoȝ tunc px̄ seqñ ꝛ plenar̄ complēт virtute cuius dimissionis p̄dc̄us Rog̃us in mesuagiū illud, cum ptiñ, ad quod ꝛc̄ intrauit ꝛ inde de tali statu possessionaт fuit et postea p̄dc̄a eccłia vacauit p mortem p̄dc̄i Ric̄i Maltoñ postea q, p̄dc̄us Rog̃us de mesuagio illo, cum ptiñ, ad quod ꝛc̄ virtute dimissionis p̄dc̄e sic possessionaт ad eccłiam illam p̄sentauit p̄dc̄m Walt̃um, Clicum suū, qui ad p̄sentac̄oem suam fuit admissus ꝛ institutus in eadem tempore pacis tempore dñi R nup Regis Angł sc̄di post conqm̄ postea q, p̄dc̄us Wiłłs Bruys de p̄dc̄o mesuagio, cum ptiñ, ad quod ꝛc̄ obijt sc̄itus post cuius mortem idem mesuagiū, cum ptiñ, ad quod ꝛc̄ descendit quibusdam Isabelle Elizabeth ꝛ Matiłł vt consanguineis ꝛ hered p̄dc̄i Wiłłi Bruys videłł filiabȝ Rob̄ti filij Wiłłi filij p̄dc̄i Wiłłi Bruys ꝛ postea p̄dc̄a Isabella cepit in virum quendam Wiłłm Appulby ꝛ p̄dc̄a Elizabeth cepit in virum Ricm̄ Eglesfeld ꝛ p̄dc̄a Matiłł cepit in virum Rob̄tum Brouñ qui quidem Wiłłs Appulby ꝛ Isabella Ric̄us ꝛ Elizabeth Rob̄tus Brouñ ꝛ Matiłł vt in iure ip̄aȝ Isabelle Elizabeth ꝛ Matiłł post finem t̃mini triginta annoȝ p̄dc̄oȝ in mesuagiū p̄dc̄m, cum ptiñ, ad quod ꝛc̄, intrauerunt ꝛ inde sc̄iti fuerunt in dñico suo vt de feodo ꝛ iure ip̄aȝ Isabelle Elizabeth ꝛ Matiłł ꝛ sic inde sc̄iti de eodem Mesuagio, cum ptiñ, ad quod ꝛc̄, feoffauerunt ip̄m Wiłłm Eure hend sibi ꝛ her̄ suis imppm̄ virtute cuius feoffamenti idem Wiłłs Eure fuit inde sc̄itus in dñico suo vt de feod ꝛ sic sc̄iт p̄dc̄a eccłia vacauit p mortem p̄dc̄i Walt̃i ꝛ adhuc vacans existit ꝛ ea r̄one ad ip̄m Wiłłm Eure ad eccłiam p̄dc̄am ad p̄sens ptinet p̄sentare absq, hoc q̄d p̄dc̄us Rog̃us fuit sc̄itus de aduocac̄oe p̄dc̄a vt de vno grosso p se put p̄dc̄i Rob̄tus Ingilton ꝛ Margareta p narrac̄oem suam p̄dc̄am suppoñ."

(Case deferred until Octave of Hilary, then until Quinzaine of Easter following, and then until Morrow of St. John Baptist, when nothing more—no judgment being entered up.)

Errata and Addenda.

Vol. ii., Part 1.

Page 16. Add note to William Marshall of Much Hadham. "He had lease of the Manor of Scrooby, co. Notts., 17 Elizabeth, 1574-5."—Raine's *Blyth*, p. 129.

Page 55. *For* Thomas Hill *read* Thomas Gill.

Page 63. *For* Kinton *read* Kirton.

Page 75. Line 35. Elizabeth Sowby. In the transcript of this Register the name is Sorebie.

Page 106. Note to Inquisitions:—

43-44 Elizabeth. John Marshall. Lincoln. John Marshall of Owmbie, co. Lincoln. Died 6 Aug., 42 Elizabeth, 1600. John Marshall is his son and heir and aged 40.

14 James. Richard Marshall. Durham. Inq. at Durham, 13 June, 10 James. Richard Marshall, of Denton, co Durham, gent., died 10 May, 6 James, Cuthbert Marshall, gent., is his son and heir, and aged 18. Court of Wards, Trinity, 14 James I.

Vol. ii., Part 2.

Page 59. Line 16. *For* 22 March *read* 23 March.

Page 84. *For* Alexander Burder *read* Alexander Burdet.

Page 85. Anne, wife of Thomas Marshall, was daughter of John Vaughan, and his issue was by her and not by Frances Saunderson.

INDEX OF NAMES.

C.

I.

J.

K.

L.

M.

N.

S.

T.

U.

V.

W.

Y.

INDEX OF PLACES.

A.

B.

C.

U.

W.

Y.

INDEX OF CHRISTIAN NAMES OF MARSHALLS.

Names are usually given under their modern spellings. When a person has two or more names initials only are given.

Wives are indexed as Marshalls, as well as under their maiden names in the Index of Persons.

ROBERT WHITE, PRINTER, WORKSOP.

www.ingramcontent.com/pod-product-compliance
Lightning Source LLC
Chambersburg PA
CBHW060521030726
47498CB00004B/1032